Pretending He's Mine

By Mia Sosa

Love on Cue
Acting on Impulse
Pretending He's Mine

The Suits Undone
Unbuttoning the CEO
One Night with the CEO
Getting Dirty with the CEO

Pretending He's Mine

LOVE ON CUE

MIA SOSA

AVONIMPULSE

An Imprint of HarperCollinsPublishers

Excerpt from *Crashing Into Her* copyright © 2019 by Mia Sosa.

PRETENDING HE'S MINE. Copyright © 2018 by Mia Sosa. All rights reserved. Printed in the United States of America. No part of this book may be used or reproduced in any manner whatsoever without written permission except in the case of brief quotations embodied in critical articles and reviews. For information, address HarperCollins Publishers, 195 Broadway, New York, NY 10007.

Digital Edition APRIL 2018 ISBN: 978-0-06-269039-5
Print Edition ISBN: 978-0-06-269040-1

Cover design by Nadine Badalaty
Cover photography © Dean Drobot/Shutterstock

Avon Impulse and the Avon Impulse logo are registered trademarks of HarperCollins Publishers in the United States of America.

Avon and HarperCollins are registered trademarks of HarperCollins Publishers in the United States of America and other countries.

FIRST EDITION

17 18 19 20 21 HDC 10 9 8 7 6 5 4 3 2 1

Para minha mãe. Obrigada.

Pretending He's Mine

Chapter One

Julian

A WOMAN IN my condo is experiencing a toe-curling orgasm—and to my knowledge, this is the first time I'm in no way responsible for it.

Because this dumpster fire needs more tinder, the person bringing herself pleasure within the confines of my not-so-humble abode is my best friend's younger sister.

I'd prefer to sustain a thousand paper cuts than listen to her moans, the catch of her breath, the rustling of the sheets around her body. But she's crashing at my place, and she left the door of the guest bedroom open—just a tiny, torturous crack. The sliver of soft light coming from the adjoining bathroom beckons like a portal to another world. *Come,* the deep, booming voice of James Earl Jones says. *The embodiment of your hidden and fucked-up fantasies lies in this realm.*

I squeeze my eyes shut. Dammit. This isn't right. It's a personal moment, and I shouldn't be privy to it. Summoning what's left of the self-control that's served me well for more years than I'd care to admit, I turn away from the light and slink down the short hall to my kitchen. There, I refit my wireless headphones and find a tall glass for the water that brought me out of my room.

I'd resigned myself to remaining as far away from Ashley as possible while she stayed the night. Instead, an innocent trip to the fridge has left me thirsty for something else altogether. I'm not even sure why I took off my headphones as I passed her room. But I did. And now I know what she sounds like when she comes.

I need to shut down this line of thinking immediately. But hell, the portal is open, and despite my good intentions, I'm tempted to step through and explore this other world.

No. I shouldn't. I *really* shouldn't.

Picture her in pigtails and remember what it was like to help her stand after an epic fall on the bike she loved to ride.

Forget that she's now a sexy woman, and banish any inappropriate thoughts about her to a parallel universe that will never intersect with this one.

Although temporary, the solution is simple. Fifty push-ups will round out my workout and help stifle my libido. With my get-over-my-lust-for-Ashley plan in place, I set the glass in the sink, cut the light switch, and spin around. A warm body skids into me, its owner's soft mouth brushing against my bare shoulder.

She shrinks back and yelps.

Instinctively, I tug Ashley forward, steadying her and mentally unbalancing myself in the process. With my chest flush against hers, I try to memorize the way we fit together, greedy to gain something from this unexpected contact.

"Julian? Please tell me it's you."

The tremor in her voice pulls me out of my stupor. I breathe heavily through my nose as I drop my arms and step back slowly. Turning to the counter and grasping it for support, I eke out, "It's me, Ashley."

As she sighs in relief, the memory of her curves imprints itself in my brain like a freshly inked intricate tattoo, simultaneously mesmerizing and painful.

Fuck the fifty push-ups. I'm going to need a hundred.

Ashley

THAT WAS A test.

In the event of an actual sexual emergency, I would be climbing Julian's body like a cat in heat. Julian dislikes cats, however, and he dislikes women who invade his personal space even more. Still, *this* woman needs to know if her lifelong crush is attracted to her.

Hence, Operation Fake Orgasm.

Moments ago, I sat on the bed in Julian's guest bedroom and flipped through the copy of *Sports Illustrated* I'd lifted from the magazine rack.

I moaned. I groaned. I smacked my lips. There were a few *yeses* in there, too. Then a high-pitched cry. To heighten the atmospherics, I rustled the sheets with my free hand.

Meg Ryan would have been proud.

Did I do all this knowing the door to the bedroom was open? Affirmative. Will the ruse reveal whether Julian's attracted to me? I should know in a minute.

He's staring at his hands, which are gripping the edge of the kitchen counter as though he needs help remaining upright.

"Sorry," I say in a tentative voice. "I didn't realize you were out here. I just wanted a glass of water."

He raises his head, and after a sweep of his surroundings, his gaze finally lands on me. In a matter of seconds, he regards me with undisguised interest, his rich, dark brown eyes cataloguing my face and body. Then he shuts down his perusal with a repeated shake of his head. Oh, yeah, I *know* that move. He's summoning his willpower, and the fact that he needs to do so is promising. Very promising, indeed.

Before I can revel in that knowledge, however, he straightens and taps his ears, pulling out his headphones with a flick of each wrist. "Hey. I've been in my own world here."

My eyes blink repeatedly, so much so that the kitchen appears to be bathed in strobe lights. "You've been listening to music?"

Oblivious to my disappointment, Julian smiles and his adorable dimples greet me. "Yeah, I was working out. Didn't want to disturb you."

My ample chest deflates. Drat. Operation Fake Orgasm was a waste of time. But wait a minute now. That's neither here nor there when I consider that Julian's bare chest is in my field of vision. I haven't seen it since my last year of high school—and Julian's last year of college. Oh. *Oh my*. There have been significant developments in the interim. He still possesses the smooth brown skin I yearned to caress. But maturity—and probably the effects of a heck of a lot of exercise—has etched itself into the dips and planes of his torso, broadening the span of his shoulders and hardening his stomach. How would the landscape change if he contracted his muscles in response to my touch? God, I'd love to know.

"So, care to tell me why you left your brother's place like a thief in the night and showed up on my doorstep this time?" he asks. "I mean, you're always welcome to crash here, but I'm curious."

His voice, a commanding baritone that glides over me like a swath of silk, draws my attention to the strong column of his throat. Even in college, Julian spoke like a man well beyond his years, but now that he's older, his voice complements his persona, the perfect accessory for any outfit or occasion. My brain perceives it as perpetual foreplay, and my body responds in kind. Shit, I'm going to need a cigarette after this conversation. But I don't smoke. I'll take a precoital nap, then. Is that a thing? If it isn't, it should be.

He lifts his body and settles on the kitchen counter, and my gaze returns to the small and large muscles of his arms and abs as they flex in tandem, a well-choreographed dance of tantalizing body parts. Needing something to do with my twitchy hands, I search for a glass.

"Upper cabinet above the sink," Julian says.

After grabbing one, I face him. "I unexpectedly needed a place to stay and figured Carter could take me in. But I didn't think through the implications."

He raises a brow. "Which are?" Then he tilts his head to the side, and a slow smile appears. "Oh, I know. He just returned from being on set in Canada."

"Yes. Exactly. He and Tori are getting reacquainted. Loudly." I grimace. "So, so loudly."

Absently running his hands over his chin, he regards me with narrowed eyes. "What's wrong with your place in Hoboken?"

It's a simple question—with a complicated answer.

Last week, I would have said nothing. But that was before my roommate's seedy boyfriend cornered me in my kitchen and squeezed my ass as I rinsed out my favorite coffee mug. That was also before I slammed said mug against the side of his face. My roommate, Elisa, screeched when she saw the streak of blood on his cheek. His injury was superficial, but her response to what had prompted it hurt me deeply. In the end, she blamed her boyfriend's wandering hands on my "tight" pajama bottoms.

Luckily, my latest stint as a flight attendant meant I could get away for a few days and distance myself from the terrible situation. Still, as long as either Elisa or her boyfriend occupy the apartment, I won't be returning.

Which means I'm homeless. But Julian doesn't need to know all of this. For his own good. Because if he found out what had gone down, he would head to Jersey for an unfriendly visit with Elisa's boyfriend and trouble would follow. So I tell him the truth, the *partial* truth, and nothing but the *essential* truth. "My living arrangements are in flux right now. I'm working on finding another place to live."

Understanding smooths out his furrowed forehead. "And staying with Carter while you figure things out isn't an attractive option, I take it?"

I chuckle. "He *literally* has his hands full with Tori. True love—it's a bit much, you know?"

Julian tilts his head back, his expression dubious. "Oh, c'mon. Are they *that* bad?"

"First, he's my brother. Second, he's my brother. Third, from what I could tell before I left, they're spreading their DNA on every surface of his house. I'm worried one morning I'll find a pubic hair in my cereal."

Julian shudders and pretends to retch. "Stop, please."

Satisfied I've made my point, I nod and purse my lips in displeasure. "Now you know how I feel."

"I'm sure your parents would welcome you with open arms."

I inwardly cringe at the thought of returning home. "I think you meant they'd welcome me into their nosy arms and pepper me with questions about my purpose in life. I know they mean well, but I'll pass."

He tilts his head as if to downplay my objection. "Would going home be such a bad thing?"

Um. Yes. I'd rather describe my colorful sexual history in graphic detail to my parents than return to Connecticut for more than a two-day visit during the holidays. Plus, Julian knows I hate my hometown and all the bad memories I left there, which is why I simply stare at him in response to his ridiculous question.

He drops his head, his fisted hands lightly pounding his thighs, but he says nothing.

After a half-minute in which I struggle for something to say, Julian lifts his head and swallows hard. A sense of foreboding blankets the room, the mood inexplicably darkening despite the brightness of his stark white kitchen. Finally, he says, "If you need a place to stay while you sort out your living arrangements, you can stay here. In one of the guest bedrooms."

I register the even and emotionless tone of his voice before I notice his matching expression. Goodness. Does he abhor the idea of my staying here *that* much?

I thought…I don't know what I thought. Maybe Julian's dating someone and he doesn't want me to interfere with his lifestyle. Maybe to him I'm still Carter's annoying sister, and he only suggested I stay here to keep his best friend and client happy.

He stares at me, his mouth slightly open as though he's holding his breath.

Or maybe, *just maybe*, Julian suspects being in close quarters with me would test his resolve to keep our relationship platonic. Although his reasoning is unclear, his lack of enthusiasm for spending more time with me is not.

That's why I'll accept his offer. Because I need to know once and for all whether Julian's attracted to me. If he isn't, I'll move on. If he is, I'll climb his body like a scratching post—for a few weeks, at most—and then I'll happily take him off my "to-do" list.

"I won't stay long. Promise." I give him a reassuring smile. "And I'll be traveling for work a lot, so you won't even know I'm here."

"I doubt that," he says under his breath.

Ha. Given what I have in mind, I doubt that, too.

Chapter Two

Julian

FOR THE FIRST morning in years, I'm lying awake in bed, my gaze fixed on the ceiling. I stare so long and hard at a small crack in the plaster that in a split second of grogginess, I wonder whether my eyes caused it.

Today's no different from the dozens of weekdays before it. Except Ashley's in my home. And now I know what she sounds like when she pleasures herself. Worse, my brain takes this new information and synthesizes it with its overblown sense of my sexual prowess and concludes that I'd do a far more masterful job of making her come. I grit my teeth. Fuck. *Not* what I should be thinking about as the sun rises—or any other time for that matter.

I throw back the covers and jump out of bed, dropping to the ground seconds later to perform my customary fifty push-ups. After going through my morning routine, I lay out my favorite ash gray suit; a crisp, white shirt; and my navy and silver don't-mess-with-me-today tie.

As I put on each component of my outfit, my equilibrium gradually returns. *This* is who I am. Julian Hart. Hollywood agent. I *chose* to be this person. And I can't forget the person who made my current circumstances possible: Carter. Yes, he's my best friend, but he's also the reason I've made a name for myself in this industry. We've managed to maintain our friendship and working relationship without incident for years, mostly because I set boundaries that allow me to separate "Carter, my best friend" from "Carter, my client." I can't fuck this up. Screwing around with his younger sister is not an option. Period.

Before leaving my bedroom, I peek out the door—and catch myself. What the hell am I doing? I'm not going to be a prisoner in my own home simply because Ashley's around. I straighten to my full height and stride down the hall—and pull up short when I find her rummaging through the cabinets. She's wearing a tank top and leggings, thank God. As it is, I'm spellbound by the way her long, dark hair brushes over her shoulders and back. More skin than that would have knocked me on my ass.

She's muttering as she darts from one cabinet to the next.

Not wanting to frighten her, I clear my throat. "Can I help you find something?"

She spins around, wide-eyed—and braless.

Oh, come the fuck on. Seriously?

I glance at the walls, the counter, the top of her head—basically, anything that doesn't have pointed nipples at its ends.

"Good morning, roomie," she says. "I'm looking for food."

Thankful for a reason to remove her from my line of sight, I open the fridge and list the stuff I already know is in there. "Tomatoes. A bunch of other fruits and veggies. Cottage and cheddar cheeses. Milk and juice." I straighten and point behind her, my gaze locked on the floor. "Granola and oatmeal in there." Then I chance a glance at her, limiting my view to the area above her shoulders.

She screws up her face and purses that sensuous mouth of hers. "I was looking for eggs, bacon, muffins, a doughnut even."

"Sorry, I don't have any of that."

She comes from behind the counter and tugs on my suit sleeve. "Did you sell your soul to the devil in exchange for not having any joy in your life? You strike me as the kind of guy who would make a perverse deal like that."

I step back and smooth my suit. "Cute, but the answer is no. Besides, I'm so happy with my life I'm bursting at the seams."

She claps her hands together and cackles. "Well, you've still got a sense of humor, so all's not lost."

Yeah. That sounded laughable to my own ears, so I can't be mad at her for knowing what's what. Some days the monotony of my life is dreary as hell. "I can pick up a few things before I come home tonight."

"Oh, don't bother." She fills a glass with orange juice and takes a long gulp before setting the cup on the counter. "I'm going to explore the neighborhood today. I'm sure I'll find a grocery store along the way."

"There's a Whole Foods about a mile west. Straight down Wilshire Boulevard."

She squeals and jumps up and down. "Their bakery is *the best*."

No, your bouncing tits are *the best*. I snap my eyes shut. Dammit. I pivot like a cadet in training and grab my keys off the table in the foyer. "I need to head out. Lots of stuff going on at work. I'll ask the doorman to give you my emergency keys. We can get a set made for you this weekend." Why can't I stop talking?

She raises a brow. "No breakfast?"

"No…I'll grab a smoothie from the shop in the office lobby."

She bites her lips and peers at me, her head tilted to the side. "Right. Sounds delicious."

Can she tell I'm itchy to put some space between us? I need to do a better job of masking my attraction to her. "Enjoy the day, Ash. And don't get into any trouble while I'm gone."

She pouts at me. "Where's the fun in that?" A saucy wink follows. "Besides, trouble is my middle name."

I don't doubt it. And that's exactly what I'm afraid of.

WITH MY *DELICIOUS* green smoothie in hand, I pass through the double glass doors of Sync Creative Management's main floor. As usual, the frenetic activity hits

me like a battering ram. My colleagues are loud, probably owing in large part to the industry adage that the
only people worth listening to are the ones who can
make themselves heard. I pass a small conference room,
where an agent is engaged in a shouting match with the
speakerphone, and ten steps from there, a cubicle station,
where Marie, my assistant, sits in the cubby closest to my
office, her space decorated with cheerful knickknacks,
including a collection of Mickey Mouse–ear hats.

She hurries to meet me. "Good morning and fair
warning. Quinn is on a tear and wants to see everyone
from the TV Group in Salon B at noon."

David Quinn is the head of our group. Being ornery
isn't just a mood for him; it's his essence. His signature
cologne should be called *eau de asshole*. Still, if he's calling a meeting at noon, it's for a good reason. The lunch
hour is when agents make deals—or try to—and while
lunch in this town lasts longer than an hour, noon is
when we emerge from our offices searching for deals to
feed the beast.

"Any idea what the meeting's about?"

Marie chews on a fingernail as she shakes her head.
She lives in a perpetual state of worry, fully aware that
her job security is tied to the success of the four agents
she works with. "No clue."

"It'll be fine, Marie. If Quinn were mad at me, he'd
ream me out first thing in the morning. That's part of his
charm."

My reassurance does the trick, and she laughs. "You're
right, of course."

"Messages?"

She nods. "Tons of them."

"Let's discuss in my office, then."

After Marie leaves, I work nonstop, speaking with several casting agents, a talent scout pitching on behalf of a child actor, and a client who's lost somewhere near Stage 15 of Warner Brothers Studios. In between the marathon conference calls, I read the latest news on casting decisions and a summary of which shows writers and producers plan to pitch during the upcoming pilot season.

With five minutes to spare before the noon meeting with Quinn, I get a call from a director who wants me to read the script of a movie he claims is tailor-made for Carter.

It's not. Carter's already told me so. The director's reputation for verbally abusing people on set precedes him. But I listen and pretend to be enthusiastic about the project, because the degrees of separation between this guy and a studio exec might matter one day. Unfortunately, my long-term strategy makes me late to Quinn's meeting.

I hoof it down the internal stairs to Salon B and look for a seat in the back of the room.

Quinn sets aside the papers in front of him and looks up when I enter. "How good of you to join us, Julian."

I'm not apologizing for doing my job, so I give him a fuck-you smile. "Pleasure to be here, sir."

To Quinn's right, his assistant coughs into her hand. Glenda's a sweet woman who deserves a million of her favorite Peanut M&M's for having the fortitude to work with him.

I snag a seat by the window, its steel gray shades lowered completely because Quinn's allergic to sunshine, and whisper to Doug, another agent in the group. "What's going on?"

"Someone jacked up a contract," he says under his breath. "Quinn hasn't identified the fucker yet. Now he'll be on our ass for weeks."

This is true. Quinn looks for any excuse to ride us harder, to remind us that we're one bad deal away from being shown the door.

Our boss sighs and gets to the point. "Let's discuss what happened."

The gist is that an agent screwed up a negotiation on behalf of a client, and it's tied the client's hands on future television opportunities. In short, an embarrassment to the agency and a major blunder vis-à-vis our client. Not one we can't correct given the client's star power, but the process of doing so makes us—and the client—look bad.

Quinn works his jaw like he's chewing on a T-bone. "If you don't have the skill or experience to negotiate a deal for one of your clients, say so. Get help. Don't fuck around on my dime." After his gaze circles the room of approximately forty people, he settles his contemptuous stare on a lone figure sitting outside the inner ring of attendees. Adam Manning. Poor guy. "Need I remind you that the Film Group has been complaining about the redundancies in the agency for ages. We're not Worldwide or APA. We can't afford to get shit wrong. Do you know how we compete with the big dogs in Hollywood? By getting it right. Every. Time."

Damn, here we go again. There isn't a week Quinn doesn't remind us of our humble origins. Ten years ago, Worldwide Management Agency, a behemoth in this town, laid off more than a dozen of its agents as part of a restructuring effort. SCM's founding partners, including Quinn, were among the ones let go. Pissed and unemployed, they opened their own firm, initially to dominate the industry and make WMA fall to its knees. But with the benefit of time and perspective—and a bitter dose of reality—SCM's partners now focus on nabbing future breakout stars before they realize how talented they are. We're the little fish in a big pond. Quinn's still insecure about his foothold in the industry, though, and he has a perpetual scowl on his face to prove it.

"Don't embarrass me out there," Quinn continues. "You have questions? Get answers. The legal department is here for a reason. You're all dismissed."

Everyone except Quinn jumps to their feet.

He points at me. "You. Stay."

Shit. What the fuck did I do now? I scroll through the list of possible transgressions. Nope. I got nothing. So I amble toward him with as carefree an expression as I can muster. "What's up?"

He motions for me to sit. "I heard there was some chatter at the GLAAD awards about Hollywood's whitewashing problem. Your name was mentioned. Care to explain?"

What's to explain? So I might have gotten impassioned during the discussion, and yes, there might have been a studio exec or two in the group of people mingling, but it's a well-known problem, and I'm not the first person to share my thoughts on the topic. "Agents and casting directors talk, Quinn. It happens. The issue came up. I shared some of my views. That's all."

He presses his lips together and leans forward, his hands clasped on the conference table. "Since this seems to be a day for reminders, let's review why you're here. You have a shit ton of small clients, but your marquee player is Carter Stone. Your *job* is to keep Carter Stone gainfully employed, so this agency can be gainfully paid. Your *job* is to keep Carter Stone happy, so he'll want to work with SCM and continue to make us money. You do Carter no favors by pissing off the very people who want to work with him. Do not fuck up the opportunities you've been given."

Well, he's never pretended to be a nice guy, but goddamn, he's not mincing words today. "Carter and I go way back, Quinn. He's not going anywhere."

"Don't be so sure, Julian."

My stomach churns. Does Quinn know something I don't? Is Carter thinking about cutting me loose? I try to recall a clue or two from one of our recent conversations, but nothing out of the ordinary comes to mind. But maybe he picked up on my lack of enthusiasm for the business? Dammit. I *hate* being racked by self-doubt.

"Look, I'm not trying to be a prick," Quinn continues. "I know he's your friend, and you've done a fine job of managing your relationship so far, but you've always assured me that you and he keep work and personal stuff separate."

I nod. "We do."

"Did it ever occur to you that the dynamic you've cultivated makes it just as easy for him to sever your working relationship?"

I swallow the lump in my throat. It goes down like a boulder covered in spikes. "No."

"Well, you should. So make yourself indispensable. Don't do anything to make him question your partnership. Because I'm not sure there'd be enough work to justify keeping you if he left, and your comments about the industry's problems could make finding another agency position difficult." He shrugs. "I'm just looking out for you, my man."

He's not, and we both know it. Quinn's only interests revolve around SCM and the money it makes him. But as much as I don't want to, I see his point.

Quinn drums his hands on the glass table as he peers at me. "Before you go jumping to conclusions and confronting Carter, let me be clear. I haven't heard anything about him wanting to fire you. But it stands to reason that if he wanted to, he could say, 'It's just business, nothing personal,' and you'd be hard-pressed to debate him on that point."

Well, fuck. Nothing like getting my ass handed to me by my prick of a boss. Especially when he makes me question one of the most important decisions of my life. To Quinn, this is about a threat to my job, which alone would be devastating. To me, though, it means much more. When I chose to become an agent and represent Carter, I crushed my father's dream that I'd join his business and continue his legacy. But I forged ahead, convincing myself that my success would be enough proof—not only to my father but also to me—that I'd selected the right path.

If Carter fires me, the strain I put on my relationship with my dad would have been all for naught. And where would that leave me? I'd be a Hollywood agent without an A-list client. And any other A-list actor who might have sought my rep would view my and Carter's "amicable parting" as a red flag. *Failure* with a capital *F* is what I'd call it.

None of this can happen. *I won't let it happen.* So from here on out, Carter's career is my highest priority.

Chapter Three

Ashley

MEANDERING THROUGH WHOLE Foods is a sensory experience. The well-lit bakery section boasts utilitarian aluminum stands filled with thousand-grain breads and ginormous muffins; less than a foot away, two plexiglass-covered cases display rows upon rows of mouthwatering cookies. And the aromas. God, the aromas. If the scent of fresh-baked bread were bottled as a perfume, I'd spritz it on my wrists every day.

I close my eyes as I sample the cherry hand pie. The filling is thick and tart, and the flaky, buttery crust melts on my tongue. "Oh, that's *so* good."

Beside me, Tori laughs. "People are staring, Ashley. Perhaps you and your cherry hand pie should consider getting a room."

"Ha." I motion for Tori to get her own bite-sized portion. "You've *got* to try this."

She wrinkles her nose and shakes her head. The curls that aren't stuffed under her royal blue baseball cap swing around her shoulders. "No, thanks."

"Oh, c'mon." I bump her shoulder with mine. "It's filled with ingredients even a personal trainer would approve of." Bending over, I read the card next to the platter. "Eggs from cage-free, non-GMO-fed hens and unbleached, unbromated flour."

"What's bromated flour?"

I shrug. "I have no idea, but whatever it is, it *isn't* in these babies."

Ignoring me, she reaches into a bin and pulls out a loaf of hearty bread dotted with seeds. Frankly, it's what I imagine French bread would look like if I slathered it with butter and rolled it on the forest floor.

"I'm not a fan of cherries," she says. "But I'll take some of this home." Then she peers into my empty basket. "Aren't you buying anything?"

I purse my lips and shake my head. "At these prices? No way. I plan to sample my way to a satisfying lunch and hit the Vons I passed on the way here."

She rolls her eyes and pulls me toward the hot and cold salad bar. "Let's grab some food. My treat. We can eat in the dining room."

After grabbing a literal pound and a half of food, I follow Tori upstairs to the indoor café. We toss our bags on an empty chair and sit across from each other at a table overlooking an underwhelming view of the produce department. Below us, a bawling toddler throws her back out in a fit that reminds me of the snippy airline passenger I dealt with last week. The child's mother is not amused, and a showdown is imminent. My money is on the kid.

Tori wrestles open the lid of her container and sighs heavily.

My gaze snaps to her face. "What's wrong?"

She drops her shoulders and pokes around at her food. "I feel bad that you left last night. I'm sorry if Carter and I made you uncomfortable. Again."

I wave away her apology. "Oh, Tori. Don't worry about it. You guys deserved an evening on your own. It was no big deal to spend the night at Julian's."

Well, it *was* a big deal, but not in the way Tori might expect. My mind replays the moment when I saw his trim waist and bare chest. Somehow, I manage to stifle a moan and attack my lunch instead.

"What was that?" Tori asks.

Fork in midstab, I look up and pretend not to see her narrow-eyed gaze and knowing smile. "What was what?"

She purses her lips in the universal *don't give me that bullshit* expression. "That look. When you mentioned Julian. Like you were hot and bothered."

"Hot and bothered? Tori, honey, I'm embarrassed for you. Delete that expression from your brain. Also, it might be time for prescription glasses. You're seeing things that aren't there."

She tilts her head and shakes it. "No, my vision is crystal clear, so spill." She scoots closer to the table and leans in. Realizing a juicy secret isn't immediately forthcoming, she sits back and pouts at me. "Oh, c'mon. Isn't this the benefit of having a sister-in-law? Another person to share your closely held secrets with?"

"You're not my sister-in-law yet," I grumble.

Her face falls, and all I want to do is kick myself in the shins. *Don't be a brat, Ashley. You know she's right.* This is exactly the benefit of having a sister-in-law. I break out into a conspiratorial smile. "If you must know, I've had a crush on him for years…but that's all it'll ever be."

"Why?"

We'd need all day to parse out the reasons, starting with the most important one: I'm not even sure Julian's all that interested in me. There's more, though. Lots more. "Dating my older brother's best friend would be awkward. Period. And Julian's his agent, too. Imagine what would happen if it worked out between us? How that might affect Julian's decision-making? What he'd feel comfortable telling his own girlfriend? And if it *didn't* work out? Yikes. I know he's already uneasy about representing Carter. A failed relationship with me would send him into a tailspin."

Tori makes a big show of pondering my answer, her lips smacking together as she slowly chews on a spear of broccoli. When she's done, she daintily dabs her lips with a napkin. "Interesting that you mentioned a relationship. I was just talking about you looking *hot and bothered.* Which makes me wonder. Is this a crush…or something more serious?"

My cheeks warm under her scrutiny. It *can't* be anything more serious. I know where Julian's first allegiance lies, and it isn't with me. I might come second to Carter in just about every aspect of my life, but I'm not interested in setting myself up to be second best in my own love life, too. "It's a crush, of course."

"But do the same reasons apply, then, if you're just messing around?"

Now she's speaking my language. "Okay, yes, I'll confess to being super curious about what he's like in bed. I mean, the man is hot, in a strong-and-silent type of way, and the idea of satisfying that curiosity…" I fan myself and blow out a breath that ruffles my bangs. "Good thing we'll be living together for a bit."

Tori's eyes grow big as saucers. "What? Since when?"

I shrug and slather a pat of butter on my roll, pretending this development isn't making me giddy with anticipation. "Last night he offered to let me stay in one of his guest bedrooms. Until I figure out a permanent living situation. And I accepted."

Tori returns the conspiratorial smile I gave her minutes ago. "Well, that should be interesting."

"It should be something, all right. We'll either kill each other or spend the foreseeable future in bed."

"Julian?" Wearing a half smile, she shakes her head. "Don't hold your breath on any sexual marathons. As far as I can tell, the man lives and breathes his job. He'd fit you in between six and seven in the morning and again from eleven to midnight."

"It's true. I don't recall him ever mentioning a girlfriend, and believe me, I've asked. Even my few attempts to ferret out information from Carter turned up nothing."

Tori nods. "Same."

"Eh. So we'll go at it before dawn and the witching hour. I'm good with that."

"I wish you nothing but luck and sex-by-appointment." Then, with a toss of her hair, she sets aside her food, leans in, and pins me with a stars-in-her-eyes gaze. "Carter and I have news, too."

Holy shit, she's pregnant. I scan her face for clues to her condition, but I don't know what the hell I'm looking for. A glow? Bags under her eyes? Besides, who's to say she's far enough along to show any signs?

She gives me an exasperated sigh and bops me on the nose. "I'm not pregnant, Ashley."

"Oh." I give her a sheepish grin. "So what's the news?"

She leans in another inch. "Carter and I are getting married."

I can't suppress the *duh* expression that crosses my face. "Yes, I know."

"No, I mean we're getting married at the Williamson Family Reunion."

I draw back. Now I'm the one who's confused. "The reunion in three weeks? What? When? How?"

"On Sunday. The closing brunch isn't just a brunch. It's a wedding. But only a few people know. My parents. Your parents. A close friend of your mother's who's a local caterer and who's also sworn to secrecy."

"Mrs. Chapman."

"Yes, that's her."

I sop up the sauce from my chicken curry dish. "Why the rush?"

"It isn't a rush, really." She picks at her fingers as she explains. "If we could have married a year ago, we would have done it in a heartbeat. But things were too hectic with my move to California and the fitness studio opening. We're ready now. And Carter and I wanted to avoid the paparazzi as much as we could."

"And a reunion in Connecticut is your cover?"

"Well, we're hoping that if any paparazzi find out we're in Carter's hometown, they'll quickly become bored with the family-friendly activities and leave before the big day."

These two sure know how to complicate their lives. If it were me and I had their means, I'd shuttle everyone to a remote island and get married on the beach—no shoes required. "Why not elope?"

Tori's eyebrows disappear under her cap. "Because I don't want to be disowned. It's bad enough I'm not getting married in a church. My parents would never forgive me if I deprived them of a wedding altogether."

"This could backfire, you know."

"Of course it could. But trying to make this work is half the fun. You can't imagine the planning that's gone into this. If we pull it off, we'll go down in the annals of supersecret celebrity weddings. One Hollywood couple invited their guests to a birthday party and surprised everyone with a wedding instead. We can, too."

"And Julian didn't balk? I would have assumed he'd want Carter to get all the publicity mileage he could from his own wedding. I can't imagine any agent would be happy about it."

Tori drops her chin and stares at the magazines on the table. A man nearby scrapes his chair against the floor as he stands, the sound not as jarring to me as Tori's silence. My gut clenches. Dammit, Julian doesn't know. He's Carter's *best friend*, for goodness' sake. I stretch out my arm and place my hand over Tori's. "You're going to tell him, right?"

Tori nods, her eyes round and earnest. "Eventually, yes. And don't pout."

I curve my lips into a weak smile.

"Okay, sure, maybe in the back of our minds, we were worried he'd put on his agent hat and object, but that's *not* the main reason we're keeping him in the dark. We want to give him plausible deniability with Carter's publicist. *She's* the one who's going to have a fit."

It's not all in Julian's head, then. Being Carter's agent *does* affect their friendship. Is that tough for him to accept? Is that the reason he's so conflicted about his place in my brother's life?

"Anyway," Tori continues, "we told everyone to wear their Sunday best for the closing brunch, so whatever you were planning to wear will be fine for the ceremony, too. Don't trouble yourself with getting anything special."

I dig into my trough of food to avoid meeting her gaze. "Oh, that's good, I guess." Truth is, I hadn't settled on an outfit because I hadn't planned on attending the reunion. A three-night stay with my extended family isn't my idea of a good time, and if my cousin Lydia is there, it'll be a special kind of hell. Now that I know Tori and Carter's plans, there's no question I'll be at the wedding. But *only* the wedding. Which means I need an excuse to parachute in for the nuptials. Oh, and I need to keep Carter and Tori's secret from my new roommate.

I sigh on the inside. This isn't going to end well, is it?

Chapter Four

Julian

As I scan Fig & Olive's main dining area, I'm reminded of a core principle I learned in business school: End every meeting on a positive note. In other words, if you've got potentially negative shit to share, say it up front. So I set aside my dish and place my elbows on the table. Here goes. "Your sister's going to be staying at my place for a while."

Carter blinks at me. "Excuse me? What—"

I put off his line of questioning with a lift of my hand and motion for our server's attention with the other. There isn't enough liquor in the world to loosen me up for this conversation, but I'll drink anyway. After ordering a whiskey sour, I settle into my chair. Amid the sea of people sitting at white linen-covered tables, Carter draws people's attention, his superstar-next-door good looks custom framed by the room's skylights and strategically placed palms.

"What's this about Ashley?" he asks.

The whispers and murmurs of the late-lunch crowd remind me how awkward representing your best friend can be. Twenty feet away, an agency colleague talks with her client, probably discussing the latest offer for a recurring role in a sitcom she'd gloated about last week. Meanwhile, I'm telling my client his sister's moving in with me.

If I could rewind the last twenty-four hours and rescind my offer to let Ashley stay with me, I would. Her presence in my home is an unknown variable, a factor that could jolt my and Carter's relationship out of sync and create a rift between us. Still, maintaining the status quo isn't as important as being there when she needs my help, no matter how hard it'll be for me to share my personal space with her. Now to convince her brother my intentions are honorable. "I'm not sure what she told you, but Ashley doesn't just need to crash somewhere for a few nights. She's been displaced. Something went down with her roommate, but she won't tell me what. Anyway, she needs a place to stay, on a temporary basis, and since I have two extra bedrooms, I offered one of them to her."

Carter scrunches his face as he pushes the food around on his plate. "Why can't she stay with me?"

"Tori."

He jerks his head up at the mention of his fiancée's name. "What the hell does that mean?"

I raise my hands in surrender, immediately regretting my lack of tact. "No disrespect, Carter. Really. It's just…well, I imagine it must be hard to live with two people in love, especially when one of them is your older brother."

His cheeks bloom with color. "All right, I get it."

The server arrives with my drink. Perfect timing. I take a sip and forge ahead. "Listen, I hope this doesn't need to be said, but I'll say it anyway. Ashley's like a little sister to me. She'll be safe, and I'll treat her with respect. You have nothing to worry about."

Carter draws back and regards me with a pensive expression. "I appreciate the blood vow, but I'm not worried."

That stings. Does he think Ashley and I are so incompatible nothing would ever happen between us, or is he confident she would never entertain the idea of being with me? And why the hell do I care? "Oh, well, good. That's a relief."

Carter chuckles. "Yeah, you'd never go for Ashley. She's way too flighty. Your perfect woman is a workaholic like you, keeps a to-do list for everything, and wears starchier suits than yours."

"Fuck off with that noise," I tell him as I smooth my jacket sleeves. "My suits aren't stiff."

Carter shakes his head. "*That's* your comeback? You're hopeless, bro. Anyway, given how uptight you are about being my agent, I can't imagine you'd ever want to muddy the waters even more by trying to date my sister. Shit, even I can see how that might make things weird. But I know you well, J, and I'm not concerned."

I tug on my tie as guilt settles on my shoulders. If he knew the trajectory of my thoughts about Ashley the past eighteen hours, he'd retract those words and question the fuck out of my motives. His point remains spot-on, however. Messing around with Ashley would turn the waters to sludge.

"I do think this could be good for Ashley, though," he continues. "Maybe you'll be a stabilizing influence. Show her that committing to a plan and following through on it isn't the worst way to live your life."

"Ashley's not lost, Carter. She's headed somewhere and enjoying herself along the way."

"Yes, well, I hope wherever that somewhere is, she finds a steady job there. And a permanent place to live."

"I hope you don't talk like that in front of her."

"Of course not. This is between us. I worry about her, Julian. I want her safe, happy, settled."

"I want her safe, happy, and settled, too. But she's twenty-six, not fifty-six, man. And I'm pretty sure she'd like a say in how that happens. Give her a chance to stumble. You did."

"You didn't," Carter grumbles.

"Which only means I'm a late stumbler. I'm going to fall on my ass eventually, I just know it."

He grins at the prospect of that. "This, I can't wait to see."

I slide my glass back and forth in front of me. Huh. That didn't go as terribly as I expected it to. He's accepted the idea that Ashley will be living with me for a short time, underscoring the trust between us. "What about you and Tori? You're good?"

Carter's slow smile says it all. "Yeah, yeah, things are great. We're adjusting to our schedules, but when we're together, I'm blissed out. She's stressed about the gym, though. Doesn't have enough employees to meet the demand."

Tori's fitness studio, Every Body, caters to anyone and everyone—young, old, differently abled, hard core and soft core, among others. "Is she hiring more staff?"

"She's working on it."

I nod absently, my mind already focusing on the business matters we need to discuss. Carter's reaction will tell me whether it's too late to heed Quinn's warning. This go-round I gulp my cocktail. "I want to give you a heads-up about something. Work-related."

Carter sits up. "Go ahead."

"Barry Sanderson mentioned you in passing when I saw him at the GLAAD awards."

He lifts a brow. "Yeah?"

Sanderson is an A-list director known for blowing through the megabudgets of his action films. He describes it as his character flaw, and the studios indulge him because he makes movies everyone and their grandmother wants to see. "He said he has his eyes on you. Interested in getting you to sign on for more than one film. Said he'd be contacting me soon to give me the details."

"Holy shit." Carter drums his hands on the table. "That's huge."

"That *could* be huge. He could've been blowing smoke up my ass, though, so until he calls, I'll try to find out what he's working on."

He nods, his eyes shiny and bright. "Yeah, yeah. Of course. We don't want to get ahead of ourselves."

I don't tell him that I'm nervous about this potential deal. Nor do I mention that I'm not equipped to handle multifilm contracts, not on my own at least. My commercial and television expertise only travels so far, and he'd be tied by this agreement for years. But this is what Carter expects of me, and I don't want to disappoint him. Plus, Quinn's "advice" is fresh in my mind. "If it's what you want, I'll do my best to make it happen."

"Then it's settled." Carter lifts his drink. "I predict even bigger things for us, man. Just like we always dreamed."

He doesn't sound like a man who wants to fire his best friend, but Carter's one of the most talented actors I know—and I know many. I suppose I could ask him outright if he's unhappy with our working relationship, but I'm not sure I'd want to hear the answer before I get the chance to secure this megadeal for him. If anything, his enthusiasm renews my resolve not to disturb our arrangement. I clink his glass with my tumbler. "Yeah. To us."

He shakes his head. "We're a long way from Weston, huh?"

Weston. Damn, I haven't thought about our days there in a long time. It's where Carter and I met, his family having been assigned to help me acclimate to life as a boarding school student far away from my Atlanta neighborhood. They checked on me several times a month, inviting me over for dinner on the weekends. At the time, my parents were building their careers and couldn't afford to bring me home for Thanksgiving, Christmas, *and* spring break, so I spent some of those holidays with the Williamsons.

"You guys became my home away from home, and I appreciate it."

Carter extends his hand for a fist bump. "And now you're returning the favor by taking Ashley in, and I appreciate that. The good part is, she travels a lot, so she won't disrupt your flow."

I'm slow to connect my fist with his because I know the truth: She's only been at my place for one night, and my flow is officially disrupted.

ASHLEY'S BACKSIDE GREETS me as I walk into my condo. She's stretching to place a couple of mugs in an upper cabinet, her long legs highlighted by the yoga pants she's wearing.

Of course.

I need to maintain the status quo with Carter. Keep his feathers unruffled. Focus on proving my continued worth as his agent. Refrain from anything that might make it awkward for us to work together. Yet his younger sister, the one member of his family with the potential to permanently burrow herself under my skin, is playing house in my kitchen—at my invitation.

She turns her head and looks at me over her shoulder, genuine affection in her eyes. "How was your day?"

I unknot my tie and slide it off my neck. "Fine." Not counting the stern warning from Quinn and an unshakable sense that my career isn't as solid as I once thought, it was…fine. "Had a late lunch with Carter."

"Cool."

I expect questions, but she poses none.

Instead, she finishes unloading the dishwasher and wipes her hands on a towel. "Thanks for leaving a set of keys with the doorman. He's a talker."

"Benny takes the social aspects of his position very seriously."

"I told him I bake the best chocolate chip cookies ever, and I think he was seconds away from dropping on one knee and asking me to marry him."

"His wife and four children might take issue with that."

"Did you know he has two grandchildren? They're twins, and from what I saw in the many, many pictures he showed me, they're adorable."

That Ashley knows this her first full day here surprises me. It took months for Benny to share anything about his personal life with me. Then again, whenever Ashley and I talk, she gives me her undivided attention. Benny must have experienced that as well.

"Have you eaten?" I ask. "I know it's late, but I could get something delivered."

"Is that what you do on weeknights?"

"Yeah, if I'm home. Eating usually happens on the job. There's a Japanese place a few blocks away that's pretty good." I cross the kitchen and dig in a drawer. "I should have a take-out menu in here somewhere."

"Sounds perfect."

Bent at the waist, we pore over the menu together, settling on a couple of rice bowls to share. Ashley peruses the desserts page, and her hair falls forward to cover her profile. I'm overwhelmed by the urge to push her hair back and see her face again. Instead, I grab the phone and call Ziki, hoping the concentration necessary to relay the order correctly will leave no room for my brain to betray me. Thank goodness, it works.

I cover the phone's speaker. "Dessert?"

She shakes her head. "Nah. I'm thinking the bowls will be more than enough."

After I give Benny the heads-up that we're expecting a delivery, I turn back to Ashley. "I figured we could talk logistics while we eat. Schedules, house rules, etcetera."

Her face relaxes. "I was hoping you'd say something like that."

"I'm going to get out of this suit before the food arrives."

Her gaze lands on the span of my shoulders, and her lips twitch. "Okay. I'll finish putting away my things."

I glance at the shopping bags by the door. "That's all you have?"

She nods. "For now. I sent most of my stuff in Jersey to storage. And it doesn't make sense to clutter your place for a temporary stay. My clothes should be coming early next week, and I have a carry-on with what I'll need until then. I live my life from a suitcase anyway."

She's fidgeting as she talks. Maybe I'm not the only one unsettled by our new arrangement. "Which bedroom did you choose?"

Wrinkling her nose, she says tentatively, "The one…closest to yours?"

Damn. We've hit upon the most significant flaw of my place. The master bedroom shares a wall with the larger of the two guest bedrooms. I'm guessing the architect probably wanted to maximize the views from the eastern side of the condo, but the result is a lack of privacy that only matters when I have visitors—or a roommate. "That's fine. You'll enjoy the sunrise."

She smiles brightly, and I can't help staring at her mouth. It's wide-set, the peak of her upper lip always left of center as though she's reacting to a private joke. I'd like to kiss that mouth so greedily her lipstick smudges across her face. *Breathe, Julian. Get your act together.* "I'll be back in a few, and then we'll talk." I escape the living area, unfastening my cuff links as I go. An ice-cold shower is calling my name.

Minutes later, the doorbell rings as I'm toweling off. I don't want Ashley to pay for our meal, so I throw on a pair of sweats, mildly nervous about freeballing around her. This is my domain, though, and going commando here is nonnegotiable. If a man can't let his balls hang free in his own home, then it's no longer his sanctuary.

I reach the door just as Ashley pulls out a few bills from her purse. "I've got it, Ash."

She turns and scans me from head to crotch. Her cheeks turn a lovely shade of pink as she gets an eyeful. "Oh, okay."

Maybe freeballing wasn't one of my best ideas.

As I settle up with the delivery person, she shifts to my left and stares at her bare toes. Am I making her uncomfortable? I'd hate it if that were the case, so I scramble to say anything to distract her from my underwear-free state. "Your second toe's just as long as your big toe."

Her head shoots up, and her eyebrows snap together. "What?"

"Your toes. Second piggy's just as long as your big piggy. My mother once told me never to trust a person whose big and second toes are the same length."

She shakes her head and snatches the take-out bag from my hands. "I can't even with you." But as she walks away, I detect a soft chuckle coming from her general direction. Achievement unlocked, and it feels good.

We engage in casual conversation as we prepare our plates, interrupting the flow every so often when she needs help finding something in my kitchen. Then we move to the dining area, a small nook that sits on an elevated platform near the floor-to-ceiling windows in the living room.

I dig into the *oyakodon* bowl, a mixture of rice, chicken, eggs, and scallions, while Ashley gorges on *katsudon*, murmuring her appreciation.

She uses her chopsticks to hold out a piece of fried pork. "Want some?"

Without thinking, I lean forward and part my lips. Our eyes meet as she drops the meat into my mouth. She watches me chew, her gaze never wavering. An unspoken battle ensues, although I'm not sure what's at stake. All I know is I don't want to avert my eyes first. Maybe I want her to think she doesn't scare me, which isn't true at all. She terrifies me. When I'm with her, it's hard to remember why I shouldn't pursue her. When she reciprocates my interest, like I think she's doing now, it's damn near impossible to remember anything at all.

Fuck it. I know when to stand down. I take a big sip of water and clear my throat. "Let's discuss how to make this work."

She sets the chopsticks across the rim of her bowl and places her elbows on the table, steepling her fingers. "Okay."

"Let's begin with what might annoy us. That's usually a good place to start. Complete this sentence with the first thing that pops into your head. It really annoyed me when my roommate—"

I gesture for her to finish.

"Left me on the toilet with no tissue within arm's reach." She crosses her eyes as soon as the words are out.

"I can't unsee it."

She laughs as she picks up her bowl again. "You asked."

"Okay, okay," I say on a chuckle. "That won't be a problem. You'll have your own bathroom. It'll be up to you to ensure you have the appropriate…supplies."

"What about you?" she asks. "I'm guessing you have a long list."

"I should be offended by that remark, but it's true. I hate when people leave dishes in the sink. There's a dishwasher for a reason. Also, it's not cool to leave only a gulp of milk in the container. My roommates in college did that all the time. It pissed me off. If there's not enough to fill a cereal bowl, it's time to buy another carton."

"What else? There's more, right?"

"I hate the smell of microwave popcorn. It makes my stomach turn. I'm not saying you shouldn't eat it. Just give me a warning, and I'll steer clear of the kitchen when you make it."

"What about your hours? I like to play my guitar in the evenings. That okay?"

"I didn't know you still played."

She drops her gaze, and her hands disappear underneath the table. "It's just a hobby."

It's not like Ashley to be shy about anything, and I'm tempted to lift her chin and ask why she's hiding this aspect of herself from me. But touching Ashley would be dangerous, so talking will have to do. "That's quite a hobby. You were what? Twelve? Thirteen when you started? I've probably had twenty hobbies in that span."

She perks up. "Oh, yeah, like what?"

Interesting that she sidestepped my question. I'll let it slide for now. Besides, there's more than one way to get an answer. "Golf."

"How'd that work out for you?"

After taking another sip of water, I say, "It didn't. Got into it mostly for my job. But golfing requires talking with your partners, and I didn't have the patience for it."

"You're an agent. How can you not have the patience for talking?"

I shrug because I honestly don't know the answer. I've asked myself the same question many times in recent years. "Hard to explain. The conversations just felt fake. Forced. And so damn boring. I'm not a golfer, but I know how to advocate for my clients. You want to talk to me about industry trends? Fine. You want to talk to me about handicaps? Big yawn."

"Did anything stick?"

"Cooking."

She sets her bowl down, places one of her hands on her chest, and grabs my wrist with the other. "Stop. You cook?"

My gaze zeroes in on the way her soft fingers close around my arm, their warmth wrapping around me in a way I suspect she didn't intend. I give her a self-satisfied smile, hoping to appear unaffected by her touch. "I do."

"Like what? Scrambled eggs? Spaghetti?"

"More like eggs Benedict and bucatini with mushrooms."

She covers her forehead with the palm of her hand. "Enough, please. Any more of that and I'll orgasm right here."

More images than I can process flash in my brain. Ashley bent over a table, my body covering hers. Ashley on top of me, her long legs tangling with mine. Ashley coming long and hard, her body shuddering underneath me. And given what I heard last night, I know the soundtrack that would be playing in the background. It's too much to handle. The circulating air changes course, pushing all the coolness out of the room. I take a long breath, pulling the remaining heat into my lungs, and my body tenses. "That. You can't *do* that."

She flutters her eyes and then regards me with innocence under the veil of her long lashes. "Do what?"

The vixen. She knows what she's doing, and she doesn't possess an ounce of shame about it. "Make sexual references around me. That's not who we are. Together, I mean."

She's the sweet, shy girl who used to trail after Carter and me when we played hoops in the front yard. Except she isn't. Not anymore. When I wasn't looking, she grew up. Picked up a ton of sass—and a mouth made for long, slow kisses. It's unsettling in the best and worst ways.

She compresses her face like she's tasted something sour. "Who are we then?"

"We're old family friends. Roomies for the short-term. Let's not make it awkward."

She blows out a long breath, pretending to be put out by my practical suggestion. "Well, if we're talking about awkward, let's address the elephant in the room." Under her breath, she mutters, "Literally."

I lean in to hear her better. "What?"

"C'mon, Julian. Your lack of underwear, that's what. Your dick was practically swinging at me like a bat when you walked in here. For a minute, I considered ducking."

My head snaps back. I'm not entirely sure I've heard her correctly. Did Ashley just say something about my junk? I shake my head as I try to regain my mental footing. This is her superpower—keeping me off balance—and I don't like it. So now it's clear. Whether or not I freeball, while Ashley's here, this place will no longer be my sanctuary.

Chapter Five

Ashley

TOO MUCH?

Maybe. But Julian needs to think of me as more than Carter's younger sister, and what better way to spur that process than to discuss his dangling private parts?

Julian works his eyebrows in a fascinating display of confusion, embarrassment, and disbelief. Up, down, scrunched together, all in under four seconds. He drops his head, avoiding my gaze, and then he rises, his bowl and glass in hand. "On that ridiculous note, I think I'll head to bed."

What? He's not even going to address it? I place a hand on his wrist to stop him, momentarily distracted by the strong pulse that beats under my fingers. I take so much pleasure in touching him, he should charge me for the privilege.

He doesn't say a word as he slowly sits back down, his mouth agape and his brows furrowed.

"I was just *kidding*, Julian. Sort of. The point is, we should be talking about states of undress, too. Like, I'll promise not to run out here in my bra and panties, and you'll promise not to grab a beer from the fridge in your skivvies or something. Isn't that how this should go?"

He swallows, and my gaze settles on his Adam's apple. I'm tempted to proposition him this minute. To ask that for just one night, he'll pretend I'm not *Ashley* and think of me instead as a stranger he desires. But Julian's too pragmatic to accept such a proposal. He'd say no without much thought and avoid me for the rest of my stay. If I'm going to have any chance with him, I'll have to get him to the point where he's incapable of rational thought. And that's going to take time. *And machinations.*

He shakes his head as though he's been pulled out of a trance, and then he sighs as he scrubs his face. "We'll both agree to be fully dressed when we're in the common areas, okay?"

"That works. And I won't be here for long stretches of time anyway. I'm too junior to know my flight schedule well in advance, but most weeks I'll be gone four or five days."

Julian smiles at the news. I'm not bothered by his obvious relief. It means there's something about my presence that makes him uncomfortable. And given the way he was staring at my mouth only minutes ago, I'm guessing the discomfort relates to our mutual but unspoken attraction. Well, that's what I'm hoping at least.

He rises from the seat, taking his bowl and glass with him. "This will work out fine, then. During the work week, I'm usually not home until ten or so, and most weekends I've got somewhere to be. We'll be like two ships passing in the night."

Ah, Julian. That's unlikely. Because if all goes according to *my* plan, we'll be like two ships colliding in the night. And hopefully, we'll *both* get wrecked.

IT TAKES ME less than twenty-four hours to break our agreement, but I didn't orchestrate this, I swear.

Yes, I have a perfectly logical explanation for walking through the house in a tiny towel. A fellow flight attendant doubles as a beauty consultant, and a few weeks ago, she convinced me to try an organic cleanser. A cleanser that requires *refrigeration*. He wasn't supposed to be here—it's just past seven in the evening after all—but there he is, staring at me from the doorway because I'm wearing the linen closet equivalent of booty shorts. *One day* after promising not to walk around in my underwear. Well, I'm not even wearing undies, but I get it: spirit of the agreement and such.

"Sorry! I just needed to grab something," I say.

For a few seconds, he peruses my face and body, and the heat in his eyes blazes across my skin. I swear time suspends, as if I could bridge the distance between us, steal a kiss, and return to my original spot before he blinks an eye.

After a shake of his head, he turns around. "I'll give you a minute."

I scramble to the fridge, grab the bottle, and hightail it out of the room, yelling "all clear" over my shoulder. As I wash my face, I listen for evidence of his movements. He runs the kitchen sink and slams a few cabinet doors. A minute later, when I collapse onto the bed, my face freshly scrubbed and moisturized, I hear a soft click, suggesting he's retreated to his bedroom.

Given Julian's reaction to seeing me close to bare, I suspect subtlety is the only way to get him to let his guard down around me. If he senses a threat, he'll institute measures to protect himself against it. And one thing's now clear: I'm a threat.

I throw on my roomiest pair of sweatpants—the ones I usually wear the second day of my cycle—and a loose T-shirt. Then I pull my acoustic guitar from its case and tiptoe to the living area, figuring the sound will be less obtrusive to Julian if I'm not propped against the wall that abuts his.

After sitting cross-legged at one end of Julian's plush navy couch, I strum a few chords, tightening the strings to get my prized instrument in tune. I sing the first verse of the song I wrote when my roommate accused me of trying to seduce her boyfriend—by "parading" in my own kitchen in sleep clothes:

You never got to know me
Never really wanted to
You thought you had me figured out
All along my heart was true
You chose him over me

> *I didn't want to face*
> *That in your mind*
> *I'd always be second place*

I shouldn't have been surprised that Elise sided with her boyfriend. We'd maintained a healthy distance, never pretending to be best friends. It was a convenient arrangement, born of our need to share living expenses and nothing more. Notwithstanding the evidence of her man's wandering eyes, she wanted to believe he was as wrapped up in her as she was in him. His unwelcome hands on my ass fucked up the narrative.

The day it all went down, I used my artistic license and poured my frustration into these lyrics, accompanying them with a D-minor chord progression that matched my sullen mood. Tonight, I tweak the song's opening, making slight alterations that don't improve it in any meaningful way. Stasis. It's suffocating. Makes me want to spring to my feet and move around. Sighing overdramatically, I place the guitar beside me. I never finished the song. And maybe I never will.

"Don't stop."

I look up and find Julian leaning against the entryway, one hand resting above him on the doorframe. Seeing him like this, stripped of his power suit and dressed in sweats and a loose T-shirt, I want to peel his other layers and get to the man beneath the polish. What does he like to do? Who does he spend time with? Is he happy? What drives him? I hope my newfound access to him will provide the answers to these questions. For now, though,

I need to avoid playing this song. It captures a moment of vulnerability, a state I don't like sharing with anyone.

I wave him off. "Oh, I was just messing around."

He pads across the floor and joins me on the couch, tucking one leg under him and angling his body in my direction. Then he grabs a slate gray pillow and places it on his lap.

For a moment I'm consumed by other questions: Is he still letting his balls hang free? Is that the reason for the pillow?

"Why do you do that?" he asks.

Obsess about his balls? Not sure. Although that's probably not what he's referring to, right? *Bad, Ashley. Heel.* "Do what?"

"Minimize your guitar playing."

"I don't," I say in an assured voice.

"You do," he says with equal confidence. "You said it was a hobby yesterday. Today you're just messing around. Yet you've been at it for more than a decade."

"Hmm. I never noticed." And I'm surprised he did. The men in my life tend to be oblivious to anything unrelated to their own needs and wants. "The deal is, I'm composing a song, but I'm stuck."

"How many songs have you composed?"

"A hundred, maybe?"

He leans forward, his eyes widening as if he's looking at me through a microscopic lens, and I freeze, my limbs rigid from being pinned to his petri dish. Somehow, I tamp down the urge to flee the room. "What? What's that look for?"

"*One hundred* songs?" he says, his voice rising an octave.

Oh. That. I shrug because I know the crap I've composed. "Give or take. I don't know for sure. And some of them are terrible, believe me. I wrote a dozen my thirteenth summer alone. So much angst."

He massages his chin as he regards me with a pensive expression. "That may be, but you don't write over one hundred songs for the fun of it. Ever thought of pursuing it as a career?"

"No."

He waits for more, giving me an encouraging nod.

"Well, *maybe.* Okay, yes, I did, for like two seconds. But I dismissed the idea a long time ago."

"Why?"

"Because I have realistic expectations. How many singer-songwriters do you know?"

"One."

"*Other* than me."

He lowers his chin, a hint of a smile softening the hard angles of his face. "None."

"Well, there you go." I point to the guitar in my lap. "*This* won't pay the bills. Besides, Carter's the star in our family."

"But it's your dream. I can tell."

"How?"

"Because you've kept at it for over a decade. Because you've written over a hundred songs in that time. Because your face lights up when you strum that guitar. And when we were going over the house rules, your one true concern was whether you'd bother me if you played."

His words alone move me, but pair them with his soothing tone, and I'm swoony putty in his hands. I wish I could lay my head in his lap, close my eyes, and ask him to repeat what he just said. But that would be weird, right? Yeah, of course it would. More to the point, Julian's picking up on things I'd never notice on my own. Makes me wonder what kind of expression I wear when I'm playing.

"When I was a teenager, I wanted to perform at local festivals and fairs. To get a sense of what it would be like. But my mom was busy with her counseling duties at Weston, and my dad was shuttling Carter to auditions in New York. Once, I even worked up the nerve to perform in the middle school talent show. Neither of my parents showed up. Said they had the wrong date in their calendar." I grip the neck of the guitar and fiddle with the tuners, suppressing the grimace that usually accompanies that memory. "Anyway, it just…never happened for me. I'm good with that."

And besides, how likely would it be for my family to have two successful children in the entertainment industry? It happens, sure, but it's still rare.

"What about teaching guitar? To kids? Or other adults like you who are scared to follow their dreams?"

"Julian," I warn, my voice low and tight.

He takes a deep breath and releases it. "Fine. But I know one thing. If you ever decide to pursue music as a career, you'll need an upgrade. It's looking a bit battered."

I scoop up the guitar with both hands and wrap my arms around it. "Hush your mouth. This is a Taylor 300 series. Sitka spruce stop. Mahogany neck. The company doesn't make that combination anymore."

Julian regards me with a raised brow. "I'm guessing there's a good reason for that."

Yes, time and the sun's rays have aged the wood, and okay, the metallic star stickers I placed on it each time I finished a song are peeling at the edges, but she's a beauty. Caressing the sides and top, I whisper, "He doesn't know what he's talking about, Melanie. You're special, and anyone who can't see that isn't worth your time."

"Melanie? You named your guitar *Melanie*?"

"I did. She's named after my favorite teacher in grade school, Ms. Adams. I was eleven when I got her, mind you. Now take it back."

He holds up his hands. "All right, all right, I take it back. She's a classic. Would you and Melanie be willing to play something for me? A song that you're proud of?"

I wink at him. "What do I get in return?"

He drops his jaw, and then his gaze snaps to mine. His expression is playful as he studies me, but much to my disappointment, he ultimately refuses my bait. Shaking his head, he pokes the inside of his cheek with his tongue. "You get free accommodations in my home, you ingrate."

Hmm. Yeah, no. We're nowhere close to breaking the friendship barrier. Any other person would have recognized my question as an attempt at flirtation. But not Julian. He probably still pictures me in braces. "I was kidding."

"You do a lot of that."

"And you don't do enough of it. You're so formal all the time. Makes me wonder if you wear a three-piece suit in bed. *With* suspenders."

His eyes crinkle at the corners, and he smiles broadly. "I wear my birthday suit in bed, and I'm very relaxed there, a fact you'll have to trust me on."

I want to pout, but that's not going to help my cause, so I pucker my lips at him instead. "Or you could prove it to me."

His eyes shutter closed. "Don't."

"Don't what?"

"Don't take this somewhere it shouldn't go. Carter's my best friend *and* my client. I've spent way too long navigating that relationship, and it's not easy. I'm not going to make it harder by messing around with his sister. We are never going to happen."

A boulder sits on my chest, flattening me *and* my spirit. "Never?"

His dark eyes soften as he shakes his head. "Never ever. Let's just leave it, okay?"

Well, there it is. The answer I've been seeking. His reasons are sound—and my objective was selfish. I wanted to satisfy my curiosity and fulfill my teenage fantasies. Julian wants to preserve a friendship *and* protect his livelihood. I take a deep, cleansing breath and exhale on a sigh. "You tend to overthink things, but in this instance, you're right." I point an accusing finger at him and give him a stern look. "*Just* this once."

"Now about that song…"

I fake a yawn and rise from the sofa. "We'll have to do it another time. I'm suddenly very sleepy."

"I'm sure you are," he says with bemusement in his voice.

Before I leave the room, I stare at his bowed head and gather the nerve to ask another question. "Under different circumstances, though, would you…"

Without looking up and without hesitation, he says, "Definitely."

The certainty in his voice makes my gut twist. Damn. Maybe it would have been better never to know the answer. Because, yes, his admission heals the light bruise on my ego, but it also makes the loss tangible.

Chapter Six

Julian

I SUFFER THROUGH another restless night and drag myself out of bed the next morning. If I'm not careful, the quality of my rest will depend on whether Ashley's around, and that's not healthy. After sleepwalking through my morning routine, I take several groggy steps to the kitchen and make myself a protein shake. When I unscrew the lid of the whey powder, the particles rush out like a small storm cloud. The floor and my face are among the casualties.

I mutter to myself as I get down on all fours and clean up the mess I've made.

Not long after, Ashley snorts above me. "You okay down there?"

"Yeah, I'm fine," I mutter. "Just a little mishap."

The truth is, despite what I know to be the rational thing to do, I spent way too much time last night imagining a scenario in which Ashley and I were lovers, not friends. It was a cruel exercise, and my brain and body are battered as a result.

"That's what you get for not making yourself a proper breakfast. Eggs, bacon, hash browns. No powder involved."

"That's a weekend meal," I say as I take one more pass at the floor with a damp dish towel. When I stand, I find a fully dressed Ashley wringing her hands. "What's wrong?"

She jumps at my question and repeatedly shakes her head as she answers. "What? Nothing's wrong. Why'd you ask?"

"Ash, it's six o'clock in the morning, you have the day off, and you're awake. Something's wrong."

Her shoulders drop. "I didn't sleep well. It'll pass, I'm sure. Figured I could explore the neighborhood more before I leave for my next trip."

Given how we left things last night, I'm guessing her thoughts weren't all that different from mine. As long as they remain unspoken, we should be fine. "When do you have to check in?"

"Tomorrow night. Red-eye to Chicago."

I feel like an insensitive shit for not thinking of this sooner. Ashley's not familiar with my neighborhood, and all I've done is point her in the direction of the nearest Whole Foods. I should have offered to show her around. My phone, which is always either in my pocket or within reach, buzzes on the counter, a fitting reminder that my time is rarely my own. I swipe it up and read a message from one of my clients letting me know she's on time for her New York audition. It's a small miracle, and I'll take it. Turning back to Ashley, I say, "I have to head into the office soon. Won't be back until late, so…"

She straightens. "Oh, don't worry about me. I'm in LA. Entertaining myself won't be hard."

As I watch her and consider my schedule, she pulls her lower lip into her mouth and scans the space. We're dancing around each other, and I place the burden on myself to correct that. Fortunately, I know exactly how to. "Hey, a potential client invited me to a play at the Pasadena Playhouse tonight. An experimental show of some kind. It's supposed to be groundbreaking and"—I make air quotes—"'edgy.' Want to join me?"

Her eyes brighten, and her pinched expression softens. "Sounds like fun."

"I won't be able to take you. Too much going on at work. But I'll arrange for a car to pick you up. How does that sound?"

She nods. "Great. What time?"

"Be ready at seven."

She gives me an ear-to-ear smile. "Perfect. I'll be ready."

See, Julian? That wasn't so bad. The awkwardness between us is only temporary. Ashley and I will be fine. Years from now, we'll sit together with our respective spouses and laugh about how we avoided a catastrophe. I'm certain of it.

I SEARCH FOR Ashley when I arrive at the theater, but I don't see her anywhere. After confirming she hasn't called or sent me a text, I lean against a column in the lobby and check my email as I wait for her. A few minutes later, Ashley spins through the revolving door, catches sight of me, and strides my way. Her long hair frames her face in soft waves, and she's wearing a frilly sundress and strappy flat sandals, as if she decided to cosplay as the perfect spring day. I'm not the only person who notices, judging by the people following her progress. Still, they're probably not imagining her like I am—tangled in my sheets, her back arched and her limbs trembling as I lick her swollen clit. *Jesus.* Straightening as she approaches, I put a fucking muzzle on my thoughts.

"Hey," she says in a breathy voice. "Sorry I'm late. The driver was showing me pictures of his newborn granddaughter, and I couldn't figure out a polite way to tell him a dozen pictures was enough."

People gravitate to Ashley, opening up to her in a way they'd never act with me. Maybe because I don't give off vibes that I want to hear anyone's life story. Still, Ashley could get a nun to cackle in church if she tried hard enough. "No problem," I say as we walk inside the theater. "How'd your day of sightseeing go?"

"Um, not great. I kind of got sidetracked. Did you know there's an ice cream shop two blocks away from your place? You can watch the batches being made. I was mesmerized."

We're swallowed by the crowd, both content to lumber along until we get to our row.

I hand her a program. "Luna Creamery?"

"That's the one!" Her eyes brighten and grow wide. "And they have ice cream flights. I inhaled those miniature scoops of deliciousness like I was throwing back shots of vodka. I'm sorry, but fresh ice cream beats an LA tour any day."

"I've never been there. Always wondered if it was any good."

She halts midstride and squeezes my arm. "We need to get you out more. See, there's this thing. It's called fun. Are you familiar with it?"

Ignoring that wisecrack, I place my hands on her shoulders and steer her forward. It feels good to have my hands on her. Too good. I drop my arms to the sides because feeling good with Ashley isn't wise. At the front of the theater, I motion for her to proceed me. "Here we are. Row B, seats seven and eight. We've got nine, too, but none of my coworkers jumped on it."

She places her purse in the empty seat and leans over. "Who's the target?"

I chuckle at her attempt to make this an undercover stakeout. "Well, Agent Williamson, the target's name is Gabriel Vega. He's done commercial work and public theater mostly. He reached out to me a couple of weeks ago—got my number from someone he knows in the television division—and he made a good first impression."

Her playful expression turns serious. "Was that okay? Passing on your number like that? I imagine you don't give it out to just anyone."

"My direct number, definitely not. But in this instance, it was the right move. He made a compelling case."

Within two minutes of the call, Vega told me about his struggle to land quality television and film roles, attributing it in part to his Puerto Rican heritage. I suspect he's right. Tinseltown is notorious for typecasting Latino actors. Sure, there's no shortage of small parts as the neighborhood ex-gang member or the Colombian drug lord, but leading roles in which a successful Latino saves the day or gets the girl, or both, are few and far between. I can't share his concerns with Ashley—it wouldn't be appropriate, especially if Gabriel becomes my client—so I flip open the program and point to his head shot. "That's him."

Ashley stares at his photo. "Wow. He's *gorgeous*."

"You know you said that out loud, right?"

She blinks up at me, and her cheeks go rosy. "Well, consider me the one and only member of your focus group, then. If his acting and personality match his looks, you have a winner."

It's all good. She's entitled to admire another man's appearance, obviously. Just feels weird to hear her be so blatant about it. And if her interest in Gabriel is any indication, I'm nothing but a temporary diversion to her, which for my own sake is exactly what I need to be. Plus, I know something she doesn't. "He's married."

She rolls her eyes. "Why am I not surprised?"

The lights in the theater flicker, and the audience's chatter fades to indistinct murmurs.

"What kind of show is this anyway?" Ashley asks just before the curtain rises.

"Experimental improv, whatever that means. Should be interesting."

WHEN THE PERFORMANCE is over, Ashley and I stroll to center stage to meet Gabriel.

A small circle of people surrounds the cast, and Gabriel gracefully accepts everyone's congratulatory remarks. His face is open and friendly, and he carries himself with ease, all positive signs for someone wanting to be in the public eye. His face brightens even more when he sees us. After breaking away from the group, he claps me on the shoulder and shakes my outstretched hand. "Hey, you made it."

"We did. Thanks for the invitation."

Next to me, Ashley clears her throat.

"Gabriel, this is Ashley. She couldn't resist coming along and getting a taste of the LA theater scene."

Gabriel shakes her hand, too. "Great to meet you, Ashley." Then he launches into a five-minute explanation of the show concept, and I pretend to be riveted by it. Not Ashley, though. Beside me, she stretches her arms behind her and stifles a yawn.

Gabriel glances at her. "Uh-oh. I'm boring your girl-friend, Julian."

She straightens and gives him a flirty smile. "Oh, I wasn't bored. Just low blood sugar, I think. And he's not my boyfriend. We're old family friends."

"And I represent her brother," I add.

"Really?" Gabriel says. "Who's your brother?"

"Carter Williamson." She gives him a sheepish grin. "I guess you'd know him as Carter Stone."

"Oh, wow. Stone's your brother? I guess good looks run in the family."

Gabriel's spouse wouldn't appreciate this conversation; neither do I, for that matter. Time to move it along. I scan the area around us. "Does your wife attend your shows?"

Gabriel slants his head and looks at me quizzically. "My ex-wife? No, it's been years since I've seen her."

I massage the back of my head as I consider this new information. "Sorry. You mentioned on the phone that your wife always thought you overshared, so I assumed…"

He waves away the misunderstanding. "No worries. She's in my past." With a wistful expression on his face, he says under his breath, "Or I'd like her to be."

Hmm. If I'm not mistaken, Gabriel's not over his ex-wife. I make a mental note to check whether she's an actor as well.

A fellow cast member tugs on the sleeve of Gabriel's button-down. "Hey, man, we're heading out soon. You comin'?"

Gabriel nods. "Be there in a bit." He turns back to us. "Hey, I don't suppose you'd want to join me? We're going to Muddy's Bar to grab a bite to eat. It's just across the street."

I hate neighborhood bars. People are too loud, and the music is never anything I want to listen to. Plus, the possibility that some fool will drink too much and say something stupid means I never relax enough to enjoy the experience. I open my mouth to decline, but Ashley lays her hands on my chest, and her delicate touch wraps around my brain and neutralizes it.

Her eyes are wide and dancing when she speaks. "Oooh, I'd like to go, but you're my ride. Can we go? It'll be fun. And I'm so hungry I could eat granola." She winks at me, and even if it's at my expense, I like that we're sharing a private joke. Way more than I should, actually.

"Well, we can't have you eating granola, can we now? The fiber and iron might cause your body to go into shock."

She's grinning as she pushes me away from her.

Gabriel claps his hands together. "Great. I'm going to grab my stuff and make sure everything's locked up. The cast is on the hook if anyone swipes the theater's equipment. Meet you over there in ten?"

"Sure." I offer Ashley my arm. "Shall we?"

She bows. "We most certainly shall."

With our arms linked, we sprint across the avenue and duck into Muddy's Bar. The place is dark but not dank, and it appears to be overpopulated with theater and musician types. In other words, I see lots of cardigans and classic rock T-shirts. The crowd's diverse, too, which isn't a surprise in this part of town. My suit sets me apart, though. To them, I probably look like an undercover cop.

Ashley points at a table in a back corner. "Let's snag that one."

We weave our way through the crowd and settle onto the curved high-backed bench that faces the stage. A middle-aged man is performing a comedy set and swipes at his forehead with a kerchief every few seconds. There's laughter in the crowd, but it isn't timed to anything he's saying.

I lean over to Ashley and whisper in her ear. "He's bombing." Her sweet scent wafts over me, and I breathe her in. Damn, she smells good.

She stills and closes her eyes.

"You okay, Ash?"

She nods and fishes inside her purse, damn near burying her nose in it. "I'm so thirsty." Then she sets her bag behind her, presses a hand against her throat, and swallows, her other arm raised to get a server's attention. When she finally looks up again, she grimaces sympathetically at our amateur comedian. "I admire his courage, but this is painful to watch."

Before I can respond, Gabriel and a few of his castmates arrive at the table with our server in tow. We exchange introductions as she waits patiently for everyone to get situated. Once we're settled, she goes around placing napkins in front of everyone. "Welcome to Muddy's, folks. We've got three- and four-dollar cocktails tonight. They're listed here." She points to a long, narrow piece of cardstock in the center of the table. "It's also open mic night. If anyone's interested in getting on stage, you can sign up by the DJ booth."

I nudge Ashley's shoulder with mine. "What do you say, Ash? Ready to get up there?"

"I'll do it if you do it," she says without hesitation. There's mischief in her eyes, as if she knows her challenge will shut me up. And it does, because there's no way I'd ever embarrass myself on a stage. We order a round of drinks and appetizers for the table.

Ashley tacks on an order of burger and fries. A few minutes later, she rises and places a hand on my shoulder as she climbs out from behind the table. "I'm going to run to the restroom." Her casual touches should go unnoticed, but my brain seizes on those moments of contact and tricks me into thinking they mean more than they do. *Why did I agree to this?* I should have shuttled her home immediately after the show. Before she leaves, she lifts a finger as if she's scolding me. "If my burger gets here before I do, don't touch it."

Gabriel winks at her. "I'll protect it with my life."

She winks back at him. "I'm relying on you, comrade."

He rewards her with a goofy grin just as our drinks arrive. Damn, I gave up freeballing in my sweats at home for this? Eager for something to do besides watch them flirt with each other, I reach for my snifter before our server can get it off the tray.

Ashley steps away, and when I finish a sip of brandy, Gabriel slides closer. "Again, thanks for coming, man. I wasn't sure you would."

His friends get into a debate about the greatest movie remake of all time, leaving us free to chat about his work. "The show was interesting. Not what I expected."

"This isn't what I want to be doing, and some days it's hard to keep pounding the pavement in search of better work."

I've heard this complaint before. If an actor didn't question the prudence of chasing his dreams at least once, I'd wonder if it really was his dream. "But you keep going because you love it, right?"

"Right. When I have a gig, I jump out of the bed singing. It's like the whole tenor of my day changes. And when I'm acting?" He shakes his head. "Man, there's nothing like it."

The sincerity in his voice moves me. He's in the business because he loves it. And if I'm being honest with myself, I envy him. I'd love to jump out of the bed singing, but that's never happened. I like what I do just fine. It's given me the means to provide for myself and help my family. I suppose that should be enough.

Gabriel glances at our tablemates, one of whom is belting out a show tune, and lowers his voice. "Maybe you could help me get out of this rut?"

"Maybe. We should have lunch and discuss your goals. I'll ask my assistant to schedule something with you next week."

Gabriel lets out a huge breath and nods. "Sounds great."

I spot Ashley on the other side of the bar, suspiciously close to the stage. She sidles up to the DJ, and they exchange a few words. He thrusts a sheet in her hand, and she studies it for a few seconds before thrusting it back at him. She backs away, shaking her head and gesturing no, while he motions for her to come back. When she returns to the table, she wedges herself in between Gabriel and me. "Is that mine?" she asks me, pointing to the only unclaimed drink on the table.

"Yeah. Were you considering going on stage for open mic night?"

She lifts her eyebrows and purses her lips. "Nope. Just curious."

Just curious, my ass. She's tempted to get on stage but won't take the leap. I wish I knew what's holding her back.

As she nurses her drink, she sways to the music piping through the speakers, her body moving like a pendulum and brushing against mine each time she leans my way. As surreptitiously as I can, I slide an inch away from her. There's only so much I should be expected to bear.

Our server returns with the appetizers and Ashley's burger and fries. Ash's eyes bug out as she licks her lips in anticipation of getting her hands on the food. Seeing her wrap her elegant fingers around the thick burger shouldn't do anything for me—but it does. And it gets worse, because she opens her mouth wide and takes a big-ass bite, moaning her appreciation in a way that sounds torturously similar to the orgasm she gave herself the other night.

"Oh, that's *so* good." She lifts the burger to my eye level. "Want a bite?"

"No, thanks."

"It's always the hole-in-the-wall that makes the best food." She chomps down again. "So good."

Gabriel laughs. "This place should hire you to sell their burgers. You're making an excellent case for them."

She grins at Gabriel as she chews. "It's fantastic, what can I say?" She holds out her burger. "Here, try it and tell me I'm lying."

I expect Gabriel to decline her offer—people don't share food with someone they don't know, right?—but he leans over and sinks his teeth into Ashley's burger.

I shut my eyes and pinch the bridge of my nose. He's ruining my watching-Ashley-eat-a-burger experience. I'm exhausted, too, my eyes blurring as I glance at the person on stage. And now I have an overwhelming need to extricate myself from this scene. Watching Gabriel and Ashley flirt with each other isn't my idea of a good time, and I don't want to contemplate the reasons why.

After Ashley dabs her mouth with a napkin and pats her belly to show that she's full, I check my watch and lean close to her ear. "Tomorrow's a work day, so we should get going soon."

She sits up, her brows puckered in confusion. "Oh, okay." I drop several bills on the table, and Ashley does the same.

"That should cover us, yes?" she asks Gabriel.

"It's fine," he says. "No worries. And it was great to meet you."

Her smile is open and friendly when she says, "Same here," and I have absolutely no cause to be annoyed by their apparent compatibility, but still…

"Gabriel, I'll follow up about lunch," I say as I shake his hand.

"Yeah, yeah, man. Thanks for coming."

We wave at the rest of the group, its members deep in discussion and unmoved to do anything other than nod at us absently.

Ashley holds my arm as we make our way through the crowd. Out on the street, she says, "I didn't realize we had to eat and run."

Technically, *she* was eating, and now *I'm* running. But there's no way in hell I'm admitting that to her.

Chapter Seven

Ashley

"Is something wrong?"

We're ten minutes into the drive home, and Julian hasn't said a word. I know he enjoys silence, and maybe he's tired, but if he can converse with his clients and colleagues all day, it shouldn't be that difficult for him to drum up enough energy to talk to me.

"Julian?"

"Huh? What?" He glances at me and returns his gaze to the road, ever the careful driver.

"I asked if there's something wrong. You're giving me the silent treatment."

"I'm not. I was just thinking."

More silence. Which I must fill. "So what'd you think of the show?"

"I'd never pay to see a show like that, but it gave me some insight into Gabriel's talent. He's a dynamic guy. Charming, self-deprecating."

"Handsome," I tease.

Although only Julian's profile is in view, I know a nostril flare when I see one. "You're upset that I think he's cute. Why does that bother you?"

He sighs. "Nothing's bothering me, Ash."

"If that's true, I'd hate to be around when something *is* bothering you." Rather than play into his mood, I riffle through my purse and pull out my phone. When a man pouts, Twitter entertains. He turns up the radio dial, filling the car with the sounds of classic jazz, which only highlights the silence between us.

Twenty excruciatingly long minutes later, Julian pulls into his building's underground parking lot. I refuse to wait for him to come around and open the car door for me. Instead, I exit the vehicle and stride to the bank of elevators that will take us from the lower level to Julian's floor.

"Wait up," he says behind me.

I jab at the elevator button and pace as we wait in the dimly lit vestibule.

Julian stands against a wall watching me. "Is something wrong?"

I stop midstride and give him a blank stare. "Nope. Just thinking." Then the elevator dings.

He pushes off the wall and saunters to my side. "I deserve that."

"Do you?" I ask as I step in.

He nods, his lips pinched, as if he's frowning at himself. That makes two of us.

"Yeah, I deserve it. I told you we couldn't be anything more than friends, and the minute you showed interest in another man, I regressed and became a two-year-old. Sorry."

His honesty is refreshing. And infuriating, too. According to his logic, because he won't permit himself to eat cake, no one else should eat cake, either. *Oh, brother.* I stare at my new sandals as I speak. "Apology accepted." Then I add, "Grudgingly."

He chuckles and nudges my chin up with his index finger. "I *really* am sorry."

That tiny contact melts me, but I don't show it, because as he put it, we're never ever going to happen. "And I *really* am accepting your apology…grudgingly."

"What can I do to make it up to you?"

A few days ago, I would have made a suggestive comment. Now I know there's no point in doing so. "Make me breakfast in the morning."

"Frozen waffles and orange juice from concentrate? Done."

Like he'd have any of that in his precious fridge. I shove him away. "No, the good stuff. Waffles made from scratch. With whipped cream and strawberries. And bacon."

"Would you settle for turkey sausages? I don't have bacon."

I shake my head. "You're such a disappointment."

"You'll say otherwise after you eat my breakfast."

I search his face for signs that he's joking, but there are none. "Seriously? You're going to make me breakfast?"

"I'd be happy to. Think of it as my way of welcoming you into my home."

"Wow. I'm honored. Can I help?"

"I expect you to. I need to instruct you on the finer points of making waffles so you can return the favor someday."

I like the idea of that. Cooking in his kitchen. Cooking *for* him in his kitchen. As the elevator ascends to his floor, we smile at each other, and I'm reminded that we weren't always awkward together. After we drift inside the condo and walk quietly through the hall, each of us continues to our respective rooms and pauses at the door.

Julian gives me a tired wave, his suit still falling impeccably over his broad shoulders and his tie unmarred by a single wrinkle. "Good night, Ash."

"Good night, Julian."

We did well today, despite the earlier tension between us. He's entitled to his prickly moments, and I shouldn't be so quick to take them personally. Our relationship doesn't need to be earth-shattering. I just need to adjust my expectations. Not sure what I was so worried about. We're fully capable of having a healthy, platonic relationship. I'm sure of it.

THE NEXT MORNING, my doubts return, and I chuckle at my naïveté. Because why, oh why is the simple act of making breakfast together a challenge, too?

It's not my fault, really. Several factors are conspiring against me.

The first? Biceps porn. Holy shit, it's a thing. When he lifts the pan from the stove, his biceps flex like thick rubber bands. If he were to hold himself above me during sex, I'd see them at close range. Up, down, swivel, and repeat.

The second factor? That apron looks fucking *glorious* on him. The strings are tied snugly around his trim waist, which emphasizes the nearly perfect V formed by his broad chest and shoulders. Damn, it's hot as hell in here. I fan myself, but it doesn't help. So when I'm sure he's not looking, I grab the mister off the counter and spritz my face.

He catches the sound, though, and draws back. "Jesus. Did you just spray yourself with that?"

"Yeah. Why?" I pull on the collar of my T-shirt to let in some air.

He snickers, his eyes gleaming with amusement. "Ashley, that's olive oil. You need to wipe that off."

Great. My cheeks are on fire, and now that there's oil on them, I just might be the first human cooking surface in existence. Swallow me whole, Mother Earth.

Shaking his head at my gaffe, he preps the waffle mix while I use a paper towel to clean myself. I should use a cleanser or something, but I don't want to miss the biceps porn—or the apron porn for that matter. Besides, olive oil must be good for the skin.

"No blueberries, right?" he asks.

"You remember."

"Yeah. And I remember you love strawberries, but I'm not putting them in my waffle maker. I'll toss them on top."

"Fine with me."

I squeeze my fists at my sides when I discover there's more porn. *Whisk porn.* He's got a mixing bowl in one hand and a whisk in the other, and he's beating that waffle mix like he's its daddy.

He looks up and finds me staring at him. "Everything okay?"

I nod like a human bobblehead. "Mm-hmm."

He transfers the mix to a measuring cup and pours the batter into the waffle maker. Then he flips it over. Oooh, it's a double waffle maker. Fancy. Unaware that he's the new host of my personal cooking show on the Julian Channel, he bends at the waist and wipes the metal plate with a kitchen towel, giving me a DVR-worthy view of his butt. His Nielsen ratings would go into the stratosphere every time he made that move.

"Can you wash the strawberries?" he asks.

Sure, no problem. *That ass is going to get someone arrested one day.*

"Ash?"

Julian's voice snatches me out of my happy place. "What?"

"The strawberries. Can you wash them?"

I shake my head and push out my lower lip. "Didn't you hear me? I said, 'Sure, no problem.'"

He laughs. "In your mind, maybe, but not out loud."

"Sorry. Watching you cook requires my full attention. You're so precise, and there are so many steps." I retrieve the strawberries from the fridge and rinse them in the sink. How do I get these thoughts out of my head? What can I do to stop myself from wanting him? I should probably confiscate his apron. That would be a good place to start.

Beside me, Julian wipes down the counter. When he's done, he bumps me with his hip and reaches for a clean strawberry, breaching my personal space to get to it. I try to bump him back, but he blocks me with his body, lifts the fruit over his head, and drops everything except the crown into his mouth.

The moment he bites into it, I sway on my feet. When he slides his tongue over his bottom lip to catch the juices, I swoon. Screw you, Julian. Screw you. But not really. What I really mean is, screw *me*, Julian. Screw *me*.

His phone buzzes on the counter, disrupting my traitorous thoughts. He leans over to read the display—*there's that ass again*—and then he grimaces. "I've got to take this."

"Sure, I'll watch this while you're gone."

Already walking off, he says, "The light will turn green when the waffles are ready. Just grab them with those tongs and transfer them to a plate."

I nod. "Seems simple enough. Go take your call."

He picks up his phone and answers it, after which he disappears down the hall. In the meantime, I squirt a cup-sized amount of whipped cream into my mouth. Straight, no chaser.

When he returns, he peers at my handiwork. "Everything okay? You didn't blow up my kitchen while I was gone?"

In return for that smart-ass comment, I shake the whipped cream dispenser and spray a dollop on his nose. Julian says nothing, his body frozen except for the furious blinking of his eyes. I have no idea if he's a physically playful person as an adult, but judging by the shock on his face, I might have overstepped my bounds with that move.

"Are you upset with me?"

He continues to stare at me.

"It's just whipped cream," I say tentatively. "It'll come right off." I grab a paper towel and reach out to wipe his nose, but he shoots out his hand and grabs my wrist before I can clean him. I yelp when he spins me around, caging me with one arm and grabbing the canister with the other hand so quickly that I don't have time to protect myself from the whipped cream he shakes onto my face. And it's *not* a dollop.

"Oh, you're going to regret that," I say as I lunge for the can.

Laughing louder than I've ever heard him laugh, Julian sidesteps around me and circles the counter. I chase after him, slipping on a streak of foam and dropping to my knees. I let out an inelegant "oof" when I hit the floor.

He's kneeling at my side within seconds, his arm draped over my shoulder. "Ash, are you okay?"

"I'm fine," I say as I use my fingers to wipe the whipped cream off my face. Then I gather as much of it as I can and run my hand over his cheeks and jaw, finishing my masterpiece with a cap on his eyebrows.

Julian widens his eyes and says, "Oh, now you're going to get it." He wrestles me to the ground and straddles me, securing my arms above my head so that I'm trapped under him. His thighs lock against my hips like steel bookends. He studies my face as though he's riveted by it, and if he were to let me go, his hot gaze would still root me to the spot. Then he leans over—so slowly I forget to breathe for a moment—and presses his cheeks against my forehead, transferring the cream from his face back to mine.

I shriek at the onslaught, turning my head from side to side to avoid getting more of the sticky sweetness on me. "Ack, Julian, I'm going to be a mess after this." Laughing, I flail against him in weak protest as he tries to pin me down. In the middle of our tussle, we bump noses, causing us both to freeze. Our mouths hover inches apart, and our gazes lock. My heart gallops in my chest, and my fingers grasp the ends of his shirt. This could be it. God, I want this to be it. His eyes narrow on my lips. Boldly, I raise my head off the floor, hoping he'll meet me halfway, but a moment before connecting, Julian pulls back on a groan, swings one of his legs around, and sits cross-legged next to me.

"Sorry," he says. "We got carried away."

Foiled. Nevertheless, I sit up and laugh. "No, getting carried away would look a little different from what just happened."

"Okay, we *almost* got carried away, and we agreed not to go there, remember?"

Jumping to my feet, I say, "Yes, I remember." As I wipe my face with a damp paper towel, I say, "I'm going to eat breakfast now. Are you joining me?"

He rises to his feet slowly. "It's all yours."

I look up, finally meeting his gaze. "You're not eating anything?"

Coming within inches of me, he wipes his face as he speaks. "No, my father's in town, and we have plans to meet for breakfast at his hotel."

"Well, then, I really do feel special."

He dabs at my nose with his towel. "You should. Always. Because you are."

How am I supposed to be satisfied with a platonic relationship when he makes offhand comments like that? Or when he touches me so casually? It's enough to make me want to smother him in his sleep. Kidding. Maybe. "That's sweet of you to say. And I truly appreciate this delicious breakfast. Your homemade waffles and I will be enjoying each other while you're gone." I circle the counter and pick up my plate, content to stand as I eat.

After grabbing his dress shirt off a nearby chair, he puts it back and buttons it briskly. "So I probably won't be home before you head to the airport. Do you need me to call a service for you?"

I shake my head as I wolf down a bite of his peace offering. It's firm on the outside and soft on the inside, just the way I like them. And he wasn't stingy with the butter. Yum. "A coworker's picking me up. I'm all set."

"Okay, well—"

The condo's intercom buzzes, and we both turn our heads in its direction.

"Expecting someone?" I ask.

Julian's gaze clouds. "No." He strides across the floor and hits the talk switch. "What's up, Benny?"

"Michael Hart is here to see you. Says he's your father?"

Julian furrows his brows. "Yeah, yeah. Send him up, Benny." He slips into his suit jacket, and then he paces as he waits for his father to arrive.

I met Julian's dad once, at his graduation from Weston. Mr. Hart was personable, charming even, but I don't know much about him. Julian's mother, Valerie, on the other hand, visited him a few times at school when she was traveling for work, so I have a better handle on her. Not surprisingly, she adores Julian.

The doorbell chimes, and Julian throws open the door. He and his dad fall into a bear hug, exclaiming "Dad" and "Son" simultaneously.

I grin as I watch their display of affection. Mr. Hart is a handsome man, an older version of Julian with salt-and-pepper hair and a wiry frame.

Julian walks backward as they enter the living area. "What are you doing here? We agreed to meet at your hotel."

Mr. Hart tilts his head and purses his lips. "We did?" He shakes his head. "I had it in my head that we were meeting here."

"Yeah, I made reservations at the restaurant there because…never mind. It doesn't matter. We can walk back over and catch up. Unless you want to go some-where else?"

"No, that's fine—" He spots me, and his eyes go wide. "Oh, hello. You're..."

Brows pinched together, he struggles to remember my name. I reach out a hand. "Ashley Williamson, Carter's sister."

He smiles. "Right, right. Good to see you again, Ashley."

"Likewise." I glance at Julian, who's staring at me with a blank expression, and then I point at my plate. "So I'll just finish this in my room and leave you two to catch up."

Julian returns to life and grabs his keys and phone off the counter. "No need, Ash. We're heading out anyway."

"It's fine," I mumble. "Lots of errands to run before I head out. Take care, Mr. Hart. I'll see you early next week, Julian. And thanks again for breakfast."

"It was my pleasure, Ash."

Whoa. Julian's voice is low and soft, and heat trav-els down my spine in response to it. I chance a glance at his face and find his dark brown eyes heavy-lidded and trained on me.

"Take care of yourself," he says as he follows his father out the door.

With my sumptuous plate of strawberry-topped waf-fles in hand, I rush to my room in search of my battery-operated boyfriend. After all, Julian *did* tell me to take care of myself, and given my current state of sexual frus-tration, I have plans to do just that.

Bzzzz.

Chapter Eight

Julian

"What's she doing here?" my father asks.

I hit the elevator button before I answer. "She needed a place to stay for a short time. I got her out of a jam."

"Is that your specialty now? Getting the Williamson kids out of jams?"

"Dad," I warn. "Let's not, okay?"

He presses his lips together as though he's forcing himself not to speak his mind.

If there were any aspect of my relationship with my father I'd change, it would be this. The tension that surfaces whenever we discuss the Williamsons is a continuing reminder that he's disappointed in me—disappointed in my career choices, specifically. I abandoned our plan to work together and chose to work with Carter instead.

But all I can do is show him I chose correctly and hope one day he agrees.

"Ashley needed my help, and I gave it to her. And yes, I offered because she's like family."

My father glances at me dubiously and then studies his wingtips. "She's an attractive girl. Are you and she…?"

No. The answer is no. But if he asked different questions, I'd give him different answers. Do you like her? Yes. Do you like having her in your home even though you're big on maintaining your personal space? Yes. Do you think about her more than you should? Hell yes.

"Nothing's going on."

His face relaxes. "That's good, I guess. No sense in getting yourself tangled with her when you're working with her brother. Too messy."

The elevator dings, and its doors slide apart. I seize the opportunity to glide inside and leave this part of the conversation behind me. We're both tending to our own thoughts during the short ride down. I can't argue with him because he's right. Giving in to my attraction to Ashley would be messy. After this morning's close call, I appreciate the reminder.

When we get to the first floor, I turn to him. "Would you like to walk back to the Kimpton? I made a reservation for ten."

In a rare move, I asked Marie to field my calls this morning and to forward only those she deemed an emergency or too important not to answer. Few people would get me to do that, but my father will always be one of them.

"Sure, it'll give us a chance to talk."

We exit the elevator, and I wave at Benny as we pass him. Out on the street, I pull out my sunglasses, and my dad does the same.

He clears his throat as he cleans his shades with a kerchief. "This girl—"

"Woman," I say.

"Right. What's her name again?"

I pull on my bottom lip as I squint at him. My father's meticulous attention to detail is legendary, so his inability—or unwillingness—to remember Ashley's name surprises me. "It's Ashley, Dad. And I'm not sure why we need to discuss her at all."

"Okay, never mind," he says as he puts on the sunglasses and strides down Wilshire Boulevard without me.

I quicken my pace to catch up with him. A part of me wants to ask about the company, but it's a tender subject between us. Still, I don't want him to think I don't care, because I *do* care, just not in the way he wants me to. "So how's business?"

My father started Hart Consulting fifteen years ago. HC gives products and services their identities, helping them build customer recognition and loyalty. Although not one of HC's clients, TOMS shoes is a case in point. When it's mentioned, most people think of the company's philanthropy. You buy a pair of their shoes, and TOMS gives away a pair of shoes to someone who can't afford to buy them. HC builds that recognition, devising a brand message and getting it out to the world.

My father slows and shoves his hands in his pockets. "We're at a crossroads. The Philadelphia office is in shambles, and I can't be in two places at once."

"What about sending Nicole?"

My older sister would covet the chance to get out from under my father's micromanaging umbrella. She works with him in the Atlanta office, which is also why she's quick to volunteer for business travel.

"Nicole's not ready for the responsibility. One day she will be. But time is the one thing we don't have."

I stop in the middle of the block. "Why the hell not? What's going on?"

He halts and faces me. "We need a big contract to justify the Philadelphia outpost. A major player. One of the sports teams. Or the chamber of commerce. *Something.* Otherwise, we're going to have to consider closing that office. My life's work gutted."

"The business in Atlanta is your life's work, and it's not going anywhere."

"I guess as an outsider looking in, it's easy for you to make sweeping statements like that. But I've devoted myself to this company for more than a decade. It's not that simple."

I'm an outsider now? Okay. I get that he's worried about his business, but the personal dig is beneath him. "I'm hesitant to say that everything will work out somehow, but that's how I see it. You and Nicole will figure it out. You always do."

"Thanks, Son." He opens his mouth and snaps it shut.

"Say what you want to say, Dad."

He places his arm around my shoulder and pulls me in close. "I didn't mean to be so harsh. That was uncalled for. It's just—"

"Don't worry about it."

We drift apart and stroll along the boulevard, each of us content to continue the way in silence. When we reach the Kimpton Hotel's entrance, I turn in, but my father walks past it, unaware that we've reached our destination.

"Yo, Dad." I wave at him. "We're here."

He looks up, shakes his head, and smiles. "Right. I'm a little distracted by everything that's going on."

He's always pushed himself too hard, and now is no different. I clap him on the shoulder and steer him through the double doors. "Let's get you some food."

Once we're inside the restaurant, the hostess motions for us to follow her, and after we're seated, my father excuses himself to go to the restroom.

I check my phone and find an email from Marie among the flood of messages. A colleague, Sooyin Liú, stopped by my office and wants to speak with me when I get in. I'll check in with her after breakfast.

A glance at my watch confirms my dad's been gone for more than five minutes, but a few seconds later, he strides through the restaurant and retakes his seat.

"Sorry about that," he says. "To my surprise, it's a single-stall bathroom."

I wave off the apology. After our server greets us and takes our drink orders—a black coffee for me and a mimosa for my father—we peruse the menu as we catch up.

"Tell me about Mom," I say.

My father takes a visible breath, smiles from ear to ear, and stares off into the distance wistfully. "She's great, Julian. Been making hints about wanting to travel more, but I don't know when we'd have the time. She's busy, too."

My mother owns her own jewelry-making business, and after putting in over a decade of hard work, she's sitting on a profitable venture—with a QVC contract in negotiations.

"And she'll never stop wondering when one of her children will give her grandbabies," my father adds.

"If I ever adopt, she'll be the first to know."

"You and your sister will be the death of us."

"With all this talk about grandbabies, I'm sure you and Mom will be the death of *us*."

My father leans forward, placing his elbows on the table and making a steeple with his fingers. I brace myself for the lecture on finding time to cultivate a life outside the office. Delaying the inevitable, our server returns with our drinks and takes our meal orders.

When he leaves, my father asks, "Didn't your mother and I give you something to aspire to? Don't you want to share your life with someone?"

"Of course I do, but I'm in no rush to get serious with any one person. Plus, when would I? Anyone who'd be understanding of the demands on my time is just as busy as I am. A relationship typically requires that the two people, you know, relate."

"And in the meantime?"

As punishment for all my past misdeeds, images of the moment Ashley and I almost kissed assault me like several blows to the body. The portal's opening again. *No, get the fuck out of my head, James Earl Jones. Turn away from the light, Julian.* And what's with this line of questioning anyway? "Wait. Are you asking me about my *sex* life?"

My tone is just as bewildered as I am.

Grinning, he lowers his chin and rubs the back of his neck. "All right, forget I asked. I'll tell your mother no children are forthcoming."

I grin back at him. "You do that."

Never mind that my stomach's still churning as I consider the number of times Ashley's infiltrated my thoughts this morning. It's a problem, and I have no clue what to do about it.

AFTER BREAKFAST WITH my father, I return to my building's underground parking lot and jump in my car for the short drive to Sync Creative Management's offices in Century City. When I get to my office, Sooyin is sitting in one of two guest chairs facing my desk. No boundaries, this one.

"Please make yourself comfortable when I'm not around," I say to her back, amusement in my voice.

She lifts her head from the notepad it's buried in and gives me a quick once-over. "No need to tell me something I already know. Listen, I don't have much time today, so I wanted to catch you as soon as I could. Nice tie, by the way."

This is Sooyin in a nutshell: sarcastic, brisk, priceless. When she joined the agency's Film Group a few years ago, we bonded immediately, in no small part because her arrival meant I was no longer the only person of color in the agent ranks.

I point at the door. "Open or closed?"

She sets the pad on her lap and lowers her voice to a whisper. "Closed. Definitely. You're the last stop on my reconnaissance mission."

Sooyin's penchant for cloak-and-dagger operations is well known. She once spearheaded a brutal prank on Milton, a cutthroat colleague who'd screwed her out of a client lead. Her revenge? Circulating false rumors about a breakout star seeking new representation. Everyone was in on it but him. Milton spent hours trying to get an introduction to the coveted celebrity and still more hours studying the actor's TV and film credits. Through it all, Sooyin asked for updates and counseled him on his strategy. She eventually disclosed the truth to him in a staff meeting several weeks later. The main takeaway: Do not fuck with Sooyin.

I shut the door, round my desk, and settle into my chair. "What's going on?"

She leans forward, her chin-length dark hair swishing across her cheeks like windshield wipers. "Did Quinn tell you what happened?"

"Had a meeting about it a few days ago. Your group must be having a field day with this one."

She nods. "Word is they're giving Manning the boot next week. Gavin and his cronies were giddy about it, the jerks. I thought for sure he was going to blow his load when he told us about it. Off the record, of course."

Gavin is Sooyin's boss. He's an asshole, and if he had his wish, every single agent in the TV Group, including my boss, would be gone. "I'm not surprised. Gavin wants to whittle our division to nothing. Manning gave him the excuse he needed."

"Exactly. So don't do anything to get fired, all right? I won't survive here without you."

"Awww, Sooyin. That's two compliments in less than ten minutes. You feelin' okay?"

She gives me the middle finger. "That's a fact, not a compliment. Just don't screw up."

I don't *want* to screw up, but I also don't know what I don't know, and it occurs to me that Sooyin could help. "Look, I'm hoping to strike a multiyear film deal for Carter Stone—"

"Hang on," Sooyin says as she rises from her chair. "The door's been closed for too long. I don't want anyone to think we're banging."

She's right. Closed doors at SCM spark curiosity, an unfortunate side effect of working in a cutthroat industry that thrives on secrecy.

After she opens the door and sits again, I come around and take the chair next to her. "I need a little tutoring. Give me a primer on what I should be thinking about. The pitfalls I should be avoiding. Strategy pointers."

She draws back. "You do realize I'm technically your competition and I could use this to my advantage."

I smirk at her. "You wouldn't. You can't survive this place without me, remember?"

She considers me for a moment, her lips puckered in concentration. "Yeah. If it were any other client, I'd tell you to hand him over to me, but you and Carter Stone are attached at the hip. Fine. When would you like to do this?"

"How about we meet at my place early next week? I'll order takeout for your troubles."

Crossing her arms, she slides her legs forward and regards me with suspicion. "You do know I have zero interest in you."

I scrub a hand over my face and grin at her audacity. "Yes, Sooyin. You've made that clear more times than is necessary. Truly."

She waggles her eyebrows and accompanies the move with a wicked smile. "All right. Let's do it. I can't wait to check out your bachelor pad."

Dammit. How could I forget I have a roommate now? Courtesy dictates that I check with Ashley first, but I've already asked Sooyin over, and I wouldn't feel comfortable uninviting her. Ah, what the hell—it's just a meeting with a colleague. I can't imagine she'd care all that much.

Chapter Nine

Ashley

IT'S GOOD TO be home. My temporary home, that is.

I'm fresh off a four-day trip with too many destinations and long layovers in between. As a junior member of the cabin crew, I can't control my schedule to any significant degree, and I'm questioning whether I possess the stamina to wait for the perks of seniority to materialize. It's an exhausting job. My bed is calling and I'm answering. But not before I stuff my face, which I'll do as soon as Julian arrives with our takeout from Ziki.

Just when I thought things might get awkward between us, he texted last night and offered to bring me dinner tonight. How sweet.

I throw open the refrigerator and forage for an appetizer. True to form, Julian filled it with fruits and vegetables. I gnaw on a carrot in frustration, wishing it were a chocolate-covered pretzel. Minutes later, just past seven as he promised, Julian walks through the door with two large paper bags in his hands.

He's wearing a light gray suit, his burgundy tie hanging loosely around his neck. His heavy-lidded gaze sweeps over me, and his eyes brighten. "Hey, welcome back."

I raise my hand in a weak wave as I take in the differences in our appearances.

I'm in a pair of oversized pajama bottoms and a sweatshirt that stops midway between my thighs and knees. True lounging-around-the-house wear. Meanwhile, he looks like he's just made a major deal and needs to make a pit stop before going back out to celebrate. The man wears a suit so well. A scenario flashes through my brain, one unrelated to our attire. In it, Julian's come home from work, and I've just returned from a trip, and he crosses the room with purpose, intent on greeting me with a kiss. And once he opens his arms, I jump into his embrace and wrap my legs around his waist. With hunger in his eyes, he walks us to the nearest wall—any of them will do—and his strong hand splays against my chest, slides down to my breasts—

"Hungry?" he asks.

Dammit, Julian. You were just about to tweak my nipple. I squeeze my eyes shut and then open one eye, hoping and praying that I didn't say that out loud. "Uh, yeah. I'm famished."

He places the bags on the kitchen counter and removes the recyclable containers inside.

There's enough to feed a football team. "Wow. That's a lot of food. I'm not *that* hungry."

He licks his lips, and his gaze darts around the room. "I forgot to mention that a colleague of mine is coming over. To discuss some work stuff. I don't know what she likes, so I decided to get a sampling." He clears his throat and fumbles with the task of opening the containers. "Should be something in here that'll work."

My hands slow as I pick up a rice bowl. Julian's nervous. Does this mean he's interested in this woman?

Oof. A besotted Julian would take some getting used to. But I'm strapping on the Spanx—big girl panties won't cut it—and giving him my support. "That's really thoughtful of you. I'm sure she'll appreciate it."

He pauses in his preparations, and with his head tilted to the side, he stares at me for a few beats. "Yeah. You're right."

I nudge him with my shoulder. "So you like this woman?"

He snaps his brows together. "I wouldn't say that exactly. We're colleagues…and friends."

"The same way you and I are friends?"

He gives me a rueful smile. "No, it's different."

I grasp onto the only subtext that makes sense. She's different because being with her doesn't present the same problems being with me would. Worse, he's hoping to do something about it but feeling sheepish about throwing it in my face. I fake an encouraging nod. "Well, there you go, then. Do you know how she feels about you?"

He thinks about my question for a moment, his gaze zipping around the room. But before he can respond, the intercom buzzes, and he rushes across the room to answer it. "Yeah, Benny," he says into the speaker.

"It's Frank, Mr. Hart. Benny's gone for the day. I have Sooyin Liú here for you."

Julian smiles at the speaker. "Great. Send her up, Frank. And thank you."

Witnessing Julian's excitement firsthand deflates me, so I burrow into my humongous sweatshirt for much-needed comfort. I'll say hello to his friend and make myself scarce.

Minutes later, she rings the doorbell and Julian throws open the door with a flourish, bowing to her and inviting her inside.

She crosses the threshold carefully, amusement in her smile and a question in her gaze. "Well, fancy meeting you here."

Wearing a fitted black pantsuit and peep-toe stilettos, Sooyin spins around as she takes in Julian's living space. Her graceful turn confirms she's lovely at every angle. Drat. Seriously, her hair is sleek and sharp, and I'm questioning whether she has pores. Is that even possible, not to have any pores? She startles when she sees me and looks to Julian for an explanation.

He smooths the tops of his thighs and leads her to me. "Right. Sorry. Sooyin, this is my temporary roommate, Ashley. A friend of the family."

I give her a broad smile, tamping down the green-eyed monster growling in my ear. Julian likes Sooyin, and my disappointment over that fact should have no bearing on how I treat her. "It's great to meet you."

Up close, her attractiveness hits megalevels. But what nearly does me in are her eyes. Her friendly gaze shimmers, as if the brightness within her finds its outlet there. But as she looks between Julian and me, her eyes narrow, giving me a glimpse of what she's like when she focuses on something—or someone. "Great to meet you, too, Ashley."

Julian strides to the counter. "I have food. Wasn't sure what you wanted." He looks at me, making an admirable effort to include us both in the conversation. "Do you have what you need, Ash?"

"I'm good, thanks." The rasp in my voice is such an inconvenience in times like these.

Sooyin peeks into the bags. "Just to clarify. I'm Chinese American."

Julian looks at her askance and blows out a slow breath. "I *know* this. Is there a rule prohibiting you from eating Japanese food?"

Sooyin shakes her head and winks at me. "Just wanted to be sure we're on the same page."

He smirks at her. "The page that says you're ridiculous? Yeah, we're both on it."

With a laugh, she shoves him to the side and lifts the lid off a container. "Let's eat. My time is valuable."

Aaaand I'm done. I can't watch anymore of their banter. "Hey, guys, I'm beat, so I'm going to grab my bowl and eat in my room. I'll probably fall asleep with my face in it. Nice to meet you, Sooyin."

Julian whips his head in my direction and scans my face and body, a pensive expression suggesting he's looking for signs of my exhaustion. "You're welcome to stay, Ash. We're just going to stuff our faces and work."

"Well, I'm going to stuff my face and sleep." I pick up my bowl and utensils and vanish like a magician. If I could disappear from the unit without getting dressed I would. But tonight, I draw the line at putting on outside clothes.

Inside my room, I lean back against the door and take a deep breath. That wasn't so bad. Yes, it's hard seeing your lifelong crush share chemistry with someone else, but Julian and I agreed we wouldn't act on our attraction, and if Sooyin makes him happy, then I'm happy for him.

Sarcasm alert: Yay.

GRRR. I CAN'T sleep, and I'm thirsty. The superagents in the next room are interspersing their chatter with an occasional chuckle (him) or a laugh (her), and it sounds like they're getting along well. They won't appreciate my reappearance, but dehydration isn't cute, so I trudge out of my room and down the hall, stomping the last few steps near the entryway to broadcast my arrival.

Julian, who's sitting across from Sooyin at the dining table, snaps his head up when I cross the threshold. He's changed into jeans and a dark blue T-shirt that emphasizes his muscular biceps. "Hey, you. Can't sleep?"

I make a big show of yawning. "Thirstiness beat out grogginess."

Sooyin lifts her head from the pages in front of her and smiles at me. Then a phone buzzes between them. I'm not sure if it's hers or Julian's, but the answer becomes clear when he leans over and reads the screen, blowing out a frustrated breath after the ringing stops and starts again. "I need to take this." He swipes up the phone and brings it to his ear as he strides down the hall, presumably to his bedroom.

I chance a glance at Sooyin and pad across the floor to grab a glass from the cabinet.

"He's a great guy," she says. The hesitation in her voice suggests she's feeling me out, trying to get a read on whether I have my own designs on her love interest.

"He is," I agree. "And a catch, too."

She removes the eyeglasses perched low on her nose. "A bit grumpy, though, no?"

I smile at that description. "*Serious* is a better word, I think. But he's smart and loyal, and he makes the people around him feel protected."

"Including you."

I turn to her then. "Including me. But I'm not a threat if that's your concern."

She grins at me. "I'm not a threat, either."

My heart thrums in my chest. Is she saying what I think she's saying? "You and he aren't…you mean…you're not—"

"Interested in him romantically?" She shakes her head. "No."

My gaze flies to her face as her meaning sinks in. "Oh." Now I'm feeling protective of Julian's feelings. "Does he know?"

She nods and leans back in her chair. "He most certainly does."

I slump against the refrigerator. Apparently, I'm terrible at reading a situation. "I assumed you and he were interested in each other, or at least he was interested in you. I asked him outright, and my assumptions were fairly obvious, but he didn't correct them."

She tips her head up and ponders that bit of information. "Very interesting. He told me you're Carter Stone's sister."

"I am."

"What's that like?"

I point an index finger in her general direction. "Just like that."

Her eyebrows snap together. "Sorry?"

"People think of me as Carter Stone's sister rather than Ashley, a woman whose brother happens to be Carter Stone."

She nods. "That's a big difference, and I didn't mean to offend you."

I put up a hand. "Forget it."

"Julian's guilty of it, too, am I right?"

I collapse onto a counter stool. "God yes."

"I might be out of line for saying this, but being out of line is my thing, so I'll say it anyway. I don't think he does it to discount you. It's for a different reason, I suspect."

"Meaning?"

"In the last few minutes, I learned that you're a flight attendant, that you're here only temporarily because you got into it with your roommate, although he doesn't know exactly what happened, and that you've written over a hundred songs."

"He told you all that?"

"He did. And if he failed to disabuse you of the notion that he's interested in me, consider what he might gain from that. If he doesn't trust himself around you, he might be inclined to manufacture reasons for you to stay away." She sits up and shakes her head. "Goodness, who invaded my body and made me your therapist? I'll shut up now."

Julian breezes into the room and stuffs his phone into the back pocket of his jeans.

I jump up, rush to the sink, and focus on filling my glass.

Maybe Sooyin's right that he wants to create a barrier between us because he's not confident in his own ability to fight our connection. But I can't forget that Julian himself made it clear we're never ever going to happen.

I can no longer ignore the truth. I'm wasting my energy here, and it's time to move on.

Chapter Ten

Julian

It's Friday at last, and tomorrow is a unicorn: a Saturday without any commitments. Sure, that could change at any moment, but I'm at least looking forward to the *possibility* of enjoying a rare day off.

The unit is dark when I enter it. To make sure I'm alone, I sweep through each room, ending my house check at Ashley's open door. I poke my head inside and find a mess. Clothes strewn everywhere. Makeup brushes and lids peppering the dresser. And a bright white bath towel on the floor. Someone was in a hurry this evening, but where did she go?

We haven't seen much of each other this week, and I have no idea whether she's due to travel for work soon. She should have left a note or texted me to let me know where she would be. There's no need for us to keep tabs on each other, of course, but she doesn't know LA well, and I'd hate for her to be out alone at night. Dammit, my mother has invaded my body, and it's not cool. Get a grip, Julian. She's a grown woman, and she can take care of herself.

After showering and reheating leftovers, I sink into the couch with my plate in my hands and a beer on the side table. I'm five minutes into the local news when Ash gets home—and my jaw drops.

Ashley's like a little sister to me.

Ashley's like a little sister to me.

Ashley's like a little sister to me.

Nope. She's not. At all.

That explains why the curvy outline of her body taunts me. Why I'm entranced by the way her flowery skirt swishes around her firm thighs as she walks. Why I want to *be* the silk tank top skimming her body and softly draping over her full breasts. I want. Yeah, that's it. *That's* the feeling. Pure, unadulterated want.

"Hey, there!" she says in a cheery tone. "Looks like you're in full relaxation mode."

My gaze travels with her to the fridge, where she pulls out a beer bottle. She grabs the opener off the counter and makes quick work of the cap.

"Fun night?" I ask.

She drops her shoulders and pouts. "It sucked." Then she tosses her head back and takes a long sip. When she's done, she says, "The guy couldn't stop talking about himself. I don't even think he asked me a single question. And he wore yellow socks with naked boobs on them, the Neanderthal. Let's mark this day as the last time I let a coworker set me up." She plods across the room and plonks down next to me. "Why is dating so hard?"

Ever experience a moment when you wonder whether you've awoken from a monthlong cryogenic sleep? Yeah. That. Because...Ashley's dating? Since Tuesday? And I'm supposed to act like this is an expected turn of events?

But it is, my inner rational person says. She can do whatever she wants, and apparently what she wants is to date. So why the fuck am I unhappy about it? No, I should just be supportive here. "It's like going trick-or-treating, that's why."

She shifts sideways and frowns at me. "Trick-or-treating? Explain."

I turn my body to face her and wedge a pillow between us—for comfort. "Okay, do you remember when you went trick-or-treating as a kid? You were excited about it. Talked about it for days. Planned your costume, your walking route. Got so excited about the candy you'd get to eat."

She waves her hands around in frustration. "Yeah, yeah. I remember all that. But how does that relate to dating?"

"Well, when you went out, you didn't know what you'd get. Some neighbors gave you crappy treats. Tons of Whoppers or Tootsie Rolls. The stuff no one would trade other candy for. That's your Neanderthal with the boob socks, right there. And you learned not to go to those houses in later years, right? But first you have to get the Whoppers or Tootsie Rolls or whatever before you scratch that house off your list."

She puts a hand over her mouth and laughs, and then she wiggles her butt into the sofa cushion, settling into a more comfortable position. "This is fascinating. Do go on."

"Okay, then there were the sickening neighbors who didn't even give you treats. They gave you a fucking trick. I mean, what the hell? Yeah, you know it's a possibility, a risk of jumping in the trick-or-treating pool, you might say, but no kid wants a trick rather than a treat. A trick *and* a treat, yes, but a trick *instead* of a treat, hell no. So those folks, those are your cheaters, and they're the worst of the worst, but yeah, they're out there, and all they want to do is steal your joy."

Her gaze clouds. "I hate those fuckers so much."

"And then there are those neighbors who lure you in. They give you treats every year, but one year, after they've lulled you into a false sense of security, you turn around to walk down the front steps and they trick you. You feel so betrayed, right?"

She nods enthusiastically. "Right, right. It's like a sucker punch."

"But then there are the houses that give you the primo candy. The Kit Kats, the M&M's, the Twizzlers."

She leans over and slaps the pillow between us. "I *love* Twizzlers."

"You might even get lucky and get the king-sized versions of your favorite candies."

She wriggles her eyebrows. "Oooh, I love the king-sized versions."

Of course Ash would go there. I draw back and wag my finger at her. "I think you're distorting my analogy. Anyway, the thing about those primo houses is that everyone knows they're a sure thing, so everyone rushes to those houses, and they end up running out of candy. So the key is to get to them first. Otherwise you might never get the candy you crave. Instead, you'll be stuck with a jar of candy corn or worse, a granola bar."

She pretends to shudder in disgust. "Granola bars make me sad."

"So yeah. It's not easy to date, but if you approach it with the right strategy and rely on what you learn from your experiences, you'll eventually get the Twizzlers you want."

She stares at me, her eyes unblinking. "Wow. Just wow. That actually makes sense, in a warped, not-everything-lines-up-logically kind of way." She nudges my shoulder. "You're a witty guy, Mr. Hart."

Jesus. Did she think I had *no* sense of humor? I lean my forearms on my thighs and study my bare feet. I can be witty. When I'm around the right people. And apparently, she's one of them. "Yes, well, I've probably maxed out my charm credits, so I'm going to be dry and humorless for the remainder of the year."

She reaches over and sets her hand on my wrist. From this vantage, her whiskey-colored eyes dominate my mental picture frame. My heart pounds, a steady drum in my chest.

"Thank you," she says softly.

"For what?"

"For helping me put that terrible date in perspective."

"You're welcome."

My voice is low and gruff, too many days' worth of want and frustration packed into my consonants and vowels. I shake out my hands and stretch my neck to ease the tightness in my muscles.

She throws her head back against the sofa and puffs her cheeks out. "I just want to enjoy someone's company, you know? Go to a nice restaurant from time to time. The movies. Have decent conversation."

"You could do all that with me."

With the back of her head still resting against the couch, she turns her head toward me. "Sex, Julian. I'd like to have sex, too." It comes out as a growl, as though she's rabid with the injustice of it all. "And not in fifteen-minute increments, either, because you're too busy to fit me into your schedule."

Ouch. I'm not a fifteen-minute man under any circumstances. To me, thirty minutes is a quickie. But pleading my case would be crude and pointless. "Can't help you there."

"Won't."

"Excuse me?"

She raises her head, and we stare at each other. "There's no physical impediment to us having sex." Her gaze dips to the area between my thighs. "That I know of."

I swallow hard. She wants me. I want her. But taking that irreversible step is far from simple. "No physical barrier, at least."

She sighs. "You know what? Never mind. I'm not entitled to sex with you, and I'm being an ass right now. Can we talk about something else?"

That's an excellent idea, because there's nothing more torturous than talking about fucking with a person you want to fuck but won't. "Do you remember when your cousin Lydia put your training bra over her sweater and teased you about being flat-chested?"

I shut my eyes and cringe. *Nice going, Julian. Mention an embarrassing moment from her childhood. That's sure to break the tension.*

She grimaces as she trots down memory lane. "God, Lydia was such a snot. I think she studied every mean-girl cliché she saw in a movie and tried to emulate each one." She squints at me, smiles triumphantly, and presses her luscious tits together. "Meet Last and Laugh. They're quite a pair."

I gulp, my throat dry and scratchy. *No, no, no, no. Do not look at them, Julian. Don't do it.*

While I'm focused on *not* looking, she snaps her eyebrows together. "And what in the world made you think of Lydia?"

"You'll see her at the family reunion in less than two weeks."

"Not if I can help it."

I draw back. "You're not going?"

The exasperation in her expression intensifies. "*Of course* I'm going. I wouldn't miss my brother's wedding for the world." Then she widens her eyes and winces. "Dammit."

I sit up. "Hang on. The reunion is a wedding?"

She drops her head to her chest. "They're going to kill me."

"Carter didn't want me to know?"

"They wanted it to be a surprise for pretty much everyone except their immediate families."

Her comment pricks my skin like a stick jabbing a tender wound. Right. I'm not immediate family. "Oh."

She raises her head, her gaze soft and earnest. "Julian, whatever you're thinking, don't. Carter didn't tell you because he wanted you to have plausible deniability with colleagues and industry folks. He didn't want to put the pressure on you to keep this quiet."

That passes the sniff test, I guess. But I can't imagine how they expect to pull this off. "So everyone's going to show up and they'll say what? 'Surprise, we're getting married'? Is that how this is supposed to work?"

"No, they're actually planning reunion activities. Football, a cookout, a trip to the spa. The closing brunch will be the wedding. The hope is that the paparazzi will believe it's a reunion, get what they think they need, and leave town before the wedding day."

Makes sense to me. Most paparazzi can't afford to pay out of pocket and follow any one celebrity for long anyway. Still, I can't help thinking that *People* magazine would be all over photos of Carter and Tori's wedding. The publicity could be tremendous. As Carter's friend, however, I understand why they'd want to avoid the circus. "It's a great idea, and wild as fuck."

Her eyes flicker with excitement. "I thought the same thing. And if any two people can pull this off, it'll be them."

"So how are you going to avoid Lydia?"

Everyone in the family knows Ashley and Lydia will never be best friends.

"Easy. I'll show up for"—she makes air quotes—"'the closing brunch.' I'll slip in and out and avoid Lydia or any of the other small-minded people who tortured me during my misspent youth."

"But what about everything else? Football, the cookout. Your parents, Carter, Kimberly. Everyone will want you there."

"There'll be so much going on that they won't even realize I'm not around. Besides, if I get there any earlier, I'll be forced to talk to Lydia and the rest of my catty relatives. I don't want to be a distraction, and if I see any of those people, I don't think I'll be able to be civil."

Over the years, Ashley's made a few comments about the shitty behavior of people in Harmon. I've taken them as snide observations about a place too small for her personality. But her reluctance to spend more than a single day in Harmon and her remark about being "tortured" make me pause. I'd already graduated from Weston when Ashley started high school, so my knowledge of that period in her life is incomplete. "What did the people in Harmon do, Ashley?"

Her face hardens, and her body tenses as though she's steeling herself for the impending effect of her memories.

"No one pulled my hair or took my stuff or anything like that. They just…said mean things about me. The common theme was that I was a slut, for being with one boy with loose lips. And when Carter left for LA, the joke around town was that I'd follow him after high school… and spend all of my time on the casting couch, doing what I do best."

"This was high school? Shit. What dicks. People like that don't know you, and they don't deserve to. And they were jealous, of course."

She shrugs. "Of Carter, maybe. And they took it out on me."

"Look at you now, though. They'll eat their words."

She cocks her head at me and snorts. "I'm a flight attendant, Julian. I'll be walking into the mile-high club jokes as soon as I arrive."

"Oh, c'mon. Lydia's older. Everyone's older. They have to be over it by now."

"You'd think so. But no. I went home for the holidays last year, and although I didn't see Lydia, I did see the others. They're less obvious about it…because, Carter. Still, the undercurrent of pettiness is there, and for obvious reasons I can't avoid Lydia this time. Oh, and she just broke up with her boyfriend. Mom says she's been a bear lately. And I'm sure she's still holding on to her crush for you."

I cock my head back. "Me?"

"Yes, you," she says with a bored expression. "She was miffed that you were the one boy who wouldn't give her the time of day. You didn't know?"

"She was a little girl. I wouldn't have paid attention to her even if she'd been the only person in town, and she wasn't."

"You never noticed how Lydia always appeared at our house when you were stuck at Weston during a school break?" She slaps her hand on the sofa cushion when I stare at her blankly. "Oh my God, Julian, I suffered through sleepovers with her when you were around. Only then did she pretend to be my friend."

"I had no clue."

"Well, I don't think she's going to let you remain clueless when she sees you for the reunion. And maybe that's not a bad thing. If she's preoccupied with you, I might be able to suffer through her presence when I'm there." She arches her back and yawns.

Don't stare, Julian. Don't you fucking do it.

She stands and pats my thigh. "Don't look so traumatized. You'll have a great time." Stretching enough to expose her midriff, she yawns. "I'm headed to bed. Thanks again for cheering me up."

"Good night," I say.

"Sweet dreams," she says as she shuffles away.

I make a valiant effort not to study her smooth calves, but I fail. Everything about her—her left-of-center smile, the rasp in her voice, the way she moves, our easy conversations—draws me in and slows me down. Makes me want to dive in and swim in her.

After she disappears down the hall, I collapse against the sofa cushion, exhausted by the strain of not giving in to our attraction. The prospect of spending four days in Harmon and interacting with Lydia has no appeal, but I'll do it for Carter and Tori. And if Ashley chooses to swoop in and stay for only a day, that's probably for the best anyway. We're managing being in close quarters largely because one of us usually is gone. But if we spend a significant amount of time together, while I'm on vacation no less, I'll do something stupid. No question about it.

Chapter Eleven

Ashley

I WAKE TO voices in the condo. Although I'm groggy, I know a woman's laugh when I hear it. Goodness, is he out there with a booty call? Worse, is it someone he's dating? Sooyin, maybe? No, it couldn't be his gorgeous colleague—she made it clear she wasn't interested in Julian—so it's got to be the former. Or...*Stop it, Ashley. It could be anyone. And you're moving on, remember?*

After groaning into my pillow, I turn onto my back and listen for a clue as to the mystery woman's identity. I bolt upright when a fist pounds against my bedroom door.

"Get up, bacon breath. Your favorite brother's here for a visit."

I smile at the sound of Carter's voice and yell back. "You're my *only* brother."

He continues to speak to me outside the door. "I'm confident that if you had more than one, I'd still be your favorite."

"That's conceit, not confidence."

"Confidence, conceit. To-may-to, to-mah-to. Get out here. Tori's with me."

"Well, you should have said that first." I pull back the covers and drag myself out of bed. Opening the door, I greet him with a genuine smile. "Hey, potato head."

He peeks around me and scans the bedroom. "You good? Everything okay?"

His dark hair is in disarray, the tuft at the front that refuses to stay put sticking up in the air like a shark's fin rising out of the water. We favor each other, except he's got ice blue eyes like my older sister, Kimberly, whereas mine are maple-syrup brown. Seeing him now, it's both easy and hard to believe my older brother makes people swoon when they see him on the big screen. To them, he's a heartthrob. To me, though, he's just Carter. My funny, sweet, and *overprotective* brother. I palm his face and push him away. "No, you can't come into my room. Also, your snooping skills are weak. Didn't Mom teach you the art of being subtle about your nosiness?"

"Must have missed that lesson." He yanks on a lock of my hair—to distract me—and then he tries to wedge himself inside. "Along with the one about how to stop worrying about your pip-squeak of a sister."

Ruthless in my mission, I tickle him in his ribs, and he backs away.

"Brush your teeth and get out here, stat," he yells over his shoulder.

"Whatever," I grumble on my way to the bathroom. Spinning around before he leaves, I tell him, "By the way, Kimberly's my favorite sibling, just so we're clear."

He pretends to shove a dagger in his chest and stumbles out the room.

A few minutes later, I join everyone in the living room, where Julian and Tori are chatting on the couch and Carter's swiping through his phone.

Julian notices me before they do, and my breath hitches when his gaze roams over my face and body. I'm tempted to call out, *You want some of this, doncha?* Getting a rise out of him would be fun. But given the way he's looking at me, I bet he's rising on his own just fine.

Tori glances at him, catching Julian's lazy inspection, and a crease appears between her brows as she registers that she no longer has his attention because it's focused on me.

Oh, Julian. You're such a dope. If only you'd relax and live for the moment. Just once. Or twice. Or, hell, three times—so I get the full Julian experience.

After a shake of her head, Tori jumps up, her long, curly hair fanning around her shoulders as she crosses the room. She enfolds me in a hug. "Ahhh, it's so good to be able to jump in a car and drop by to see you."

I give her an equally effusive embrace. Tori's quickly becoming one of my favorite people. I wish I could travel back in time, transport her to my childhood, and tell her my silly secrets as we paint each other's toenails and listen to P!nk. "Well, the good thing is, now that I'm around, I can help with wedding prep if you need it."

Her eyes go wide as she scrunches her brows, and then she cocks her head in Julian's direction, as though she's mentally telling me to keep quiet about the pending nuptials. Carter looks up from his phone, a stricken expression compounding my guilt.

"He knows." My disclosure comes out in a pathetic wail. "It just slipped out in conversation. I'm so sorry."

Their heads whip around, and they both stare at Julian.

Carter recovers first. "I hope you understand, man. I wanted you to be able to say you knew nothing about it. Especially with Dana, who will flip her shit when she finds out."

Dana is Carter's publicist, and from what I can gather, she gets miffed when Carter doesn't inform her of matters that might—or in this case, *should*—get press attention. Her client's wedding qualifies.

Julian, looking delectable in a black tank and his favorite gray sweats—and wearing underwear this time—waves his explanation away. "Are you sure you didn't keep this from me because you thought I'd press you to make a big splash of it?"

Carter rubs the back of his neck. Busted.

"Because if you'd consulted me about it, I would have at least had you consider the potential for getting your name out there in a big way that makes you even more marketable than you are now. And it wouldn't have to be a big—"

"Julian," Carter interrupts, raising his voice. The tightness in his eyes hints at his annoyance.

I'm not accustomed to witnessing tension between these two, and Tori isn't either, it seems. We exchange worried glances and wait.

After several seconds of taut silence, Carter sighs heavily. "Just be happy for us, okay? This is what we've decided to do."

Julian's chest rises as he draws in a slow breath. "Fine. And of course I'm happy for you." He grins, but his gaze remains cloudy. "But let's keep my knowledge between us, okay? Quinn will be on my ass if he thinks I didn't dissuade you from doing this."

Carter nods, his expression softening. "Deal." He clears his throat. "Hey, listen, do you think your parents would come?"

It's a peace offering, and Julian accepts it.

"For the wedding? I'm sure my mother would love to."

I suspect no one missed that he didn't say anything about his father.

Tori, who's been chewing on her bottom lip with a vengeance, sighs in relief. "I'm so glad we can be open about this now." She turns to me. "You do have something in mind to wear, yes?"

"Not yet, but don't worry. I won't show up naked."

Julian coughs into his hand, and Carter pats him on the back. "You all right, J?"

"Yeah, I'm fine. Just a little parched." He rushes to the sink and fills a glass with water. Leaning against the counter, he chugs until his watery eyes clear.

Tori quirks an eyebrow at him and returns her attention to me. "Anyway, you'll be arriving Thursday, right?"

I stare down at my toes. "Um, no. I don't think I can." Glancing at her confused expression, I try to shove away my guilt. "But I'll be at the wedding, of course. And you'll be so busy you won't even miss me."

Out of the corner of my eye, I see Julian staring at Tori and me.

Carter, who's now slouching in a chair, straightens and pins me with a questioning gaze. "You don't want to be there?"

"With you guys, yes. In Harmon, no. The outer layers of our clan are more than I want to handle. And it's not just Lydia. It's Uncle Richard and Aunt Carol, who'll undoubtedly have hundreds of questions about my love life."

"Carol is Lydia's mother?" Tori asks.

"Yes," I say.

In fact, every time I see Aunt Carol, she asks me whether I've "sown my oats yet," probably because Lydia's spun a tale about my sexual exploits that bears no resemblance to the truth. It's gross, and annoying, and I don't want to deal with it. So yeah, I'll show up for the wedding, make nice with my extended family for Carter and Tori's sake, and spend time with my true loved ones another time. But I'm not staying any longer than necessary.

Carter chuckles. "Well, I'm guessing Lydia will be busy flirting with Julian, so you probably won't have to deal with her."

Julian pushes off the counter and throws up his hands. "Was I the only one who didn't know Lydia had a crush on me?"

Carter and I answer at the same time. "Yes."

Tori laughs. "If it's any consolation, I wasn't aware of it, either. But of course, I didn't know any of you then."

Julian smirks at her. "Oh, you've got jokes now, too."

Carter stands and pulls Tori to his side. "You should be happy about that. It means you're in her inner circle."

Because pettiness sometimes gets the best of me, I can't help emphasizing the painful experience Julian *shouldn't* be looking forward to. "Now that Lydia's broken up with her high school sweetheart, she's...how did my mother put it...oh, right, she's a free woman and raring to go."

Julian winces and grips the back of his neck. "This is beginning to sound like a nightmare. And you know what? I'm not sure I'll be able to take off that much time. It's a well-known fact that agents never rest."

Carter's eyebrows snap together. "You told me you'd already worked out your vacation schedule."

This time Julian's the one who's busted, and he wears a sheepish smile to prove it. "Right."

"Just tell Lydia you have a girlfriend," Carter offers, his fingers tapping away at his phone. "It's not like she'd be able to call you on that."

I snort. "You say that like an out-of-sight girlfriend would make a difference to her. I assure you, it would not."

Tori studies Julian and me, her gaze swinging between us, and then her eyes go wide. She thumps Carter on the chest several times. "Wait. I have an idea." She holds out her hands in a hear-me-out-first stance, her eyes glittering with mischief. "What if you two pretended to be dating? Just for the weekend?"

When I see Julian's stricken expression, I slap a hand against my mouth to stem the cackle waiting to burst from my throat.

That's an excellent question. What if, Julian?

Chapter Twelve

Julian

I'VE NEVER EXPERIENCED a brain fart—until now.

This is not the blessedly quiet and uneventful Saturday I was looking forward to. Not even a tiny bit. That awkward moment when I failed to take off my agent hat and congratulate Tori and Carter on their impending nuptials was the first disruption. This harebrained scheme to pretend I'm dating Ashley is the second.

While I try to absorb the force of the Mack truck that just hit me, Tori turns to Ashley, her hands fluttering with excitement. "If you two are a couple, you won't have to deal with your nosy relatives." Turning to me, her eyes bright and hopeful, she says, "And *you* won't have to deal with Lydia, either."

Carter stares at her, an incredulous expression on his face. "I'm not sure that's going to solve anything. It might lead to more questions." His throat snags. "And what are you envisioning? That they'd be kissing each other in front of everyone?" He shudders. "Or that they lie to our parents? Seems like a lot of acting just to get out of a few annoying conversations."

Tori glances at the ceiling and shakes her head. "You're overthinking this, Carter. People who date don't have to engage in public displays of affection. They're just spending time together. Haven't you ever asked someone to join you at an event so you could turn to them if things got awkward or uncomfortable?"

Carter nods. "Well, sure, but—"

"See? That's all I'm talking about here." She peers at Ashley. "What do you think? Would you stay the entire weekend if Julian was there as your plus one? And before you answer, chew on this. From what I hear, your parents love Julian, so there'd be no reason to lie to them."

Ashley—the traitor—makes a show of rubbing her chin and considering it. "It's not a terrible idea." She flicks her gaze my way. "I think I'd be able to endure the weekend if Julian were there to shield me from the pettiness."

Those damn irresistible eyes of hers sparkle with amusement. The urge to kiss away her smirk is strong. So fucking strong. "I'm flattered."

She pouts as though she's mimicking me. "Oh, c'mon, Julian. I adore you as a person, not just as my boyfriend-for-hire. It's a perfect solution. And think about this. You could even say with a straight face that we're living together. Besides, would pretending to be my boyfriend for four days and three nights be *that* much of an imposition?"

Yes. Yes, it would. How am I supposed to battle my attraction to her if we're pretending to date? I've already screwed myself by inviting her into my home. This would multiply the risk factor by thousands.

Tori takes up the argument. "It's my wedding, Julian. And I want her there for the duration. Do it to keep this bride happy. *Please.*"

Dammit. That's guilt-tripping at its finest. With Tori's flair for theatrics, I might have to sign her as a client, too. My gaze shoots to Carter for help.

He shrugs and shakes his head. "I have three words. Tori. Bride. Wedding. What would you do if you were in my shoes?"

Tori makes sickeningly sweet kissy faces at him. "*No me jodas, mi amor.*"

Carter thrusts out his hand in her direction, as if to say, *There's exhibit A.* "See there? She tells me not to fuck with her while making goo-goo eyes at me. I know where my bread is sliced, toasted, *and* buttered. So it's good to meet you, future brother-in-law."

"*Pretend* future brother-in-law," I say, although I feel silly for clarifying that obvious point.

Tori claps her hands. "So you'll do it?"

I study Ashley, her hopeful expression slowly making me warm to the idea. "This is what you want? It'll make it easier for you to be there?"

She nods. "It'll make it easier for me not to drop kick Lydia into the next town, at least." I don't respond, so she continues, her hands opening and closing into fists at her sides. "All right, seriously, I just don't want to be the center of anyone's attention. This is Carter and Tori's time to shine. With you there, I think my family will curb their condescending ways, and I'll be less anxious about the whole ordeal."

"Okay, I'll do it. *Just* for the weekend."

But Ashley's eyes go wide. "Oh, wait a minute. Would Sooyin be upset? Would she expect you to take her, I mean?"

I haven't thought about Sooyin since she came over to explain the finer points of negotiating film deals and Ashley conveniently assumed I was interested in her. "We're not at that point. She wouldn't care." In fact, she wouldn't give a rat's ass if I pretended to be Ashley's boyfriend.

Ashley shimmies. "It'll be fun, Julian."

No, no it won't be. But I'll deal. Because that's what I do.

Carter opens the pantry door and peers inside. "Got any bagels or pastries or something?"

"He does not," Ashley says behind him. She shifts him to the side and pulls out a paper bag. "But I have coffee cake muffins."

She announces this like a villain who's finally watching her evil plan come to fruition.

I set out glasses and dishes while Ashley separates the muffins from their liners. Then she and I stand at the sink together, working seamlessly to rinse a bunch of fruits to add some nutrition to this makeshift breakfast.

"Think quick!" she says.

But I'm too slow to catch the red grape that bounces off my nose. "Let's try that again."

She pitches another grape, and I easily catch it with my mouth.

"You're a man of many talents, Mr. Hart."

I wink at her. "You don't know the half, Ms. Williamson."

Carter clears his throat. "Are you going to share the breakfast with us now?"

Ash and I smile at each other and push the serving plates closer to our guests. *Our guests.* Yeah, I like the sound of that. Dammit. I need an intervention, obviously.

We stand behind the granite counter while Tori and Carter sit on stools opposite us. As we eat, they fill us in on the details of their faux family reunion. The best news? Tori's mother and sister, who co-own a Puerto Rican restaurant, will be treating us to a welcome dinner. I'd gnaw off my right hand for properly prepared fried plantains. The mushy versions at the deli salad bar near my office are an abomination.

"My mother doesn't get the point of reunions, so she's confused," Tori explains. "In our family, everyone attends an event, no matter how small. A few of my second cousins even attended my kindergarten graduation. She doesn't understand why Carter's relatives need to be tricked into coming."

"Well, it's not just about being tricked into coming," Carter says as he brushes crumbs off his shirt.

My instinct is to grab the dust pan and clean up after him, but years of home training have taught me that you never clean up while guests are eating. It's fucking hard, though. Carter attacks his muffin like he learned how to eat only recently—like yesterday, in fact.

Ashley puts a hand on mine, mouthing, "We'll take care of it later."

Tori watches us with interest, so I pretend to be disinterested. But shit, that felt familiar, and not just in a *we're roommates* way.

"We also need to make sure they shut their big traps," Carter continues. "My family doesn't know how to be discreet about anything."

Tori slaps his hand away when he tries to swipe a grape off her plate. "I'm excited to see everyone." She leans over and drops her head on Carter's shoulder. "And to marry this man."

He turns his head and plants a soft kiss on her forehead. I'm happy for him. He's found "the one" a lot sooner than I imagined he would.

We talk for several more minutes, and then Tori rises from her stool.

To Carter, she says, "Let's go, hot stuff. My class starts at eleven." Then she pulls out a pair of huge sunglasses and a baseball cap, mainstays of her life now that she's in the public eye. Carter, the goofball, does nothing more than try to pat down his cowlick.

He polishes off the muffin as he stands.

"Carter said you're understaffed. Hire anyone yet?" I ask Tori.

"Banking on getting my girl Eva to relocate. I'll work on her during"—she makes air quotes—"'the reunion.' I can't wait—"

"Hey, Tor. You said we had to go."

Still facing me, Tori throws up a hand at him. "I can't wait to see her."

Then, with a wink to each other, Tori and Ashley hug before Carter pulls Tori out of the unit.

After closing the door, I lean against it and zone in on Ashley, who's filling the dishwasher—and whistling.

When she's done, she turns to me with a half smile. "So, you ready to practice?"

I shake my head at her, a sense of ensuing danger prickling my skin. "Practice what?"

"Pretending to be my boyfriend."

Damn. I'm noping out of this conversation. Right now. "We can wing it, Ash. I'm going to—"

"But wouldn't it be fun to cram for the final exam?" she asks, wagging her eyebrows.

"Ash," I say, drawing her name out in a warning. "Stop messing around already."

Her lips quirk up at the corners. "Okay, okay."

My phone buzzes on the dining table. I walk over and peek at it with one eye, muttering that it better not be related to work.

Quinn's name and image pop up, as if I've conjured him from my nightmares. I answer the call with fake enthusiasm. "David, what's up?"

Ashley picks up a magazine on the coffee table and drops onto the sofa. I watch her flip through the pages as I listen to my boss.

"Julian, I know it's the weekend, but I'd like your help."

"What do you need?"

"A little birdie tells me Brielle Loughlin isn't happy with KMB." Quinn says this in a stage whisper.

He means Kantis, Moor, and Belle, one of the leading agencies out here. And Brielle's a television award circuit darling. No film roles on her résumé yet, but it's only a matter of time. I know where this is going before he says anything else. Tonight, the Television Critics' Association hosts its annual awards ceremony at the Beverly Hilton. Brielle will undoubtedly be there. Which means Quinn undoubtedly wants me there, too.

"You'd like me to attend the TCA Awards and lay the groundwork?"

He chuckles. "Yes, exactly. Don't even pitch her a soft sell. Just get on her radar. I'd do it myself, but I've got a lot going on, so…"

Bullshit. He'd never do this himself. Poaching clients is frowned upon in the industry, and David doesn't want to sully his own reputation by engaging in any activities that might have even a whiff of impropriety. So he asks me to do it. A soft sell I'd say no to. But speaking with an actor in the industry, just so there's a face she can associate with our agency, I have no problem doing. "Tickets?"

"All electronic this year. I've got two. I'll forward the email."

"Sure, I'll take care of it."

"I knew you would." He doesn't say this as if he appreciates my willingness to do his bidding. Rather, he says it matter-of-factly, as if saying no never was an option.

"Later, David."

Ashley sets the magazine on her lap. "Work beckons?"

"Unfortunately, yes."

I swipe at my phone to refresh my email. As promised, Quinn's forwarded the electronic tickets to the awards event.

Two tickets.

I should ask her to join me. An event outside the house doesn't have nearly as many risks as hanging out together at home. Besides, I enjoy her company. Her running commentary on the evening's events would be more entertaining than the awards ceremony. "What are you doing tonight?"

She grins, her eyes wide in anticipation because she overheard my end of the conversation with Quinn. "No plans. Why?"

"Want to rub shoulders with a few celebrities?"

She gives me a filled-to-capacity smile that makes my chest ache. "Hell yes."

That settles it, then. We're getting out of our painfully close quarters and hanging out in public, and I'm well aware that's the safest place for us these days.

Chapter Thirteen

Ashley

As Julian guides me through the lobby of the Beverly Hilton Hotel, I try to suppress any hint that I'm star struck. It might surprise him to know that the sister of a Hollywood actor can be awed by celebrity sightings, but it's true. This is Carter's world, not mine, and purposefully so.

What a world, indeed. Marble in a variety of neutral hues dominates the cavernous lobby, and I count several massive chandeliers before we pass through the doors of the International Ballroom.

"This is where the Emmy Awards are held," I say. There's no mistaking the wonder in my voice, and I wince, knowing experiences like this one are commonplace to Julian.

"Yeah. Surreal, right?"

I'm gratified to hear a touch of wonder in his voice, too, and I resolve to get out of my head for the evening and enjoy myself.

He pulls out his phone and shows his screen to one of the four members of the hotel staff stationed at the double doors. She scans his phone, hands us programs, and wishes us a wonderful evening.

We weave our way through the rows and rows of tables to find our own. Along the way, Julian slows, turns around, and asks, "How do you want to be introduced? Do you want anyone to know your Carter's sister?"

I shake my head vigorously. "No, I'd prefer just to be your date." My cheeks warm when the words register in my own brain. "I mean, I know it's not a date, date. Just. Well, I'm here with you and that's it, okay?"

He regards me with furrowed brows and a small grin, an expression that reads as both amusement and confusion, as if he's entertained by my fumbling but isn't sure he should be. "Right. I understand."

He pivots and stuffs his hands in the pockets of his suit pants before he resumes the trek to our table. His jacket lifts a bit in the back, and there's no way I'm not sneaking a peek at his butt. Oh. *I spy with my little eye a very nice ass in front of me.* And I'm so absorbed by the view that I fail to lift my gaze when Julian reaches the table and spins around.

My head crashes into his chest. "Sorry." I don't dare look in his eyes as I lie. "Thought I saw something shiny on the floor. An earring maybe."

He ignores my explanation, suggesting he's aware I made it up. "I was just wondering if you wanted me to grab you a drink from the bar."

"Sure, a glass of white wine, please. I'm going to use the restroom while you're gone. Meet here?"

He nods. "Be back soon."

I ask a passing server to point me to the restroom and trail behind two women headed in the same direction. To my right, I see three child actors, stars of my favorite sci-fi series on Netflix. I stifle the urge to hound them for clues about the upcoming season. I don't want to be *that* person.

When I return to the table, a wineglass sits at my place setting, and a few feet away Julian chats with a woman. I seize the rare opportunity to observe him in his element. He carries himself with ease, a commanding figure who draws the attention of those around him. After a minute or so, the woman by his side laughs, mirroring his relaxed demeanor. They shake hands, and then she slips around him and disappears into the throng of people shuffling to their tables.

I jolt when a man drops into the seat beside mine.

He wears a carefree smile, but his assessing gaze skips across the faces in the ballroom, suggesting he's working even now. He offers me a hand. "Mark Berry, senior features writer for *Inside Hollywood*."

I take it. "Ashley Williamson."

He peruses my face and body as though their very purpose is to entertain him. "Let me guess. An aspiring actress?"

He poses the question to my breasts, and for a horrifying moment he appears poised to bury his face in my cleavage.

In my head, I ask, *And what about you? An accomplished asshole?* But I rein in my annoyance and simply say, "Nope. Just fangirling."

Julian appears next to me and lowers himself onto his chair, his arm crossing in front of my chest before he and Mark greet each other with a complicated manshake, as though they're choreographing pirouettes with their fingers.

He gives me a sideways glance. "You okay?"

I take a sip of the wine before I answer. "I'm great."

I mean it, too. My dress floats over my skin and flatters my body at every angle. I'm in the company of a handsome man who treats me well. And I'm free to stargaze without the usual need to answer questions about my famous brother.

Mark smiles at me. Now that he realizes I'm with Julian, I matter. What a prick.

He leans over, his attention directed to Julian. "Been meaning to speak with you about an angle I'd like to explore for a feature. Maybe even a series."

"Oh, yeah?" Julian says as he absently scans the room.

"Been thinking about shaking things up a little. A three- or four-part series on diversity in Hollywood."

"Or the lack thereof," Julian notes.

"Exactly. And since you're one of the few agents of color out here, I thought it would be great to get your take on some of these issues. I heard you on that panel at the Agents in Industry Conference. You were vocal in a way

I hadn't anticipated given that your fortunes are tied to the gatekeepers."

Julian hesitates to respond, as though he's weighing his words carefully, and given the reporter's lead-in, I imagine that he is. After a lick of his lips, he lifts his chin, his gaze determined—defiant even. "It's not an easy topic to tackle during a thirty-minute panel. I mean, lack of representation is only the tip of the iceberg. There are plenty of inequities—in salaries and the quality of roles, for starters. And we could talk about the misogyny women of color deal with for days." He pauses and takes in a deep breath before he continues. "Look, I recognize it's regarded as either a divisive subject or something I'm not supposed to talk about altogether, but I care about these issues. Others? Not so much."

He speaks with such passion about the subject that I'm enthralled. The two guests next to Julian nod, likely recognizing the truth of his statements.

Mark leans back in his chair. "And that's why I'd like to interview you. Game?"

Julian blows out his breath as he considers the request. "Let me think about it. I'll let you know."

Mark rises from the chair. "I'm around all next week if you want to chat."

Julian nods. "Sure. Good seeing you."

Mark acknowledges me with a two-fingered salute. "Ashley."

I tilt my head in his direction and give him a weak smile. He strikes me as the kind of man who thinks he's made more of an impact on someone than he truly has.

After Mark leaves, Julian asks, "Did I miss something between you two?"

I give him a weary sigh. "Typical male bullshit. I was nobody until he discovered we were together."

Julian purses his lips and nods slowly. "Then he won't be getting that interview he wants so badly."

"Julian, no. This is an important issue. He didn't say anything overtly asstastic. He's just a creep."

"I'll bear that in mind as I consider his request. There are tons of reporters who could tell that story."

I'm touched that he's offended on my behalf. Makes me proud that past me always thought he was crushworthy. Present me wholeheartedly agrees, even though I know nothing will come of this infatuation.

After the ballroom lights dim, the event passes in a blur of monologues, applause, and acceptance speeches. I recognize many of the actors called to the podium, but they're over one hundred feet away, so I can't do much more than marvel that we're in the same room. By my side, Julian leans in every few moments, saying something in my ear, reaching for the bread basket, or exchanging a look when we react to a joke on stage. Being this close to him is both easy and unbearably stimulating.

When the ceremony is over, we shuffle out with the rest of the attendees, a clump of bodies plodding along until the funnel disperses. Julian hands the valet his ticket, and we wait under the concrete awning that covers a third of the circular driveway. The chill in the air makes me shiver. Noticing, Julian removes his jacket and drapes it over my shoulders.

"May in LA is cooler than I thought it would be."

He smiles. "LA tip: Always bring a sweater."

"So noted," I say, my teeth chattering as though I'm trapped in a blizzard.

Julian purses his lips. "Shit, you're so cold." He opens his arms. "Bring it in, Ash."

I don't hesitate to burrow into his chest, and with his jacket covering my shoulders and back, I'm now cocooned in Julian-made warmth. His body stands like a pillar that won't budge, until I dare to place my arms at his waist and he contracts against my touch.

I don't retreat. Instead, I deepen the contact, curling my fingers around him and squeezing.

Julian's car pulls up, and he practically leaps out of my embrace. Saved by the valet.

With his jacket still draped over my shoulders, I slip into the car, and Julian closes the door when I'm settled inside. Watching him through the windshield as he strides to the driver's side, I chew on my bottom lip, frustrated with myself for pushing him where he doesn't want to go. It's not fair to him. I mentally slap my hand and channel Carter's typical admonition: *Stop being a brat, Ashley.*

For a few seconds, Julian stares at the steering wheel, gripping it with both hands.

"Ready to go?" I ask.

He jerks his head before turning it in my direction. "Yes. Sorry. Was just thinking about something."

"What's that like?"

He laughs. "You know full well what that's like. I'd be surprised if your brain ever shuts off."

"True."

In fact, it's currently working at full capacity, alternating between imagining lusty, sweaty, no-holds-barred sex with Julian and suppressing my dirty thoughts as I know I should. So fine, we've decided not to act on our attraction to each other, but why should I be the only one tortured as a consequence? Isn't there some fun to be had here? Then I remember Sooyin's theory that Julian is pretending to be interested in her to keep his attraction to me at bay. Testing her hypothesis would be amusing, wouldn't it? "So tell me about Sooyin. What's your plan there?"

He glances at me sideways and swallows before he answers. "Plan?"

"Well, yeah, if you're interested, what do you intend to do about it?"

He clears his throat as he turns the steering wheel, his gaze trained on the road ahead. "I like her. But I'm not going to push. I…uh…I'm just going to let things happen naturally."

Such bullshit, Mr. Hart. "If you need any tips on how to approach her, I'm here for you."

In a rare safety violation, Julian removes one of his hands from the wheel and slaps it on his thigh. "You're precious," he says, his deep, rich voice laced with laughter. "I think I can handle it on my own, thanks."

I shrug. "Okay, but you're missing out on the opportunity to learn some closely held secrets about what women really want."

He perks up. "Now I'm intrigued."

"Ha. I knew you would be."

He motions for me to get on with it. "I'm waiting."

"Okay, where to start. Oh, I know. Many guys send flowers to let a woman know they're thinking about her. It's sweet. And yes, we appreciate them. But do you know what works even better than that?"

"What?"

"Pick. Up. The. Fucking. Phone. *Call her.* At random times. Not every day or, Jesus, definitely not every hour, but when you can. Just to say 'Hey, hello, I'm thinking of you.' That's the best kind of foreplay, and guys don't do it enough."

"It goes both ways, you know."

"Of course it does."

We reach his condo, and he drives into the underground parking lot. After easing the car into a parking space, he asks, "What else?"

I climb out of the car and wait for him to lock it. "Okay, here's one I encounter more than I care to. Not every woman wants a serious relationship."

He stops short and throws his hands over his chest, pretending to be shocked. "What the hell? Are you serious?"

I clip him on the shoulder. "Yes, I'm serious. Sometimes women want someone to hang out with. They're not always looking for a life partner. And I find guys act in ways designed to avoid a long-term commitment when half the time the woman doesn't want one either."

"Is that the story of your love life?"

"Yes, yes, a thousand times, yes."

I hand him his jacket, my gaze automatically zeroing in on the way his shirt stretches across his chest as he slips his arms inside.

We pass Benny on our way through the lobby and wave at him.

Stepping into the elevator, Julian waits at the threshold until I enter. "Okay, this has been an eye-opening discussion. Give me one more."

My last tip comes out with much thought. "It's a marathon, not a sprint."

He swallows before he speaks. "I'm not clueless, so I can guess where this is headed. It's not a race to the big finish, right?"

"Exactly. Sure, sometimes a quick bang does the job. Other times, you can't help yourself, and it's got to be all-consuming and clumsy and so rough the guy's dangling belt buckle digs into your thigh and you notice scratch marks the next morning. But mostly, we want to be savored. We want to know that you'd happily spend the entire day making us shudder and gasp and cry out in pleasure and that your face between our legs is a fucking joy, not a chore."

The elevator dings, and I step off. But when I turn back, Julian's still inside, his keys in one hand and his face pointing to the ceiling.

I laugh. "I've blown your mind, huh?"

He drops his chin to meet my eyes, and I'm unprepared for the force of his stare. It's stormy, needy, *hungry*. His gaze drops to my mouth before he pushes off the wall and stalks my way. He's not being coy. Far from it. He's telling me in no uncertain terms that he wants me. Goose bumps dot my skin, and my heart bangs against my chest like a stampede of horses is trampling over it.

I don't wait for Julian to reach me. Instead, I rush toward him, and when our bodies meet in the middle, I throw my arms around his neck and press into him. He braces my face, and I rise on my toes, desperate to get my lips on his mouth.

Before his mouth comes down on mine, he asks, "Ash, what are we doing?" He doesn't wait for an answer, nor do I give him one.

Not in words, at least.

Chapter Fourteen

Julian

ASHLEY AND I are kissing like the world is on fire and this is how we want to take our last breaths. I gently suck on her bottom lip as I pull her close, and she gives me a delicious moan that I'll remember forever. I'm a kid charging through the schoolhouse doors for recess, and her mouth is my playground. Good Lord, my fantasies were underwhelming compared to this. We tug on each other, hands grasping for purchase, until I grab her ass and lift her against the wall, my erection pressing against the junction of her thighs.

The whoosh of the closing elevator doors reminds me that we're outside my home and any one of my neighbors could find us.

With my chest heaving and my cheek resting on her chest, I whisper, "We need to get inside."

Ashley caresses my back, her touch feather soft. "Yeah."

She slides to the ground and rights her clothing, while I search my pockets for my keys. They're not there, though, and then I spin around and discover them on the floor outside the elevator. Dropping them is atypical, but so is what just happened. I swipe them up off the ground and open the door.

Ashley glides inside, and I follow her seductive trail. The door isn't even closed when we reach for each other again. She slips her hands inside my jacket, ghosting her fingers up my back as she nuzzles my jaw. I spin her around and use my lower body to press her against the nearest wall, and then I'm on her, unleashing all the want that has kept me up at night for more weeks than I'd care to admit. My lips are everywhere, trailing soft kisses over her bare shoulders, along her collarbone, under her chin.

Through it all, she whispers words of encouragement that make my gut clench in anticipation of being inside her. "Julian. Yes. God, I want this. So much. Please."

All day. All night. Soft and slow. Rough and fast. Whatever she wants, and however she wants it. I'd like that for her. But what the fuck am I doing? *Think, think, think.* She's Carter's sister. And I resolved not to do anything that would make him question whether we should continue to work together. With all my talk over the years about not doing anything to blur the lines between our personal and professional relationships, I'd lose all credibility if I tried to pretend that dating his sister doesn't qualify. I'm not rocking the boat; I'm upending it and smashing it into a thousand pieces against a rocky shore.

But it's hard to care about all that when this amazing woman is nuzzling my neck and making soft, breathy noises against my ear.

She lifts the skirt of her dress and guides my hand to the thin waistband of her underwear. "Touch me, Julian."

Oh fuck, oh fuck, oh fuck.

Her breath is warm against my face, and I lean into her, unable to resist the promise in her eyes. Even so, I try. "I'm not sure we should do this, Ashley. It'll complicate everything."

My efforts to approach this rationally disintegrate when she whispers, "Do you want me to do it for you? Would that make it easier for you to let go?" She nips at my earlobe, sending a jolt that pulses through my body. "If you want this, give me your hand."

I'm powerless to deny her, mesmerized by the strength and passion in her voice, so I give her my hand, and she draws it inside her panties, threading her fingers with mine so we both can give her pleasure. The heat of her pussy is like a siren's call, and my dick swells against my fly. With her gaze boring into mine, she presses against my fingers, guiding one of them to skate over her slick folds. "I want this, Julian. Just this once."

I harden even more at the prospect of replacing that digit with my cock. But this isn't the time for contemplation, because she's not done with me. Not even close.

"More?" she asks.

I groan at the thought of what's to come. "God, yes."

She circles two of my fingers and pushes them inside, letting out a long moan that never seems to end. She's taking what she needs, and I'm more than happy to give it to her. Her other hand clasps my shoulder, and she buries her face in the crook of my neck. "Yes, Julian. Do something. Please."

An invisible hand slides up my chest and tightens its fingers around my throat, forcing me to choke out words that are best left unsaid. "You're incredible, Ash. Fucking perfect. Keep going—just like that."

She lifts her head, narrowing her eyes into slits. "You want to absolve yourself of responsibility? Pretend it's me and only me making this happen? I won't let you."

Without preamble, she withdraws her fingers and stares at me defiantly. I don't react, in part because I'm dying to know where she plans to take this. And partly because…I'm just dying, teetering on the edge of control, loving the feel of her pussy and tying myself in knots over it.

"Touch me, Julian. All by yourself."

Unwilling to deny her request, I brush my fingertips against her clit, and then I slide my digits inside her, stroking her slowly. When she rocks against my hand, setting her own urgent pace, I know she wants to come like this. My mind is racing with the implications of what we're doing. This is Ashley. My fucking fingers are inside her, and she's so wet, they're practically gliding on ice. If that weren't enough, she's generating so much body heat, she's making me sweat, too.

I'm vibrating. Everywhere. And my toes are flexed so tightly in my shoes that I'm sure to cramp up at any moment.

"It's so good," she moans against my ear. "But I need more."

I should stop, but the selfish corner of my brain convinces me that I can't leave her dissatisfied. Seeing her this way, her mouth open and glistening, her eyes glazed and unfocused, fuels me. I use my feet to spread her wider, then I dip my leg between hers. I slide her hands up against the wall, caging her torso with my frame. "Ride my thigh," I murmur against her jaw. "Make yourself come."

I draw back slightly, fascinated by the way her golden brown eyes darken. Without a word, she slips her arms around my neck and lowers her body. She's writhing against my thigh, undulating in a slow and steady rhythm, and when she appears to hit the right spot, she throws her head back, a sensuous goddess consumed by lust. "Oh God. Yes, yes, yes."

What the fuck was I thinking? This isn't any less tempting. Now instead of envying my fingers, I'm jealous of my quads. My mouth lands on her throat, and I suck hard. She's sweet and salty, like pretzels dipped in chocolate.

"Oh," she says, a note of surprise in her voice. She lowers her head and cradles the sides of my face. "More, damn you. I won't get off like this."

The challenge in her voice compels me to prove her wrong. "You will."

I reach in between her thighs, push her panties to the side, and spread her lips, flexing my thigh so her clit rubs the muscle there. Then I grab onto her ass and slide her back and forth against me, creating the friction she needs.

She digs her fingers into my arms and buries her face against me, her cheek smashed against my shoulder. Her mouth hangs open as she cries out her pleasure, shouting *yeses* and *ahs* that tell me she's coming. And it is such a fucking turn-on. I have nowhere to put my passion, nowhere to go for my relief, and the pleasure I feel from watching her orgasm intensifies as a result, as though I'm coming vicariously through her. After letting out several high-pitched cries, she collapses against me, breathing harshly in the aftermath.

My phone is vibrating in my pocket, but I ignore it, choosing to massage her thighs instead. Eventually, we straighten, and I help her smooth her dress, neither of us looking at the other. The enormity of what we did hits me in waves. We can't go back. It happened. And we can't go forward, either. But *fuck* I want an encore, and next time she won't be riding my thigh.

My phone vibrates again.

"Answer it," she says softly. "I'm going to freshen up."

I pull it out of my pocket and answer, grateful for the lifeline but unable to focus on the call until Ashley slips out of the room.

"Julian."

Unfortunately, it's Quinn, and my lingering erection bids a hasty retreat. "Yeah, Quinn. As requested, I introduced myself to Brielle. She was friendly, and I think we're on her radar now."

"Good. But that's not why I called. I didn't send you to the awards to get on your soapbox about diversity again. Alienating our clients costs us money, and people in this industry talk, so pull your shit together when you're in public, okay?"

"David, I was doing my job, cultivating a connection with an influential reporter—"

"I don't care. I'm not sure how many ways I can tell you the same thing. You can think it if you want to, but don't share it when you're on my dime. Got it?"

And then I hear the dial tone. *Motherfucker.*

I drop the phone on the couch and toss Quinn out of my head. I'll deal with him on Monday, when we've both had a chance to calm down. I need to address a more pressing issue anyway. How do I explain to Ashley that I let my attraction for her override my good judgment and it can't happen again? What do I say that won't make her feel like I'm rejecting her? Is there a way to make clear that I'm not thinking only of my own needs and wants, but hers, too?

I trudge down the hall as if I've been summoned to the principal's office, and when I'm outside Ashley's bedroom, I mentally prepare myself to knock and say what I need to say.

But Ashley beats me to it, swinging open the door with purpose and stopping short when she sees me. "Oh, shit, Julian. You could lose a man part tiptoeing around like that."

Unable to meet her gaze, I stare down at the floor, fumbling for the words to make this right. "I...thought we should...uh, talk. You know, about what just happened."

"Oh good," she says.

My head snaps up at her easy, friendly tone.

She's wearing a hint of a smile. Before she continues, she takes a deep breath, and then it all comes out in a rush. "That was a mistake. You know it, and I know it. I mean, you're Carter's best friend, and that's just awkward. Not to mention he's your client, and I know how difficult it is for you to manage both sides of your relationship. So yes, while your thigh is the stuff that nonpenetrative sex dreams are made of, let's consider this a mutual momentary loss of our common senses and agree never to speak about it again."

I can't stop blinking as I try to process what I heard. Am I hallucinating that shit about my thigh?

"Say something," she urges.

The notion that I'd be able to forget what she looks like when she comes is absurd, but lying to ourselves is one of humankind's most widely used self-defense mechanisms. I swallow hard before I speak. "Uh, yeah. I was going to say the same thing. Well, not that stuff about nonpenetrative sex, of course, but...okay, we're cool, then?"

She nods as she bites the edge of her bottom lip.

I begin to turn around but freeze when she reaches out and grazes my elbow. "Yeah?"

"I've got a hectic travel schedule before the reunion, so I'm going to arrange to return to New York after my next trip. I'll head home from there."

"So, we'll just meet in Harmon?"

She nods.

"And we're still doing this?" I ask.

She raises a brow. "Pretending to be dating? Definitely." Eyes wide, she places a hand on her chest. "Oh, unless you've changed your mind?"

"No, no. I said I'd do it, and I will. Now that we're on the same page about remaining just friends, it'll be fine."

"Right."

I'm not sure she needs an echo, but I don't know what else to say. "Right."

But in my head, an ominous voice says, *Wrong, Julian. Something's going to go very wrong.*

Chapter Fifteen

Ashley

HOME, BITTERSWEET HOME.

As I stare at my parents' modest pale yellow colonial, I'm reminded of the warmth and laughter that filled our house for as long as I lived in it. With its simple white shutters and the trellis that never was sturdy enough to climb, this place served as my childhood oasis. That I needed an oasis at all is the bittersweet part.

My mother appears at the screen door, a mixing bowl and wooden spoon in her hands. "Ashley, get in here and save me from this kitchen. I have no idea what I'm doing."

Very true. She's known for many things, but cooking is not one of them.

I pull my carry-on over the circular brick-paved driveway and up the front steps. Mentally calling dibs on the swing seat on the farmer's porch, I enter the house and take a deep breath. "Something's burning," I say as I park my suitcase by the umbrella stand.

Moving like the Road Runner, my mother kisses my forehead, scrambles to the oven, and peers through the glass window. "Oh shit. My corn bread."

I set my purse on the table and wave away the acrid air. "Did you set the timer?"

She stuffs her hands in the oven mitts. "That makes too much sense, sweetie. I'm a let's-just-wing-it kind of chef." When she opens the oven door, a cloud of smoke whooshes out and she coughs. "That'll teach me to cook."

"Should have left it to Dad," I mumble.

"I heard that, smart-ass."

"Sorry." I can't help grinning. "What can I do to help?"

She tosses the muffin pan on the stovetop, and it clanks against the burners when it lands. "Sit. Have a cup of coffee with me. We bought a Keurig, so I can't screw that up."

"All right, let me run to the bathroom first."

When I return, I fiddle with the K-Cups, deciding on a Colombian blend. While I wait for my mother's cup to brew, I study her.

"What?" she asks.

"Nothing. You look good." And she does. Her short wavy hair is graying at the sides but otherwise retains the rich chocolate brown color she's had for decades. Faint lines bracket the corners of her mouth, highlighting the sassy smile that always graces her lovely face.

"You do, too," she says, cupping my chin. "Beautiful, really. And I'm so glad you're home."

We switch places in front of the coffeemaker. "I'm glad to be home."

"It's not nice to lie to your mother," she says over my shoulder.

I spin around just as the machine's ready button lights and the coffee drips into my cup. "*I am*. Well, glad to be here for Tori and Carter. And to see you, and Dad, and Kimberly. The other folks?" I shrug. "Eh. It'll be fine."

We take our coffee and sit at the kitchen table, a striped maple monstrosity that my father and Carter made when we were teens. Neither my father nor Carter wanted my help. Instead, they built it together, a male-bonding project that spanned an entire summer and left me outside literally spinning my wheels on the upgraded bike my parents gave me for my birthday.

"Where is everyone?" I ask.

"Carter and Tori went to the airport to pick up her family. Your father is at the hardware store looking for an extension cord that'll reach the gazebo. Kimberly's taking the kids to get haircuts. And most of our guests will be here this afternoon. A few stragglers won't get here until Saturday."

"Are you excited?"

The dreamy expression on her face is answer enough. "One of my babies is getting married. I'm ecstatic."

"Tori's lovely."

My mother lets out a happy sigh. "The minute I met her I knew she was the one for Carter. I'm so glad they figured it out."

"Me, too. He has less time to worry about me now."

"Yes, but now *I* can pick up the slack."

I take a sip of my coffee. "No need to. Truly. Am I staying in my old bedroom?"

My mother lets me change the subject—because yes, there's no doubt in my mind that if she wanted to press it she would. "I'm putting the young folks in the guest house. You'll have more fun there. Everybody else will stay here. But bear in mind, as far as I know, Carter and Tori are *not* sleeping in the same room."

Over the years, my mother's refused Carter's many offers to buy her a new home. Instead, she compromised and gave him permission to build a guest house on the back end of the property. With my father's help and waivers from the local permit office, he oversaw the construction. It has four bedrooms, a fully equipped kitchen, and four bathrooms, so calling it a guest house is a bit of a misnomer.

"I was thinking you and Tori's best friend could share the room with the double beds, but if you want to stay with the old folks, that's fine, too."

"Why? Is Lydia staying?"

Although she still lives in Harmon, I imagine Lydia's fear of missing out would compel her to hang around anyway.

"She's not coming."

Yes, yes, yes. My brain and heart high-five each other. "She isn't?"

"Nope. Aunt Carol says she's got some big work-related trip she couldn't postpone. But Aunt Carol and Uncle Richard are driving up from Pennsylvania. Let's see, I figure we'll have"—she uses her fingers to tick off the names—"Carter and Tori in one bedroom, Tori's sister, Bianca, in another, Julian gets his own, and you and Eva in the fourth."

"Got it. That's too bad about Lydia, though. We'll miss her."

My mother snorts. She knows very well that my cousin and I get along like opponents in *The Hunger Games*. "I'm sure you will." She narrows her eyes. "Kind of undermines your reasons for wanting to pretend to be dating Julian, huh?"

"You know about that already?"

"Carter and Tori filled us in on the plan when they got here."

I take a sip of my coffee before I answer. "Yeah. I guess you're right. It's no longer necessary. I mean, Aunt Carol will be a pain in the butt, but I can handle her. And if Lydia isn't here, she might even tone down her pettiness."

"You don't seem relieved by any of this. Is there something you're not telling me?"

My mother should have been a detective—or a hound dog. She can sniff out intrigue and cover-ups like a veteran sleuth. And if I want some semblance of peace this weekend, I should be honest with her.

"So I might have had a tiny little crush on Julian in my teens," I say, pressing my thumb and forefinger together to emphasize the insignificance of my infatuation back then.

My mother waves me off. "I knew that. But I'm more interested in what's going on in the here and now."

"Are we really having this conversation?"

She scrunches her brows and shakes her head. "Is there any reason not to? You're twenty-six years old, sweetie. And I *do* know where babies come from."

My forehead hits the table. "Oh God."

She lays a hand on my hair and smooths it. "If it'll make you feel better, I'll start. Your Dad and I still—"

"Stop, please," I say. "I applaud whatever you and Dad are still doing, but I don't need to know about it."

She gives me a toothy smile, the wrinkles at the corner of her eyes deepening. "There, there. It'll be fine. Take a deep breath and tell your mother what's going on."

I do as she says. "I like Julian." I take a furtive glance in her direction. "I'm attracted to him. But we agreed that it doesn't make sense to do anything about it. Plus, I'm not looking for anything serious, so why complicate things for what's essentially a desire to scratch an itch? I don't want Carter in my business just as much as Carter doesn't want me in his."

She listens and sips her coffee, a neutral expression denying me any clue as to what she thinks about the situation.

"Thoughts?" I ask.

"Well, I guess on some level I understand his hesitation. Men can be weird about these things. And he's got the added factor that he's never truly been comfortable acting as Carter's agent. Carter's said as much on more than one occasion. So I get it. But I'm not sure I understand what's holding you back."

"It's just...he'll always be Carter's friend first and foremost. That's just a fact. They have so much history together. If Carter and I had a fight, Julian would definitely take Carter's side. Goodness, it's in his own professional interests to. Can't you see how dicey that could be? I don't want to be with anyone who won't put me first."

My mother tuts. "I think you're underestimating Julian and yourself, but if all we're talking about here is, as you put it, 'scratching an itch,' why would all this matter?"

I dip my chin into my cowl-necked top. Because scratching an itch with your brother's best friend isn't something you can pretend never happened. And okay, yes, I like Julian way more than I should. "You're right. It doesn't matter. The smartest thing to do is step aside and get out of their way."

"Sounds a lot like the reason you didn't want to go to Weston."

She never fails to bring up this sore spot between us. When I was fifteen, I begged my parents to enroll me in the local public school rather than the town's day and boarding school. My mother was a guidance counselor at Weston, so they would have received a significant tuition discount, but I couldn't bear the idea of going to school with Carter. By then, he was regularly appearing in commercials, and I knew it was only a matter of time before he landed a major role. I didn't want to be part of the madness, didn't want people to think they could get to him through me, and I didn't want to become known only as Carter's sister.

"It's just how I feel, Mom."

"Fine. It's certainly not my job to push you. I will say this, though. I love Julian dearly, and if you happened to date him for real, I'd be happy for the both of you."

"Carter wouldn't," I grumble.

"Hard to say what Carter would think, but in the end, this is about you and Julian."

Before I can respond, the screen door creaks, alerting us that someone's arrived. Judging by the number of voices, it's quite a crowd.

Carter and Tori stumble into the kitchen, laughing and jostling each other as they find their footing. Behind them, three women, two of them almost certainly related to Tori, take tentative steps inside as they scan the room. An older man who must be Tori's dad brings up the rear, a roughly carved wooden cane at his side.

My mother rises from her chair and holds out her arms. "Lourdes, it's so good to see you."

She must be Tori's mom.

"Susan, good seeing you, too," she says as she steps into my mother's embrace. Lourdes turns to the younger woman who favors her. "And you remember my older daughter, Bianca, yes?"

"Sure, sure," my mother says. "So glad to have everyone here."

A striking black woman with a halo of chestnut brown curls steps up and holds out her hand. "I'm Eva, Tori's partner in crime. Thanks so much for letting me stay in your beautiful home."

My mother gives her a warm smile. "My pleasure, dear."

Lourdes leans back and looks over her shoulder. "Psst. Pedro, *ven aquí*."

Tori's father stops perusing the framed pictures at the kitchen's entrance, wipes a hand on his slacks, and comes forward. "Hi again, Susan."

They shake hands, and then my mother announces, "This is my daughter Ashley."

From there, we bustle around the kitchen, engaging in small talk, riffling through bags for phones and chargers, and going over sleeping arrangements.

A few minutes later, my niece and nephew barrel through the kitchen with my older sister, Kimberly, in tow. My father shows up next and pulls me into a bear hug. Another stream of introductions and reintroductions follows, and if some of these people weren't related to me, I wouldn't be able to keep it straight.

Beside me, Eva snorts. "Jesus, we need name tags."

"I know, right?" I say. "I'm sure my mother bought some. Luckily for us, we'll be away from the hub."

Together my parents ransack the fridge, pulling out beverages and large Tupperware bowls.

Amid the bustle, I slip out and escape to the living room. With fevered hands, I send Julian a circumspect text:

Circumstances have changed. Abort operation. Stand down. Copy?

He responds within seconds:

Got it. Be there soon.

Although it would have been fun to pretend to be his girlfriend, I'm relieved I won't have to. The pressure is off, and we won't need to engage in any awkward interactions that'll leave me wanting what I can't have. Best of all, my barracuda of a cousin won't be around to criticize me and make snide remarks—or flirt with Julian. Smiling, I return to the kitchen and immerse myself in the flurry of activity.

"We've got three types of salads—chicken, pasta, and garden," my mother explains. "Oh, and meatballs. We can nibble on this to tide us over until dinner."

Everyone scrambles to wash their hands, and then we all pounce on the food. There isn't enough room for everyone to sit, so a group of us—Carter, Tori, Eva, Bianca, and I—retreat onto the porch.

I'm leaning against the railing with a paper plate in my hand when two cars pull up. Shielding my face from the sun, I peer through the window to make out which family members have joined us and see Aunt Carol sitting in the passenger seat. Ugh.

Worse, the rear passenger window of the first car lowers to reveal Lydia in the backseat. She throws her arm out and waves. "We're here, everybody."

Dammit. Why is she here?

Then the rear door of the second car opens and Julian climbs out.

He's wearing a gray T-shirt and jeans that sit low on his trim hips. His eyes are hidden behind aviators, but his full smile is plain to see. My heart trips and quickly recovers, as if it's a person stumbling in the street when she knows someone's watching. The driver sets Julian's bag beside him, along with a guitar case that looks an awful lot like mine. Stunned, I watch Julian slip several bills into the guy's hand.

Lydia climbs out of my uncle's car and spins to face Julian. "Well, well, if it isn't Mr. Steal-My-Heart in the flesh."

Her play on Julian's last name makes me want to gag.

Behind me, Eva says, "Oh, my lord. Please tell me that's the last time I'll hear that."

"Unfortunately, it won't be," I tell her out of the side of my mouth. "I guarantee it."

Then the circumstances hit me upside my head like a ton of bricks falling from the sky. Lydia's here. And I told Julian to stand down. But he doesn't know why. Shit.

What the hell do I do now?

Chapter Sixteen

Julian

ASHLEY BOUNDS DOWN the steps, jogs toward me, and launches herself into my arms. "I missed you, baby."

Her voice rings out, purposefully loud and calibrated to travel.

"What's going on?" I murmur against her ear.

Not that I'm complaining about holding her in my arms—she's warm and curvy and smells like apples—but she texted me less than ten minutes ago to tell me to *stand down*.

She burrows into me and tilts her head back. Staring at me intently and wearing a yes-I'm-happy-to-see-you smile, she slides her hands up my back, places them around my neck, and pulls me in for a kiss.

My grin vanishes, replaced by lips parted in confusion. But I'm alert enough to settle my hands on her waist and assume the role she obviously wants me to play. And I approach it like I'm auditioning for a career-defining part. Why should Carter have all the acting fun?

Our lips connect, and the need to taste every part of her consumes me within seconds. She's pliant in my arms, sending me to a space that settles my nerves but causes my muscles to tense. It's both soothing and electric to be with her this way, comforting in that I already know we have chemistry, daunting in that I know there's nowhere for this to go. I'm feeling so much, I don't know which way is up. But damn. The texture of her mouth, the way her soft skin brushes against my jaw, the low groan that erupts from the base of her throat, it's all so fucking promising, and I want more. She opens her mouth wider, taking me in deeper, and I'm lost. I trail my hands up the sides of her body, seeking an anchor, and reach under the curtain of her hair to pull her closer.

"Julian," she whispers.

Her voice is breathy and needy, and I want her to repeat my name a thousand times.

"Julian, what the hell, man?" someone barks out.

That's *not* the kind of repetition I was hoping for.

Carter.

Fuck. I'm mauling his sister in front of him, so I understand exactly where he's coming from. I turn in his direction but avoid his gaze. Tori, understanding the ruse is in play, elbows Carter in the side and flicks a glance to Lydia. He rolls his eyes in response.

"You two are *dating*?" Lydia asks, an incredulous tone intensifying her high-pitched voice.

"Not just dating," Ashley replies with a lift of her chin. "We're living together, too."

Lydia shakes her head. "Wow. I mean, wow. Yeah, just wow."

I think it's safe to conclude she's surprised by the news. Now that she's pursing her lips, it's also safe to conclude she's annoyed.

"Interesting choice," she tells me in a flat tone.

I squeeze Ashley's shoulder, staring lovingly into her eyes. "Any other choice would have been idiotic."

Ashley buries her face against my neck. "Awww, you're so sweet, Care Bear."

Care Bear. What the fuck? That's grounds for immediate termination of this farce. I won't just play this game, I'll win it. "Not as sweet as you, Love Biscuit."

She narrows her eyes at me, but any retaliation is forgotten when she spots the guitar case by my feet. "Is that Melanie?"

Lugging around a guitar case through the airport wasn't easy, but the excitement in her voice fills me with a quiet contentment I haven't experienced in a while. "There's your baby, all right." I step closer and whisper. "I figured you might want her around this weekend. For comfort."

She wraps her arms around me and squeezes me tight, speaking softly against my ear. "Thank you."

After I throw my travel bag on my shoulder, Ashley clasps my hand and leads me toward the house, Melanie at her side.

Ashley's mother, Susan, rushes out, her gaze zipping around the scene like a gnat. "Carol. Richard. Glad you got here safely." Her gaze falls on Lydia. "I thought you were traveling?"

Lydia appears thoughtful for a moment, her front teeth worrying her bottom lip. "The meeting was postponed unexpectedly. Someone on the team fell ill, so we'll be rescheduling it for next month. I can stay all weekend, and since everything's happening here, I'd love to stay over too, if that's okay."

"Of course," Susan says without hesitation.

Lydia's mother instructs her husband on the finer points of carrying luggage as she walks beside him to the front door. "I assume we're staying in the main house?" she asks Susan.

Ashley's mother nods. "Yes."

Carol barrels up the stairs, and a round of introductions ensue.

Lydia hangs back.

Ashley's mother pats her on the hand. "You can stay in the cottage with the other whippersnappers."

Out of the corner of my eye, I see Ashley jerk. Her mother shrugs, a pained expression suggesting she understands the arrangement isn't ideal but can't think of a reason to alter it.

"There are four bedrooms. Julian, would the pull-out couch work for you?"

"Why would he need to do that?" Lydia asks, her eyes narrowing on Ashley and me. "They're already living together, so it shouldn't be a big deal for them to stay together here, right?"

Beside me, Ashley whimpers.

Ashley's mother doesn't miss a beat. "You're right, of course. It's totally up to them." Then she grins. "In fact, I think that makes the most sense under the circumstances." Leaning into Ashley, she says, "Just don't broadcast it to your father."

Lydia looks at us expectantly.

"Yeah, of course it's not a problem to share the room with Ash," I say.

Carter grunts. Tori laughs.

A woman I've never seen before cackles. "I'm sensing tension. Where's the popcorn? This is can't-miss-stuff right here."

I can tell by the delight in her eyes at our obvious discomfort that she's trouble. And considering I've just signed up to spend three nights sharing a bed with Ashley, I'm confident there's more trouble to come.

ASHLEY AND I listen for the sound of Lydia's footsteps to fade before we softly close the door. The bedroom we're sharing contains four pieces of furniture: a dresser made of light wood, a rocking chair in the corner, a small nightstand, and a king-sized bed that serves as a wink and a nod to the thoughts I'm trying to suppress.

I can practically hear Missy Elliott's "Get Your Freak On" in the background.

"It'll be fine," she says. "It's a big bed." She's going for a reassuring tone—I think—but now she's biting her bottom lip as she spins around and scans the room. "Cozy, right?"

One person's cozy is another person's worst nightmare, obviously.

"If it'll help, I can sleep on the floor," I offer.

Her eyebrows snap together. "No, that would be ridiculous and uncomfortable. We're adults. We can handle sleeping in the same bed. I'll stay on my side, and you'll stay on yours."

As proof of the maturity she undeservedly ascribes to me, I plop onto the bed and rest on my elbows. The mattress is firm, just the way I like it. "So what happened? One minute you were telling me to stand down, and the next minute you were swallowing my face."

She plops down next to me and falls back with a sigh. "My mother told me Lydia wouldn't be here, so I figured there was no need to pretend that we're dating. But then she showed up, and I didn't know how else to tell you to disregard my text." She sits up on her elbows and pins me with a disapproving glare. "And I did *not* swallow your face. If I'm not mistaken, your hands were seconds away from palming my ass."

Guilty as motherfucking charged, but I'm not snitching on myself. "I was just trying to get my bearings. You caught me off guard. Speaking of which, when you told Lydia we're living together, it occurred to me that we never agreed on how long we've been dating."

She wriggles her nose and shrugs. "A year?"

"Damn. That's serious."

"Yeah," she says on a laugh. "That's like a decade in Ashley years."

"Don't do that," I tell her.

"Do what?"

"Talk about yourself in the third person. It freaks me out."

She laughs more heartily than warranted by the circumstances. "You sound like Carter. He hates it, too. You two are more alike than you'd ever admit."

"He's had quite an influence on me."

She tilts her head to the side. "And that's a good thing, right?"

"Yeah, of course it is." But how do I explain the small voice in my head warning me that he's influenced me *too* much? "It's just…sometimes I wonder what my life would be like if I hadn't chosen this path."

"Agenting?"

I smooth the comforter. "Yeah."

"It's not too late to find out."

She says this like it's a simple proposition. Like I can just drop everything and switch gears at a moment's notice. Like I haven't spent my working life building a reputation as an agent on the rise. That's Ashley for you, though. She follows her whims wherever they take her. In truth, some days I wish I could be that way, too.

A knock on the door causes me to spring up from the bed. When I open it, Tori slips inside, a clipboard in her hand.

"Hi, I'm your friendly family reunion coordinator here to tell you what's on tap for the next few days." She winks at us. "Join me in the living room?"

She's all smiles, and I fully believe she's having the time of her life, but I also suspect she'd shank us if we messed with her plans. This woman is no joke. So I'll do whatever she wants to do, and I'll wear the brightest smile she's ever seen while doing it. "We'll be there in a minute."

Ashley sits up. "I'm going to freshen up. Out in a sec."

Tori gives us a curt nod. "Excellent. I'll be waiting." Then she pivots and does an about-face like she's an active-duty commanding officer who's just dismissed her troops.

A few minutes later, Ash and I shuffle out of the room to find everyone gathered around for their instructions.

Carter, who's always eating, noshes on an apple as he waits for his fiancée to begin. The woman I now know is Tori's best friend, Eva, flips through a home-decorating magazine. Lydia, meanwhile, riffles through an accordion business folder—to highlight how important she is, I guess—and generally pretends to be put out by the need to even be here.

"Can we get on with this?" she says without looking up from her ministrations. "I'd like to rest before dinner."

Tori and Eva exchange a look, and Eva mouths something to her. Whatever it was, it makes Tori stifle a laugh as she shakes her head.

After consulting her clipboard, Tori clears her throat. "Okay, people. Here's what we have planned. Tonight, we're just relaxing. Bianca and my mother will be treating you to a few dishes from our upcoming cookbook, *Puerto Rico Over Easy*, which will be out in the fall and is available now for preorder."

"You have no shame," Eva says.

Tori nods enthusiastically. "You speak the truth, *chica*. And where was I?"—she consults her clipboard—"Aha. Tomorrow morning is free time, but whatever you do, you'll have to be back around eleven because we have a zip-lining outing scheduled for noon."

My heart palpitates, and my mouth goes dry. "Zip-lining?"

Ashley whips her head in my direction, probably in response to the strangled tenor of my voice. "You okay, Julian?"

"Yeah, yeah," I say. "I think the day is catching up with me, that's all."

Inside, however, I'm trying to stem the panic that's threatening to make me light-headed. I'm not a fan of heights, and the idea of swinging through the air on a steel cable is about as appealing as cleaning a bathroom toilet with my bare hands.

Lydia twists her face into a grimace. "I'll pass on zip-lining. I'm not the most athletic person in the world, and I just got my nails done."

After hearing Lydia's announcement, Tori smiles. "Next, we'll have the opportunity to enjoy a peaceful afternoon at a local spa. Get our nails done and such. Lydia, you'll probably want to pass on that, too...since you just did them."

"Oh, no, the spa would be great," Lydia counters. "I'm long overdue for a pedicure."

Ashley cocks her head. "Wait. There's a spa in Harmon? Since when?"

Tori shakes her head. "No, that would have been too easy, but I found one fifteen minutes away, near Derby."

That's good, I guess. After I lose a few years of my life catapulting myself through the air, I'll need a deep-tissue massage to relax me.

"On Saturday, Carter's niece, Izzy, has a soccer game in the morning. Carter and I need to…um…do something in preparation for Sunday's brunch, but the rest of the family is welcome to support Izzy in her last soccer game of the intramural season. In the afternoon, we'll have the family cookout and flag football. I was thinking it would be nice to hang out Saturday night. Head to a local bar for drinks or something."

"Uh, probably not a great idea," Carter says. "We might attract too much attention."

Tori pouts. "As you can see, I have not quite mastered the ins and outs of dating a celebrity. Okay, what if the women hang out here for an adult slumber party, and you and Julian can hang out with my dad at the house? He's been itching to try out the new pool table in the study."

Ah. She doesn't want to spend the night before the wedding with Carter, but she can't say so outright because Lydia's here. How cute.

I nod. "That works for me."

Her smile grows brighter. "Then we'll finish the weekend with Sunday brunch."

"Sounds perfect," Eva says.

The rest of us murmur our agreement.

Carter stands and takes the clipboard out of Tori's hands. Before she can object, he folds her in a tight embrace and whispers something in her ear. She nuzzles his neck, then pulls him toward their bedroom. With her free hand, she waves at us. "Carry on, friends."

Eva yells after them. "Get your eggplant, *mama*."

"We're going to change for dinner," Tori yells back.

Eva snorts. "Is that what the kids are calling it these days?" Then she rises and stretches her arms over her head. "I think I'll change, too. For real. See you soon."

Which leaves Ashley and me with Lydia.

She taps the top of the folder as she studies us. "So how long have you two been dating?" she asks.

Ashley and I jump on each other's words, saying *about*, *almost*, and *a year* within seconds of each other.

"And you're already living together, huh?" she asks rhetorically. "Tell me the truth, Ashley. Did you have a crush on him when you were younger?"

Ashley narrows her eyes at Lydia. "You know I did."

Lydia stares wistfully at a spot behind Ashley. "Oh, that's right. I remember you cried the first time he came to visit while he was in college. You were upset because he didn't notice that you were *all grown up*." She shakes her head and smirks. "I'm happy for you. This must be a dream come true."

Lydia reminds me of the typical mean girl in a movie in which the high school underdog gets her revenge. Except this isn't a film, it damn sure isn't high school, and judging by the sadness in Ashley's eyes, the wounds Lydia's inflicting on her are real.

I can't take any more of this woman's ridiculousness, so I pull Ashley into my arms and draw her close, ignoring her wide-eyed expression. "I don't know if it's a dream come true for her, but it's certainly a dream come true for me." Then I lift her chin and place a soft kiss on her parted lips. "Imagine discovering that your perfect match has been within arm's reach for years."

I don't falter as I say these words, and for a moment I'm struck by the possibility that they came easily to me because they're true.

Ashley settles her head in the crook of my neck and grasps the back of my head, as though she's drawing strength from my performance.

Except it might not be as much of a performance as she thinks—for me, at least—and that's an unwelcome development.

Chapter Seventeen

Ashley

I BITE THE inside of my cheek as I watch Lydia slink away down the hall. I suspect most people have experienced her brand of pettiness at least once in their lives. But we're no longer in high school, and she doesn't appear to have matured much since then. Worse, she's a relative whose presence I can't avoid the next few days. Serenity now.

When her door closes, I drop my arms and step out of Julian's embrace. "Thanks."

Julian takes a deep breath and rubs his hands down the front of his jeans. "Sure, no problem. I think we're doing a decent job convincing her we're dating."

Right.

I'm trying to be an adult about this. Trying to remember the reason we both agreed to this charade. Trying not to trick myself into thinking we're a couple. But the line between fiction and reality is blending before my eyes, and I'm struggling not to want things I shouldn't. Not just temporary things, but permanent ones. Dammit. I need to manufacture a reason to put some space between us, even if it's only for a few minutes. "I'm going to—"

"Let me guess. Freshen up? You do a lot of that."

I ignore his observation, and although he follows me to the bedroom, I don't acknowledge his presence before I slip inside the bathroom. After patting my cheeks and forehead with a cool washcloth, I reapply my lipstick and venture back outside.

Julian's on the phone, his back to me as he holds his cell phone against his ear. "Yeah, yeah, of course I'll make myself available to read it. Carter will love that story line and the potential for sequels. And with your magic touch at the box office, Sanderson, this could be a lucrative collaboration for everyone involved. Thanks for following up. I'll wait for your call, and we'll go from there." He stuffs the phone in his back pocket and claps triumphantly.

I step forward, and the bamboo floor creaks under the pressure.

Julian spins around and dips his chin in embarrassment, his gaze focused on his feet. "Uh...I thought you were still in the bathroom. Got a little excited there about something. Work never goes on vacation, unfortunately."

"Sounded like good news, though."

He looks up. "Still in its early stages, but it could be."

"For Carter?"

He presses his lips together and shrugs apologetically. "Yeah, but I really can't say more. It's his business."

Okay. So he doesn't want to talk about Carter's work. I can understand that. Still, it's a sobering reminder of the reasons I shouldn't want a future with him. His need to carve out separate spheres between his personal and work lives means there are parts of his life he won't ever want to share with me. This probably would be the case with any of his clients. Because it's Carter, though, it chafes. "Sure. I get it."

The tension around his eyes disappears. "Ready to head to dinner?"

"I'm so hungry I'll risk eating my mother's food."

He waggles his eyebrows. "Luckily for us, we won't have to."

"Oh, that's right. Lourdes and Bianca cooked tonight. Well, what the hell are we waiting for then?"

Laughing, we race to the door and jockey to be the first one out, and then we quietly walk along the gravel path to the main house. Once inside, I spot Tori connecting her phone to the speakers in the living room.

Eva jumps up from the couch and strolls in our direction. When she reaches us, she playfully pokes Julian's chest. "Whatever you do, don't let them convince you to do the Electric Slide, okay? People think whenever there's music and more than one black person in a room that dance is sure to follow."

Julian chuckles. "It's true, though."

Eva cackles and pushes him away. "No, it's not, dammit."

"What about Tori? She's black, too."

"Yes, but she's Latina, so she's expected to salsa her way through life."

Tori snorts. "So, so true."

Julian tosses his head back and grins. "Ah, okay. Well, don't worry. I don't know the Electric Slide anyway."

Eva purses her lips in mock disbelief. "I *know* you know that dance, Julian."

He laughs. "Oh, yeah, how do you *know* this, Eva?"

She waves his question away. "Do you have a sister, and is she married?"

"Yes, and yes," he answers.

"Did she have a traditional wedding?"

"She did."

"Then *someone* in her wedding party danced the Electric Slide. I'd bet money on it."

Julian shakes his head, his eyes lit with amusement. "Can't argue with that, either, because it's true."

Tori drags Eva to the center of the room for an impromptu dance party. "C'mon, woman. Let's burn some calories before we eat."

"I'm starting to get flashbacks to the time you tortured me in your Zumba class, Eva," Carter says from the sidelines.

Eva waves him over. "Get your butt out here, then, and show us what you learned."

We all join in the fun, making use of the available space in the center of the room. Giving up on trying to follow any steps, we dance together in a circle, until Eva backs up and slams into a man I've never seen before.

He shoots out his arm to steady her. "Whoa, there. Be careful where you're going, pretty lady."

Pint-sized Eva looks up at him, her short, springy curls dancing around her. "Be careful where you're standing, Thor. Mere mortals can't survive crashing into you."

The guy isn't as huge as Thor, nor does he possess Thor's golden locks, but he's towering over Eva, and his pecs *are* impressive.

"Anthony," Tori says excitedly. "You made it."

Anthony's gruff exterior softens the moment his gaze settles on Tori. "*Princessa.*"

Tori dives into his arms and squeezes him tightly. "I'm so glad you're here."

Carter saunters over. "Anthony, the cousin from California, right?"

They shake hands.

"Right."

"Good to finally meet you, man."

"Same," Anthony says.

"Everyone," Tori says with a bounce. "This is my cousin Anthony. He's like a big brother to me."

Anthony turns his head in Eva's direction. "And who's this Tinkerbell?"

Eva freezes, and a small vein appears at her right temple. "I'm Eva, an adult woman with a black belt in tae kwon do who doesn't appreciate being called Tinkerbell."

He holds up his hands in surrender. "Warning issued and heeded. I won't make that mistake again. But as a sixth-dan black belt, I'd be remiss if I didn't point out that someone with tae kwon do training shouldn't be so quick to show her temper."

Eva huffs. "Someone who knows nothing about me shouldn't be so quick to give me his unsolicited advice."

Julian and I glance at each other and step away from the fireworks.

Carter jumps in to bring the situation to a simmer. "So, Anthony, Tori tells me you're a stunt coordinator. You've probably worked with a few of my stunt doubles."

Anthony shifts to Eva's left, deftly moving outside her verbal firing range. "Ever work with Jack Henson? He's one of my guys."

Julian joins them. "I know Jack. He did stunt work for one of my clients. Not for Carter, though. He's too delicate for physical roles like that."

Carter draws back, and his mouth goes slack. "I could wrestle you to the ground in five seconds flat."

Julian laughs, his expression calm and unconcerned. "I doubt that. Besides, Tori wouldn't want to you to get any bumps or bruises this weekend, so this isn't the time to be issuing any challenges." Julian grabs his chin. "Can't do anything to mar that pretty face of yours."

Carter's eyes narrow, and the corner of his mouth quirks up as he pulls away. "Well, aren't you a lucky one, then?"

I watch the guys mess with each other, enjoying how easily they get along, until Eva pulls Tori and me to the side. "Help me, ladies. I don't know what's happening. It's not like me to bite someone's head off like that. Anthony's hotness short-circuited my brain."

Tori takes Eva's hands. "I say this as your very best friend in the world, don't go there. He's emotionally unavailable."

Eva waggles her eyebrows. "Oooh. A challenge. My favorite kind of project."

Tori throws up her hands. "Don't say I didn't warn you. And what about Nate?"

I'm having trouble keeping up with who's who, but I love that they're including me in their circle. "Who's Nate?"

"My former boss," Tori says. "He's currently backing my new studio. And he's in love with Eva."

"Correction," Eva says with a shake of her head. "He's in love with the idea of being in love, and I'm not ready to be the princess in his fairy tale."

"Hey, ladies," Lydia says as she slides into an open spot next to me. "What are you talking about? And who's the new man candy?"

"He's my Mr. Goodbar, so back off," Eva says.

I burst out laughing. "I think I love you, Eva."

She gives me a hip bump. "I think I could grow to love you, Ashley. I need to vet you a little more before I can be certain."

I return her wink, and we smile at each other.

My father emerges from the kitchen ringing a bright red cowbell with his school's alma mater printed across the widest part. "Dinner is served. Please make your way to the dining room." He bows as he backs out of the room.

Eva tugs on my sleeve as we walk down the hall. "Where's everyone? Our family's reunion is usually ten times this big. Like we have enough people to field two football teams."

"The Williamsons are a small bunch. And most of Tori's extended family is in Puerto Rico. We'll get a few stragglers Saturday, including my grandparents on my dad's side. Just wait until you meet Grandpa James. He's a hoot."

A hand lands on my waist, and I look down to see Julian's arm pulling me to him. He brushes his lips against my temple without losing his stride. A frisson of electricity pings around in my belly like a pinball.

"I'm hungry," he says nonchalantly, as if touching me is second nature to him and I should treat his affection as commonplace. I shoot him a questioning look, and he leans into me. "Don't look so taken aback. We're dating, remember?"

Uh, I won't forget that we're *pretending* to be dating anytime soon, but that doesn't mean I'm not surprised when he acts like my boyfriend. Or that I'm not freaked out about enjoying it so much.

We snag the seats next to Tori and Carter, with Julian sitting closest to Carter. Unfortunately, Lydia and my aunt and uncle take the chairs across from me. But I don't worry myself over that minor annoyance and instead focus on the culinary delights in the middle of the table. It's a feast fit for anyone with a pulse.

Tori's mother explains our options, which are plated in large, shallow bowls and passed around family-style. "We have our version of *bacalao*, a fish stew. *Arroz con pollo*, which is rice with chicken and vegetables. *Pasteles*, which are like *tamales* but made with plantains and taro vegetables, and finally corn fritters for anyone who doesn't eat meat. *Buen provecho.* Enjoy your meal."

My mother brings her hands together and smiles at Tori's mom. "Lourdes and Bianca, thanks so much for this wonderful food. I can only hope that Randall's barbecue skills on Saturday can live up to this."

"Way to put on the pressure, Susan," my father says. "With a wife like you, who needs…" He's a smart man and knows how to avoid a chop across the throat, so he winks at my mother to make clear he's joking.

The bowl exchange ensues in earnest after we bless the food, only to be interrupted by my father, who stands and raises his water glass in the air. "I also want to welcome the Alvarez family in our lives and in our home. We're thrilled that Tori and Carter have found each other, and we can't wait to see what else is in store for them."

Everyone follows suit, and we clink glasses as we shower the couple with *awwws* and *hear, hears.*

Dad clears his throat. "And I just wanted to take a moment to recognize and congratulate Carter on his nomination for a Screen Actors Guild Award. We're proud of you, Son."

We raise our glasses higher. Kimberly and I glance at each other, and she rolls her eyes. We love Carter dearly, but there's no question our parents sometimes forget their two daughters are in the room when our brother's around.

Across from me, Aunt Carol scoops a spoonful of rice onto her plate. "Ashley, where are you working now?"

She says this in a loud, clear voice, and the smirk that appears on Lydia's face confirms my suspicion that the question was planned. The chatter around the table continues, but the pounding in my ears deludes me into thinking everyone's gone quiet and is paying close attention to the exchange.

"I'm working as a flight attendant. Mostly domestic travel, but I've had a few international assignments as well."

She purses her lips as she takes in my answer, reminding me of my high school English lit teacher, the one who looked at the class with disdain and thought the material was well over our heads.

"But don't you want something with more permanency? A job that'll keep you in one place?"

Sure, I think about it often. But there isn't much that captures my interest like my music does, and the odds that I'd be able to make it my career are slim. I'm exploring other possibilities, wisely engaging in due diligence, and that keeps me from panicking about the lack of direction in my life. No way I'm sharing this with Aunt Carol, though. "Permanency isn't a priority for me these days. There's plenty of time to settle somewhere. I have an exciting job that allows me to see different places and meet fascinating people." I turn and smile at Julian. "And a boyfriend who keeps me grounded. Life is good."

"And Lydia tells me you're living with Julian?"

"Yep," I say with a pop of my lips. "See? I'm perfectly capable of making a commitment."

She pretends not to have heard me. "Speaking of permanency, Lydia received a promotion recently. She's now the manager of her marketing division."

Lydia shakes her head, the barest hint of a frown on her face. "Mom, no one wants to hear about that."

This is the first time I can recall Lydia not wanting to be the center of everyone's attention. Makes me wonder how much of her personality is attributable to her mother's conceited ways. I try to paste on a bright smile, wanting desperately for it to be genuine but knowing it isn't. "That's great news. Congrats, Lydia."

"I guess it must be hard," Aunt Carol says. "Living in the shadow of your siblings."

I'm not wrong when I say the room's gone quiet now, and out of the corner of my eye, I see Julian set down his fork and push his plate back.

"Carol," my mother warns. "Don't be obnoxious."

"What?" Carol asks as she helps herself to more food. "I'm just saying. Kimberly was a track star and is now a successful high school coach being wooed by several colleges. Carter's a Hollywood heartthrob. Shoot. Even I wouldn't want to be their siblings."

Julian leans forward, his gaze fixed on Aunt Carol. "Ashley's perfect just the way she is, and she's got layers you don't even know about. Like, she's a talented musician. Did you know she's composed over one hundred songs?"

"You have?" Carter asks, the pitch of his voice rising.

"You never told us," Kimberly says as she cuts Izzy's meat into small pieces.

"It's nothing, really," I say.

Carter clucks his tongue. "But why aren't you out there trying to make a career of it?"

This is exactly what I wanted to avoid: an inquisition. I know Julian meant well, but telling the family about my music only makes me more defensive. It's my life, and I get to decide how to live it. "Because maybe it's just a hobby. Because maybe everything's not about being the next big whatever. People can be perfectly happy without aspiring to be something *more*."

"Well, I think it's wonderful that you're still playing guitar," my father says. "If you enjoy it, how can that be a bad thing?"

"Exactly," my mother says. "Lourdes and Bianca, this food is amazing."

Tori's mother and sister smile proudly.

Tori waves her hand in front of what's left of the dishes. "And if you'd like the recipes, you can find them all in one place in our upcoming cookbook, *Puerto Rico Over Easy*. Available for preorder now."

Lourdes and Bianca shush Tori.

"What?" Tori asks. "Our publicist says we have to get the word out."

Bianca snorts. "I'm sure the publicist didn't mean for you to hawk our book at every opportunity."

Tori bares her teeth in embarrassment. "Was that overkill?"

She cringes at the chorus of *yeses* and *definitelys* that follow.

I'm grateful they're no longer talking about me, but the damage is done. When I'm finished with my meal, I quickly excuse myself. "I'm feeling a little under the weather. I think I'll head to bed early tonight."

I rise from my chair, and Julian does the same.

"No, no," I tell him as I lay a hand on his arm. "Hang out with Carter. Catch up with my dad. I'll see you later when you...um...come to bed."

"You're sure?" he says, his gaze locked on my face.

I nod. "Yeah." Impulsively, I bend down and kiss his forehead. "Later."

He holds my hand until the distance between us forces him to let go.

I know he wants to comfort me. The concern in his eyes tells me so. A part of me wants that from him, but another part of me realizes that an empathetic pat on my back or a squeeze of my shoulder wouldn't be enough. I need more. Which he won't give me.

Space it is, then.

Chapter Eighteen

Julian

EVERYONE'S MOVED TO the living room, where Carter, Tori, Eva, and Bianca are playing poker. Beside me on the couch, Carter's dad describes the grill he's planning to buy. He even pulls out his phone to show me the model. Titillating stuff.

Lydia and her mother are in a corner chatting, their heads close together. I wouldn't at all be surprised if they were devising another plan to insult people. They do it to mask their own feelings of inadequacy, and anyone who isn't Ashley can see it. But she's probably been their target so often she's given up on trying to understand their motives. I want to go to her, but I want to give her space, too.

"There are a couple of options," Randall says as he points to his phone. "See here, this one has a warming rack, but with this one, I can add on a pizza oven. What do you think? Which would you choose?"

"That's great. Should produce excellent meats."

Randall chuckles.

"What?" I ask, turning my head to look at him.

"You're not paying attention, Son. I asked your opinion on—"

Susan calls me to the kitchen before Randall swipes left again, and I jump up to answer her call. "Excuse me, I'm being summoned."

When I enter, Ashley's mother motions for me to join her at the table.

I drop onto a chair. "What can I do for you? Need help in here?"

She brings a coffee mug to her lips and takes a sip before she speaks, her eyes never straying from mine. "You're not having a good time, and I know why."

I laugh off her comment, unsure where she's headed with the observation but sufficiently aware of her skills at uncovering feelings I prefer to keep hidden. "I'm enjoying myself just fine. Don't worry about me."

With only the top of her face visible over the cup's brim, she says, "I'm not worried about you. I'm worried about her. And you are, too."

I exhale and squint at her. "It's that obvious?"

"Maybe not to them, but it is to me. I spent a year trying to crack your shell, remember?"

She's right about that. I came to Weston reluctantly, resentful that my parents had shipped me to boarding school supposedly to broaden my horizons and expand my educational opportunities. Ms. Susan, as I called her then, counseled day school students, but she also served as my host mother, the person entrusted to watch over me while I was away from home. I moped around when I came to visit, and Carter, who was two years my junior, was a pain in the ass who was goofy as hell and wanted me to be the older brother he never had. I wasn't down with it, until a classmate tried to bully him and my protective instincts kicked in. Slowly, I let the family in, and they've become a permanent part of my life.

"I remember." I grab the back of my neck and raise my face to the ceiling. Ah, who am I kidding? I *need* to know she's okay. I stand abruptly. "I'm going to check on her."

She gives me a full-blown smile. "I was hoping you would."

I creep from the kitchen to the short hall leading to the front door, but my attempt to leave undetected is thwarted when I collide with Lydia.

"Oh," she says. "Leaving so soon?"

The best I can come up with is to yawn and stretch my arms wide. Hey, acting isn't my strong suit, and I never claimed otherwise. "I'm beat. Going to head to bed early."

She wrings her hands in front of her, opening and closing her mouth a few times. Finally, she drums up the courage to speak. "I liked you, too. She knew that. I just… I just wanted you to know."

I'm not sure what I'm supposed to make of this revelation. Does she want me to think Ash betrayed her by dating me? Is she suggesting that I should be with her instead? Why does she think it's even remotely appropriate to corner her cousin's boyfriend and undermine her in this way? "Ashley might not see what's going on yet, but I do. You're jealous of her, aren't you?"

With a hand on her chest, she scoffs at me. "That's absurd. You don't know what you're talking about."

"Actually, I know exactly what I'm talking about. Sure, you pretend it's about your years-old crush on me, but it's more basic than that, isn't it? You envy the way she lives her life. The way she makes friends so easily. Her decision to leave Harmon and immerse herself in different experiences. The way she refuses to tie herself down simply to check off a box based on other people's definitions of success. You want that for yourself."

She scrunches her face, pretending there's no basis for my observations. "I don't envy Ashley in the least. I think your feelings for her are clouding your judgment." After an exaggerated flip of her hair, she storms off.

I chuckle as I watch her go. She's growing older, sure, but she's definitely not growing up. I'll give Lydia this, though: She unwittingly stumbled on a fact I can no longer deny. My feelings for Ashley *are* clouding my judgment—and I don't think that's going to change anytime soon.

MY PRETEND GIRLFRIEND is asleep by the time I enter the bedroom. Only the top of her head and several long strands of her hair poke out of the cocoon she's created with the comforter. Frankly, I'm relieved. The prospect of sharing a bed with her while suppressing our mutual attraction makes me consider sleeping in the tub. But

I'm too tall for that, and now that she's snoring lightly, I can slip under the covers without the awkwardness we'd experience if we both were awake.

I grab my toiletry bag and dip into the bathroom. After a quick shower and edge trim, I brush my teeth and hit the light switch. I'm wearing a T-shirt and long pajama bottoms because anything less would be weird.

Ashley's snoring loudly now, and the vibration in her throat makes her sound like a dog growling at a perceived threat. And her body is draped over 80 percent of the mattress. Maybe I *should* sleep on the floor. But after I fail to find any sheets or blankets in the closet, I climb into bed and settle on the slice of surface area she hasn't commandeered. Whispering her name, I nudge her over with my arm and left leg.

Except she reacts wildly to my touch, and in the scramble to untangle herself from the comforter, she rolls over the edge of the mattress and hits the floor with a loud yelp.

"Fuck, Ash." I jackknife off the bed and lean over. "You okay?"

She rubs her elbow. "Ow. What the hell happened?"

"Something spooked you in your sleep. Not sure what." *I'm going to hell for this lie.* "Bad dream, maybe?"

She turns her head back and forth, trying to orient herself. Then she widens her eyes in horror. "Was I snoring?"

"Hell yes."

She groans and lies back down on the floor. "This day needs a do-over."

I flip my legs around and climb out. Then I step over her, placing my feet hip-width apart around her body, and hold out my arms. "C'mon, Ash. No more feeling sorry for yourself."

She takes my proffered hands, and I haul her up.

Still grasping my hands, she squints up at me and asks, "Did I miss anything?"

"Nothing at all. It wasn't the same without you."

I'm stunned by how much I mean this. When she left, my enthusiasm for being there went with her; it's as if she's slowly taking pieces of me I'll never get back. I drop my hands and put space between us. "Let's get to bed. Tomorrow's a new day."

She nods absently, and then we both climb back into bed and settle under the covers.

The mattress dips as she turns on her side to face me, and I roll over to meet her gaze. Her dark brown hair fans out on the pillow, begging for my touch, but I wedge both hands under my face to avoid doing something stupid.

"Thanks for today," she whispers.

She's so beautiful, her face cast in shadows in the dimly lit room, and I do nothing but stare at her for a few seconds, until I realize I might be giving off creeper vibes. "You're welcome. But I'm not sure I did all that much. And given how Lydia tried to corner me in the hall, I think you're doing me the bigger favor here."

She lifts her head off the pillow, her eyes narrowing on my face in an attempt to see my expression in the dark. "What happened?"

"Nothing, really. She just wanted me to know she had a crush on me a long time ago. I'm chalking it up to a need for closure."

"For your sake, let's hope so." Without warning, she reaches out and traces a finger along one of my eyebrows. "I never noticed how defined your eyebrows are. Do you wax them?"

I'm thrown by the change in subject. But also, does she expect me to put sentences together when she's touching me? Needing an excuse to put space between us, I pretend to be offended and draw back. "That's insulting. No, I don't groom them. This is nature at its finest."

She smiles into the pillow, exposing the curve of her neck, and I draw on every ounce of my willpower to refrain from leaning over and kissing her there.

"For years," she says, "I wondered if you had a sense of humor. Now I know you do."

"Let's keep that a secret between us. My rep as a no-nonsense agent would be ruined."

She snuggles into the pillow and rests her cheek against it, the playful glint in her eyes sobering. "Do you enjoy what you do?"

If I wanted a reminder why a relationship with Ashley wouldn't work, this is it. I can't answer her truthfully, not without revealing my lack of enthusiasm for a career that directly affects her brother's livelihood. Would she share my confidences with him? Inadvertently, even? Still, I'll admit I'm tempted, for the simple reason that I'd *like* to talk to her about this. I can't ask my father for advice. He's permanently poised to tell me *I told you so*. And as much as I like Sooyin, she's a colleague, too, so speaking with her about my discontent wouldn't be wise.

Ashley reaches out and guides my chin so that I'm forced to meet her gaze. "Hey. I'm a good listener, and nothing you say will go beyond this room."

There's no judgment in her eyes, only affection, and her assurance is exactly what I need to hear. "Sometimes I wonder how I got to this point. One day, Carter asked me to look over his records because he was worried his agent was skimming him. The next thing I know, I'm interviewing for a position as an agent intern in LA. The rest, as they say, is history. I'm not sure I thought it through in the way I should have."

"What would you have done otherwise?"

"Worked with my father. He'd been angling for me to help him run the business since I left home to attend Weston. That was the plan, and to this day, he has no problem reminding me that I didn't follow it. We have a great relationship otherwise, but I hurt him when I chose to work with Carter."

"But what about the work? Apart from what you do for Carter? Is that fulfilling?"

"To be honest, not all that much. I mean, I love it when my clients fulfill their dreams. Knowing they've found their passions is inspiring, but sometimes it reminds me that I'm lacking my own passion, a sense that I'm making a difference somehow. That's when I can practically hear my father telling me I'd regret being an agent, that I need to focus on making my own dreams. Other times, I want to kick myself for being greedy, for wanting more than

I already have. So what if I barely have a personal life to speak of? What does it matter that I work long hours? This is the path I chose, and for the most part I've been successful at it, so shouldn't I just suck it up?"

She places a hand on my cheek, stroking my skin, and I can't help leaning into her touch. "Your career path isn't etched in stone, though. You have time to adjust, time to figure out what makes you happy. That's what I tell myself, at least."

I could tell her that figuring out what makes you happy is pointless if you don't do anything about it, but I don't want to make her defensive. Despite what she told everyone at dinner, I know Ashley has a dream, a goal potent enough to get her out of bed every morning. But she's afraid to go after it, scared that she'll fail. That's a discussion for another day, though, so I simply say, "Thanks for listening."

"Anytime."

She stares at me, her hand lingering on my face. I tilt my head, chasing the softness of her touch, and in a moment of weakness, I brush my lips against her fingers. Her small intake of breath roars like a strong gust of wind in the small room. We both nudge our bodies forward, until we're less than an inch apart, sharing the same air and panting like there's not enough of it to sustain us both.

God, I want to just let go and give in so badly I'm investing all my energy in trying to suppress this feeling. I groan for the both of us. "We shouldn't."

"I know," she says, her body arching in frustration.

"But I want to."

I'm not sure what's possessing me to be honest. It doesn't help the situation at all.

She falls on her back and stares at the ceiling, while I remain on my side and stare at the rapid rise and fall of her chest. I envision myself covering her naked body with mine, rolling my hips against her soft thighs, digging my hands into her ass and sliding my cock inside her until the fullness makes her gasp.

She squeezes her eyes shut, as though she's in physical pain. "It's nice to know I'm not the only one feeling this way."

"You're not, I assure you."

Again, Julian. What the fuck? Close your mouth and go to sleep.

"Good night, Ash."

"Good night."

She turns on her side, leaving me staring at her back.

And wanting her.

Chapter Nineteen

Ashley

I DO BELIEVE that's morning wood nestled against my backside.

Batter, batter, batter, schwing.

Julian's arm is resting on my waist, and I can easily imagine starting each day like this. If I move, I'll wake him, and that would be unnecessarily rude. Since I'm a considerate person, I'll lie here and let him sleep. *Such a chore.*

He was wearing a shirt when we went to bed last night. Now, though, his chest and my shoulders are making skin-to-skin contact, and the twisted T is draped over the footboard. Okay, maybe I'll shift a bit. Just to get more comfortable.

The hand on my waist slides to my hip—and freezes.

Any minute now, he'll spring away, and we'll have a good laugh about his morning woodpecker.

Any minute now...

Any. Minute. Now.

But he lightly squeezes my hip, and oh God, the urge to draw his hand between my thighs makes that empty space ache.

I fake a light snore, and he snatches his hand away.

"Shit," he whispers as he rolls on his back.

I don't want Julian to beat himself up over this, so I yawn and stretch and generally pretend to be waking from a deep, uninterrupted slumber. The moment he shifts, I climb out of bed and escape to the bathroom.

When I return minutes later, he's resting his elbows on his knees and cradling his temples. The view of his smooth, broad back transfixes me. I'd love to kneel behind him and massage his muscles. I'd like to be the person who gets to do that for him. But I know his position, and as much as I wish this weren't the case, I'm not the person he needs.

I stride across the room and throw open my suitcase, hoping the sudden activity will change the tense energy in the air. My back is to him when I say good morning.

"Mornin'," he slurs.

His rough voice scrapes against my skin, a worthy substitute for the five-o'clock shadow I wish he'd sweep across my breasts. Out of the corner of my eye, I watch him slide his arms behind him, extending his torso, and then he raises his face to the ceiling.

What a cruel, cruel man.

To stop myself from staring, I focus instead on choosing my outfit for the day. "It's been a while since I've gone zip-lining, but I remember the harness doesn't do very nice things for your crotch. It's like you're signing up for a wedgie, or worse, a camel toe. I think I'll go with leggings."

He straightens and massages the back of his head. "How many times have you done it?"

"Four, five times maybe. Did it in Costa Rica once after my first international flight. There's nothing like soaring above the treetops and seeing waterfalls and wildlife on your way down. It was so fast, too. Like flying through the air."

He stands abruptly and rushes to the restroom. Nature calls, I guess.

When he reemerges minutes later, water droplets dot his forehead, as if he splashed his face, and his lips are set in a thin line. Maybe my assumption that he's a morning person is wrong.

Well, I'm not poking that bear, even if he poked me first. I gather my clothes and toiletries and whizz past him to the bathroom. Before I close the door, I say, "It'll be yours in ten minutes."

"Take your time," he says in that gruff voice that makes me wish we were having drowsy morning sex.

As promised, I'm done quickly, and I leave the room in search of coffee. I find Tori and Eva sitting at the table in the small eat-in kitchen, chatting and each nursing a mug.

"Well, good morning, sunshine," Tori says.

"Damn, you're glowing," Eva says. "Am I the only one not having sex on a regular basis?"

For a few seconds, I do nothing but blink at her and shake my head. Oh, right. Eva doesn't know Julian and I aren't really dating. The question is, should I tell her? I don't know her very well, but I'd like to. And I trust my future sister-in-law to surround herself with good people. After filling my mug with coffee, I join them at the table.

I listen for sounds of Lydia.

"She's at the main house," Tori says. "Carter's gone, too. It's just us."

I think this might be the first time a girlfriend has known what I was thinking without me saying so. My joy might be a bit out of proportion to the circumstances, but whatever, I love it.

Leaning in, I say, "Julian and I aren't really dating. It's all a ruse."

Eva scrunches her face. "Why?"

I sigh. Yeah, Ashley. Why? "Well, as you can probably tell, there are a few pains in the asses in my family, and I thought my time here would go more smoothly if they thought I was seriously dating someone. I have a reputation for being a bit of a rolling stone, and I thought Julian's presence would deter them from asking questions about my life and future."

Eva sets down her mug and peers at me. "Sounds like you thought wrong."

"Seems that way, but now we're stuck with the charade through Sunday."

"You're a very convincing couple," Eva says. "Are you saying there's nothing there, there?"

I chance a glance at Tori, who's all ears while she sips her coffee. "Are we attracted to each other? Sure. Will we do anything about it? Nope."

"Why the hell not?" Eva asks, a touch of exasperation lacing her tone.

I lift an eyebrow.

"Sorry," she says. "I think the sexual tension is getting to me. Y'all need to take care of it—for the sisterhood."

"It's not that simple, I assure you."

"It never is," she mumbles.

I sigh into my cup. "I don't want to compete with my brother for Julian's time. And Julian's always been uneasy about mixing his personal and business lives. Being Carter's agent is his exception. Dating me would upset the order of things."

"Well, let me ask you this then," Eva says. "Why do you think he agreed to the charade?"

Now that's an easy one. "Lydia. She's been after him forever. This served his purposes, too."

"Wait. You say he's not comfortable representing Carter because of their personal connection?"

I nod. "That's right."

"But he agrees to a fake relationship with his client's sister so he can dodge a woman who has a crush on him?"

Eva and Tori share a knowing look.

"Ding, ding, ding," Tori says. "I'll take Things That Are Obvious for six hundred, Alex."

I pinch my lips together, unsure what to say. I know he's attracted to me, but could there be more to this for him than lust? As usual, I have no answers, so I groan instead. "This is a mess and—"

The door to our bedroom opens, and Julian walks out in a pair of shorts that are no match for his powerful thighs. "Morning, ladies."

Tori and Eva both say, "Good morning, Charlie" and high-five each other.

Eva waves her hands excitedly. "Oh, we could take *Charlie's Angels* to the next level." She stands and drops into a fighting pose. "I call dibs on the middle, though. I can rock a Farrah Fawcett wig like a boss."

"Who'd play Charlie?" Julian asks, grinning. "I can't act at all."

"Not sure I agree with you there," Eva says with a smug smile. "But to answer your question, I'd choose Chris Pine. No, what am I thinking? Idris Elba. Definitely. Could you imagine that British accent wishing you good morning?" She flutters her eyelashes. "I'd be like, 'Good morning, Idris' and drop my panties in the same breath."

Julian stares at her with a blank expression. "Okay, that's my cue to leave. Where's Carter?"

"He's with his mother," Tori says. "And I need to say hello to my parents before Susan takes them to the flea market." She rises from her chair. "We'll meet outside at eleven thirty, okay? The zip-lining center is twenty minutes away."

Julian swallows hard and smiles. "Can't wait."

But the sheen of perspiration on his face suggests he's lying through his bright white teeth. Huh. What's that about?

"JULIAN, YOU DON'T look so great, man," Carter says as he clips a part of the harness around his right thigh. "You okay?"

Julian nods as he breathes out. "I'm fine."

We're under a canopy of tall trees at Sunny Creek Adventure Park. Our instructor checks that each of our harnesses is secure and gives us a thumbs-up. After a ten-minute safety briefing, he leads us to the first set of trails and points to the color-coded flags at their entrances. "The flags will tell you the level of difficulty. Blue is a less-challenging trail. The climbing bridge is suspended at thirty feet. Green is at fifty."

Carter and Tori smile at each other.

"Green, right?" Carter asks, and Tori nods enthusiastically.

Anthony, who looks compelling in his athletic wear and totally in his element, turns to Eva. "We should do this in pairs. What's your pleasure?"

"Not to be paired with you," Eva replies.

Anthony chuckles, the muscles in his chest flexing as he does. Oh, I bet he could make his pecs twerk.

"Suit yourself," he says as he follows Tori and Carter up the ladder leading to the green trail.

Eva rolls her eyes and jogs after him.

"Fifty feet, you say?" Julian asks our instructor.

"Yeah. But you'll get wonderful views from thirty feet, too."

Julian licks his lips like he's trying to quench his thirst from that act alone. When he's done, he rubs his fingers over his mouth as he considers the trails. I've never seen him indecisive about anything, but he's hesitating now.

He's scared.

I grab his hand. "Care Bear, I'm not sure about green. Could we do blue instead?"

His gaze darts to my face, and then the tightness in his pinched expression disappears. "Yeah, let's do it. But call me Care Bear in public one more time and I'll tell everyone your snore sounds like a running lawnmower."

I scrunch my brows and give him the evil eye. "Rude."

Our instructor waves us off, shaking his head at our antics. "Have fun, folks."

I climb the ladder first and wait for Julian on the first platform. Ahead of us, a woman snaps the suspension lock to the steel cable that runs the length of the bridge and beyond. Once engaged, the harness system prevents anyone from advancing without being secured to the cable.

Julian pulls himself up over the ledge, giving me an awesome view of his broad shoulders and ripped arms. He stands and peeks around me to survey the bridge. "You've done this a bunch of times. Why'd you decide on this one?"

I go for a nonchalant tone. "Because you're afraid of heights."

His chest caves, and he drops his chin. "I can handle heights when I'm in the cabin of a plane. But suspended in air with only a thin cable between me and the dirt below? I'm terrified."

I'll admit to being gratified that he shared this with me and no one else. "We'll get through it together, okay?"

He grunts. "We'll see."

"C'mon, Julian, let's approach this with a little positivity."

He straightens, rolls his shoulders, and puffs out a breath. "Okay, let's do this."

We work together to get through the trail, pausing only when the next suspension bridge looms a short distance away.

"That's higher than the last one," he observes.

"Try looking up instead of down in between steps."

He raises his face to the sky, and the sun highlights the planes of his face, like it's gathering energy directly from him. Then he opens one eye and steps forward.

"You're doing great, Julian."

"How are you doing over there?" Carter bellows from a higher platform to our right.

"Awesome," I yell back.

"I can do this," Julian chants. "I can do this."

"Yes, you can," I whisper near his ear.

He shivers, and I step back to give him the room he needs to advance. As he grows more comfortable with the climb, I point out the creek below us and a hummingbird that whizzes by.

"Thanks for having patience with me," he says, stepping forward to the next challenge bridge.

I readjust my gloves and slap my hands together before unclipping my harness from the last cable and snapping it onto the new one. "The zip line is coming up after this."

Behind me, Julian stumbles. "I might need an airlift."

"No, you won't. You're going to handle the zip line like you handle a negotiation for one of your clients. Make it your bitch."

He laughs. "Okay, that's not how I handle my business, but I get your point."

We approach the zip line, where a member of the park's staff waits to assist us.

"How ya doin', folks? Who's going first?" the woman asks.

Julian steps up. "Do you mind if I go first, Ash? I need to get this over with."

"Not at all. Go for it."

The woman rechecks Julian's helmet and helps him secure the harness to the cable. "This one's a steep fall, so you might feel a little queasy on the way down. Luckily, the landing is clear. Lots of dirt and no branches. You know how to hang on, yes?"

Julian reaches up and hangs on to the handles of the pulley that'll soon be gliding with him in the air. "Yeah."

"Okay," she says. "Just let me know when you're ready, and I'll help you with a push."

Julian scans the area, his pupils dilated to I'm-going-to-die size. "Okay."

She places a hand on his back.

"No. Wait. I was saying okay to letting you know when I'm ready, not telling you I am, in fact, ready. Hang on a minute."

He mutters something to himself.

"You don't have to do this, you know," I tell him.

"Um, yeah, he does," the woman says. "Unless we think an airlift is necessary. It's not safe to double back." She speaks into her walkie-talkie. "Code green on Trail Blue."

Well, this is escalating in a way I hadn't anticipated. What to do? What to do? He's frightened. So he needs a distraction. Then it comes to me.

"Can you give us a sec?" I ask the woman.

"Sure," she says, stepping away.

I face Julian. When his eyes are trained on mine, I lean over and whisper. "Just so you know, watching you today in those cute athletic shorts has been a hell of a turn-on. Your ass is amazing, and I've wanted to grab it all day. In fact, I'm so horny my nipples might poke holes through my shirt."

He jerks and drops his heated gaze to my chest.

Then I push him.

Chapter Twenty

Julian

MY HEART HAS grown wings and is fluttering like that hummingbird we saw a few minutes ago. Holy shit, I fuckin' did it.

After removing my helmet, I spin around and shake out my arms as I watch Ashley fly down the zip line. That amazing woman pushed me where I didn't think I could go.

She screams her joy through the entire descent, her face dominated by a carefree smile that fits her adventurous personality.

"That was fantastic," she says with exhilaration in her voice as she lands on her butt.

Then I remember her tits. Specifically, what she said about the state of her nipples. And I remember *why* she said it. To help me overcome my fear.

Before I can think better of it, I haul her up, lean down, and kiss her.

It's awkward as fuck since she's still tethered to the zip line and wearing a helmet. But she doesn't let a bit of climbing equipment stand in the way of reciprocating. She moans into my mouth and throws her arms around my neck. I cup her jaw, my thumbs gliding against the soft patches of skin there. Ashley's hands grasp the back of my neck, massaging my tension-filled muscles. Heat curls down my spine, and I imagine what it would be like to spread her body on a bed and kiss every tantalizing inch of her, from her temples to her adorably peach-painted toes. Damn, what would it be like to sink into her?

Somehow a voice in the distance pierces through what little level headspace I have left. "Keep it moving, you two," it bellows.

We spring apart, the dazed expression on Ashley's face undoubtedly matching mine. A line has formed on the other end of the zip line, and a man with his young child glares at us. Understandable. He probably didn't expect to have *the talk* with his little boy while swinging through the woods.

Ashley recovers first and waves at the park employee, yelling back a terse "Sorry!"

Without a word to me, she unclips the cable and descends the short set of stairs that mark the end of the trail.

I plod after her, cursing myself for sending mixed signals. She trots through the clearing that will lead us back to the park entrance, not bothering to wait for me.

"Ash, hang on," I say.

She doesn't pause or falter but presses ahead, and I'm forced to sprint to catch up with her.

"Ash, stop."

She pretends not to hear me.

I run fast enough to surpass her, then I block her path. "Ash, please. Stop. I'm sorry."

She raises her chin and regards me with sad eyes. "You're not being fair, Julian. I can't keep up with you. One minute you're adamant that we shouldn't act on our attraction. The next minute you're snaking your tongue down my throat." Her eyes go wide as soon as the words are out, and she presses her fingers against her temples, a small smile lifting the corners of her mouth. "Dammit." She narrows her eyes on me. "Did your brain go there, too? Because I just envisioned something longer and thicker than a snake."

I drop my head into my chest and laugh so heartily my chest rumbles. "Yeah, my mind went there. You're a bad influence."

"It *is* longer and thicker than a snake, right? I'm asking for science."

"Well, it's not boa constrictor thick, but it's not a garden snake, either." I shake my head. "How'd we come to this?"

She snorts. "We should both stop talking. It's safer that way."

I take one of her hands and squeeze it. "The adrenaline took over. And I loved that you helped me through the worst of it. I got so caught up in the moment, I didn't think it through. And I'm sorry. I'm so sorry."

"It's just…it's hard to keep this straight in my head. I know I was a participant, too, but let the record show that you came at me first."

I throw up my hands, fully prepared to accept my part in this. "You'll get no argument from me. I—"

"Hey, you two," Tori says, walking up to us with Carter and Eva trudging behind her. "You're supposed to be climbing, not talking each other's heads off."

"Where's Anthony?" I ask. In truth, I'm grateful for the interruption because it's getting harder and harder to rationalize my conflicted feelings.

"I chewed him up and spat him out on the trail," Eva says.

Tori rolls her eyes. "He's using the restroom. What are you doing over here?"

"We just finished," Ashley says. "I wasn't feeling the height on that one, so we decided to take the blue trail."

I'm not letting her fake this for me. "Actually, I wasn't the one feeling the height on the green trail. She took pity on me."

Tori, Eva, and Ashley link arms and head down the gravel-filled path.

Carter hangs back. "You're not good with heights, J?"

"Not like this, no," I reply.

"Well, what do you know. Every superman has his kryptonite, I guess."

He's right about that. Except my true kryptonite is his baby sister.

In other words, I'm fucked.

AFTER A QUICK stop at the cottage to pick up Bianca and Lydia, the group splits into two cars for the ride to the spa: Carter and I take his rental, and Kimberly drives the women in her minivan. Anthony begs off joining us, claiming he wants time to catch up with his aunt and uncle, but given the way he glared at Eva when he climbed out of the car, I suspect he's using his relatives as an excuse.

According to Carter, a hefty payment ensures both the spa's discretion and private accommodations. We even enter through a side door, and the staff whisks away the women before Carter and I settle on our services.

Fifteen minutes later, Carter and I are in the steam room, sitting across from each other and wearing white towels around our waists.

"So you ready for the big day?" I ask him.

He slaps a hand on his stomach and leans against the tile wall behind him. "More than ready, J. She's my heart. And she makes everything better. My day is brighter with her in it. Sleep is better. Shit, life is better, period. And I almost fucked it up. But now we're together, and I'll be able to call her my wife in less than forty-eight hours."

I sit back and close my eyes, breathing in the hot, sticky air and enjoying the way it's easing the tension in my muscles. "I'm happy for you, man."

And I truly am. Carter doesn't let many people into his life, but I'm glad he opened his heart to Tori. She keeps him grounded, and I know I can count on her to have his back, too.

He chuckles. "Be honest, though. It's killing you that we're not making a splash of our wedding, isn't it? You probably cried a few tears for the lost opportunity to turn this into the event of the season."

"I won't lie. I did cry a few tears. On the inside. But being your agent comes second to being your friend, and at the end of the day I want you to be happy. If this is what it took, then I'll support you one hundred percent." I listen for a response. Carter's steady breathing makes me wonder if he's fallen asleep on me. "You still with me over there?"

"Yeah, I'm here. It's just..." He leans on his thighs and pinches the bridge of his nose before he speaks. "When we told you about the wedding and we had that... moment at your place, I realized how your role as my agent could cause a rift between us. And I know I give you a lot of shit about your need to separate your work and personal lives, so I just wanted to tell you that I get it now. We're family, but we're business partners, too. It's a balance, and I want to thank you for making sure we don't tip the scales in a direction that could fuck this up."

I smile at him, but inside I'm sighing. "Sure."

He's right, of course. I've done an admirable job keeping my work and social relationships from blending. It's the reason Carter and I have worked together this long without killing each other. But there's a woman somewhere in this spa who could upset the status quo, and every moment I spend with her makes me want to tilt the scale in favor of spending all my personal time with her.

"Everything all right with you and Ashley?" he asks. "I'm not sure your charade had the intended effect."

"You're right about that, but unless we want to own up to the lie, we're stuck with it until Sunday. It's not a big deal. We're adults, and we know how to handle ourselves in this situation."

My monologue hangs in the air, a warning to back off even to my own ears. Because despite my discomfort with the subtext of this conversation, I know I'm right. Ashley and I don't need anyone's help resolving the situation. We can tie ourselves in knots just fine on our own.

"No need to get defensive. I trust your judgment, so I'll let you two work it out." He chuckles. "I have to say it's been surprisingly entertaining watching you pretend to be interested in her."

I laugh it off and slide to the edge of the bench, my legs crossed at the ankles.

Little does he know there's no pretending involved.

AFTER A LATE dinner with the family, "the whippersnappers," as Susan has dubbed us, return to the cottage. Ashley and I haven't talked much since the zip-lining episode, just a little back rubbing and hand holding to keep up appearances, so I'm anxious about tonight. When we're finally alone together in the room, it's clear I had good reason to be concerned. She flinches at my every movement, as if she's poised to take flight if I get close to her. My conversation with Carter this afternoon left me just as tense, so I know exactly how she feels. But I can make this easy on us both by putting some distance between us. "Listen, I'm thinking it might be a good idea for me to sleep out on the couch tonight. I can go out there after everyone's gone to bed, and then I'll sneak in here early in the morning."

I expect her to protest, but she flops down into the rocking chair, sagging in relief. Then she blows out a breath, and with her eyes shiny and bright, nods. "Okay, yes. I think that makes sense. It'll make things less awkward, you know?"

"Yeah."

She runs her hands over her thighs, smoothing the creases in her shorts, and her gaze darts around the room until it lands on her guitar case.

"You need some time alone with Melanie, don't you?"

She jerks her head back, and her lovely mouth falls open. "How'd you know?"

"I know you."

She wears a thoughtful expression, her mind somewhere beyond this room. "Not many people do."

"I know that, too."

She pouts at me and shakes her head in frustration. "I liked you so much better when you were my teenage fantasy or a tasty piece of eye candy."

"And now you're lying."

She jumps up from the chair, grabs a pillow, and throws it across the room, aiming for my head. "Get out. And stay out. We have no room for irresistible men who will make our lives more complicated."

I dodge the pillow easily and lob it back at her, but I miss my mark. "Okay, I'll leave you alone with your precious guitar. I need to make a few calls anyway."

She laughs and heads into the bathroom. Before she closes the door, she pokes her head out. "Enjoy the sofa." And then she disappears.

"You're going to miss me, admit it," I call after her.

She peeks out again and sticks out her tongue. "I'll admit it. Now go."

I haven't had this much fun with a woman in a long time. It's fucking addictive.

I JERK AWAKE, unsure what interrupted my X-rated dream about my best friend's sister. But I solve the mystery within seconds, opening my eyes to a pajama-clad Lydia standing by the couch. Suddenly I'm wondering if I'm trapped in a horror movie.

"Hey," she whispers.

She says this as though it's unremarkable to be hovering around me while I sleep.

I run a hand down my face and sit up. "Everything okay? What's up?"

She places her hands at her hips. "What's up? That's *my* question." She waggles her eyebrows and lifts her chin in the direction of the bedroom where Ashley and I are staying. "Trouble in paradise?"

There's no mistaking the hopeful gleam in her eyes and the happy curve of her lips. *Think, Julian. Think.* Why would I be out here if Ashley and I aren't fighting?

"No, not at all," I say, my gaze jumping around the room. A print copy of *The Hollywood Observer* saves me. Pointing to it on the coffee table, I explain, "I...uh...I wanted to read a bit." After lifting the paper, I rise and stretch. "The light was bothering her. I guess I fell asleep."

Hearing this, Lydia drops her shoulders and her smile slips. "Oh, okay. I'm going to make some tea. Want some?"

"No, thanks."

"Well, good night, then."

"Good night," I reply.

And then she just stands there, waiting for me to go into the bedroom, which I do—reluctantly, I might add—because what else *can* I do?

I open the door softly and tiptoe in. Not surprisingly, it's dark in here. The moon's glow coming through the window casts shadows in the sparsely decorated room. I squint to make out the shapes of the furniture and hear the bedsheets rustle. Still as a statue, my eyes survey the scene, adjusting to the dimness of my surroundings. My gaze travels over the bed, registering that one of Ashley's arms—the source of the rustling—is hidden under the covers. My heart gallops in my chest, and my breath quickens. She's not doing what I think she's doing, is she? No fucking way. This *must* be a continuation of my dirty dream.

In a fog, I take a step back, ready to bolt out of the room, and reach behind me for the doorknob. Then it happens. With her other arm stretched behind her and her eyes squeezed tight, Ashley lifts her head off the pillow, shudders, and releases the softest of gasps. "Julian."

Damn, damn, damn. Not a dream at all. She's thinking about me and getting herself off. I buckle from the pleasure and pain of witnessing it. Of their own volition, my lips part, depriving me of time to filter my words. "*Oh, fuck*, that's hot."

Chapter Twenty-One

Ashley

MY EYES FLY open, and Julian's frozen form greets me.

No, no, no, no, no. This can't be happening.

I cover my mouth with my hands. "Oh God." The burning around my ears, face, and neck must be the precursor to going up in flames. What to do? What to do? My brain jumps out of my body and yells at me: *Get the hell out of here, Ashley!* Right. I spring out of bed and dash to the bathroom, mumbling, "I'm going to be sick."

Inside, I pace the span of the small space, the cold tile serving as a temporary reprieve from the five-alarm fire scorching the rest of my body. I can't even look at myself in the mirror. I know what I'll see there: a woman with a flushed face whose chest is heaving and whose hair is plastered to her neck. "Oh God, oh God, oh God."

A soft knock on the door makes me jump like a scared cat.

"Ash, are you okay in there?"

His voice is tender with concern. Or is that pity? I drop my head against the door and groan.

"Ash, talk to me," he says, his voice now laced with worry. "I'm sorry about…interrupting. I didn't realize what was going on until it was too late."

"Stop. I don't think I can ever talk to you again. There's no recovering from this, Julian. I might as well pack my bags and catch a flight somewhere far away. I hear Iceland's nice."

The sound of his chuckle comes through the door clearly.

"It's *not* funny, jerk."

He clears his throat. "Sorry. Can you…can you just open the door, so we can talk?"

I suppose I can't stay in here forever, but I'd like to. I'd *really* like to. Blowing out a breath that puffs out my cheeks, I swing the door open and face the wall of Julian blocking my way. "We'll pretend this never happened."

He steps back and nods. "Okay."

I raise a finger at him. "No jokes. No comments. No innuendos. Got it?"

He holds up his hands and continues to back away. "Okay, okay. I didn't see or hear anything."

I busy myself by fluffing the pillows and straightening the comforter. "Just out of curiosity, what *didn't* you see or hear?"

He shakes his head. "What? I just told you I didn't see or hear anything."

"But you *did* see or hear something."

He places his hands on his hips. "And you told me not to comment about it."

"Right. Okay."

I scurry under the comforter and burrow like the woodland creature I'd like to be. The mattress dips, but Julian's body isn't anywhere near mine. I throw back a corner of the cover and peer at him. He's sitting with his back to me, a hand gripping the back of his neck.

"Why'd you come in, anyway? I thought you were going to sleep on the couch. There's a bathroom out there, so it didn't occur to me that you'd need to come..."

My voice trails off. Good God, Ashley, you're making it sound as if you planned a night of masturbating to visions of him in your head.

"Lydia," he says, as if her name alone explains everything.

"Lydia?"

"She found me out there and wondered if we were squabbling. I told her I was reading and must have fallen asleep."

"Oh." Okay, sure, it's not every day your teenage crush finds you calling out his name in the throes of a fantastic self-induced orgasm, but what's done is done, and I can't change what happened. Mortifying, yes. World-changing? No. But dammit, my cheeks are still blazing. "I'll survive." I laugh nervously. "It's not like you haven't seen me come before, right?"

"Would any of this be easier to handle if I told you I've done it, too?" he asks over his shoulder.

"Masturbated? You, a man, masturbates. That's hardly earth-shattering information."

He twists his body to turn to me, his eyes dark and heavy-lidded. "No, I meant I've thought about you while I touch myself."

Oh. *Oh God.* My belly flutters wildly, and a rush of warmth travels between my legs. I do believe we've entered the foreplay stage of these proceedings, and I am here for it. "Yes, that helps. Thanks for sharing."

I squeeze my eyes shut. *Thanks for sharing?* What is wrong with you today?

He doesn't respond, but he does jump up and draw in a loud, ragged breath. Now that his hands are gripping the back of his neck, his profile reveals the impressive boner straining against his sweats.

Fuck me.

No, seriously, Julian, fuck me.

But he won't want to, right? Because the man has willpower the likes of which I'll never possess. Nevertheless, let's have a little fun with this, shall we? Anything to help me set aside my own embarrassment. I slide my back up against the headboard and whisper. "Show me."

He snaps his head in my direction. "Show you what?" His voice is strained, tight because he's trying to control his arousal and achy because he isn't succeeding.

"Show me how you think of me and touch yourself. It's only fair. I showed you mine, now show me yours."

He rubs at his brows and paces the room, not hiding either the guarded look in his eyes or the hard set of his jaw. "You can't be serious." He leans over and swipes up a T-shirt from the open suitcase by the rocking chair. "I'm going to take a walk."

His hand is on the doorknob when I say, "I really wish you'd stay. Think of it this way. You wouldn't be touching me, if that's your concern. You'd be doing what you just admitted you've done before. This time it would be in front of me. That's the only difference."

He tightens his hold on his shirt and the doorknob. "That's a *big* difference."

"Promises, promises."

My quip causes him to spin around, and I sag against the headboard when a flicker of a smile passes across his face. He'd never do it, but for a few seconds, it was fun—and arousing—to imagine that he would.

"Jesus, Ashley, you really are something, you know that?"

"I know." I slide down onto the mattress and stab at my pillow to find my spot. "But seriously, just come back to bed. I can forget about being caught in the act if you can."

A beat of silence follows, and then he drops his shoulders, his expression dazed and wary. "Okay."

I turn on my side, hoping to give him a moment to collect himself, and when the mattress dips, I scooch forward to avoid any chance our bodies will brush against each other as he settles in. I don't detect any movement under the comforter, so I gather he's decided sleeping on top of the bedding is safer.

"Good night, Julian." I twist my head and say over my shoulder, "Oh, and if you need to take care of…well, you know, I won't be offended." Then I turn over and smile into my pillow.

"Shut up, Ash."

He speaks in a low and gruff voice, his vocal foreplay skills in play. I blow out long, even breaths, both to control my reaction to him and to lull myself to sleep. The slow, insistent ticking of the clock above the dresser helps to relax me, and minutes later my droopy eyelids close. Not long after, Julian lets out a frustrated sigh and shifts. I listen for more signs of his distress, preparing to ask if everything's okay, when a soft hiss fills the air and the mattress vibrates under me at a steady pace.

Oh my God. Is he…is he jerking off? Does he think I'm sleeping? My chest tightens when I consider the possibility that he knows I'm awake and wants me to hear the evidence of his desire for me. I'm tied in knots, unsure what to do. Face him and watch? Pretend I'm unaware? Jump his bones? The odds are low that he'll continue if I turn around, so I remain still, squeezing my eyes shut and supplying my own images to accompany the sound of Julian's heavy breathing: His cock is long and thick and pulsing in his hands. The faint hair at the base of his dick hits the underside of his hand each time he strokes himself from root to tip. With parted lips and eyes at half-mast, he rests his free hand on his stomach and massages it, his muscles contracting against his fingertips.

Turned on by my own imagination, I moan and clench my pussy, shifting ever so slightly, which causes my pajama top to scrape against my sensitive nipples.

He freezes, and I press down on my bottom lip, inwardly cursing myself for making noise.

"What...what the fuck am I doing?" he whispers. Several strong beats of my heart later, he speaks again. "Ash? You awake?"

With my head still turned away from him, I confess. "Yeah, I'm awake."

He groans. "I'm sorry. I—"

"Don't stop touching yourself. It's okay. I want you to."

He doesn't answer, but after the tenth ticktock of the clock, the bed's vibrations resume and pick up speed, the soft slap of wet skin and his tortured breathing bouncing off the walls as though they're being broadcast in surround sound.

"Oh shit," he grunts. This time there's no hiding the tremors coming from his side of the bed. Then a soft string of words follows. "Yes, that's it, baby. Right there, Ash. Yes. Yes. Fuck. Aaash."

The bliss in his voice wraps itself around me, caressing me like strong, confident hands. The throbbing between my legs narrows and settles on my nub, and for a second I wonder if I'm coming, too. Jesus. When the shaking stops, I blink my eyes open and wait. Seconds pass before he eases out of the bed, and then his shadow blankets my side of the room as he creeps to the toilet. The door closes softly. Moments later, water splashes in the sink, and I let out a breath I didn't know I'd been holding.

This is my ghost. Ashley Williamson is dead.

As far as I am aware, no book provides guidance on how to face a man the morning after he masturbated next to you. "How's it going, Handsy?" Nah. Too literal. What about "How'd you sleep, Slickster?" A tad crass, I suppose. I'm not sure what to say or whether to acknowledge what happened, but I'm certain that Julian is close to succumbing to my charms. Pushing him over the edge wouldn't be all that difficult. The more important question is, should I even try?

A woman who wants to protect her heart and who knows Julian's identity begins and ends with his career would tread carefully here. If Julian were faced with a choice between risking his professional ties to Carter and nurturing a relationship with me, I doubt he'd decide in my favor. But does it need to come to that? I'm not entirely convinced it does. Maybe Julian's fixation on creating separate spheres of his life is a stroke of serendipity, laying the groundwork for a situation where he can be with me *and* continue to work with Carter. Or maybe I'm so desperate for him I'm coming up with excuses to justify scaling the invisible wall between us.

I catapult out of the bed when he shuts off the shower, mentally preparing myself to face him. In the meantime, I gather an outfit and clean underwear. With my clothes in my arms and a foot tapping against the floor, I try my hand at a greeting.

"Hey, it's no big deal," I could say. "We both had it *coming* to us."

Heh. While making light of last night's debacle probably is the safest option, stoking our tension seems more beneficial to me in the long run.

"Last night was a revelation, and I'd like us to take our relationship to the next level."

No, too obvious.

Julian peeks out, scattering my thoughts as if they were a thousand feathers flying out of a torn pillow.

Wearing an easy expression and a half smile, he says, "Now we're even. No jokes. No comments. No innuendos. Got it?"

I'm amused that he's thrown my admonition back at me, and it's only fair that I oblige him. "Got it."

His head and torso disappear inside again, and he shuts the door.

Sure. Got it. But he can't erase my memory, and we have one more night together. The possibilities, Mr. Hart, are endless.

THE KITCHEN IS already abuzz with activity when Julian and I come in. My father's marinating meats for this afternoon's cookout, and Lourdes and Bianca are eating breakfast. I love seeing our two families come together, and I can't wait to gorge on whatever Dad's making. To my delight, my aunt Carol is nowhere to be seen.

Carter and Tori are visiting the town clerk, one of my father's poker buddies, to pick up their marriage license, and although Carter assured Tori they didn't need a witness, she insisted on bringing Eva along "just in case."

Kimberly bounds down the stairs with my adorable niece and nephew in tow. "Izzy, make sure your cleats are in your bag."

My sister rustles around the living room, gathering Izzy's athletic socks, car keys, and her phone, while Julian and I wait near the front door, watching the storm of activity from a safe place.

She stops her Tasmanian Devil routine long enough to notice we're there. "Oh, hey. Where are you headed?"

"With you. To Izzy's game, of course. We'd like to cheer her on, too."

Kimberly's eyes go wide. "Oh. Um, okay." She leans into me. "Just so you know, the team's in a bit of a *Bad News Bears* situation, Izzy excepted. This won't be the World Cup or anything close to it."

"Yes, I figured, Kimberly."

"And her coach is—"

"Mom," Izzy yells from the mudroom. "I can't find my cleats." The panic in Izzy's voice sends Kimberly whirring past us.

"Good morning, everyone," my mother says at the top of the stairs. "I'll be down in a sec to prepare coffee. And don't you dare leave without me."

"Mom, it's a Keurig," I shout up to her. "There's nothing for you to prepare."

"Well, shoot. Now I know how cashiers feel about those automated checkout machines at the grocery."

"Making coffee's not your job, though," Julian points out. "It's not the same."

"Thank you, Julian. You were always quick to make me think a little deeper. Today's no different." They exchange smiles, a look of affection passing between them.

Izzy's cleats accounted for, Kimberly leads the charge out of the house. "We'll take my Dodge."

Julian and I come to an abrupt stop behind her.

"Do we have to?" I ask in a whiny voice.

Kimberly grins. "Get in, brat."

Julian rounds the minivan and pretends to examine it like it's a foreign object. He presses a single finger against the windshield. "Is it contagious? If I get in this thing, will I turn into a soccer dad? What's next? Wearing black socks with sandals?"

Kimberly rolls her eyes. "Jesus, I didn't know I'd be driving four children to the game. My own kids are enough, thank you." She stops in front of me and squeezes my wrist. "And you? What have you done to the real Julian? The one who never cracks a joke."

"I upgraded him for the newest version." I lean toward her and whisper, "This one *feels* and *laughs*."

"I can hear you," Julian says, his lips pursed in feigned outrage.

"I know."

He playfully swats my ass. The move is so unexpected, the sound of it registers like an explosion in my ears. Julian, apparently surprised himself, shuffles back, his eyes wide and his expression grim. "Sorr—"

I cover my mouth with both hands, striking a pinup pose that lifts my ass. "Oh, I wasn't expecting that." Then I wink at him. "Do it again."

"Hey," Kimberly bellows. "Watch yourselves around my kids." Then she asks, "Does anyone know if Lydia's coming?"

Shit, I hope not. "She's probably still sleeping." I scramble around to the sliding door and motion for Julian and the kids to get inside like we've just committed a bank heist and we're making our getaway. "Let's go, people. Let's go."

I turn around and watch my mother's progress. She's holding the handrail as she descends the steps, her movements slow and careful. Watching her, I feel a fist squeeze my heart, because she's getting older, and so is my dad. "Mom, everything okay?"

"Yes, dear," she shouts back. "Your dad and I were a little too spirited in the bedroom last night, if you know what I mean. Hip's out of whack, I think."

Kimberly snorts, and my eyes nearly roll out of my head.

"That's *your* mother," Kimberly says as she rounds the van.

Julian and I climb into the second row while Izzy and Donovan take the third. My mother clicks her seat belt into place, claps, and looks at Izzy. "Let's go kick some butt, sweetie pie."

Kimberly groans. "Mom, it's youth soccer. This is about teamwork, growth, personal satisfaction. Winning isn't everything."

My mother draws back. "But it is a thing, right? I mean, winning *is* the goal of the game, isn't it? That's why we keep score, yes?"

Kimberly grumbles.

Julian taps Donovan on the knee. "What about you, buddy? No sports for you?"

Donovan pulls his head out of the book he's reading. "I don't like to sweat. It's uncivilized." He says this with all seriousness, and I struggle to hold in the laugh that's bubbling up at the base of my throat. This kid is *so* speaking my language.

Julian and I smile at each other, and I want to swoon at the carefree man who's taken over his body. A few days away from work has done wonders to relax his typically high-strung disposition.

The soccer field is less than a ten-minute ride away. When we get there, Izzy scrambles over us and exits the car as soon as it stops. Julian gets out and comes around to help my mother out of the van, which only makes me swoon more. Together, we pull out the camp chairs in Kimberly's trunk. I raise my head at the sound of a vehicle traveling over gravel close by and groan when I see Lydia parking her car.

Wonderful. Just wonderful.

"Hey, guys," she says in a cheery voice. "Thought I'd join you and watch the game."

This isn't a state-of-the-art field by any means. We've got grass, two goals, and a bunch of portable chairs along the sidelines. Lydia's typical scene doesn't feature sports or dirt, so I'm immediately suspicious of her intentions. "The more the merrier."

Up ahead, Kimberly chases after Izzy, who stops in front of a tall man and smiles up at him while she shields her eyes from the sun. Bending to Izzy's eye level, he ruffles her hair, pats her on the shoulder, and consults his clipboard. Something about him triggers a memory, but I can't place him.

Until my gaze settles on his smile. Max Drummond.

My high school boyfriend.

For three months, we were inseparable. Believing we were in love, I didn't hesitate to lose my virginity with him. Two weeks of daily sexcapades later, he dropped me and started dating Lydia. It's the stuff of a John Hughes film—without the kick-ass soundtrack and Molly Ringwald.

I'm so annoyed with myself for caring about this silly episode in my life. Still, I can't pretend to be unaffected by seeing him again. He's Izzy's soccer coach. Blech. If there were any rocks around, I'd kick them. Worse, Lydia made a beeline for him and is chatting him up like they're old friends.

"Why are you wearing that sour face?" Julian asks.

I jolt at the sound of his voice. "Oh, it's nothing."

"Oh, it's something," he counters.

Then I remember the reason for this farce. "Ex-boyfriend at twelve o'clock."

Julian follows the mental hour hand and leans over. "Amicable breakup?"

"Not exactly. He ditched me for Lydia."

"What a dick," Julian replies.

"Trust me, there wasn't much of that going on, either."

Julian hisses and crooks his fingers to mimic fangs. "Damn, you're poisonous. I'll have to remember that."

I shrug, miffed at the circumstances and irritated by Julian for some inexplicable reason. "I'm guessing I'll never see your schlong, so you have nothing to worry about." Oh, *that* explains my mood. The day's turned to crap, and I'm sexually frustrated, too.

Julian chokes on a laugh. "Schlong?"

I pat him hard on the back, forcing myself not to be grumpy. "Indeed."

"I'm going to pretend I didn't hear that." He straightens and points at Max. "So what's his deal now?"

"I have no idea, nor do I want to."

Which isn't exactly true. I'd love to hear that he regrets ever breaking up with me and dating Lydia instead. I'd love to know that if he had to choose all over again, he'd choose me. I freeze in place, stunned by the direction of my musings. Maybe I'm not as mature as I like to think I am.

"Are you sure you don't care?" Julian asks.

I turn my head and peer at him, meeting his knowing gaze. "I shouldn't care, but I do. How juvenile is that?"

"It's not juvenile at all. He hurt you at a time when you were feeling vulnerable. You wouldn't be human if you weren't at least curious about what he's been doing since then. It's only unhealthy if you let it consume you."

I wish I could carry Julian's wisdom in my pocket and fish it out whenever my insecurities threaten to overwhelm me. Actually, I'd prefer for him to always be available as my sounding board. He's excellent at it.

Julian taps my mother on the shoulder. "Mama Williamson, what's the deal with Izzy's coach?"

She looks up at him from her chair. "Max?"

Julian nods. "Relationship status."

"Single as far as I know. Dated a teacher at the high school about a year ago, but I think she moved out of town."

He points his chin in the general direction where Max and Lydia are standing. "And what about those two?"

"They usually avoid each other like the plague," my mother says. "Not sure what's different this time."

"Huh," Julian says, studying Max and Lydia with a pensive expression. "She's competing again."

I tilt my head at him. "Who?"

He thrusts his chin in Lydia and Max's direction. "Lydia. When it comes to you, everything's a competition. You have a boyfriend, she steals your boyfriend. You have friends, she ostracizes you to ensure they no longer hang around you. Isn't that what happened in high school?"

I nod grimly. "Yeah."

"You get a fun job traveling the country, and her mother makes sure to announce her daughter's been promoted. She's jealous of you, baby, and you've been dealing with it so long you've started to think of everything as a competition, too. It's even spilled over to your relationship with Carter, hasn't it?"

I conveniently set aside his observation about my brother and focus on Lydia. "Why would she be jealous of me?"

"Now don't get me wrong. You're nothing special."

I clip him on the shoulder. "Watch it now."

He snickers as he massages the spot, his eyes squinting in mock pain. "Will you give me a sec? I'm trying to make a point here. The thing is, it's not about you being different from everyone else. I mean, look at the incredible women at this reunion alone. But for whatever reason, Lydia recognizes all of *your* great qualities and doesn't see them in herself."

"My great qualities, huh? And what are those?"

He purses his lips playfully, aware that I'm fishing for a compliment. "Oh, I don't know. You're funny as hell, for starters. And you're down-to-earth. You care about other people's happiness more than you care about your own. And…"

The things he sees in me will soon render me a puddle of feelings on the ground, and I'm okay with that. But he's hesitating, too, and I need to know what he doesn't want to say. "And what? Tell me."

He threads his fingers through mine and pulls me closer to him. My gaze locks with his, and a shiver runs through me at the look of hunger I see there.

"You're so fucking sexy I can hardly think straight," he says. "The more time I spend with you, the more time with you I want." He raises our clasped hands to his mouth and kisses each of my knuckles, one by one.

We need a room, ASAP.

"Psst," my mother says out the side of her mouth. "Ex-boyfriend's staring. But also, remember we're at a children's soccer game, okay?"

Julian laughs. "Don't worry. We can accomplish what we need to and still keep it PG."

Bummer. That's so boring.

"Come," he says. "I think we should say hi to Max before the game starts."

Hand in hand, we walk over to the Renegades sideline. At first, I hesitate to approach Max, but Julian gives me a gentle nudge.

I paste on a smile born of fake confidence. "Max Drummond, is that you?"

Izzy's coach adjusts his baseball cap and widens his eyes when he registers that it's me. The corners of Lydia's mouth sag when she spots us.

"Ashley?" he says with excitement in his voice. "No friggin' way."

"It's me, all right."

He directs his charming smile at me, and I forgive myself for being taken in by him at seventeen.

"Well, if it isn't the one who got away," he says. "Never thought you'd come back here long enough for me to see you."

That description throws me, but I laugh to cover my confusion. "Right."

He swings his gaze between Julian and me, probably trying to gauge the nature of our connection. "Oh, hey. I'm Max."

Julian gives him a firm handshake. "Ashley's boyfriend. Good to meet you."

In so many words, Julian has told Max that's all he needs to know about him.

"Listen," Max says to me. "Obviously, I need to coach this game, but I'd love to catch up with you afterward. Just a few minutes of your time?"

I gulp. Do I want to give him any more of my time? I suppose I could. And while I do that, I can also show him I'm living my best life without him. "Sure, sure. I can spare a couple of minutes."

"Great," he says. Then he lifts the whistle hanging on a cord around his neck and blows into it. "Let's go, Renegades. Huddle up."

The game is entertaining. Izzy is fearless in her defense of the ball, but what makes the day are the few times when her teammates kick the ball into the wrong goal. Max takes it all in stride, encouraging them despite their flubs. A few times, he glances my way as he laughs at a play on the field. In those moments, Julian finds a way to touch me, and it gives me a small thrill to be the subject of his affection, even if it's aimed at making Max envious.

At halftime, Julian stands behind me and wraps his hands around my waist. I lean back and rest my head against him, enjoying the solid feel of his body against my backside.

"Having a good time?" he asks against my ear.

"I am. It's great to see Izzy dominate the field. She's got skills, and she knows it."

"Your ex-boyfriend appears to be paying more attention to you than the game."

"That's your fake boyfriend radar."

He stiffens, and for a few seconds I wonder if I've taken a misstep somehow. But I quickly dismiss the thought when he plants a kiss on my cheek.

Julian holds me tighter. "I understand you might want to make him jealous, but he doesn't need to know anything about you. He's your past, and that's where he should remain. None of these people matter as long as you're confident in who you are and where you're headed."

He's right—in theory. The problem is, while I may be confident in the person I am today, I'm not confident in where I'm headed, and I wonder if I'll ever be. "If you think that's all true, why are you working so hard to make him jealous?"

He pauses before he answers, and I *so* wish to know what's going on in his head. Finally, he says, "Because it's my job and I agreed to the assignment. But I'd be remiss if I didn't point out that this is busywork."

A glance at my mother confirms what I suspected. She's watching us with interest. If I were in her shoes, I'd be watching us with interest, too. And he's right, of course. I don't *need* Julian to pretend to be my boyfriend. That aspect of the plan was fucked from the beginning, but fessing up to our machinations would make us both look bad, and although I can't look any worse in the eyes of certain members of my family, I do care what they think of Julian. He doesn't deserve their snide comments, and I don't want to open him to their criticism.

Besides, I'm enjoying this pretend relationship far too much to put an end to the charade now. I still don't know what to say to Julian's observation, though. Thankfully, Max blows his whistle again, signifying the start of the second half. I try to focus instead on Izzy's game, but my brain keeps processing that to Julian, this is just an assignment. Which shouldn't be such a terrible thing, but I'm shocked to discover that I'm disappointed.

Twenty minutes of internal angst later, I cheer when Izzy's team easily wins the game, and then we all rush over to congratulate her. Even her brother gives Izzy a thumbs-up with the hand that isn't clutching his copy of *Dork Diaries*.

After speaking with a few parents, Max jogs toward us. And I have the overwhelming urge *not* to talk with him. What purpose would it serve? Julian's right. Lydia showed up to remind me that he chose her almost a decade ago, but why should I care? She's not my competition, no matter how much she wants to be.

I tug on Julian's sleeve. "I think you're right. He's in my past. Quick. Can we just go? Let's meet everyone at the van."

Julian smiles and caresses my cheek. "I thought you'd never ask."

I'm stunned by the intimate gesture, my plan to sprint to the car derailed by the softness of his touch. But I'm robbed of any prolonged enjoyment when Julian bends his knees and scoops me over his shoulder. I yelp at the unexpected action, although I'm secretly delighted that he can lift me with such ease. Goodness, he's strong.

Max calls out my name. "Hey, Ash. I thought we were going to talk?"

With my ass perilously close to Julian's face, I raise my head and yell back. "Sorry, Max. There's been a slight change of plans."

"Damn skippy," Julian says as he strides away like he's carrying a three-pound bag of apples.

But there's another change in plans that Julian might be less enthusiastic about. Because in that moment, I have an overwhelming desire to make this fake relationship real.

Chapter Twenty-Two

Julian

I SET ASIDE my plate and pat my belly. "Stick a fork in me because I am done."

Pushing my torso away from the table, I scan the backyard and the people milling around. Carter and Tori couldn't have asked for a nicer day for their barbecue. The sun is beaming, and the breezes are strong enough that we're forced to hold down items on the picnic table with makeshift paperweights.

We're now joined by Ashley's grandparents on her father's side, as well as a few cousins Ashley said she hardly knows. Although he's sitting at a different picnic bench from mine, Grandpa James is studying me, his index finger steadily tapping his bottom lip. I pretend not to notice and use my peripheral vision every few minutes to confirm that his attention is still directed at me.

Ashley nudges me with her shoulder as she wipes her mouth with a napkin. "Hey, Care Bear, I'm going to grab some more of that *hand-tossed* salad. Want some?"

I crane my neck to get a good look at her face, but her expression is blank. Still, I know she purposefully emphasized the word *hand-tossed*. With my eyes narrowed into what I hope are intimidating slits, I lick along the front of my teeth. "You promised there'd be no innuendos, Love Biscuit."

She straightens and gives me a sheepish grin. "Sorry, you're right. I couldn't resist."

"That's fine. I'll exact my revenge later."

I'm surprised she didn't refer to the hand-tossing incident sooner. Technically, neither one of us is immune to being ribbed about it, but I'm more disciplined than she is, and I've kept my promise not to mention it again.

Doesn't mean I'm not thinking about it. Because I am. *A lot.* The moment Ashley called out my name at the height of her orgasm plays like a song on repeat in my head. It's the last thing I should be thinking about hours before our final night together in the same bed. Her brother will be sleeping down the hall, for Christ's sake.

You didn't consider that when you were jerking off next to her, though, right? No, I'm ashamed to admit I did not. In fact, I now realize Carter hasn't taken up much of my headspace the past few days. There's no room, not when Ashley's around.

"You're out for revenge, huh?" Ashley asks. As she rises from the bench, she shivers. "Oooh. I'm *so* scared."

A few feet away from us, Tori blows a whistle. "Gather around, folks. It's time to play football."

Ah, revenge is near.

"Correction," she continues, holding up a single finger, "it's time to play *flag* football."

Damn it, revenge is elusive as fuck.

Collective moans and groans fill the air around me. Tori snaps her brows together and continuously blows the whistle to drown out the complainers. "Did I mention that each member of the winning team will receive a prize?"

Tori's announcement sufficiently motivates enough people to make two teams. After Tori and Carter drift away and bow their heads for a private discussion, they return to the circle of potential players and call out the people on their respective teams.

Kimberly and her daughter, Izzy, are on Carter's team. They're joined by Bianca, Carter's dad, and me. Tori's band of misfits includes Ashley, Kimberly's son, Donovan, Anthony, who's rubbing his hands in his teammate Eva's face, and Tori's dad, Pedro, who warns that he won't *mean* to trip anyone with his cane but says it might happen nonetheless. Lydia sits on the sidelines with the remaining grown folks but volunteers to keep track of each down.

Tori and Carter then pass out belts with plastic flags attached to them with Velcro. I've never played flag football, but I know the rules are similar to tackle football, except we can't...tackle. This game would be ten times more fun if I could wrestle Ashley to the ground, but I'll take advantage of any chance to chase after her—especially when she's wearing shorts that do wonderful things for her round ass and strong thighs.

The teams huddle up, and after the coin toss—and a few minutes of trash talk, mostly between Carter and Tori—we position ourselves at the line of scrimmage. Anthony bends over, preparing to pass the ball backward through his legs while Ashley and Eva jostle each other to work out who will receive his pass.

"Go, Eva, he's waiting for you," Ash says with a wicked grin.

"Don't make me do it," Eva says through gritted teeth. "There's no way I'll be able to concentrate with his butt in my face."

Anthony overhears this, of course, because *everyone* on the field can hear her. "Ah, baby, let my tush be your guide."

Eva grumbles her assent and readies herself for the pass. After the snap, she tosses the ball back to Anthony, and our team converges on him. He's freakishly nimble and gets the team's first down easily. Next down, he snaps the ball to Ashley. Kimberly, the former track star, chases after her like...well, a track star, but before she can swipe a flag off Ash's belt, Tori calls a time-out.

"You can't do that," Carter says with a laugh. "The ball isn't dead yet."

"It should have been first down," Tori counters. "Ashley ran more than ten yards with the ball"—she points to Lydia—"but our *ref* is on the phone."

Sure enough, Lydia's pacing and talking on her cell phone, a finger pressed against her other ear to drown out the noise from our game. "Sorry, there's an emergency at work," she explains to everyone within earshot. "They need me to run through a work-around."

Bianca rolls her eyes. "You mean I did all that running for nothing? *Mierda.*" She arches her back and circles the group with a pained expression on her face. Pedro and Randall, both out of breath, sneak away during the break.

"I think that's all for us," Randall says over his shoulder.

I sidle up to Ash and pat her on the back. "That was a mighty run there, Champ. Proud of you."

Winded and bent at the waist, she huffs out, "Thanks, Care Bear. Too bad it doesn't count." Then she looks up at me and smiles, squinting because there's no shade to be found. She's damp from her sprint across the backyard, her skin glowing and her eyes bright, and before I know it, I'm pulling her up into my arms, so I can nestle my head against her neck and breathe in all her goodness. My desire for her isn't pretend. This feeling is as real as it's ever been for me. And I'll be damned if I fight it anymore.

She melts into me, as though she's trying to meld our bodies, and her hands, strong and possessive, grip the back of my neck. We stay in that position for several seconds more, until Susan shouts, "Okay, you two, we get it. You're smitten with each other, but it's called flag football, not hug football."

With our chins dipped like children who've just been scolded, Ashley and I leap away from each other, and I busy myself tying my sneaker. Kimberly strides near us and slows. "I get that you're faking, but you're doing a helluva great job. Makes me wonder why it's been so easy to pull this off." Then she winks at us and saunters away. I rise, meeting Ashley's gaze and noting the color in her cheeks. We share a smile. I'm not averse to keeping secrets with her, but is her secret anything like mine? Does she, too, want to be with me, regardless of the consequences? I'll make it my goal to find out tonight.

A commotion at our temporary sideline snags my attention. Susan sets her body in front of Lydia, halting her niece's incessant pacing, and puts out a hand. Lydia, with her phone still at her ear, turns over the whistle to Ashley's mom and resumes making sweeping hand gestures to accompany her very important phone conversation.

Susan motions everyone back to the field. "Okay, whippersnappers, let's get this game back on track."

The teams hustle to their spots and face each other, and Susan blows the whistle. This time, I receive Izzy's snap and scurry around a pile of people, aiming to advance at least ten yards. Ashley, with fire in her eyes and her jaw set in determination, overtakes me and reaches for a flag at the front of my waist. I fake her out, sidestepping her with a shake and pivot worthy of an NFL highlight reel. The sound of her footsteps at my heels pushes me to run faster, and I'm so close to reaching the ten-yard marker that I slow down while holding the football in one hand and waving it triumphantly in the air. Behind me, Ashley says, "Oh no, you're wearing shorts like the ones you wore for zip-lining. Shit, Julian, you know what that does to me."

An image of her bouncing breasts flashes in my brain and brings me to my knees, the impact causing the ball to fly out of my hand. Horrified, I yell "No," and it registers as dramatic, pained, and in slo-mo. Ashley stretches out her arms and catches the ball midair. With remarkable speed, she runs toward her team's post, cheering triumphantly as she crosses the goal line.

Carter jogs toward me. "What the hell, J? What's with the butterfingers?"

I stumble to my feet and smooth my hands on my shorts. "Sweat, man. The ball was too slick to hang on to."

I've lost count of the number of lies I've uttered this weekend. I don't even know who I am anymore. Maybe that's a good thing, my inner voice whispers. Given how little I've thought of work and how much I'm enjoying the time off, maybe it is. But the lying—both to myself and to Ashley—must stop.

But not *quite* yet.

I take a step and wince.

"What's wrong, man?" Carter asks, his brows drawn together.

I take another step, this one tentative, and then I buckle from the alleged pain, grabbing for my ankle. "Shit. I think I twisted it."

Carter bends his knees and pulls my arm over his shoulder. "I've got you."

Ashley rushes over, her brows knitted over wide eyes. "What is it?"

Her voice is laced with concern. I'm probably going to hell for this, too. "Not sure, exactly. My ankle feels funny."

"Here," she says to Carter, draping my other arm over her shoulder. "I've got him. I'll take him back to the cottage. He needs to elevate his foot and get some ice on it."

Carter objects. "Ash, I can help."

She shakes her head. "Carter, he'll be fine. Go out there and finish the game. End it on a high note. For Tori."

Carter looks back at his fiancée. "Okay. But if you need anything, just send me a text."

Ashley nods. "Will do."

"Thanks, man," I say to Carter.

He gives me a hard pat on the back. "Take care of that ankle. I'll check on you later."

We limp across the backyard, a few people shouting their wishes for me to feel better. I wince again when we pass the front of the house. "Hang on. Let me catch my breath."

"It really hurts, huh? Maybe we should get an x-ray."

I vigorously shake my head. "No, not at all. It'll be fine. Probably just need to rest a bit." I take a deep breath and lean on her again. She's so soft. "Okay, I'm ready."

We resume our trek to the cottage.

Beside me, Ashley worries her bottom lip. "I feel so bad about this. It was my smart-ass remark that made you drop to your knees, wasn't it?"

Might as well strap me to a sonic submarine going to hell. "It's okay, Ash. I'll be fine."

Finally, we reach the cottage, and I lick my lips, my body thrumming from the knowledge that we're seconds away from being alone.

Once inside, she whirls on me, her eyes narrowed like a judgmental cat in an internet meme. "Care to explain why you lied about your ankle?"

Well, damn. Guess I'm busted.

Chapter Twenty-Three

Ashley

JULIAN'S NOT KNOWN for playing games, so I'm curious to hear his excuse for faking an injury. I cross my hands over my chest and lean against the cottage door. "Well?"

The fraudster shakes out his hands and legs before he speaks. "How'd you know I was lying?"

"Outside, when we started walking again, you switched the foot you were limping on."

He scratches his jaw. "Yeah. I'm not a good liar, which arguably is commendable."

Oh, jeez. Is he for real? "No, Julian," I say with laughter in my voice, "not *being* a liar is commendable. Whether you're skilled at it is beside the point."

He twists his hands as he paces. It's an unusual demeanor for him, so I'm anxious to hear the reason for this latest ploy.

"Listen," he says, stretching out his neck. "I was planning on telling you as soon as we got inside. You just beat me to it."

"You're still not answering my question. Why the fakery?"

He stops in front of me. "I wanted to speak with you alone, without everyone around…and under circumstances where I could be reasonably certain we wouldn't be interrupted."

Goodness. Such an ominous preamble to whatever statement he needs to make. What could it be? "Should I sit down for this?"

He tilts his head. "Not particularly, no."

"Okay, then what's going on?"

He lifts his shoulders and blows out a slow breath. "I can't stop thinking about you. Every fleeting touch between us, every time we share a joke, every time we talk, every time I'm around you—all of it makes me ridiculously happy, and I refuse to believe there's something wrong with that feeling. I know we agreed it would be a bad idea to be together, but the more I'm around you, the more I'm convinced it's the *only* idea that makes sense." He pauses and rubs two fingers over his mouth before he licks his lips and continues. "Will it complicate my relationship with your brother? I suspect so. Will I need to work doubly hard to ensure it doesn't? Of course. But dammit, Ashley, if you're feeling anything close to what I'm feeling, I'd like to try."

My heart squeezes in my chest as though someone's trying to fit it through a pinhole. Did Julian just confess to wanting me? No, more than that, wanting to *be* with me? I look down at my clenched hands, a few seconds away from pinching myself, and then I return his steady gaze. His brows are knitted, and he's peering at me with such focus he doesn't appear to be blinking.

"Tell me what you're thinking," he urges.

I've spent so much time convincing myself that a relationship with Julian would never happen—and that I didn't want one anyway—I'm unsure how to process the possibility that it could. Our reluctance stems from good and valid reasons, among them the risk that our being together would further complicate his ability to serve as Carter's agent, and for me there was the added worry that I'd be the loser in any fallout. But as Julian pointed out earlier, I'm not in competition with anyone, not Lydia or Carter, and if we're willing to meet the challenges openly and honestly, I'd be a fool not to give us a chance.

I shoot out my hand, grab the front of his T-shirt, and tug him flush against me. When I rise on my toes, our mouths are centimeters apart, the soft puffs of his breath tickling my nose. From here, I can fully appreciate his impossibly long and thick eyelashes. It's a common theme where Julian's concerned—long and thick—and I'm discovering it's my favorite combination. Forget peanut butter and jelly, long and thick is where it's at. "I'm in if you're in."

The heat in his dark gaze intensifies. "I'm not in yet, but it's going to be so fucking good when I am."

I draw back. "Are we talking about the same thing?"

He moves closer and cages me against the door. "I'm talking about being inside you."

Oh God. Julian inside me. I tense everywhere, and a frisson of electricity begins at the nape of my neck, travels over my breasts, and settles on my clit, the tingling making its way down my body like falling dominoes. Desperate for more contact, I sweep my cheek across his five-o'clock shadow. "I like where this conversation is headed." He swallows hard. I tilt my head and press my mouth against his Adam's apple. His sun-kissed skin smells warm and earthy, like a cinnamon stick dipped in brandy, and I'm eager to lick every inch of him.

But that's not going to happen now. Because Julian spins me around, gathers my hair to the side, and runs his strong hands down my back and over my butt. "Your ass looks amazing in these shorts but—"

The sound of crushed gravel warns us that someone's approaching. I spin around and face Julian, who's doing a terrific impression of a deer caught in headlights.

"Hey, Julian, you feelin' better in there?" Tori yells.

Outside the door, Carter asks, "Babe, why are you yelling?"

"Oh, was I yelling?" Tori replies. "I'm a loud woman, what can I say? And you love me, don't you?"

Carter doesn't respond verbally, so I'm guessing he's responding in other ways.

"She's covering for us," I whisper to Julian.

"Yeah, she's probably right that we shouldn't spring this on him now. He should be focused on them."

I nod, grateful—and relieved—that we agree on this. "Quick, get on the couch and put your leg up."

Channeling his inner long jumper, Julian hops three times and leaps on the couch. He places a throw pillow on the coffee table and rests his foot on it while I scurry to the fridge, grab some ice, and throw it in a plastic sandwich bag. Because I'm as devious as Julian, I put a small amount of water in the bag, too, so it appears that some of the ice has melted.

Nice touch, Julian mouths.

Tori enters the cottage with my brother following closely behind her, his hands on her shoulders as he steers her inside. Carter's gaze bounces around the room, taking in the scene, and then he focuses on Julian.

"Hey, man, how you feelin'?"

"Much better," Julian says. "Your sister's an excellent nurse. How'd the rest of the game go?"

"We won," Tori says with a triumphant smile. "Despite Donovan's complaint that he was, and I quote, 'perspiring' too much."

I grin, picturing Donovan wiping his sweaty forehead, a look of disgust on his face.

"I'm glad you're feeling better." Carter collapses onto the armchair across from Julian. "Listen, I'm supposed to collect you and bring you to the house. Poker night with my dad and father-in-law. We're supposed to make ourselves scarce because the women are hanging out here for the evening." He hangs his head. "Tori's not even sleeping with me. They're having a slumber party out here."

Dammit. That's *not* what I'd hoped to be doing this evening. "We are?"

Tori nods. "Yep, that's on the schedule. I know it might sound silly, but I don't want to share a bed with Carter the night before we marry. It's not about"—a tinge of rosiness appears on her cheeks— "sex. It's just…I think it'd be nice for each of us to have an evening alone to reflect on the momentous step we're taking."

It's a lovely sentiment. It truly is. But I can't pretend I wasn't envisioning a different end to the day, one in which I'd be reflecting on Julian's body parts.

Julian and I glance at each other. I'm sure his plans ran along the same lines.

"The ladies are gathering snacks from the fridge," Tori continues. "They'll be here soon."

Julian jumps up from the couch. "All right, let me make a pit stop before we head out." He strides through the living area with no apparent limp.

"Damn, you really are feeling better," Carter says from his chair.

Julian pauses, his back to us, and then he resumes walking, this time more slowly. "Yeah, it must have been a cramp or something."

"I'm…uh…going to grab some stuff for the slumber party. Should be getting dark soon." I rush out of the room and close our bedroom door.

Julian pops his head out of the bathroom. "It's for the best."

My stomach drops at the shuttered expression on his face, and I drop onto the bed. Is he having second thoughts about us? So soon? "What's for the best?"

He comes out with a small towel in his hands and dries off his face as he sits on the bed. "Think about it. Do we really want our first time together to be this quiet affair, us both holding back because other people might hear us? I don't want you to be distracted or reserved." He places a single finger under my chin and slowly turns my head toward him so that I'm forced to meet his gaze. "I want us to be able to shout and cuss and wail if we need to, and I think we will…need to, I mean. Plus, being in the same bed without doing what we both want to do? That'd be torture."

I exhale. He isn't changing his mind. Quite the opposite. But all this talk about having sex is a poor substitute for actual sex, and I'm strung so tight that even sitting here now I can feel the ache between my legs. *Woman, get a hold of yourself.* "Okay, when you put it that way, I'm forced to agree." I flop back and stare at the ceiling. "I'm still grumpy about it, though."

He falls back next to me. "So am I."

"Good. So tomorrow we'll have loud, grumpy sex."

He turns on his side, and I do the same. Then he nudges his face forward, and our lips meet. It's a soft kiss, just a brush of our mouths, but there's so much promise in it that I'm vibrating with the need to have him inside me.

"It's a date," he says.

Screw the date. I want loud, grumpy sex, and that's final.

"WOULD YOU RATHER date a guy with chronic bad breath—that *can't* be corrected—or a guy whose penis is too large for your vagina?"

After reading the card, Kimberly slaps her hand on the couch and snorts. "Eva, where the hell did you get this game from?"

Eva, who's draped over Tori like a lap blanket, waves her glass of champagne. "An online sex store, if memory serves. Aren't they great?"

Clad in pajamas, the women are lounging in the living room, consuming bubbly and inhaling leftovers from this afternoon's picnic. We'll be spending the night here as Tori requested, and I'm already devising a plan to get a spot on the pull-out couch; that king-sized inflatable mattress in the corner looks as comfortable as the floor.

After licking the barbecue sauce off my fingers, I say, "That's an easy one. I'd go with the extra-large dick. Halitosis is a deal breaker. Plus, a guy with a large penis can still make use of his tongue, and there's no rule that says his dick needs to go all the way in. Besides, only twenty-five percent of women regularly orgasm from penetrative sex."

Several beats of silence pass before everyone bursts out in laughter.

"Damn, Ashley," Tori says with tears in her eyes. "You sounded like you were defending your thesis."

Bianca blows out a raspberry, a bored expression on her face. "Does this game have any questions geared toward women who enjoy having more than just dick on the menu?"

Oh. Okay. That's a good point.

Eva flips through the cards and waves one in the air. "Here's one. Would you rather have your parents catch you having sex or catch your parents having sex?"

Bianca throws her long hair forward to cover her face. "Oh God. Pass."

"I caught my parents having sex once," Kimberly offers.

I slap her thigh. "Shut. Up. You did? When?"

"In high school—"

"No, don't share the details. Not with me at least." Obviously, my parents can have all the sex they want, but I don't need to know about it. I jump up and shuffle to the kitchen to grab another beer. After I pop the bottle open, I spin around and watch everyone. It's been a great weekend, and I'm so glad I came. Although pretending to be Julian's girlfriend didn't quite work out in the way we'd planned, I'm not complaining. In fact, this weekend exceeded my expectations. Plus, it got me to this moment. If I had shown up tomorrow as originally planned, I would have missed out on spending time with these fantastic women.

My gaze strays to the left side of the room, where Lydia's work papers are strewn all over the dining table. She chose not to join us, explaining that she's behind on another project that she can't put off any longer. After

Tori told her a professional photographer would be snapping pics at brunch, she ran off to her place to find something to wear and prep her hair, the messy evidence of her major project temporarily forgotten. I feel bad that she needs to work this weekend, but I'll admit to being relieved she isn't around. When we're together, my guard is up, and it's exhausting.

Tori stretches on the couch and rises to her feet. A few seconds later, she joins me in the kitchen. "Hey, I've been meaning to ask you something, and please, please, please don't feel like you have to say yes, because you don't, but Carter and I were talking about tomorrow, and we thought it might be nice if you would sing during the reception, with your guitar as accompaniment."

My stomach roils, and my palms will be slick in seconds, I'm sure. I've never sung or played my guitar for a large audience. That alone gives me the jitters. But making my debut in front of my family? I generally don't bite my nails, but I'm gnawing on them now. Will they think I'm trying to be someone I'm not? Or think I'm ridiculous for fancying myself an entertainer when everyone knows that's Carter's department?

Tori nudges me. "Earth to Ash, you still with me?"

I shake my head and give her a weak smile. "I'm here."

"I can see the idea doesn't appeal to you."

Her voice is soft, no hint of reproach in it whatsoever. But I feel like I'm letting her down somehow. "It's not that I don't want to, Tori. It's just…I didn't plan for this, and I'd be too nervous."

"Sure, sure," she says, waving me off. "No worries at all. Tomorrow's going to be perfect no matter what."

I drop my chin into my chest. "I'm sorry. I guess I'm not as much of a badass as I lead people to believe."

She throws her arm over my shoulder and pulls me in for a smothering hug. "There's more than one way to be a badass, you know. And if you think about it, pushing through your fears to accomplish a goal is pretty badass in and of itself."

Her smile chases away my worry that she's upset with me. I owe her the favor of not rejecting the idea outright. "I'll think about it, okay?"

"Of course. Like I said, no pressure. If the mood strikes you, get up on that stage and sing your pretty little heart out." She tries to stifle a yawn but fails. "Okay, time for us to head to bed. Tomorrow's a big day."

My mind drifts to the vow Julian and I made earlier. In less than twenty-four hours, we'll be having loud, grumpy sex. Tomorrow's a big day, indeed.

Chapter Twenty-Four

Julian

CARTER AND TORI'S wedding day begins with thick, gray clouds overhead, and I easily picture Tori wailing at Mother Nature for bringing them less than perfect weather. I'm pulling up my trousers when Ash stumbles into the bedroom, her pajama top askew and her hair matted on one side. My heart thrums, confirming that she's adorable to me in any state but particularly appealing when she's sleepy and disheveled. She grumbles a terse good-morning on the way to the bathroom, but I catch her wrist and pull her to me for a brief detour.

When she realizes I'm poised to kiss her, she grimaces, shrinks back, and covers her mouth. "No, don't. Morning breath. Beer, barbecue chicken, chips and guac. You don't want any part of this."

I playfully shove her away. "You're right. Thanks for the warning."

Her eyes grow wide, and she grumbles some more. Stepping forward, I cut off her unintelligible remarks by placing my mouth on hers. But I don't take the kiss further. My hands remain behind me, and only a sliver of space separates my naked chest from her torso. I speak against her lips. "Your move." Then I step back and wait.

Her gaze darts to my bare shoulders and returns to my eyes before she snakes her arms through the spaces formed by mine and digs her fingers into the small of my back. "This is an important test of any relationship, you know. A morning breath kiss is a declaration of commitment. Are you ready to take such a big step?"

She's smiling as she speaks, but I'm taking her question very seriously. Yes, I want to be committed to her. In my mind, that's settled. What's still left to be determined is how to navigate this unexpected development so that it doesn't bite me in the ass.

I don't alter my stance. Keeping my hands off her allows me to focus on the kiss and all it's meant to communicate. I dip my head and capture her bottom lip between my teeth, scraping it gently before I suck it into my mouth and release it. Watching her reaction is its own pleasure.

Her pupils flare, and then her lids fall closed. "Yes. More, please."

I spread my legs wider, giving myself room to shift, and then I drop butterfly kisses up her neck to her chin, eventually working my way to her lips and grazing them with the tip of my nose.

"Julian," she whispers.

Her voice, breathy and strained, changes the sound of my name, the longing she injects into it making the word almost unfamiliar to my ears. It's not the cry of arousal that I've heard before, two nights ago most recently. This time she speaks it like a lover, like someone who knows I am hers and doesn't want to wait any longer to have me.

My erection, full and heavy, answers, pressing uncomfortably against the zipper of my pants. That discomfort jolts me out of the moment. We can't do this here and now, despite the clawing need in my gut to fuck her for hours. I rest my forehead against hers as we both slow our labored breaths.

"I promised Carter I'd help him double-check everything outside."

She nods, a look of regret dampening the lustful expression she wore seconds ago. "I told Tori I'd help her get ready." Under her breath, she says, "It's the least I can do."

Am I reading her correctly? Is that *sadness* in her eyes? I pull her close, my lips feather soft on her temple. "Did you have fun last night?" I pull back and tip her chin up when she sighs. "What is it? Did something happen?"

Ash furrows her brows and shakes her head. "No, nothing like that." She pulls out of my arms and sits on the bed. "Tori and Carter asked me to perform for the reception."

I join her on the bed and squeeze her thigh. "That's fantastic, baby. Good thing I brought your guitar." Wagging my brows, I tap my temple. "My forward thinking saves the day."

"I told them no."

I sit on that news a minute. Obviously, it's her decision to make, but I wish she would have said yes. When will she realize her music is her passion? When will she stop pretending that she's satisfied switching jobs every six months and leaving her living situation to chance? I predict she'll be defensive if I ask these questions, so I start with something easy. "Why'd you say no?"

"I'm not a performer, Julian. I've never played my instrument in front of a large audience. Tori and Carter's wedding isn't the place to make my debut."

"Why not? It's mostly family. They'll support you."

"Or they'll think it's laughable that I'd want it for a career."

"It's clear you've thought about it. Do you?"

She pinches the fabric of her pajama pants and shrugs. "I don't know what I want."

I suspect she won't want to hear this, but committing to her means I won't hold back my thoughts, even if I run the risk of pissing her off. "Here's the thing. I think you know what you want, but you're afraid to go after it. I understand. Your brother's a big star, and how the hell could you compete with that, right? And your sister's a single mom raising two kids, and she's kicking ass as a high school coach, and what have you done in comparison, right? If that's not enough, your aunt's a crabby mess who sees everything as a competition and raised her daughter to think the same way. So I get it now. If you don't try for what you want, you won't ever fail." I shrug, pursing my lips into a no-big-deal expression. "There's a certain logic to that, I guess." I raise my index finger in the air. "But here's the wrinkle."

She opens her mouth in mock outrage, suggesting she knows I'm bullshitting. "Can't wait to hear it."

I take her hand and squeeze it. "This isn't about Carter, or Lydia, your aunt Carol, or anyone else. You're *enough* just as you are. So this is really about *you* and what *you* want."

She pouts at me. "I think you're overstating the situation, and your reverse psychology isn't working."

My head is still attached to my neck, so I'll safely assume she doesn't want to bite it off. I'll keep going. "Oh, yeah. How many jobs have you had in the past three years?"

She squints as though she's mentally calculating the answer to my question. "Four."

"And how many apartments have you rented in that time?"

"Four." She points a finger at me. "But this last one wasn't my fault. My roommate and her boyfriend were douches."

"Okay. And what about that one semester in college? What happened there?"

She frowns. "That was a disaster."

"So you left."

She nods, her chest visibly deflating at the same time. "Yeah, I left."

I place my arm around her shoulder and draw her in for a hug. "You have a beautiful voice, and you're a gifted musician. It's okay to be afraid to fail. That just means it's important to you. But *not* trying to do something that's important to you for fear of failing? That's a waste."

Someone bangs on the door, depriving her of the chance to respond. "Hey, you two. We have a wedding to attend, and Ashley, we need to help the bride get ready. Save the sexual gymnastics for later."

Ashley shakes loose of my hold and shout backs. "Getting ready now, Eva."

We both rise. She grabs her toiletries while I slip into my shirt and jacket.

"How do I look?" I ask, holding my hands out to the sides.

She surveys me from head to toe and gives me a soft smile. "Handsome. Now I need to take a shower and get this funk off me."

"You do that. I didn't want to say anything before, but you're smelling a tad ripe."

She sticks out her tongue and dashes into the bathroom. Before she shuts the door, she pokes her head out. "I should clarify. I didn't say no to Tori when she asked me to play. I told her I'd think about it. Thanks for giving me more to think about."

Is it possible to smile with your whole body? Because my grin feels like it's bursting from my chest. "You're welcome, baby."

THE CLOUDS BREAK before ten o'clock, the sun arriving like an honored guest whose appearance is vital to the festivities.

Carter and I stroll around the perimeter of the seven-by-thirty-foot tent and tug on the poles staked in the ground. The setup is simple and designed for easy build and breakdown before and immediately following the wedding and reception. Someone's done this safety check, we're sure, but when it comes to Tori's special day, we're not leaving anything to chance.

"You have the ring?" he asks.

I pat my inner jacket pocket and pretend to be alarmed. "Shit. Where is it? I had it a minute ago."

Carter's eyes go round, and his body sways as though he's going to faint. "Tell me you're joking."

I grasp his shoulders and steady him. "I'm joking, man. I've got you."

He takes a deep breath and releases it through his nose. "Just wait until you're in my shoes. I'll remember this and pull some similar shit, for sure."

A vision of Ashley pops into my head. I'd stagger from the implications of my subconscious if I wasn't standing in front of her brother. "I wouldn't expect anything less of you, my friend."

We give each other a quick hug.

"Hang on. I need a pic of you two together," a voice to our right says.

Carter's grin spreads into a full-blown smile when he sees its owner's face. "Jewel, I can't believe I'm saying this, but it's so great to see you."

His personal assistant cuffs him on the shoulder. "Ha-ha. Careful, Mr. Stone. Or is it Williamson today?"

"It's Williamson for these purposes." He winks at her. "I want my marriage to be legal and all."

Jewel bumps me with her shoulder. "Hey, J-Money."

Christ. I've told her several times I hate that nickname, but she never listens. Another tactic is in order. "What's up, Cubic Zirconia?"

She screws up her face at me. "Did you just try to make a...*joke?* It was a bad one, but still, the effort alone is impressive."

Yeah, even I must admit that was bad. If Ash were here, she'd pat me on the back and give me a sympathetic smile.

"Hello? Julian?"

I shake my head loose of Ashley-related thoughts. "Yeah, what's up?"

She raises the smartphone in her hand and motions for us to stand together. We comply with her directions, and she snaps a pic. Jewel grins at the result as she views it on her phone. "*Awww,* look at you guys. Hashtag besties forever."

Carter shakes his head and hits her with an overly dramatic eye roll.

"Don't be ungrateful, mister. If it weren't for me, you'd have your publicist on your ass."

Carter trembles in mock fear. "Does Dana know?"

Jewel's eyebrows rise an inch. "Are you kidding me? If she knew, she'd be here *with* the paparazzi. Nope. She doesn't know yet, but I think she suspects something's going on. She's been asking lots of questions, and I've been deflecting. Just being your phenomenal personal assistant, as usual."

I laugh. Carter calls her his personal pain in the ass. I've seen them in action enough to know the feeling's mutual. "Is that what he told you PPA stands for?"

Carter elbows me in the side and pulls Jewel away. "C'mon. I'd like you to meet my mother."

I spend several more minutes checking the stability of the stakes in the ground, which is why I'm kneeling when Ashley descends the steps of the back porch, a small bouquet in her hand. If I weren't on my knees already, I'd buckle at the sight. Her light blue dress skims the top of her knees, and its rounded neckline reveals only the slightest swell of her breasts.

She walks carefully along the brick walkway leading to the garden and heads straight to me, her eyes shiny and playful. "Hey, handsome man. Ready to get your best friend hitched?"

Aware we have an audience, I pull her into my arms. There's no artifice in my smile when she nuzzles my neck and breathes in my scent. "I smell good, don't I?"

She laughs. "You always do."

"Weddings tend to bring out the romance in people, right?"

She tilts her head and regards me with a suspicious glint in her eye. "Yeah, I guess. Why do you ask?"

"If we're a couple, shouldn't we be affected by the mood, too?"

Her face clears, and she gives me a lopsided grin. "Ah, I see what you're getting at."

I cradle her face and pull her closer, and her eyes flash with a hunger that mimics my own. The kiss is chaste but tender and manages to be both promising and frustrating at the same damn time. After we slowly drift apart, she leans against me and lets out a happy sigh. Her affection moves me in the most elemental of ways, grafting itself onto my skin and burrowing bone-deep. Whatever happens after this is anyone's guess, but even now she's made a mark on me as permanent as the tattoo at my hip. I raise our clasped hands to my mouth and kiss the back of her hand.

When I look up to survey the backyard, I see Lydia staring at us. Our eyes meet, but she quickly hangs her head and studies her phone.

Then I spot my parents in the last row of chairs under the tent. Given their furrowed brows, there's no mistaking their confusion. Well, Julian, I guess you've got some explaining to do.

"We made it just in time," my mother says. She grasps my shoulders and spins me around. "How are you feeling? Everything good?"

I let her inspect me, knowing this is her way of assuring herself that I'm okay. "I'm great, Mom."

The multiple bracelets on her wrist jangle as she strokes my cheeks. "My sweet boy, you look good."

"So do you." She looks ageless, in fact. Her beautiful brown skin is smooth and unlined, and her short hair is impeccably styled as usual.

She waggles her eyebrows. "You and Ashley look good together, too."

My father grimaces and plonks down onto a rattan chair on the back porch. "When did this happen? In Philly, you said nothing was going on between you two."

"It was LA, Dad, and yeah, I was telling you the truth then."

"So, in that short time you two started dating?" he asks.

I shake my head. "No, listen, it's not what you think." I've always been honest with my parents, and I don't want to start lying to them now. Still, I'd need a set of flowcharts to explain why and how we got to this point. I decide to give them the abridged version. "All right, here's the deal. When we first got here, Ashley and I were pretending to be a couple, for reasons that aren't important. Then something happened, or maybe it's been happening for a while and I'm just now admitting it to myself." I shake my head, trying to sort it out in my own mind. "Whatever, it doesn't matter. We're together now, and I'm happy."

My father massages his chest as he studies me. "Do you think that's wise? What does Carter say?"

"He doesn't know yet. We figured it wouldn't make sense to spring this on him today. But I'm not worried about Carter's reaction. He and I are solid, and my dating his sister isn't going to change that."

Our decision not to tell him isn't motivated by a concern that he'll be upset about it. Nevertheless, he'll wonder how and when it happened, and given my long-standing insistence on separating my personal and work lives, he'll be surprised by my choice to date his sister.

That's a conversation for another time and place, right? And a trace of doubt on my part is to be expected. I press my lips together and shove my hands in my pockets. Am I lying to myself? To my parents?

My mother is still confused. "Wait, wait, wait." She rests two fingers on her temple as she paces. "So let me get this straight. Before you came to Connecticut, you and Ashley worked out a plan to fake your relationship?"

"Right."

"And this entire weekend, you've been *pretending* to date?"

"Yes, but—"

"Excuse me," Lydia says, her face peeking out from behind the door to the back porch.

My heart crashes to the floor and jumps back up into my chest. Fuck, fuck, fuck.

She tiptoes past us. "I didn't mean to interrupt such an important conversation, but I need to get to my seat."

Did she just *wink* at me?

Lydia skips down the steps like Bambi chasing a butterfly. Over her shoulder, she says, "Hope to chat with all of you after the wedding."

"Who the heck is that?" my father asks.

"That's Ashley and Carter's cousin Lydia."

And I've just given her the ammunition to ruin everything.

Chapter Twenty-Five

Ashley

TORI'S EXPRESSION TRANSFORMS from nervous anticipation to pure joy when she sees my brother with the
wedding officiant by his side. The bride's strapless A-line
dress highlights her shoulders and the definition in her
arms, and her curly hair, which she's pinned back with
stunning orchids, frames her glowing face.

Next to her, Pedro is beaming, his smile threatening
to outshine the sun, and only a few people know that Tori
didn't want to be walked down the aisle but agreed to do
so to appease her parents.

Eva and Bianca are standing to Carter's right, while
Julian and I stand to his left. Although the bride and
groom will each have two people by their side when they
marry, Julian is the only male, and his singular presence

likely reminds many of the guests that Carter rarely lets new people in his circle.

I study Julian as Tori glides down the aisle. He's a handsome man, whether he's in a suit and tie or jeans and a T-shirt. But his attire today, the happy medium between business and casual, is Julian at his most tempting. His blue cotton suit accentuates his broad shoulders and trim waist, and his crisp white shirt, open at the collar, treats me to a bite-sized portion of the glorious chest underneath. *Get the hormones in check and focus on the wedding, Ashley.*

I snap my head front and center. When Tori and Carter reunite, they face each other and hold hands. I can't help thinking I'm intruding on a private moment, their loving expressions acknowledging the significance of what they're about to do.

The officiant shares his thoughts on the sanctity of marriage, after which he advises the guests that the couple has decided to recite their own vows.

Carter delivers his first. "When we met on that plane to Aruba, I was pretending in many ways. Pretending that I wasn't a Hollywood actor. Pretending that I didn't have insecurities. Pretending that I didn't need to let anyone else in my life. I was wrong on the first count, and I knew it. But I had more to learn, and thanks to you, I did. You're the one who made me see that unless I faced my doubts head-on, I'd never be able to love you the way you deserved to be loved…"

I glance at Julian and discover he's staring at me, perhaps sending a message of his own. Right. I get it. I'm hiding, too. I draw in a small breath and return my attention to my brother.

He speaks with conviction, his voice wavering only when the depth of his emotions threatens to overwhelm him. Not to be outdone, Tori speaks eloquently about their friendship, their passion, and their trust. A few guests sniffle in their seats. After a subtle nod from the officiant, Eva and Julian produce the weddings rings, and Tori and Carter exchange them.

"With the power vested in me by the State of Connecticut, I now pronounce you husband and wife. You may now seal your union with a kiss."

And do they. Complete with a dramatic dip that leads to dozens of clicks from the photographer's camera. It's the kind of kiss that produces happy sighs from the audience and a boisterous "Well, all right" from Grandpa James.

Before I can talk myself out of it, I slip away from the well-wishers and dash toward the cottage to get my guitar.

"WHERE THE HELL is it?" I mutter to myself as I pull up the comforter. Finding Melanie was easy, but I can't find my guitar pick anywhere. I usually keep several spares, but I left them on my dresser in California, and Julian wouldn't have known to look for them.

Think, Ashley, think. Where was I the last time I played? Last night. In the living room. On the couch. When Tori and Eva performed a stirring rendition of "Single Ladies" and begged for me to "give them a beat."

I rush out of the bedroom and smooth my hand over the sofa cushions. "Shit. Nothing." Maybe someone found it and placed it somewhere else? My gaze bounces around the room and lands on the clutter on the dining room table. I lift a stack of Lydia's papers, but in my haste, a neighboring stack teeters and falls to the ground before I can catch it. "Dammit." I drop to my knees and begin to gather the papers—random sheets of paper that don't appear to have anything to do with marketing—and then I come across a single page in blue with the words *Eligibility for Unemployment Insurance Benefits* in large bold letters at the top. It's dated a week ago.

"What are you doing nosing around in my stuff?" Lydia asks from the door.

I quickly straighten the stack and place it back on the table. "Nothing. I was looking for something and knocked over your papers. Sorry. I wasn't snooping, I promise." Continuing my search for the missing guitar pick, I lift a few documents as I scan the table. There it is. Wedged under the napkin holder. "Aha. Found it."

Lydia squints as she continues to watch me in silence.

I ignore her, grab Melanie, and hurry to the door. "Excuse me."

She's blocking me and doesn't budge. "Before you go, why don't you tell me how things are going with your *boyfriend.*"

Her mouth is curved into a self-satisfied grin, and there's amusement in her voice when she stresses the word *boyfriend.* Whatever. Lydia's the least of my concerns. My biggest concern is holding it together while I perform in front of a live audience. "Lydia, I don't have time for this. In case you haven't noticed, there's a wedding in progress."

She steps to the side. "Oh, of course. Don't let me stop you. But it'll be interesting to hear what people say when they find out you and Julian are only pretending to date. How pathetic is that, Ashley? Honestly."

What the hell? How did she find out? With just hours left to this long-ass weekend, I can't believe Lydia discovered our secret now.

She shakes her head at me as if to say *Well? I'm waiting.*

And here's the thing. I could easily concoct an explanation credible enough to confuse Lydia and leave her guessing as to whether it's true. But I'm so tired of her bullshit, and I'm tired of being anything other than who I am. I set Melanie down. "Okay, Lydia, let me break this down for you in a way you'll understand. You. Win. You're right. Julian and I pretended to be dating this weekend. I can't even remember why I thought it was a good idea, but it had something to do with you. And your mother."

God, it all sounds absurd now. I could tell her that Julian and I turned a corner in our relationship, that we're dating for real. I don't want to stoop to her level, though. "I was silly to think it would make a difference, right? Because you're just as competitive and immature as you've always been. And besides, my value isn't based on the person I'm dating. So go ahead and tell everyone Julian's not my boyfriend. And while you're at it, go ahead and explain to everyone why you've been pretending to be busy with work while you're also mysteriously collecting unemployment benefits."

Her eyes bulge, and her skin pales. "It's not what you think—"

"It doesn't *matter*, Lydia. Your loss isn't my gain. But ask yourself why you've always taken such pleasure in bringing me down. For years, you've used me to gauge how well you're doing, probably because your mother egged you on. But I'm *not* your competition, and if there's anyone you should be angry with about your feelings of inadequacy, it should be her. Leave. Me. Out of it."

I pick up the case and yank it against me, banging my knee in the process. "Shit." I storm out the door. I'm shaking, all the pent-up frustration inside me vibrating outward and hopefully leaving my body for good. With any luck, I'll get back to the reception at an opportune time to gift Tori and Carter with a song. I'll make a bee-line for the dance floor; if I don't, I'll surely talk myself out of performing.

Behind me, Lydia calls out, "Ashley, you wouldn't dare blab about my personal business. I know you."

I pretend not to hear her. Of course I won't tell anyone she's been pretending to be employed this whole time. That's not my way. But I'm tempted. *So* tempted. God, everything she said—about the promotion, the company's need for her help during flag football, and the supposed major project that couldn't get delayed—all of it was a lie. Who *does* that?

A voice in my head answers, its tone annoyingly judgmental. *You do.*

In that moment, I'm forced to face the truth. Lydia has her faults, sure, but so do I. In fact, I've been hiding so well and for so long, I don't know any other way to be. Look how easy it was for me to agree to a fake relationship with Julian. It's enough to make a grown woman want to slap herself.

Well, not anymore.

Chapter Twenty-Six

Julian

SOMEHOW, I SET aside my concerns about Lydia's discovery long enough to focus on Carter. *My best friend is married.*

We give each other a pound. "You did it, man," I tell him.

He shakes his head, a dazed expression on his face. "Yeah, I'm still stunned the lady in 12D agreed to marry me."

Given the tumultuous start to their relationship, I'm stunned, too. In any case, he wears their love well, and I'm glad Tori's the one who broke through his defenses and stole his heart. "Do you need me to make a toast or something? Tori didn't mention anything during her thirty-minute PowerPoint presentation about the wedding schedule."

His shoulders shake with laughter. "Don't let her hear you making smart remarks about her penchant for planning. The toast is up to you, though. She didn't want to pressure you or Eva to make any planned remarks." He leans in and whispers in my ear. "To be honest, we were both focused on the getting-married part. Everything else is gravy."

"All right, then. If the mood strikes me, I'll regale them with tales of your wild teenage years. So much incriminating stuff to share."

"Have you forgotten that those years were modeled after yours?"

I tilt my head at him and blow out a breath. "Good point. I'll just wish you a long marriage and call it a day."

He slaps me on the back and walks me over to the table. "Smart man."

Brunch is a casual affair, a nod to Carter's laid-back personality, with everyone invited to eat at a long rectangular table under a tent several feet away from where the ceremony was held. The waitstaff delivers the family-style spread, and the guests dawdle as they try to decide where to sit.

I survey the grounds, searching for Ashley. I'd like to speak to her about Lydia—forewarned is forearmed—but she's nowhere to be seen. Reluctantly, I sit down, trying to work out a way to protect Ashley from Lydia's barbs. A minute later, I spot Ashley leaving the cottage, and as she travels along the cobblestoned path, her guitar case in hand, Lydia appears at the door, calling out to her. The stony expression on Ash's face suggests they've already exchanged words.

Ashley strides with purpose to the small parquet dance floor, breezing past me with only a glance in my direction, and then she sets her guitar case on the ground. After approaching Tori and Carter's table, she leans over to whisper in Tori's ear. The bright smile that graces the bride's face tells me we're all in for a treat.

With a fond pat to the body of her guitar, Ashley pulls the instrument out of the case and secures the strap around her shoulder. She taps the microphone and draws back when the feedback rings out like a loud gong. "Hey, everyone. So um…for reasons I still don't understand, Carter and Tori asked me to perform a song for their wedding. And…"

She freezes, her eyes blinking furiously.

C'mon, baby, you can do this.

She glances at me, nods ever so slightly, and takes a steadying breath. "Well, you all know Tori by now, and she's not someone you want to say no to." That draws a laugh from the guests. "This is 'I Choose You' by Sara Bareilles."

She strums the guitar with confidence, and a few people in the audience straighten in their seats. When she sings the first verse, she tilts her head to the side and closes her eyes, transporting herself somewhere else. The folksy rasp in her voice fits the song, and the lyrics are custom-made for Tori and Carter. *That's it, Ash. Show them who you are.* Halfway through the song, she opens her eyes and sways her body to the music, her shoulders and chin lifting as though she's throwing off a burden that's been weighing her down. She's no longer entertaining us; rather, she's doing what she's meant to do, and I'll never forget the dazzling smile she gives us after the last note.

As she secures the guitar in its case, the guests clap long and hard, a few of them shouting, "Bravo!" and "Encore!" Tori rushes over to tackle-hug her. When they separate, Carter folds his sister into a tight embrace and plants a soft kiss on her forehead. Less than a minute later, Ash takes the seat next to mine.

I lean over and whisper into her ear. "You were phenomenal, and I'm proud of you, and I can't wait to have loud, grumpy sex with you."

She laughs and shoos me away. "Thank you."

Knowing the threat that looms, I try to give her a heads-up about Lydia. "I need to speak with you about your cousin—"

Sighing heavily, she flicks her gaze upward. "You and me both."

Eva, who's sitting to her left, snags her attention, while everyone else continues to praise her performance as they enjoy the meal. At one point, Grandpa James asks, "Why aren't you out there on your world tour?"

Ashley's eyes crinkle at the corners when she smiles at him. "It's not that simple, PopPop."

"Nothing ever is," he replies.

Ashley's aunt chimes in. "Music is a tough business. For every successful artist, there are thousands struggling to get their foot in the door."

There's always a person in a group who's an expert on everything. For this gathering, it's Carol.

"You'd have to be an outstanding talent to make it, and even then, there's no guarantee," she continues. She places a hand on Lydia's. "Better to be practical like my Lydia here. She chose a career that will sustain her over the long term."

Jesus, the woman sucks the joy out of any situation. I'm renaming her the Happiness Negator.

Ashley's grandmother scoffs at Carol. "Well, I think my granddaughter's an outstanding talent, and if she wants to be a megastar, no one's going to stop her."

I chance a glance at Lydia and register her clenched jaw. This conversation must be grating to her for at least two reasons. One, she's not the center of it, and two, Ashley is. She scoots back in her chair and relaxes into it as though she's getting ready to add to the discussion. Given that she's wearing a smug grin, I can predict what her contribution will be. If my cloth napkin were longer, I'd reach across this table and use it to wipe that expression off her face. She's licking her lips, her eyes flickering with amusement as she stares at Ashley. Then she leans forward on the tips of her fingers, as if she preparing to pounce on her—physically, mentally, or maybe both.

I can't let Lydia hurt Ashley, especially not here, in front of her friends and family—and not when she's riding the high of her performance. But how do I neutralize Lydia? There's not much I can say or do that will offset what we did or make her exposure less embarrassing for Ashley.

Lydia chuckles. "Hey, Ashley. A little birdie told me something interesting."

Ashley, who's been happily chomping on a piece of bread, raises her head and purses her lips at Lydia.

"Shit," I mutter under my breath.

Ash hears my distress, and her face ices over. She drops the roll onto her plate. "You *wouldn't*, Lydia."

Yes, she would, because she knows that unlike her, Ashley would never stoop so low. Although the truth is my best option, it isn't ideal since we agreed we wouldn't tell Carter until he and Tori returned from their honeymoon. Plus, there's no time to get Ashley's okay. But I'm willing to take a hit—from Ashley *or* Carter—if it comes to that. After grabbing my water goblet, I jump out of my chair and tap a fork against the rim of the glass. "If I could have your attention for a moment, everyone."

Carter chuckles. "Want to wait until the champagne's served?"

I gulp and stretch the collar of my shirt, realizing belatedly that I'm not wearing a tie that needs loosening. My difficulty in breathing is no wardrobe malfunction; it's wholly man-made. "Not really, no. I'd like everyone to be sober for this toast."

Grandpa James chortles. "A sober toast is a boring toast, young man."

Ashley's mother chucks a roll at him, which he deftly catches.

After the laughter dies down, I begin. "Most of you know I met Carter when I came to Weston. I was a sullen kid, upset that my parents had shipped me hundreds of miles from home." I study the group and focus on my parents. "I didn't realize it then, but they were only looking out for me, trying to help me secure a better future. I get that now. Back then, though, I resented my situation. And I didn't like my teachers, or anyone else connected to the school, until I met this loud, brash woman who took me into her home and fed me chocolate chip cookies—store bought, I later learned. Still, Ms. Susan, as I called her then, wouldn't let me sulk, and eventually she coaxed me out of my shell."

Susan smiles at me, leans over to Randall, and rests her head on his shoulder.

"Now, I also learned that Susan was part of a package deal. Her husband, Randall, and her kids, Kimberly, Carter, and Ashley, were also part of my new family away from home. And Carter followed me around like a puppy. I think he was impressed with my CD collection, and maybe he was looking for an older brother or something, but somehow we clicked. And we talked. A lot. Most of you know Carter well, so that should come as no surprise. I was never much of a talker, but with Carter, I started talking as much as he did just to shut him up."

"It didn't work," Carter shouts.

I nod. "And I'm glad it didn't. Because it opened me to something I'd never experienced before. Love between friends. He's the guy who's watched me grow into a man, and I've watched him grow into a star and so much more. But at his core, he's my best friend Carter, and I want him to be happy and fulfilled."

Carter takes a long sip of his water, his eyes sober.

"With Tori, he's just that: happy and fulfilled. I'm confident that if Carter couldn't act another day of his life, with Tori by his side, he'd be okay. Still happy. Still fulfilled. Because they center each other, hold each other up when one of them falters. A perfectly imperfect love that we should all aspire to."

I bow in Tori's direction. "So thank you, Tori, for coming into his life and for getting him in shape in more ways than one. I wish you both a lifetime of peace, love, and Netflix binges."

Susan and Randall thread their fingers together and share a sentimental look. Tori dabs her eyes with a kerchief and mouths *thank you*.

She might not have as much gratitude when she hears what I have to say next, though. Because everyone knows you're never supposed to steal the bride's spotlight. Still, I can't let Lydia embarrass Ashley in front of her friends, family, and in a few cases, people she hardly knows. "Now, Carter and Tori, I need to say something else, and I hope you'll indulge me on this one." I turn to the couple, my pleading eyes imploring them to understand the necessity of what I'm about to say. "I have a confession to make. For reasons I won't get into so as not to embarrass anyone here, I asked Carter's sister Ashley to pretend to be my girlfriend this weekend."

The clink of the utensils ceases, and a low hum of whispered conversations begins. My gaze darts to Ash, whose fork hovers near her chin. Her eyes are huge.

"And she agreed, because she's kind and giving. And unlike me, she's always up for a little fun. But something changed in the last few days. What started as a ruse became real. For me, at least. The more time I spend with her, the more I realize what I should have known before. She's the one for me."

Now Ashley sets her fork down and watches me with soft eyes.

"I just wanted to clear my conscience…not sure why exactly. Maybe it's because weddings bring out the romantic in me and I'm here with friends and family." Standing in the center of the dance floor with a microphone and my heart in my hands, I'm more vulnerable than I've ever been, but my discomfort is irrelevant if it means Ashley won't suffer.

"And I want Ashley to know when I kiss her it's not because I'm playing a role. It's because I *want* to."

A few *awwws* make their way through the tent.

Grandpa James hollers. "Son, that's the kind of move I would have made in my youth. Well done." He motions for a server. "Can we get the champagne now?"

Carter and Tori rise from their chairs. Hand in hand, they walk over to me.

The bride pulls me in for a long embrace. "Thank you, Julian. That meant the world to me."

"It was heartfelt."

She pulls back and surveys my face with her head tilted in contemplation. "All of it?"

Carter steps to my side and claps me on the back before I can answer her. "You didn't have to, but that was a perfect speech man." He clears his throat. "About Ashley—"

One more lie to top off a weekend of deceit. "It's not what you think. I can't explain now, but Lydia found out what was up. I had to do something to protect Ashley. Lydia was circling like a shark in blood-infested waters."

He pulls his head back, nodding slowly in understanding. "Ah. Got it. I can't keep up."

"Nor do you have to. Everything's under control. Enjoy your wedding, man."

He tugs Tori to him and assumes a tango stance. "Ready for our first dance, wife?"

Tori laughs and pushes him away. "Not like that, no." Then she shimmies backward, beckoning him with a crook of her index finger. They sway together in the middle of the dance floor without having made any announcement that they would be dancing as a married couple for the first time. They're doing what feels right in the moment, and I love that Tori isn't wasting her wedding day worrying about checklists.

My gaze lands on Lydia and Carol, who are talking to each other in hushed tones. Lydia's face is flushed, and when she's not talking, she's glowering at her mother. For once, her ire appears to be aimed at the correct person.

My body relaxes now that I've neutralized any pettiness Lydia planned to direct Ashley's way. But a different kind of tension surfaces when I see Ashley and her long legs striding toward me. She's wearing a flirty smile, and her eyes are flickering with interest. And all I want to do is push her against the nearest wall and kiss her so well she forgets her name, address, *and* social security number.

Before she reaches me, though, Grandpa James cuts her off and, with the help of his cane, bows like he's her subject. She curtsies and links her arm with his as they walk onto the dance floor. Cockblocked by PopPop. I can live with that—for now.

What I can no longer live with is my dry throat, however, so I stroll to the edge of the tent in search of a drink. Not surprisingly, my mother corners me as I'm lifting a ladle out of the punch bowl.

"That was quite a speech," she says. "And the truth, right?"

"Yes, *that* was the truth." I point at the bowl. "Want some?"

She takes a cup and holds it out. "Sure."

After serving her, I pour some for myself, and we drift to the side of the table, our gazes settling on the dance floor, where my father dances with Carter's mother.

"You both look good," I say. "Everything okay?"

My mother takes a sip of her drink before she answers. "We're both fine. Physically strong and still in love. Will you be coming home anytime soon?"

I turn to face her. "Not for a while, unfortunately." With my cup, I gesture at the activity in front of us. "I took off time to be here, and I'm going to be paying it back in blood, sweat, and tears when I get back. I'll be home for Thanksgiving, of course."

She clasps my hand and kisses my cheek. "Be sure you do that." Her mouth curves into a smile as Ashley approaches. "In the meantime, enjoy this beautiful day. *This* is what life is all about."

I couldn't agree with her more.

Chapter Twenty-Seven

Ashley

Now that I've filled Grandpa James's dance card, I return to my new mission: Operation Seduce Julian. When I reach my target, I take his hand. "You *want* to kiss me, huh?"

He drops his gaze to my lips, his eyes flickering with undisguised interest and palpable heat. "Kissing is only one of many, many things I'd like to do with you."

"Kisses, caresses, and orgasms, oh my."

"Exactly." With a lazy smile that matches my own, he threads his fingers through mine and pulls me close, folding me into his strong embrace. Prince's "Nothing Compares 2 U" plays through the floor speakers found at each corner of the tent, and I melt against Julian's body, letting him control the way we move to the music. I brush my cheek against his hair-roughened jaw, which leads my brain to imagine other kinds of friction I'd like to generate with him.

"Lydia found out," I whisper.

"Yeah."

"And you swooped in to protect my honor. You didn't have to, but since you did, remind me to thank you later."

He draws back, affection in his gaze. "Will do."

We're inseparable throughout the reception, even feeding each other a piece of the wedding cake. Yes, we're *that* couple, and if I weren't one half of it, I'd gag at the cuteness of it all.

After two hours of celebrating, Carter and Tori try to make their escape, but after saying good-bye to Julian's parents, Julian and I ambush the bride and groom at the cottage. Carter's on the phone in the common room, so Julian veers in that direction while I head to their bedroom in search of my new sister-in-law. The sooner everyone's gone, the sooner Julian and I will be alone.

"Hey, lady," I say as I walk through the door. "Can we do anything to help?"

Tori sticks her head out of the bathroom. "I'm going to change. Can you make sure I didn't leave anything on the floor or in a corner? My mother's going to send the rest of my stuff to LA."

"Sure." I drop to my knees and peer under the bed, not finding any missed items. Then I scan the room and spot a row of condoms on the nightstand. I raise them in the air. "Will you need these?"

She pokes her head out again and pouts. "Unfortunately, yes. I'm not taking well to my latest birth control prescription. They'll have to do until I can visit my doctor."

I give her a dubious look, pointing at the four packets. "Is this enough?"

"Hell no," she says on a laugh. "The industrial-sized package is already in my suitcase." After slipping on her dress, she emerges with a sly smile. "But you should take those. I have a feeling you'll need them."

I lift an eyebrow and give her a playful grin in return. "I have a feeling you're right."

Eva barrels through the door, huffing as though she's just sprinted in a hundred-meter race. "Oh, good, you're still here." She leans against the wall and catches her breath. "Hang on. I have something for you."

She rushes back out, and Tori and I shrug at each other.

When she returns, she's holding a small package. "Close the door."

Tori shakes her head. "The words *Eva* and *close the door* worry me."

Eva jumps on the bed and throws her head back in mock frustration. "Just do as I say, woman. For once."

I close the door, and Tori hops on the bed. Deciding this is too weird a conversation for me to fully invest in without knowing more, I approach them warily and sit on the edge.

Eva places a hand on my thigh. "Pretend he's not your brother. It'll help." Then she leans forward and removes a few items from the box, placing them down gently as though they're precious artifacts. She lifts a piece of fabric first. "Panties that'll drive him wild."

Tori raises a brow and looks at her askance. "That's butt floss."

"No, they're crotchless panties." She sticks her finger in the hole. "Easy access."

Tori snorts. "You mean an embarrassing accident waiting to happen. Next."

Eva holds up a small pink bottle. "Strawberry-scented massage oil. Creates a warming sensation. Safe for his dick."

Tori grabs it. "I'm pretty sure he'd object to any heat-producing elements near his junk, but I could make use of this elsewhere. What else?"

Oh. My. God. I know what that is.

She dangles a butt plug in the air. But it's not any ol' butt plug. It has a rainbow tail.

"I'll never think of *My Little Pony* in the same way again," I observe.

Tori puts a hand in front of her and closes her eyes. "No. Look, I'm not judging anyone's kinks, but we're not introducing unicorns into our sex life."

Eva pouts. "Okay, fine. But this you're going to love." She turns around and pulls out another item from the box, which as far as I can tell looks like a telephone headset. "An oral sex light." She reads the package: "Don't go down without it." Then she acts out "4 U Both" like she's Prince in his "I Would Die 4 U" video.

Tori and I blink at each other and fall over in laughter.

"Yes," Tori says as she wipes her eyes, "because I want to look like a miner as I go down on him."

"Heigh-ho, heigh-ho, it's off to suck I go," I say in a singsong voice.

Eva cackles. "It's official, Ashley. You're one of us now."

Carter knocks on the door, and we scramble to stuff the sexcapade items in the suitcase.

When Tori opens the door, Eva and I are sitting demurely on the bed, our hands folded on our laps.

Carter peeks in. "I don't even want to know." Then he looks at his wife. "We need to leave soon."

"I'll be out in a minute. I just have to get some plugs."

Eva barks out a laugh, and I throw up my hand to cover my mouth.

"For my *ears*," Tori explains. "Ear plugs for the plane."

He looks at her skeptically and says, "Riiiiiight."

When he leaves, we fall on the bed again, snickering and tearing up at the ridiculousness of it all until Lydia knocks on the door and sticks her head inside. Oof. She's the last person I want to see, but I'm going to do my best to be mature about it.

We all straighten and stare at her.

"Hey," she says with a weak wave. "We're heading out, so I just wanted to say bye."

As I take in her guarded expression, I'm struck by how small she seems. For years, I thought of her as this larger-than-life person who'd been responsible for my adolescent torment. But she's just Lydia. And I understand now that she treated me like shit to mask her own insecurities. It doesn't excuse her behavior, though. I mean, I've never met a single person who isn't insecure about *something*, and not all of us lash out at others to compensate for it. No, Lydia needs to own up to her mistakes, and I don't imagine she'll be doing that anytime soon.

"Bye, Lydia. I guess I'll see you at the next family gathering."

She nods. "Yeah."

"Thanks for coming," Tori says diplomatically.

Lydia gives her a stiff smile and shuffles out the door.

When she's gone, Tori rises from the bed and claps her hands. "Okay, I've got to go. Aruba awaits."

Before she zips up her suitcase, I reach in and grab the butt plug. "If you're not going to use this—"

But she snatches it away and tosses it on top of her clothes. "No. It's mine. Get your own."

Eva and I fall over each other in a heap, guffawing until Tori scrambles inside the bathroom and slams the door shut.

Well, then.

Ten minutes later, after saying good-bye to everyone, I return to the bedroom I've been sharing with Julian, the short stack of condoms tucked away in my clutch like a tantalizing promise of what's to come.

He looks up from his phone. "Everyone gone?"

I give him a suggestive wink. "They are. When are you due to head back?"

"My flight leaves at five. You?"

"Heading out in the morning." I pout at him. "If you leave tonight, I'll be all by myself here." Shrugging as if it's no big deal, I cross the room, reach into my suitcase, and pull out a black lace bra and panty set. He watches me inspect the undergarments, and I pretend not to notice. "I guess I could go back to the house and hang out with my parents."

He drops his phone on the bed and strides toward me, a wicked gleam in his eyes. "No need. I'll be missing my flight."

Excellent. *Batter, batter, batter, schwing.*

Chapter Twenty-Eight

Julian

NEVER ONE TO mince words, Ashley rises on her toes and places her mouth near my ear. "Remember when you had your fingers inside me?"

The question sends a signal from my brain to my dick: *Your fantasy is now reality. Time to engage.* I want her so badly I can practically taste her on my tongue. She'd be sweet, tangy, and fucking delicious. With my throat dry as sandpaper, I choke out a scratchy response. "Yes."

Her hand squeezes my cock through my slacks. "Can you imagine this there instead?"

Oh, I can imagine it all right. I've envisioned it a thousand times in my dreams. But for some wretched, unfathomable reason, I'm hesitating. I groan in frustration. "Are you at all worried that this could blow up in our faces?"

She laughs against my ear. "Nope. We won't need our faces for what I have in mind."

Her unconcern helps to push away my doubts. *Be more like Ashley. Live in the moment.* So I splay my fingers against her jaw and pull her in for a kiss. "Speak for yourself. I very much expect you to sit on my face multiple times."

She moans and her eyes flutter closed as she presses into me. "I've always liked the way your brain works."

Our lips connect, and said brain goes fuzzy for a moment. I'm fully familiar with suppressing my desire for Ashley, but now that we've given ourselves permission to simply enjoy each other, I'm *still* struggling to let go.

The sweetness of the wedding cake lingers on her tongue, and I should be eager to savor the taste—but I'm not.

Ashley pulls back and peers at me. "What's wrong?"

"I'm not sure."

She pats my shoulder. "Ah, performance anxiety?" She nods at me gravely. "Understandable. I have high standards."

I collapse against the closet door and massage the back of my neck. "Funny. Also, not helping."

She spins around and takes stock of her surroundings while I try and fail to get out of my head.

She regards me with those doe eyes, her lips plump from our kiss. "I think you need visual stimulation. I do, too." She stalks toward me and tugs on my slacks, unbuttoning them and pulling down the zipper, her face raised to watch my reaction. "There, that's much better." Her hands slip inside my pants and roam over my hips, her fingers brushing against my underwear. "Boxer briefs. Called it."

I'm not sure how she can remain this calm when her touch alone makes me tremble. It's fire and heat and the promise of much more. If I fuck this up, I'll never forgive myself.

She steps back, claps her hands, and toes off her sandals. "Okay, we'll focus on my needs later. Let's get you relaxed first."

Moving with more grace than I ever expected from her, she climbs on top of the bed and rises to her feet, standing in the center with her arms at her sides.

She lifts the skirt of her dress to her waist, revealing a scrap of material that's probably marketed as panties but does nothing more than cover her pussy. I'm glad she unbuttoned my slacks because my dick hardens at the sight of all that supple skin.

With a wink at me, she lets the skirt drop down. "How are we doing so far?"

I press a hand to my dick. "It's working. Why'd you stop?"

Is that me sounding like a petulant child? What is this woman doing to me?

"Tsk, tsk," she says. "Be patient and you will be rewarded."

I like the sound of that. And I like how Ashley is taking control, comfortable in her own skin and sweetly seductive now that she knows how she affects me. But I'd like to get to the even better stuff soon. "Be quick about it and you'll be coming so hard you'll see the entire Milky Way."

She bends, crosses her arms in front of her, and whisks off her dress in seconds.

My gaze roams over every dip and curve of her body, caressing her with my eyes as I imagine doing with my hands and mouth. God, she's going to bring me to my knees.

"Say something," she says, her voice no longer as assertive as it was moments ago.

"I don't think I can," I say honestly. "Give me a minute."

This is surreal. I've spent most of my adult years shoring up the gates that would lead to this, but we've thrown them open, and I don't know where to begin. So many mind-blowing possibilities.

Her hands fly up over the cups of her lace-covered bra, and she steps forward. "Maybe we should forget this."

"Don't move, Ash."

She freezes.

"I'm savoring, not hesitating." I slide my hand across my stomach and down the front of my pants. "There's a *big* difference."

Her knees wobble, and she takes in a deep breath.

"Do you enjoy following instructions, Ash?"

She juts out her chest and raises her chin. "Depends." There's the confidence again.

"On what?"

"The person giving them and the potential payoff."

"I guess we'll just have to see how this goes, then." I lick my lips and rub my hands together. "Let's start with something simple so we can ease you into this, and if there's anything you don't want to do, tell me, okay? I only want what you want."

She nods. "Okay."

I push off the closet door and run a hand over my abs. "Show me those gorgeous tits."

Chapter Twenty-Nine

Ashley

I'M GOING TO spontaneously combust. With his directive echoing in the room, my body betrays me, and I go weak-kneed. In this instance, doing what he asks gives me pleasure, so I eagerly reach up and unclasp my bra, massaging my breasts out of their cups to show him how much I enjoy following his commands.

Julian's dark eyes flash with want, and his lips part. "Arch your back. Present them to me, and don't be shy."

I straighten and thrust my chest forward. I want him to devour me, want to be tangled with him in this bed, overwhelmed by his heat and the strength of his touch. Every second before the moment he enters me registers as a form of exquisite torture, and I can't help rubbing my thighs together to take the edge off.

"Are you wet?" he asks.

His voice is low and sure, a turn-on in and of itself. And he doesn't wait for me to respond. "Of course you are. I bet if I touched you there you'd soak my fingers."

His words force a low moan from me.

"Now, remove your panties, baby."

My hands are at my waist without delay, and I'm sliding the sides of my thong down my hips, but I meet a bit of resistance, and they don't come off easily.

His eyes narrow, and his gaze centers on the space between my legs. "Fuck. You're so wet your panties are sticking to your pussy." His eyes are squeezed shut when he speaks again. "Lord, I'm a lucky, lucky man."

With my underwear finally pooled at my feet, I step out of them and toe them off the bed.

He walks slowly toward me, and I can no longer stand still. I inch my way to the edge of the mattress, waiting for him to join me. He raises his big hands and palms my breasts, massaging them until my body feels feverish from his ministrations. I fall to my knees, wanting his mouth on me. With a look of reverence on his face, he closes his lips over one breast, his teeth grazing my nipple, and I shudder from the exquisite pleasure.

"Stand up and turn around," he whispers.

When I do, he gives me further instructions. "Bend over."

Oh. The thought of bending over for him and exposing myself at his eye level turns me on as much as actually doing it.

"Can I touch you?" he asks, his voice raw and tight.

"Yes," I moan.

Then he slides a finger along my folds, and I cry out, desperate to have him inside me. "Julian, please. Hurry."

"Lie down on the bed, Ash."

I drop to my hands and knees and slowly lower myself on the bed. Behind me, I hear the rustle of his pants. Dispensing with the need for a command, I roll over and sit up on my elbows.

I'm truly unprepared for him. Standing with his feet hip-width apart, he steals my breath away. His chest and shoulders have been on my watch list for years, but Julian's naked form in its entirety is a sight to behold. Beautiful brown skin and strong thighs. His cock, long and thick, stands at attention as though it's waiting for orders from its captain. A small tattoo of an anchor covers the area where his left hip and thigh meet.

I spread my legs wide and raise my knees, beckoning him with my body's position.

He takes his cock in his hand and strokes it, readying himself for me. "Condoms," he chokes out. "Before we go any further, tell me you have one, because I know I don't."

I bite on my bottom lip suggestively before answering. "More than one."

His gaze is feverish as he surveys the room. "Where?"

"In my clutch."

He stalks to the dresser, opens my clutch, and pulls out the strip. "Do you want to put it on?"

I scramble to a kneeling position. "Please."

He inches forward and hands me the condoms. I break off and rip open a packet, pull out the protection, and stroke him before rolling the condom on.

He hisses and grabs at the air for purchase.

I scoot forward and offer him my body for support. "Shhh, I've got you."

His hands curl around my shoulders, and his hips jerk in response to my touch. Then, using both hands, I slide the protection over his cock, inch by delicious inch. Satisfied with my work, I fall back against the mattress, returning to my original position. With one hand on his erection, he climbs onto the bed and fits his body against me.

His weight presses me into the mattress, the heat generated between our joined bodies finally matching the warmth between my legs.

The air is heavy, thick from the humidity outside and the smell of our arousal in here. It surrounds us like a bubble, making me incapable of thinking beyond what's happening in this room. When he kisses me deeply, it's both too much and not enough. I want him inside me, and my stomach clenches in anticipation—and frustration.

His soft lips graze my ear. "Are you ready for me, baby?"

"Yes, Julian, yes."

He slides the tip of his cock against my entrance and waits. "You can't begin to imagine how much I want this, Ash. I'm burning up at the thought of being inside you. Is this what you want?"

"Please. Give me everything you have. I want it all."

He groans and nips at my neck. Then he centers himself and presses forward. As he works his way in, I thrust my pelvis up and rock into him. When he's filled me to the hilt, we both let out a long, ragged *fuuuuck*.

"Damn," he says on a long groan. "You're tight. And wet. And you feel so good I could stay here forever."

He raises his torso off the bed and rests his forearms on the mattress, never ceasing to grind against me.

I undulate my hips in a circular motion, meeting his thrusts each time. "Julian, yes, that's..." I'm not sure I have enough brain cells to finish my thought. My body is a live wire, an unending circuit of sensations cycling through me.

"Yeah, baby, I feel it, too," he says, his voice gentle with awe.

I reach around and grab his ass for leverage, pulling him closer each time he plunges inside. His gaze is unfocused, and then he squeezes his eyes shut and increases his rhythm.

He's controlling his movements, going slow for my benefit, but that's not what either of us needs. "You want to pound into me, don't you?"

His pupils flare before he centers his gaze on mine. "I won't last if I do."

"We have all night. I'm fully expecting a round two."

Without a word, he pushes himself up, and I settle my legs over his shoulders. The shift causes him to sink farther into me, and we both moan at the fullness from this new angle.

"Fuck me, Julian. Don't hold back."

He moves tentatively, testing his balance, and once he finds the right position, he pulls out and plunges back in.

"Oh God," I shout. "Again, please. Don't stop, don't stop, don't stop."

He sets a torturous rhythm, and I answer it each time, tightening around his cock and spurring him on. Meanwhile, my hands are everywhere, reveling in the smoothness of his skin and the hardness of the muscles underneath. I'm trying to hold onto something real so I don't float away. Within minutes, my body is flushed and trembling and the tingle between my legs intensifies. "Julian, I'm close. *So* close."

"Let go, baby. I'll be there with you."

He thrusts and thrusts and thrusts, his pace unrelenting. I chase after the orgasm, searching for the explosion of sensation that remains *just* out of reach. Then he circles his hips, a tiny swivel with a massive impact. With that one move, the tingling in my body gathers in my center and rushes out, a wave of heat washing over me. "Julian, I'm coming."

He doesn't stop, and soon he's shaking, too, roaring as he finds his own release and eventually collapses against me.

I'm spent and breathless, achy and warm. My hands roam over his back and shoulders as he catches his breath. Then he pulls back and peers at me, his eyes still flashing with desire. "Round two might break me, but I'm up for the challenge."

Round two.

What the…?

Now?

Oh God.

Chapter Thirty

Julian

I HAVE ENOUGH morning wood to populate a forest.

Not a surprise with Ashley's ass snuggled up against me. For a minute, I do nothing but take in the feeling of waking up next to her. I can't see her face, but if she enjoyed last night as much as I did, her lips should be curved into a satisfied smile even in sleep.

I'm not going to start something I can't finish, though, so I slip out of bed and dip into the restroom. A few minutes later, I return to the bedroom and find Ashley stretching on the bed.

Perfect timing.

She gives me that satisfied smile I was hoping for, and then she stretches her mouth wide and yawns. "What time is it?"

I pick up my phone from the nightstand. "Just after nine."

She bolts upright and slaps her hands against her cheeks. "Shit, shit, shit."

"What is it?"

She rolls out of the bed with a sigh, and I take a moment to appreciate the roundness of her firm ass.

Still naked, she flits around the room gathering stuff. "I need to be at the airport in an hour. Can you take Melanie back with you?"

"Of course."

She pouts at me. "I'll be gone a few days. And now there's not enough time to enjoy the afterglow."

"Is that what we're doing?"

She studies me warily. "Regrets so soon?"

How can I regret the best sex of my life with a woman I care about? "Hell to the no. Zero regrets."

She grins from ear to ear and steps into my embrace. "Good. Then we'll spend a few days apart and unload on each other when I get back. The good kind of unloading, I mean."

I waggle my eyebrows at her. "That'll be a lot of unloading."

She draws back and lifts a finger in warning. "So long as it's not unloaded in my hair, we're good."

I bark out a laugh. "No worries. My aim is impeccable. I'm talking sniper-level accuracy."

She pushes me away. "You're such a boy."

I take her hand and help her stroke my dick. "This is all man, baby."

Her lids grow heavy. "Yes, yes, it is, but we don't have time."

Dammit. Not what I want to hear. "A quickie?"

She jumps up and wraps her legs around my waist so quickly I scramble to grab her.

But a knock on the cottage door causes me to lose my grip, and she falls to the floor.

"Oh shit, Ash," I say as I pull her up.

She snorts and rubs her ass with one hand while placing a finger over her mouth to shush me. "That could be my dad."

I grab my sweats off the armchair and put them on at turbo speed. "You answer it. I'll get dressed and rustle up the sheets in the other room."

Taking my T-shirt with me, I sprint to the room Eva stayed in. I've got my head through the collar when I hear Susan talking to Ashley in the common room. "You asked me to be sure you were up. And now I see that you are. Did you have a good time last night?"

Ashley groans. "Don't do this, Mom. I can't with you."

I can imagine Susan's facial expression. To say she's no prude would be an understatement.

Susan laughs. "All right, all right. Just be glad it's not your father. He thinks Julian left last night and wondered why you wanted to sleep here alone."

"Bless you for covering for me."

"Oh, I didn't cover for you. I simply pretended not to hear him when he made that assumption. It's a handy tactic when you're married."

"I'm grateful."

"Well, I'll leave you to get ready." There's some shuffling, and then, "Julian, you might want to head out with Ashley. Just a suggestion. I'll say my good-byes now."

I poke my head out, but I don't look her in the eyes. "Take care. Thanks for your hospitality."

"Oh, dear," she says before she walks out the door. I can hear her cackling outside as she treks back to the house.

I venture into the common room, and Ashley shakes her head at me. "Thanks for your hospitality?"

I shrug. "The pressure got to me, okay?"

"But you thrive under pressure. You've said so many times."

"*Work* pressure, sure. But I crumble under I-just-boned-your-daughter-and-now-I-have-to-talk-to-you pressure."

"So long as the boning-the-daughter part is on point, I couldn't care less about anything else."

"Happy to give you a demonstration to alleviate any fears you may have."

She shakes her head and looks at her watch. "No time. I need to run to the house to say good-bye to everyone. But I'll take a rain check."

I palm her ass and pull her to me. "Fitting. Because when you get back from your trip, you're going to be drenched."

She smirks at me. "Promises, promises."

"Facts and more facts," I counter.

Now all I need to do is get through the next few nights without her. Should be easy enough, right?

WHAT SHOULD HAVE been simple turns out to be more difficult than I could have imagined. A mountain of work awaits me when I return to LA—scripts I need to review, contracts I need to negotiate, and asses I need to kick. Barry Sanderson, the eccentric director who's been making noises about wanting to work with Carter, calls and tells me to expect a hand-delivered script soon. But thoughts of Ashley permeate the frenzy, and coming home to an empty unit no longer calms me. Instead, I'm restless in her absence.

The first night, I strum on her guitar even though I've never touched the instrument in my life. The second night, I text her just to say hello, and when she doesn't respond, I imagine a thousand scenarios to explain why. When she finally gets back to me, I read her response wearing a goofy grin. The third night, I contemplate sleeping in her bed but eventually conclude I'm being creepy as fuck.

The night she's due back, I celebrate signing Gabriel Vega by meeting him for dinner. It's a welcome diversion from thinking about Ashley throughout the day. I need to get a grip where she's concerned, and my brain is slow to cooperate. It's not a state I'm familiar with. Being overworked has been my drug of choice for years, leaving me no time to think about my nonexistent love life. Enter Ashley, and I have no idea what I'm doing.

Gabriel and I are seated in a booth at Starlight, a small corner café with walls covered in framed photos of Hollywood stars.

Gabriel cranes his neck as he surveys the scene.

"Hoping to spot someone famous?" I ask him.

He straightens and faces me. "Sorry. Was I that obvious? It's just…I have an agent, man. I'm excited."

"You should be. But let's be clear, you have an agency backing you now. Not one person, okay? That's why I wanted you to meet the team, so you could go to them if you need help."

"Right. You made that clear. But you'll be my point person?"

"Yes, I'll be your person on the ground, so to speak. I'll hustle for you, talk you up, help you navigate the bullshit. It's a partnership, okay? If you ever feel I'm not doing enough for you, tell me. I might not agree with you, but I'm mature enough to recognize I'll get it wrong sometimes."

"Well, I'm glad you brought me in. We're going to do great things together. I can feel it."

Taking in his fresh face and bright smile, I can't help remembering Carter's early enthusiasm. The business chips away at that eagerness over time, but when an actor's first starting out, it's a jolt of energy that fires me up, too. My job is to channel it so Gabriel can get good work and—importantly for us both—so he can get paid. This is where I excel.

After the server takes our order, I lean forward. "Let's talk about your game plan."

We discuss his roles to date, and I suggest a few changes to his résumé. "My biggest concern for you is that it's clear from your roles so far that you're being typecast." I recall the tense conversation I had with Quinn a few weeks ago. My gut tells me the best approach would be to address the matter head-on and say outright—in black and white—that Gabe isn't interested in stereotypical roles. Quinn would murder me, though, so I settle on a temporary work-around until I know more about how he'll be received. "I'm going to focus on getting your name out to casting directors who've done right by other minority actors. As for casting calls, we'll go over those together and be sure you're on board with the role before I do any networking."

As I talk, Gabe's smile wanes. He leans forward, his gaze and elbows on the table. "And what happens if the roles are too few and far between? What do we do then?"

"Honestly, I'm not sure what we'll do, but we'll figure it out together, okay? For now, spruce up that résumé. I'll start making calls."

My phone buzzes in my pocket. Excusing myself, I pull it out and see a message from Ashley:

I'm home. See you soon, Care Bear. Can't wait.

Now I have a significant incentive to finish this conversation. The sooner it's done, the sooner I can get home. Home to Ashley.

I slip my phone back in my jacket pocket and motion for the server to bring the check. "So we're good?"

Gabe draws back and stretches in his chair. "There's one more thing..."

Hearing the hesitation in his voice, I lean forward and study him. He's not meeting my gaze, and he's fidgeting with the unused cutlery beside his plate. "Gabe, I'm your agent now. I want you to feel comfortable talking to me. Believe me, I've heard some wild tales over the years. If it's not criminal or unethical, you'll get no judgment from me."

He lets out a breath and smiles. "Yeah, I'm not sure why I'm making this a big deal. It's about Ashley…"

His use of her name hits me like a sucker punch. God, I hope this isn't going where I think it's going. I draw in a long breath, suppress all signs of the tension I'm feeling, and adopt a nonchalant façade. "What about her?"

"Well, I remember her saying that you were family friends, so I was wondering if you'd pass on my number to her?"

Yeah, it's going where I thought it was going. You know, for a man who detests when his personal and work lives overlap, I sure do confront the issue at every turn. Now how to do I put this to minimize the awkwardness? As few words as possible seems about right. "Sorry, Gabe. Ashley's seeing someone now."

He jerks his head back. "Oh. Okay." He laughs. "Well, maybe it won't work out. A guy can always hope, right?"

Dammit. He won't let the matter go unless I give him a reason to. I'm not looking forward to telling Carter I'm actually dating his sister, but there's something satisfying about the prospect of acknowledging to Gabe that Ash is my girlfriend. The server arrives with the bill, and after glancing at the total, I hand him my credit card. When we're alone again, I say, "Gabe, I'm the someone."

He squints at me. "Sorry?"

"The someone Ashley's dating. The someone is me."

"Oh." He stares at me a few seconds. "Ohhh, I get it."

I fuss with my tie and loosen it. "It hasn't been long, so yeah. That's why…"

"Oh, yeah, no. I understand. Forget I said anything, okay?" He holds up his hands. "I'm no longer thinking about her in that way."

Right. That's not how a man's mind works, but I'm not going to be unprofessional about it. This conversation itself is giving me hives. "It's forgotten."

The waiter returns with my card, and Gabe and I stand to leave. As he drops his napkin on the chair, he says, "Man, you're Carter's best friend *and* you're dating his sister. He's going to get all the great jobs, isn't he?" He chuckles as he says this, but I don't join in his laughter. Gabe and Carter aren't in the same league, at least not yet. Still, it's the first time a client has suggested that I give Carter special treatment, and although there's no truth to the implication, I'm annoyed with myself that it's even an issue.

I stop Gabe before he exits the dining room. "Look, I pride myself on being able to keep my personal life from affecting my work. You have nothing to worry about."

Gabe claps my shoulder, his voice sure. "I was just joking. I'm not worried, man."

That makes sense, I suppose. Because I'll be doing enough worrying for the both of us.

MY CONDO IS dark and eerily quiet when I walk through the door. It's not like I was expecting balloons and confetti, but I was selfishly imagining that she'd rush into the room and throw herself at me.

I stride through the hall and peek into Ashley's room. Her carry-on sits untouched on the floor, and her bed is still made. Maybe she stepped out to the store. Loosening my tie as I step into my bedroom, I drop my jaw when I see Ashley in my bed. Holy hell. She's naked—and blindfolded. I close and open my eyes to be sure I'm not imagining the exquisite vision before me. Nope. Still there. Still rocking my world.

I slip my tie off, ease out of my suit jacket, and approach the bed in stealth mode. "Welcome home, Ash."

She doesn't respond, and then I notice the slow rise of her chest. As I move into the room, her faint snoring grows louder. I press a fist against my mouth to stem my laughter. And then I realize the insanely fortuitous opportunity at hand.

I make quick work of unbuttoning my shirt and toss it behind me as I kick off my shoes. The socks must go, too, because it's a personal rule of mine, a response to the trauma of watching pornos as a teen. But that's all the time I'll spare, because I'm eager to nestle between her legs and make her come.

Like a tiger approaching its prey, I climb onto the bed and watch her reaction. She stretches awake, her back arching off the mattress, and my gaze roams over her naked skin, taking in the sight of her breasts. If I'm not mistaken, her dusky nipples are speaking to me. *Julian, suck us*, they say.

"Julian?" she asks.

"It's me."

"Sorry I fell asleep. I had big plans."

She rocks her hips, redirecting my attention to the lower half of her body.

"Don't worry about it," I whisper. "This is perfect." I slide a hand between her legs and caress her calves. "Open up, baby."

She scoots back and spreads her legs wide, giving me ample room to settle in.

I kiss her thigh before tapping it. "I want to bury my face in your pussy and make you come. Would you like that?"

She sighs. "Not really, no." After a few seconds, she laughs. "I'm *kidding*. I'd like nothing more than for you to show me your best impression of an ostrich."

I shake my head at that one, unable to suppress my grin. "Place those gorgeous legs on my shoulders, then."

"So bossy," she says.

"And yet you're doing as I say. I wonder why."

"Yeah. I know not to bite the mouth that eats me."

My forehead falls to her thigh as I laugh. This woman. "Okay, no more jokes from you. I've got serious business to attend to."

"My lips are sealed."

"That's going to make it hard for me to execute my plans."

Her laughter shakes the mattress. "Not *those* lips, silly." After a pause, she says in a softer voice, "I'm proud of you, though. Your developing sense of humor is going to add years to your life. They say—"

"Ash."

"What?"

"Shut up."

"Well, damn. If you weren't about to go down on me, I'd—" She lets out a long moan, and then she sucks in a shuddering breath. "Oh fuck. Julian, yes."

That's more like it.

Chapter Thirty-One

Ashley

THIS MAN'S TONGUE should be bronzed and given a permanent place in the nearest art museum. The placard would read, *Giver of atomic orgasms, circa 2018*.

My mouth hangs open as he presses his lips against my inner thigh, making me anticipate the next stretch of sensation he'll draw out of me. We're on round two, Julian having decided that the first orgasm was merely the appetizer. I'm giddy with anticipation thinking of my own plans for dessert. In the meantime, waiting for him to set me on fire again threatens to make me howl, and I am *not* ashamed.

The blindfold intensifies the experience, my other senses sharpening to make up for my inability to see what's happening: the rustle of the sheets when he shifts on the bed; the soft lick of his lips; the long, slow inhale when he breathes me in; the sandalwood cologne he favors.

This time, though, there's more movement than before. And then he lightly squeezes my breasts before trailing a single finger down my belly. He stops at my navel. "Should I keep going?"

"Yes," I whisper. "Please, yes."

He inches his finger a smidge lower. "Here?"

I raise my hands overhead and stretch against his touch. "More. Put your fingers inside me."

"Is that what you need?"

My encouragement rushes out as a desperate plea. "God, yes, please."

"But what if you come on my hand? Will that be enough? You'll want to fuck me, too, right?"

He stresses the word *fuck*, and my pussy throbs in response. "I promise I won't come."

The bed shifts under his weight, and then he's no longer touching me. Damn him.

"You want to make promises, huh?" he asks.

I freeze at the casual way he dismisses the notion. Is he pulling back on me? Now? I can't see his face, so I'm unable to glean any clues from his expression. I bring my legs together, unsure where this is headed and detesting how exposed I feel.

"No, baby, don't close up on me. I'm trying to tell you something and going about it badly. You want to make promises? Go ahead. I'll make them, too. I want this for as long as you want me. Us. Together. No one else. I don't think we ever made that clear."

This is huge for him, and we both know it. He's making promises without the benefit of knowing how Carter will react to us as a couple. It's huge for me as well. The cynical part of my soul warns that *not* making promises about our relationship is better than making and failing to keep them. But I want to try with Julian, because I'm confident he'll try just as hard as I will to make this work. "I wish I could see your eyes."

He takes my hand and places it on his chest. "Feel my heart instead."

And I do, the beats steady and strong against my hand, a fitting description for Julian himself. "Okay, just us."

He takes in a breath and lets it out. "Perfect. Now let's see if you can keep your promise not to come."

Oh God. Why did I make that stupid promise? He's going to wield it against me like a weapon.

"Now, if you want my fingers, you'll get my fingers. If you want my mouth, you'll get my mouth. What'll it be?"

"I want both."

"Good choice," he says. The mattress dips between my legs, and then he lays the flat of his hand on my pussy and lightly squeezes it before sliding two digits inside me.

I lift my ass off the bed to get closer to his mouth. "Julian, yes. Yes, yes, yes."

As he slides his fingers in and out, his tongue comes down on my clit, a long, strong lick that curls my toes and sends a tingle down my spine. "Jesus, Julian. More. Do that again."

He spreads me wide and licks at my clit, tiny, torturous flicks that provide just enough pressure to push me to the edge but not over it. My hands grasp the back of his head, and I grind into his mouth. Minutes of exquisite tension pass, and my brain goes fuzzy. If someone forced me to recite my ABCs on pain of death, I'd be done for.

The mattress shifts again.

Although his mouth is gone, his breath teases me, letting me know he's still close.

"You're so fucking hot here," he says. "And I wish I could take this taste with me everywhere I go." Then he closes his mouth over my nub and sucks—hard.

Shocked by the change in course, I arch my back and—oh my God, that's me wailing. A million tiny explosions go off inside me, a ripple effect of pulsing sensations that make me cry out in pleasure. "Julian, yes, yes, yes, yes, yes, yes." I repeat the word while tears slide down my face.

As I recover from the best orgasm of my life, Julian kisses the inside of my thighs. My body collapses into itself, and I can't do anything but lie on the bed. Julian still has the capacity to move, though, and he slides up my body and removes the blindfold.

My eyes adjust to the dim lighting in the room, and then I focus on his face hovering above me. "Well, hello there."

He gives me a slow smile and presses his lips against mine. "Feel free to sleep naked in my bed whenever the urge hits you."

"Keep giving me mind-altering orgasms like that one and the urge will hit me every single day."

Chuckling, he lifts himself off me and stretches. "It's been a long day. I'm going to take a shower before we continue."

I sit up on my elbow and watch him enter the bathroom.

He winks at me. "Round three begins in a few minutes." Then he softly closes the door.

Actually, Julian, round three will begin in less time than that.

THE SOUND OF the shower is my cue to slip inside the bathroom. His eyes are closed, and his face is tilted under the spray of water.

Julian's magnificent when he's dry, but he's phenomenal when he's wet. An ass that could launch a thousand ships, and a powerful back whose muscles flex mightily even when he's doing something as simple as lathering his hands.

I open the shower door and step in.

He doesn't turn around. "Couldn't wait, huh?"

I'm honest in my neediness. "I could not." Pressing my chest against his back, I reach around him and grab the soap. Then I build up a nice amount of lather and wash his cock, making sure to stroke him slowly as I rinse him off.

He groans and places his hands on the wall. I hold him firmly, pumping him at a steady pace. One of his hands slides down the wall, and his legs shake. "Fuck, Ash. That feels incredible."

I place my other hand on his shoulder. "Turn around. I want you in my mouth."

He spins to face me and leans against the shower wall. I lower myself to my knees, caressing his chest and stomach on the way down.

I take his cock in my hand, look up, and give him a sultry smile.

"Ah, baby," he says. "What a sight."

With a last lick of my lips, I open my mouth wide and get my fill of him.

He balls one of his hands into a fist and slams it against the wall. "Jesus. Yes. Take my cock."

So I do. And I leave no part of him untouched as I stroke him with my tongue. Then his hands are in my hair, pushing it to the side so his view is clear. "Fuck. Fuck. Fuck. Keep going, baby."

With that response, there's no way I'm stopping. I go faster. And his groans grow louder as he rocks his hips forward again and again, until he groans my name in delicious anguish. He shouts a muffled curse before he taps me on the shoulder. But I don't heed his warning. Instead, I palm his ass and push him farther into my mouth, enjoying the unintelligible sounds he's making as he comes.

Boneless and dazed, he struggles to pull me up and kisses me, sharing the taste of him on my tongue. "Damn, woman, you wrecked me."

I kiss his jaw and slap his ass. "One good turn deserves another, wouldn't you say?"

He squeezes mine in return. "If that's the case, we'll be at this all night."

"Good. Sleep's overrated anyway."

JULIAN'S RESTING HIS head on my stomach, lying diagonally across the bed.

"Is there something up there I should know about?" I ask him. "Bear in mind, if it's a spider, I will catapult myself out of this bed so quickly you'll definitely be injured in the process."

He cranes his neck to look at me. "What?"

"The ceiling, Julian. You've been staring at it for the past five minutes. What's wrong?"

He sighs. "Just thinking about Gabriel, who's now my newest client."

"You made him an offer. That's great, congrats." The absent expression on his face suggests he isn't in a celebratory mood, however. "Or not."

He drops his head back onto my stomach. "No, you're right. I should be excited, but…"

The hesitation in his voice doesn't surprise me. Julian's always been tight-lipped about his work. But if we're going to be together, he needs to share this aspect of his life with me, too. Otherwise, we might as well call ourselves friends with benefits. "Talk to me, Julian."

I count the seconds of silence that follow, a form of mental fidgeting as I wait to see if he'll let me in.

Eventually, he speaks. "I love his enthusiasm. I love the possibility of working with him and helping him get his due."

"You make that sound like a problem."

"It's not. But I worry that I won't be able to deliver for him, not in the way he deserves. Hollywood doesn't put out a welcome mat for people who aren't white, male, and straight."

I slide out from under him, and his head hits the mattress. Now I'm looking down at him. "You mean people who aren't like my brother."

After scrubbing a hand down his face, he looks up at me and nods. "Exactly." He bites down on his lips as he ponders the situation. "I'm racking my brain for ways to make myself useful to him without burning bridges in the business...or getting fired." He shakes his head as if to clear it. "It's just something I've been thinking about it. I'm not going to solve anything tonight, obviously."

I admire him for handling his client's careers with care. Everything I've seen about agents in popular media paints a less than flattering picture of them. Julian challenges that depiction. Even now, when he suspects roadblocks ahead, he's focused on confronting them head-on. Makes me consider my own ambitions and what I'm willing to do to achieve them. "Well, at least Gabriel's got a lot going for him." I tick off his positive attributes with my fingers. "Good-looking, charming, *and* talented. To my untrained eye, you've got someone with star potential."

"Glad you noticed."

Is that sarcasm I hear? Oh dear. I'm tickled that he's not immune to the green-eyed monster, but I'm not encouraging his behavior. "News flash. I can appreciate a man's looks and talent without having any romantic interest in him."

He mutters something, then speaks up. "Of course you can. Just ignore me."

"Easy enough."

In seconds, he springs to his knees, tackles me back down, and pins me under him, his wide smile and dancing eyes stealing my breath for a moment. Broody Julian makes me horny, but playful Julian makes me swoon.

He buries his head in my neck and nips at my skin. "Can you ignore me now?"

I force myself not to yelp or laugh, even though he's tickling me and I'm screeching inside. I whip my head around instead, pretending to listen out for a sound. "I'm sorry. Did someone say something?"

He nuzzles his way up to my jaw and nips me there, too. "What about now?"

Oh, the brush of his mouth against my skin feels nice. Really nice. "That's a little harder to ignore but still doable."

He rises above me, the corded muscles in his forearms flexing as he gets into a push-up position, and then he lowers his body in tiny increments, until I reach up, grab the back of his neck, and pull him down. "You've made your point."

He collapses behind me and turns me to the side, arranging us in a spooning position. After planting a soft kiss on my shoulder, he says, "I like being in bed with you."

"Yes," I say on a laugh. "It's where we do our best work."

He pinches me on the hip. "I'm not talking about sex. I'm talking about something else entirely." His fingers trail up my side and disappear under my hair, massaging my scalp with the perfect amount of pressure. "I'm so fucking into you, Ash."

For a moment, I simply absorb his statement, reveling in the knowledge that, as my mother would say, we're smitten with each other. I flip over to face him and place my hand on the back of his neck, pulling him close. "Same."

He draws back. "You're so fucking into yourself? That's a bit conceited, don't you think?"

I lay across him and drop my chin onto his chest. Our faces are close but not close enough to kiss. "No, Julian. *I'm* so into *you*."

He says nothing for a moment. Then he winds his hand under the curtain of my hair, grasps my neck, and pulls me down to within an inch of his lips. "Then it's time to tell your brother, wouldn't you say? I'm ready if you are."

He's got more to lose here than I do, that's for sure, but he's ready to commit anyway. It's inspiring. Makes me realize that committing to someone—or something— is an expression of love. And oh God, I *do* love Julian. "Okay, when he gets back, we'll tell him."

"Ash, if you want me to do it alone, I will."

I shake my head and grab his hands, pressing them to my chest. "No, we're a team. We'll do this together."

But there's something else I need to do on my own.

Chapter Thirty-Two

Julian

ONE OF THE many benefits of dating my roommate is that I no longer worry about freeballing in my home. A second benefit: She appreciates it, too. After the long day I've had, diving into my sweats sans underwear and sitting in front of the couch with my woman by my side sounds like heaven. Bonus points if it leads to lazy sex followed by at least six hours of sleep.

The front door to my condo flies open before I can fit my key into the lock. Ashley pulls me inside, her eyes flickering with excitement. "You're exhausted, aren't you?"

"Well, hello to you, too," I say as I open my arms out for a hug.

She snuggles into my body, cups my jaw, and plants a soft kiss on my lips. When she pulls back, she bats her eyelashes. "I know you're tired, but I'd like to show you something."

I like the sound of that. Waggling my eyebrows, I walk her backward and ease out of my jacket.

Her eyes sparkle with amusement as she laughs. "Not *inside* our place. We need to go out for me to show it to you."

Hmm. I *don't* like the sound of that. But then my attention snags on something she said. *Our place.* She thinks of this as *our place*, and I *love* the sound of that. This weekend, sometime when we're lazing on the couch, I'll broach the topic of making our living arrangement a permanent one. It's a selfish move, sure, because I want her with me all the time, but I'm hoping she feels the same way. "Do I have time to change at least?"

She eyes her slim platinum wristwatch. "Nope." And then she pulls me out the door.

"Okay, okay." I try to ease back into my jacket while she tugs me to the elevators. "Where are we going?"

Her mouth curves into a mysterious smile. "It's a surprise."

A TAXI DROPS us off in Silver Lake, a trendy neighborhood known for its hipster grunge and artisanal coffee shops.

After stepping out of the car, I study the lamplit street and turn to her. "This is where you wanted to take me?"

She bounces in place, her eyes glittering with excitement, and I can't help soaking in the positive vibes.

Whatever the surprise is, it's making her glow. She takes my hand and points across the street. "There."

A brick-front establishment with a sign that reads *Musicology* sits in the middle of the block. "What am I looking at?"

She blows out a breath as though the answer is obvious. "It's a music store. Come."

We run across the street, and I follow her inside. She strides to the back, confidence in her step. Obviously, she's been here before. Soon, we're passing a dozen small music rooms, until she stops in front of one. "This is my room," she says with a smile. "Well, not *my* room all the time, but as of today I'm renting it, and I'll be offering guitar lessons here starting next week."

I'm so blown away by her announcement that I step back and lean against the door across from hers. "Wait. You'll be teaching music here?"

She nods, her eyes wide and bright. "Yes, a few days a week until I phase out my job with the airline." She worries her lip and watches me. "And I chose this location because the indie music scene is great in this neighborhood, or so one of my coworkers tells me. Figured I could see about getting a few gigs at bars and coffee shops in the area. Oh, and I signed up for open mic night at Muddy's tomorrow night. Think you could come and cheer me on?"

"Definitely."

She breathes out. "So that's the surprise. I might go broke within a few months, my savings will only take me so far, and I'll need to pay rent at some point, but I'd like to try."

My heart expands in my chest, full of happiness for her. She's tamping down the doubt and aiming for the life she wants. I push off the wall, take her hand, and pull her close, my fingers tipping up her chin. "I'm so proud of you, baby. And don't worry about rent. My place is bought and paid for."

She looks up at me, her brown eyes blinking. "Wait. You want me to stay with you? Indefinitely?"

"I do. Would you like to?"

She rises on her toes and leans in for a kiss. It's tender and sweet, the latter because I can taste traces of sugar and berries on her tongue.

"Someone had dessert already."

Her cheeks turn rosy. "Cherry hand pie from Whole Foods. It's my new favorite."

I lick my lips as though I'm tasting her on my tongue. "You're my new favorite."

Her eyes gloss over, and she gives me a sultry smile. "Let's go home, then. I'd like to verify that fact."

I mimic a robot, my voice and movements stiff and measured. "Commencing verification process in T minus twenty."

WE DON'T GET beyond closing the door before we're smashed together in a tangle of chests, arms, and mouths. She pulls down the bodice of her sundress while I chuck my shirt and jacket behind me.

I'm toeing off my shoes when her tits appear in my line of vision. "Holy shit, Ash. No bra? If killing me was your goal, consider it done."

She laughs against my shoulder, her hands working quickly below her waist. I take a step back and see her panties drop to her ankles. They're peach colored, just like the nail polish on her toes. I scramble to unbutton my slacks, but her hands get there before mine.

She's panting as she gives me instructions. "I'll get the zipper. You get the condom. Please be quick."

My hand flies behind me to my wallet. If I don't have protection in there, I will beat the shit out of myself and then turn my body over to her for a second pummeling.

"Hurry," she says as she pulls down my zipper and tugs my pants down my thighs.

I'm still riding the high of her new venture. To me, it's one of the hottest things she's ever done. I want to be inside her and show her how fucking proud I am of her with each stroke. My fingers, the stupid fuckers, don't want to cooperate, though, and I'm having trouble sifting through my wallet. Finally, I see the packet, and I actually think I might cry in relief.

She sees the condom at the same moment she pulls my cock out of my boxer briefs. "Oh God, oh God, oh God." She grabs the packet out of my trembling fingers and sheathes me in seconds, shouting "done" like she's just completed a Quickfire Challenge on *Top Chef.*

I grab the skirt of her dress and bunch it up to her waist. "I'm sorry if I ruin it, but I need it out of the way."

Her eyes are drowsy and hooded, her cheeks suffused with heat. "S'okay. Don't care." I lean into her and slide a finger up her slit, but her hand comes down on me like a band of steel. Her eyes are fiery with determination. "No, I want you, not your fingers. And not in five minutes, not even in five seconds. Now."

More than happy to give her what she wants, I hook her leg over my arm, stretching her wide, and press my chest into hers until her back hits the door. She grasps my shoulders, her gorgeous breasts bouncing as she adjusts to the position. With my free hand, I guide my cock to her entrance, bend my knees, and push up into her in one fluid movement.

Her high-pitched cry fuels me. So I pull out slowly and slam back into her.

"Yes, that's it, Julian. *That's it.*"

"Holy fuck, Ash. Your pussy is hot and tight, and I cannot *believe* how fucking good it feels to be inside you."

Her hands slip to my waist as I fuck her harder and faster. I can't get enough of her, and I'm determined to make her come hard. I trail my free hand up her body and slide my thumb inside her parted mouth. "Bite down if you need to."

Her love-drunk eyes widen as I slam into her over and over again, and then she clamps down on my fingers, a whimper escaping her throat as she convulses around me. When Ashley's coming down, I begin the climb, my finger still stinging from her bite. She leans over, that left-of-center smile turning wicked. "This pussy is yours."

Just as she expected, I detonate, my body shuddering against her as I grip her thigh. Several explosive aftershocks hit me before it's over. Breathless, I lazily roam my hands over her body as we right ourselves. I try to catch my breath while I ease out of her, but it's a challenge. "That was incredible."

She meets my gaze, her eyes soft and her mouth plump and relaxed. "It was."

Can it get any better than this?

It can't.

In fact, within a few days I discover it can only get worse.

Fresh from his honeymoon and at my request, Carter saunters into SCM in the late afternoon wearing a hoodie, jeans, and his Blackfin sunglasses. The office stops churning, and half the personnel scramble to get a glimpse of him.

I can easily picture his scrawny teenage chest as he dribbled a basketball in front of his house. My, how times have changed.

He smiles at everyone and shakes a few hands as he approaches my office, his trademark charm in overdrive. We give each other a pound, and then he flops down onto one of the two armchairs facing my desk.

"So now my best friend, the big agent, is summoning me to his office to update me on business matters?"

I round the desk and sit. "Chill. I have reasons. And you're going to thank me when you hear what I have to say."

339 PRETENDING HE'S MINE 339

He sits up. "You have my attention."

"First, how was your vacation?"

He smiles, and his eyes light up. "Perfect. Spent most of it in bed. Hence, the perfection."

"And Tori?"

"Back to work. And trying to convince Eva to move to LA."

"Good Lord. Those two together in this town?" I pretend to shudder. "Pray for everyone."

"I thought the same thing. Tori wants her here, though, and I want what Tori wants."

I grin. "Because you're whipped."

"Definitely." He looks around the office, impatient as usual. "So why'd you need to see me?" He tucks his chin into his chest, looks up at me, and bats his eyelashes. "I mean, other than wanting to see my handsome face."

I shake my head at him before speaking. "It's confirmed. Barry Sanderson wants you to be the leading star in his next big-budget project, one the studio execs hope will be a franchise. Think *The Matrix* meets *The Hunger Games* with a little humor thrown in. He wants you to read the script, and you'll need to do a few reads, of course, but he says he knows enough about your work to be confident you're his top choice."

Carter leans forward and widens his eyes. "Holy shit."

"Holy shit, exactly. This is huge, man." It's a once-in-a-lifetime opportunity for us both. Given that he's uncharacteristically silent, I suspect he understands the significance of this development.

Carter leans back in his chair and stares at me. "You read the script?"

I shake my head. "No. We'd both have to sign a nondisclosure agreement before we can even see it, which is why I brought you in. Once he receives our NDAs, Sanderson will send a courier with two copies. Nothing's definite, but this is the first step in a major deal if you like what you read."

He massages the back of his neck as he processes the news. After several seconds, he swipes his hand down his face and gives me a *wow-this-is-happening* smile. "Okay. Where do we go from here?"

I pick up the folder with the nondisclosure forms. "I've read through them, and the legal department says this is standard verbiage, so take a look and if you're cool with it, sign on the dotted line. I'll get them faxed to Sanderson, and we should be good to go."

He rubs his hands together while he shakes his head. "Man, this is incredible." He reads through the one-page agreement and signs it.

"Give me a sec," I tell him, and then I step out of my office and arrange for Marie to fax the agreements to Sanderson. Within a minute, I get an email from the director's assistant letting me know a courier is on the way.

When I return, Carter's texting.

"I'm going to pretend you're not texting Tori after signing a nondisclosure agreement."

"You do that," Carter says without looking up. "And there's nothing incriminating in this text anyway. Just checking if she's up for celebrating some undisclosed major news."

"Hey, you could do that at Muddy's in Silver Lake. Your sister's performing at open mic night."

He looks up from his phone. "She is? She didn't tell us."

"Yeah. She figured you'd be wiped out and wouldn't want to venture out. I promised I'd be in her cheering section, though."

He nods absently. "That'll work."

And this will give us the opportunity to let him know Ash and I are together now. It's a perfect setup.

"What time?" he asks.

Before I can respond, Sooyin rushes into my office without knocking, her expression grim. She skids to a stop when she spots Carter. "Oh shoot, sorry!"

I dismiss her apology with a wave. "Don't worry about it. We're just finishing up."

Carter rises while she holds out her hand and introduces herself. "Carter Stone, it's great to meet you. Sooyin Liú. I'm an agent in the Film Group."

"Hey, Sooyin. Good to meet you, too."

"Sanderson is sending the script over," I tell her.

It's not a fact I'd publicize to any other agent here, but Sooyin's my friend, and she's walked me through the potential pitfalls of a deal with the studio, so she's fully aware of the stakes.

"Hey, that's great news," Sooyin says. "I've worked with him before. An upstanding guy in a sea of assholes." She lowers her voice. "Just so you know, Sanderson is very protective of his ideas, and he's a bit…well, let's just say he's eccentric."

"We've heard," Carter and I say in unison.

A rat-a-tat knock causes all of us to spin our heads toward the door. Without waiting for me to answer, Quinn sticks his head in. "Heard one of our favorite clients was in the hizzouse."

Sooyin and I glance at each other, our version of a mental eye roll.

Carter reaches over and shakes Quinn's hand. "Hey, how you doin', Quinn?"

"Great, great." He points at me. "This guy taking care of you? Because if he isn't, I'll throw him out on his butt in a heartbeat." Then he roars with laughter. But he and I both know he's not joking.

Carter's bland expression matches his monotone. "Julian always takes good care of me. You have nothing to worry about there."

I'm relieved he kept it professional and didn't refer to our friendship in some way. That would have irked me, and he knows it.

Quinn's smile slides off his face when he realizes Carter isn't amused. "Well, glad to hear everything's going well." He peers at me. "We'll talk later." Then he rushes out the door.

Sooyin slaps the tops of her thighs before she pushes her butt off the edge of my desk. "I need to get back to work. It was great meeting you, Carter."

Before she disappears down the hall, I poke my head out of my office. "Psst, why'd you stop by?"

She spins, shuffles back to me, and drops her voice to a whisper. "More gossip. As expected, Quinn canned Manning late last night. The scuttlebutt is that they're looking to fire three more in your group by the end of the quarter. Just wanted to give you a heads-up, but with a Sanderson deal in play, I'd say you have nothing to worry about."

Damn. Poor Manning's fate was sealed the minute he embarrassed Quinn. "Thanks for letting me know."

"Now go celebrate. We'll talk next week."

"Thanks."

After I sit back down in my chair, Carter pulls out his phone. "Pictures of the honeymoon." He hands it to me. "Check 'em out."

I bet he can't fathom that I don't have any interest in looking at them. He gets this bad habit from his father. Reminds me of my sister, Nicole, who shares photos of my niece with me *while* Sophia is sitting on my lap. Thankfully, the gods take pity on me and Marie rings to let me know the courier's here with the Sanderson scripts. Soon I'll be able to send Carter away and finish my work in time to get over to Muddy's.

Less than a minute later, Sanderson himself is at my office door.

Well, shit. This changes everything.

Chapter Thirty-Three

Julian

BARRY SANDERSON DIRECTS Hollywood blockbusters and consistently makes any list of mega power brokers. Why the hell is he in my office with a messenger bag hanging from his shoulder? Never mind. The fact is, he's here, and I need to make the most of his appearance.

Carter and I both jump up to greet him.

"Sanderson, this is a surprise," I say. "What can I do for you?"

He gives me a knowing look, his face ruddy from too much sun exposure. "You're smooth, Mr. Hart. You didn't blink when I showed up, but really you're wondering why I'm wearing sunglasses indoors and delivering the script myself, aren't you?"

Hell yes, I am. "I'll be honest. The shades are throwing me off."

Carter turns his head in my direction and tilts his head.

What? Is it a crime for me to joke around? I ignore Carter's questioning gaze.

"Heh." Sanderson removes the sunglasses and lets them hang on a gold chain around his neck. The inner fashion police in me wants to give him a ticket for that infraction. "This script is my baby, and I've been burned before, so I'm not taking any chances with this one."

"Fair enough," I say.

Carter reaches out, and Sanderson shakes his hand.

"I'm honored that you're interested in me for the role," Carter says. "I can't wait to read it."

Sanderson taps his stomach with his hands. "You're perfect for the role. I've seen your work, and you've got the acting chops I need to make this franchise a hit. Let me ask you this. About what percentage of your action scenes have involved stunt doubles?"

I motion for Sanderson to take a seat, and both he and Carter lower themselves into the chairs facing my desk as they chat. A beep from my speakerphone pulls me away from the conversation. "Yes, Marie?"

"Your mother's on line two, Mr. Hart."

My Spidey senses are on full alert because she rarely calls me at work. "Keep chatting, gentlemen. I'm going to take this quick call."

I stand and face the window looking out to the Avenue of the Stars. "Mom, everything okay?"

"Everything's fine, Julian. Is this...is this a bad time?"

The hesitation in her voice chills me. "Hang on. I need to find a quiet spot. I'll call you back in two minutes." Carter and Sanderson are deep in conversation, and I don't want to interrupt them. "I need to step out for a minute."

Carter looks up and peers at me. "Everything okay?"

I don't know, but there's no sense in setting off any unnecessary alarms. "Yeah, yeah. I'll be back in a few." I stride down the hall and slip into one of the agency's small conference rooms. I'm back on the phone with my mother within seconds. "Tell me what's going on."

She sighs. "There's no emergency, okay, but you said you weren't coming home soon and I wanted you to know."

Now my heart feels like an invisible fist is squeezing it. "Know what?"

"Julian, your father's showing signs of early dementia. Short-term memory loss. Disorientation. Trouble finding words."

The invisible hand won't let go. My father doesn't just remind me of Superman. No, he *is* Superman. A humble man with a modest background who climbed his way to the top and took others with him when he got there. He did it despite the naysayers, despite the people who put up roadblocks in his path, in large part because he used his sharp intellect to build his company from the ground up. I can't reconcile the image of him that's always been in my head with the person my mother's describing.

"It might be exhaustion," I offer. "You know what happens when you start looking up symptoms on the internet."

She tsks at that suggestion. "Sweetheart, we've seen a doctor about this. A neurologist. We'll be visiting a second one next week."

I can't disregard a doctor's diagnosis no matter how much I want to. "What does Nicole say?"

She takes a deep breath. "Nicole is in risk-management mode. To her, it's all about putting people in place to protect the future of the business. That's what she feels she can do for him."

"That's what I could have been doing for him, too. Is that what you're thinking?"

There's no hesitation in her response. "I wasn't thinking that at all. His life is not yours, and your life is not his."

I run a hand down my face. I wish it were that easy to disregard his disappointment in my choices. "Try telling him that."

"I have."

She doesn't need to say more. I know her telling him so made no difference. This explains the tenor of my recent conversations with him. His preoccupation with the state of my career stemmed from his concerns about his. "When was he going to tell me?"

A few beats of silence follow my question. Then she says, "Never, is my guess."

"I should talk to him."

"Give him some time, Julian. I don't think he's accepted it himself. And it's not like he's going to forget who you are tomorrow. The doctor told us his decline could take years. It happens gradually, but now we can prepare for it."

I drop my forehead onto the smooth mahogany table and squeeze my eyes shut. "This is…a lot to take in. I don't know what to say. So that's why he's been hounding me about building something of my own, telling me I need to focus on nurturing my legacy."

"Yes. I didn't want to tell you at Carter's wedding, but you mentioned that you wouldn't be making it to Atlanta anytime soon, and when he told me that you two had words when he saw you in LA, I realized you didn't have the right context to understand his frustration." She pauses for a moment. "It's coming from a place of love, sweetie. The doctor says the diagnosis will make your father think about his own mortality, and although he's not going anywhere anytime soon, I suspect he's trying to assure himself that everyone will be okay when he's gone. Just continue what you're doing. Go out there and be the best damn agent you can be. Show your father you chose correctly."

My head might explode from the disparate thoughts crashing into it. Will my father be okay? How much time before we notice a difference in his behavior? When he couldn't remember names or places recently, were those early signs of dementia or merely a consequence of his exhaustion? I'll need to go home to see him, but will Quinn think I'm slacking if I take yet another day off for personal reasons, especially after taking a mini-vacation for Carter's wedding? Jesus. What a fucking day it's been. A laugh gets stuck at the base of my throat. *And on top of all this, Barry Sanderson's in my office.*

My mother's voice permeates the mental fog. "Sweetheart, breathe. Dementia is an unfortunate sign of aging, but it's not even close to being the worst thing that could happen to your father. I just wanted you to know."

I take a fortifying breath and sit up. "Okay, okay. I'm fine now. I'll be home soon. In the meantime, if you need anything from me—anything at all—you call me, all right?"

"Of course, Son."

Her voice is soft and warm, full of the affection she's always given me. It's the balm I need right now. "Love you, Mom."

"Love you, too, baby."

In a daze, I plod back to the office, where Carter and Sanderson are still conversing animatedly. They both stop talking the moment I reappear.

"Everything okay?" Carter asks, wrinkling his brow as he studies me.

I'm reminded of one of the few mantras that's never let me down: *The workplace is for business, and your personal life has no place there.* Lock that shit away and get it together. I relax my features and enter autopilot mode. "Yeah, yeah, everything's cool."

Carter's face clears. "Great. Barry and I were just talking about grabbing some dinner. Says he'd be happy to talk big picture and walk us through his concept. What do you say?"

That pulls my hazy head out of my ass. I can't very well tell him I'd rather meet Ash at Muddy's, not in front of Sanderson at least.

Sanderson watches us and rises to his feet. "Do you think you could point me to the restroom? My bladder isn't as reliable as it used to be."

I walk him to the door and ask Marie to show him the way.

When there's sufficient distance between Sanderson and us, I turn to Carter. "I thought you wanted to go to your sister's open mic night?"

Carter does a double take. "Well, yeah, but Ashley will understand. It's an open mic night, one of many probably. We can catch the next one. This"—he points to the hall—"is a chance we can't pass up. I already texted Tori and told her we'll need to postpone our celebration." He squishes his brows together and tilts his head. "What's going on, J? Why aren't you as excited about this as I am?"

I don't know what to say, and that rarely happens to me. He doesn't know how much courage it took for Ashley to sign up for open mic night, but I do. He doesn't know that she's my lover and that I want to be there to support her. Still, after years of carving out separate spaces for my work and personal lives, I'd be a dick agent if I backed out on him tonight, in the midst of talks to secure him a career-defining role, simply because I'm dating his sister. He'd be well within his rights to discard me in favor of an agent who'd make his career the highest priority. Quinn would love that development. No, as much as I'd like to go, I can't risk my career over an open mic night. I blow out a breath and slap him on the back. "I'm excited, man. It's just so much happening at lightning speed. Let me send your sister a text to let her know."

Carter nods. "Cool. I'm going to use the restroom." He strolls out the door. A few seconds later, he pokes his head back into my office. "This isn't a dream, right?"

"It's very real, my friend."

Shit. I want to be happy about Carter's news, but I'm torn up about Ashley. And I won't even be able to adequately explain why I bailed on her without running afoul of the NDA. Dammit. So this is what happens when you let your personal and professional lives collide. I make a mental note as I pick up my phone: Don't *ever* do this shit again.

Chapter Thirty-Four

Ashley

OH GOD. WHY did I think this was a good idea? If my palms get any sweatier, I won't be able to play my guitar tonight. I take several large gulps of water as I scan Muddy's main room. The view of the stage from this dark, secluded corner isn't helping the situation, either. It's a small stage, yes, but this vantage point emphasizes the vastness of the room—and the size of my potential audience.

People. There are *so many* people. My chest aches at the thought of performing in front of them. I try to remember the typical advice for stage fright.

Picture everyone taking a shit.

Oh, that's gross. No.

Picture everyone naked.

How the hell does that help? My mind would imagine an orgy, bodies writhing and twisting in the room while my music sets the mood. Too distracting. Um, double no.

A giant of a man with more hair on his face than on my head lumbers toward me. Of course, I picture him naked, and there's so much hair—everywhere.

"You're Ashley?" he asks in a deep, booming voice.

I swallow and wipe the droplets of water that splash onto my skin. "Yeah."

"You're up in five."

My heart rate increases, and the fine hairs on my arms rise. I'm in the first car of a roller coaster making the steep climb before its highest, most terrifying descent. Where's Julian? He'd know what to say to calm my nerves. I pull out my phone to text him and manage a smile when I see that he's beaten me to it.

Hey, Ash. Sorry to bail on you, but something important came up. I know you'll be great. See you at home later.

Oof. *Something important came up.* My stomach plummets now that I know there won't be a friendly face in the audience. I regret not inviting Tori. She would have come through for me, but I didn't want to harass her the day she returned from her honeymoon. Focusing on my nervousness makes it easier to contain my disappointment. So much for dedicating my performance to Julian. Maybe I shouldn't do an original song. A cover would go over better with this group.

The emcee, a pretty redhead with boobs as nice as mine, jumps up on the stage, the spotlight following her as she sashays like a runway model. "All right, folks. Next up is Ashley. She'll be doing an original song, so give her some love and be kind."

The audience greets me with enthusiastic applause. Buoyed by their cheers, I swing my guitar behind me and fake a shitload of confidence as I climb the stairs. When I get to center stage, I take a deep breath, shake out my hands, and perform to a crowd of strangers, not a friendly face in sight.

I RETURN TO an empty condo. How fitting. Maybe my mood will improve if I pout, stomp around, and slam a few doors. Eh. What's the point of being overly dramatic if no one's around to witness it? Potato chips will help. They always do.

After ripping open a fresh bag, I chomp down on a handful of salt and vinegar chips as I pinpoint the source of my sullen frame of mind. I should be riding the high of my performance, reveling in the memory of the people who walked up to me after I was done and raved about my song. Instead, I'm focused on one detail: Julian wasn't there because *something important came up*.

No, this is not okay, Ashley. I need to be mature about this. He's a busy man, and he wouldn't have stood me up for a superficial reason. Tonight won't be my last moment on a stage, and next time, Julian will be there to rub my back and talk me through my jitters. Hearing the jingle of his keys outside, I wipe my face of crumbs and roll the bag closed, securing it with a bag clip before I stuff it back in the pantry.

His glassy eyes brighten when he sees me in the kitchen. He doesn't waste a second and strides to me, folding me in his arms as though touching me is his only agenda. "Hey, baby. How'd it go?"

I dip my face into the crook of his neck and breathe in his warm, earthy scent. A hint of strong liquor—bourbon, maybe—floats in the air around his mouth. "It went really well. If you'd been there, it would have been perfect."

He stiffens against me, the fingers stroking my hair slowing almost to a halt. I want to snatch back the words. I don't mean them as criticism. It's just a fact that his presence would have made the evening more special.

"I'm sorry I missed it. There was a major development at work that I hadn't anticipated, and I couldn't get away."

I kiss the spot behind his ear and tighten my hands on his waist. "Good development?"

"Yeah," he says as he runs his hands down my back. "Can't say much about it now, but yes, a *great* development."

"I'm happy for you, then." I pull away when my stomach grumbles. "I think I need to stuff my face now. I was so nervous earlier I didn't have an appetite. It's returned with a vengeance." I round the counter and search for the drawer full of take-out menus. "Want to order something from Ziki?"

He shakes his head and unknots his tie. "I'll pass, but don't let that stop you. I had dinner with Carter." He yawns.

"You did?"

That he had dinner with my brother shouldn't be a significant revelation, but it drops at my feet like a bomb. Carter's the *something important* that *came up.*

"I did," he says as he peers at me. "The development has something to do with his career."

"Why didn't you mention that you couldn't come to open mic night because you were with Carter?"

It's a stupid question. Why does it matter? But now that I've asked, I'm interested in his answer. Maybe I'll gain some insight into how he rationalized not coming to see me perform.

He cocks his head and shakes it, rapidly rubbing the back of his neck. "Ash, I'm tired. I could have mentioned it, but I forgot to. Most days, it's very easy for me to compartmentalize what I do. I was working with your brother an hour ago. Now I'm not. What difference does it make?"

I envy his ability to divide his life into sections, but my mind doesn't work that way. Knowing that Carter was the reason he wasn't there for me changes the intensity of my disappointment, as though it were a bland meal sprinkled with the right amount of spices to alter its flavors and make it an entirely new dish. I hate my reaction, mostly because it reveals a difficult truth: Where Julian's concerned, I still can't shake the lingering worry that I'll always come second to Carter.

"You didn't show up for open mic night because you were with my brother. That matters to me."

The pinched, tension-filled expression on his face broadcasts his annoyance. "I was *working* with your brother."

"Having dinner."

"Yes," he says, his voice incredulous. "My job often involves dinner, drinks, shows, whatever." He leans on the counter. "It was important. I wouldn't have ditched the show otherwise."

"What was so important?"

He straightens and purses his lips. "Are you serious? You're questioning my motives?"

The conversation is deteriorating, but I don't know how to stop it from devolving further. I just want him to talk to me. "I'm asking you to share your reasons, that's all. Is that so hard to do?"

He sighs. "In this instance, it is. Carter's got an exciting opportunity in the works, but I'm not supposed to say anything about it. Not yet. I'll tell you soon, though. I promise."

It's never pleasant being an outsider. It's even worse when your lover is one of the insiders pushing you out of the circle. I don't doubt what he's saying is true, but that's not the point. He chose Carter over me. I'm tempted to put on a mask and act as though everything's okay, but I vowed not to pretend to be someone I'm not, even if doing so reveals my flaws. "I'm not going to lie. It hurts that you were with Carter when I wanted you to be with me."

He drops his head and sighs. Seconds pass before he raises his head. This time, he's wearing a blank expression and staring off at nothing. "Can we talk about my day for a minute? One, I discovered a colleague had been fired and the agency is gunning to fire a few more. Two, I learned my father is showing early signs of dementia, and while he's fine now, I'm reeling from the news and thinking about my father's inevitable decline. Three, a director who's trying to court my biggest client showed up at my office unannounced and invited me to dinner. I made the call that accepting was the right thing to do for my client and me. Four, I came home and I'm getting reamed by my girlfriend for not attending a fucking *open mic night.*"

He imbues the words *open mic night* with such derision that I take a step back, grateful for the counter that would make it too difficult for my hand to connect with his cheek. That would be a mistake I can't take back. Nevertheless, I'm no longer willing to minimize my music, and I'll be damned if I let him pick up the slack. "I'm sorry about your father, and I wish you'd had a better day, but belittling something I'm proud of isn't the way to improve your situation."

He squeezes his eyes shut and rubs his temples. "I'm sorry. I know tonight was important to you, and I truly wish I'd been there."

"Look, this won't be the last time this issue comes up for us, and I need to be honest here, I'm scared."

He drops his head and sighs. "Of what, Ashley?"

I lean over and place my hands on the counter, taking his hands in mine. When he looks up at me with wary eyes, I continue. "Scared that you were right all along, that we're not supposed to be a couple, not with our respective baggage weighing us down. Maybe there's too much background noise for us to ever enjoy just being together. Maybe it's not healthy for either of us."

I don't know exactly what I'm trying to accomplish here. It'd be nice if he assured me that my concerns are unwarranted, but a small part of me suspects he's just as scared as I am and my voicing these fears only serves to compound his. Am I *trying* to sabotage our relationship?

He lets out a heavy sigh. "I'm scared I was right all along, too. I was hoping I wouldn't be, but I don't enjoy being put in this position. You're asking me to choose between you and my career, and that's not fair."

I slump my shoulders. "Wow. If that's what you got from this conversation, then you have more baggage than I thought."

Now that I know where his head is at, I realize Julian minimizes his accomplishments just as much as I once did. I didn't strive for anything because I didn't want to be measured against my brother and come up short, whereas Julian thinks his only true professional accomplishment is being Carter's agent.

How can one person be the source of so much angst solely by virtue of his existence? Poor Carter. He deserves better, and so does Julian. "Julian, how many clients do you have?"

He raises a brow and tilts his head at me. "Two dozen. Why?"

"So Carter's not your only client. And you manage to get those people work?"

"Of course."

"So why do you think your career begins and ends with Carter?"

He shakes his head. "That's not exactly how I see it."

"No? Interesting. Because from where I stand, that seems to be how you see it."

He clenches his jaw, and a vein at his temple throbs from the pressure. "Well, I wouldn't have those clients if it weren't for Carter, and I probably wouldn't still have my job if it weren't for Carter. My boss has told me that in so many words."

I cross my arms over my chest. "Right. Because the head of an LA agency has an incentive to tell you how much you're valued? I haven't even met the man and I can see through him. And anyway, if that's true, the problem's your boss, not you. And here's the rub. I love my brother, but I wouldn't be a decent girlfriend if I didn't point out the obvious to you."

He narrows his eyes at me. "Which is?"

Maybe I should stop here. This isn't the discussion I'd planned on. It would be easy to characterize this as an overreaction on my part and spend the rest of the evening watching TV with him—or better yet, making love. But if we don't work this out now, we'll need to work it out another time. Because I *do* want to get past this.

"Which is?" he repeats.

I drop my arms and exhale. "He's holding you back."

"From what?"

"From being the person you're meant to be."

My observation darkens the room like storm clouds rolling in. He clenches his jaw again and flares a nostril for good measure. "For fuck's sake, Ash, how does that even make sense?" He gestures up and down his body, his eyes fierce. "This *is* me. The good, the bad, and everything in between. If I'm not who you want, fine, but don't try to pretend it's because I'm lacking in some way when we both know you're just pissed about me not showing up tonight."

I rush around the counter and cup his jaw. "*Listen to me, Julian.* That's not what I'm saying at all. This isn't about open mic night. This isn't about Carter's supersecret project. This is about you, about me. About us. About where we need to be in our own lives to make this work."

He snaps his head back. "So what are you saying? You think Carter and I never should have worked together? That's something my father's been saying for years."

I take his hand, physically pleading with him to look at me. "I'm saying that people change. That people can make decisions that make sense at one point in their lives and no longer work for them later. It doesn't mean you chose incorrectly. But you're not stuck doing anything you don't want to do."

He drops his head, refusing to meet my gaze. "I'm an agent, Ash. This is what I do. I'm not stuck. And I'm never going to buy into the notion that your brother's hindering me in any way. How fucking ungrateful would I be to think that?"

I take his chin and lift his head. "He's the one who should be grateful."

He pulls away and scrubs a hand down his face. "I'll be honest now, too. I don't understand any of this. If I didn't know you better, I'd say you're searching for reasons to drive a wedge between us."

"No, I'm trying to bring us closer together."

He stares at me, his eyes cold and remote. "Well, it's not working."

A weight settles against my chest, making it difficult to breathe. My T-shirt is suddenly ten times too small, constricting my mental range of movement. Maybe that's a good thing, because the heaviness in my body is preventing me from lashing out in frustration. Isn't this what I wanted? To force us to confront these issues, one way or the other? "Friends with benefits would be so much easier, am I right?" My voice is surprisingly calm and clear, not remotely close to reflecting how this conversation is tearing me up inside.

He forces a smile. "Look, I'm really tired. Can we talk more tomorrow?"

With the broadest smile I can manage, I nod. "Sure. Have a good night."

He pivots and trudges down the hall to his bedroom, throwing back a few meaningless words over his shoulder before he disappears. "Sleep well, Ash."

In other words, *don't plan on sleeping with me.* Sometimes when you pick at a scab, you make it worse, revealing the tender sore underneath. I unknowingly did that tonight, but I don't regret it. We can't resolve our issues if we don't acknowledge them.

When I hear his shower running, I pick up my guitar and strum a few indistinct chords. At least I have this. I'll *always* have this.

Chapter Thirty-Five

Julian

THAT FUCKING CRACK in the ceiling must be a metaphor for my life. I could have sworn it was barely noticeable only weeks ago, but this morning the fucker's two inches long. If I don't repair it soon, it's going to be a bigger headache to correct in the future. Or maybe it's a metaphor for my relationship with Ashley. What the hell happened last night? We went from happy to hurting in sixty seconds flat.

After half-assing through my morning routine, I venture to the kitchen. I'm fixing a cup of coffee when Ashley comes out of the bedroom with a suitcase trailing behind her, the guitar case strapped across her back, and a large trash bag in one hand. I'm tired and cranky, and I still haven't figured out what I could have done differently to stop yesterday's conversation from veering off course. I fear anything else I say will only make the situation worse. "What's going on?"

Her hair is styled in a loose ponytail, and her skin is free of makeup, making her appear younger than her twenty-six years. Her expression is placid, the perfect advertisement for a yoga product—or a constipation remedy. "I'm staying with Lisa for a few days until I figure out where to go next."

"Lisa. Your coworker?"

"Yeah."

I want to tell her she doesn't need to leave. I want to let her know I'd enjoy having her here even though she gutted me last night and we're not happy with each other right now. But that's not what I say. "Running away as usual, I see."

Damn, I should cut off my own tongue. *Fuck you, morning. Fuck you.*

Her eyes blaze with contempt, but then she blows out a long breath and composes herself. In a cool voice, she says, "You're running, too. You're lying to yourself if you don't see that."

I set my mug down and place my hands on my hips. "So what? You want me to stop working with your brother? Is that the ultimatum you're throwing down?"

"I'd *never* presume to tell you what to do. You need to figure this out yourself, because anything I say is going to make you defensive. Just do me a favor. Whatever you decide to do about your career, make sure it's what *you* want. I'd hate for you to wake up one day ten years from now and discover you let your own happiness slip from your reach because you chose the path of least resistance."

I can't contain the sarcasm even if I tried. "Thanks. I'll bear that in mind."

She stares at me for a moment, her lips parted as if she's going to say something else. Instead, she gives me a curt nod and lifts the garbage bag off the floor. "Take care of yourself, Julian. I'm sure I'll see you around."

My protective instincts kick in as I realize she really is leaving. "Wait. Do you need a ride somewhere? How can I get in contact with you?"

"Lisa's picking me up, and you have my phone number. Carter will know where I'm staying."

My fingers are itching to take her in my arms and tell her to stay. But that wouldn't be fair to either of us. She wants assurances I can't give her, and she wants me to make decisions I'm not ready to make. "Bye, Ash."

She salutes me. "Bye, J-Dawg." Then she spins around and walks out the door.

I won't pretend it's easy watching her go, but it's for the best. Hers and mine.

I'M GOING TO strangle someone today. Hell, Marie won't come near my office, and my scruffy appearance is warning everyone else away. Good thing, too, because my patience is nowhere to be found this week, and the casting director on the line is the latest in a string of people unlucky enough to cross paths with me.

Bill Nance thinks he's God's gift to Hollywood. In truth, he's a slimy gatekeeper who got his gig by knowing important people's secrets. Unfortunately, those important people bankroll major television productions, including a made-for-TV film that should have been a perfect opportunity for Gabriel.

"Let me get this straight," I say into the speakerphone. "Gabriel walked out on an audition. Without provocation."

"Well, I wouldn't call it unprovoked, exactly." He chuckles. "Let's just say I administered a bit of truth serum first."

"Truth about what?" I say, unable to hide the annoyance in my voice.

"I told him he didn't look clean-cut enough for the role of Jacob. The part calls for a young stockbroker from a middle-class background who gets hardened by prison time. It wouldn't be believable."

"Because he's Latino."

"Right," he says without a hint of embarrassment or shame.

What a dick. I'm guessing he doesn't think I'm believable as a Hollywood agent, either.

"Look, I know how hard it is to get jobs when you're trying to get a foot in the door, so I asked him if he wanted to read for the part of José. It's perfect for him."

"Let me guess, José's a Latino inmate who befriends Jacob and helps him on his journey of self-discovery."

"Hey, you've read the script?" Nance asks.

Jesus Christ. I take a deep breath and count to three. I'd love to explain to Nance how problematic his behavior was, but I stop myself, remembering Quinn's admonition:

"Your *job* is to keep Carter Stone happy, so he'll want to work with SCM and continue to make us money. You do Carter no favors by pissing off the very people who want to work with him." The deal with Sanderson isn't inked, and I'm hesitant to ruffle anyone's feathers until it is. But signing a multimillion-dollar deal feels less important to me than speaking up for Gabriel. It's the right thing to do.

Fuck. I'm operating at half capacity, stymied by the politics of the business and my boss's threats. If I fuck up things for Carter, I fuck up *everything*.

My chest tightens. Whoa.

Where did that come from? Even I know two plus two does *not* equal five.

And in that moment, I realize Ashley's right. I *do* think my career begins and ends with Carter, and my professional relationship with him *is* holding me back. Through no fault of his, but still…*dammit*. Why couldn't I see this before? *You didn't want to see it*, my inner voice whispers.

My inner voice may be quiet, but my outside voice is loud. "No, I didn't read the script, Nance. I took a wild guess. The point is, you treated Gabe like trash, and that's not okay."

"I…didn't…uh…mean anything by it," he says sheepishly. "I thought being frank would be the best approach." He gives me a long-suffering sigh. "Look, I think you might be too close to this issue—"

"So, what? You want to speak to my boss instead? I'll dial him myself."

He clears his throat before he responds. "Hart, I respect you. You've got a great reputation in a business that brings out the worst in people. But you can't be sensitive about these things. It's business. And at the end of the day, money talks in Hollywood. Everything else is set dressing."

He's right about that. But he fails to see what I can grasp easily. Audiences are clamoring for movies that reflect the diverse world we live in. The spate of recent movies fronted by black creatives that surpassed Hollywood's expectations is just one example of how out of touch people like Nance are. And studios will follow the money if someone helps them see the forest for the trees.

"Nance, this isn't something you want printed in the *Hollywood Reporter*. Actors talk. Agents talk. And then it spreads like wildfire. Plus, you're wrong. And it's myopic thinking like yours that leads to the whitewashing of movies that would have done loads better had an actor of color been selected for the lead role. Four words: *Ghost in the Shell*."

There's no way Nance isn't familiar with that flop of a movie. With a $110 million dollar budget, the film barely took in a sixth of that during its opening weekend.

He sighs. "What would you have me do? Hire your client despite my misgivings?"

"Apologize to my client. That's it. Whether he wants to go for a role is his decision, but I'll advise him against working with people who can't see past their own biases."

"Fine. I'll call him. I truly didn't mean anything by it."

And that's one of the most fucked-up parts about this. "I'll tell him to expect your call."

I hang up, roll my chair back, and stand at the floor-to-ceiling window that looks out onto the building's courtyard. I'm running on adrenaline, and I don't know what to do with all the extra energy pulsing through me. I settle on pacing the width of my office.

Focusing on Gabriel's terrible experience has the added benefit of distracting me from Ashley's absence. It's been four days since she left my place, and I miss her more than I could have imagined. She's out of my life for sharing her honest opinion, one I'm now forced to agree with.

Not even five minutes after my call with Nance, Gabriel rings my cell. I pick up immediately and drop into my chair. "Hey, Gabriel. I was just going to call you to give you a heads-up. Bill Nance should be calling you later today."

Gabriel laughs. "He already called."

"He did?"

"Yeah. And he apologized for his comments. Said he'd be more mindful of his prejudices in the future."

"I'm not so sure I'd believe that."

"Yeah, I agree. But he tried. And I can't recall ever having that kind of conversation with anyone in the five years I've been hustling in this business. So thank you. For the first time in my career, I feel like someone in this business has my back. My instincts about you were right."

"And what instincts were those?"

"I've read your comments about diversity in Hollywood. About equal pay and representation. Your willingness to speak up and speak out sealed the deal for me. This shit won't ever change if we can't even *talk* about it. There are plenty of agents, but an agent who cares about the issues that could make or break my career, that's gold."

I'm stunned into silence. I've spent so much time justifying my position to Quinn, I lost sight of the fact that my advocacy could make a difference for actors on the front lines. It makes me want to get on my soapbox and represent them all. And it reminds me once again that Ashley tried to get me to see my value apart from my connection to Carter, but I was unwilling to listen.

"You there?" Gabriel asks on the other end of the line.

"Yeah, I'm still here. Thanks for the vote of confidence. I'll make sure you don't regret it. Look, I can't pretend to understand how you felt today, but I can relate. And I'm sorry. There will be other auditions. I'll work my ass off to make sure of that."

"With you on the case, I'm not worried. Heading off to the J-O-B now."

"Right. We'll talk soon."

The phrase my mother drilled into my head as a kid comes to mind: Don't just talk about it, *be* about it. *That's it.* If SCM wants to stand out from the crowd and position itself as a player in an already crowded market, why not brand itself as the agency that will take on Hollywood's diversity problem? Quinn gets publicity, notoriety, and a host of new clients like Gabriel, and I get a career I can be fired up about. But as much as I can imagine the possibilities, the reality of my circumstances tempers my excitement. Quinn would never go for it. He's made his position on this issue clear, and he's not interested in being a maverick.

As all these thoughts swirl around in my head, I picture my mother, her hands at her hips and her voice soft and encouraging: *Quinn's not the person to make this happen. You are.*

I wish Ashley were here to help me work though my ideas, but I stupidly pushed her away when she told me truths I didn't want to face. She's right. I *do* need to resolve a few issues before I can love her the way she deserves to be loved. And I'm not wasting any more time getting there. I pick up the phone and ring my colleague, who answers immediately.

"Hey, Sooyin, I need your help."

Chapter Thirty-Six

Ashley

LISA GIVES ME a brief hug as we prepare for takeoff. "Ready to make your last flight announcement?"

I slam a tray or two before I answer. "God, yes. I'm so ready."

She grabs the microphone and passes it to me. "Have at it, sweetie."

Burying any evidence of my glum mood, I paste on a fake smile and address the passengers. "Good morning, everyone. On behalf of the flight crew of AirStar's flight from New York to LA, I want to welcome you on board. Total flight time is five hours and thirty minutes." This time, I give them a genuine grin. "Today's flight is my last one with AirStar, so make it memorable, okay? The cabin crew will be starting drink service as soon as the captain has turned off the fasten–seat belt sign. In the meantime, please direct your attention to the front of the plane, where one of our flight attendants will go through the safety features and procedures for this Boeing 767."

Lisa grabs an inflatable life jacket and positions herself in the aisle before I continue.

"If you choose to read, sleep, or generally ignore her, you might miss out on valuable information that could save your life or the life of those around you. So one, two, three, eyes on she."

After Lisa completes the safety instruction, she returns to the galley to help me prepare the drink cart.

"Oh, shoot," she says in her thick Midwestern accent. "I forgot to announce the in-flight movie. Hang on."

The crackle of the intercom fills the cabin, followed by Lisa's chipper voice. "Good morning again, everyone. The in-flight entertainment will begin shortly. The film selection is *The Mash Up* starring Carter Stone. If you need headphones, a member of the crew will be passing through to provide them free of charge. Enjoy."

Somehow I resist the urge to crumple the can in my hands. Gah. Lisa only recently discovered Carter was my brother when he showed up at her apartment to check out my temporary digs. I grimace, remembering the flimsy excuse I gave for not mentioning him sooner: "I didn't think you'd care." With my eyes shut, I take a deep breath and exhale, annoyed with myself for hiding my brother's existence from her. It's obvious I was worried she would compare us. But so what? I'm not in competition with Carter. He has his life, and I have mine. And apart from the gaping hole in my heart now that Julian and I are no longer together, my life is a good one, with friends who are anxious to cheer me up and a possible gig with a band looking for a singer-songwriter to join them.

The gaping hole, though, is a problem. Much as I'd like it to, it's not shrinking at all, and each day I don't hear from Julian makes me question whether I should have voiced my concerns so early in our relationship.

Lisa returns, interrupting my thoughts, her innocent expression masking the devil within.

I give her the evil eye. "Traitor."

"Oh, c'mon. It'll be fun to listen to what people are saying about your brother. Kind of like our little secret."

"If someone makes a snide remark and I accidentally spill a Bloody Mary on them, it'll be on your conscience."

She gives me a smug smile. "Deal."

Sure enough, thirty minutes into the flight, I'm getting a passenger her third cup of water when her male companion chuckles.

"Good Lord, this is terrible," he says. "Where'd they find this guy? I can't stand rom-coms anyway."

I should use discretion here and let the remark go, but the dude is sitting next to the woman with the bottomless bladder who also won't keep her foot out of the aisle, and together they're an unpleasant pair. "Actually, he's very talented. Was nominated for a Best Supporting Actor award for his role in this movie."

The guy presses his lips together and gives me a condescending smile. "Awww, that's cute. You're one of those celebrity watchers, huh?"

"Not at all. He's my brother."

"Right," he says, the snooty tone of his voice underscoring his skepticism.

I can't help myself, so I pull out my phone and show him one of the photos from the family reunion. "Here we are with my mother in front of the house we grew up in."

The woman seated next to him leans over and peeks at the photo.

"Wow," the guy says. "And you're a flight attendant? Why not rest on his laurels?"

Not long ago, a question like this would have made me defensive, but now I see it for what it is: a rude question posed by a judgmental person who doesn't deserve my time. "Because they're not mine, and I'm making my own way." I dangle a bag of peanuts in front of him. "Nuts?" I pound the bag with my fist. "They might have gotten a little crushed in transit, but they're still edible."

The guy pales. "No, thank you."

When I return to the galley, Lisa asks, "Everything okay?"

I nod. "Everything's fine."

Better yet, I'm feeling pretty damn good about where I'm headed. If I can just get Julian to extract his head from his ass, I will be golden.

MY SECOND OPEN mic night at Muddy's goes more smoothly than the first. I manage to remain calm even as I wait to perform, and although I still don't know anyone in the audience—both Tori and my new temporary roommate, Lisa, are working—the crowd's enthusiastic reception last time helps to suppress my stage fright now.

When I finish the song, another original composition, the spectators clap and cheer, and I stop a few times to shake an outstretched hand as I weave my way back to the bar. I claim a stool near the cash register and signal the bartender.

"Water, please."

A man takes the stool next to me, the collar of his jacket raised to shield the bottom half of his face and a baseball cap pulled low over his eyes. *Oh brother.* I pick up the glass the bartender sets in front of me and try to glance at the guy as inconspicuously as possible. He's not dressed for a June evening in LA, and he hasn't said a word since he sat down.

I wait and glance. Wait and glance.

"Great performance," he finally says in a voice I easily recognize.

I twist my body toward him. "What the hell are you doing here?"

Carter tilts his head up, revealing his eyes, which are twinkling. "Came to see my baby sis." He lowers his hat. "But I didn't want to attract any attention."

I bark out a laugh. "You are *so* bad at this. I'm sure the bouncer's ready to throw you out on your suspicious ass."

"Just act like you're having a good time with me and I'll be fine."

I motion for the server again. "A Save the Bay IPA for my friend here, please."

He swings his gaze between Carter and me, widens his eyes a fraction, and nods discreetly. "Sure thing."

Carter reaches for my glass and takes a sip. "Sorry. This jacket is making me sweat."

Shaking my head at him as I chuckle, I reclaim my water. "Did Tori tell you I'd be here?"

"Yeah. She felt bad that she couldn't make it, so I offered to come in her place."

"You didn't have to do that, but I appreciate it anyway."

He swivels in the stool and faces me. "You okay?"

"I'm fine. Just adjusting to a few changes in my life." I'm not ready to tell him about Julian, but even if I were ready, I wouldn't know what to say. Is he in my past? Permanently? Or will we find a way to resolve our differences? I don't have answers yet.

Carter accepts the bottle from the bartender and takes a long swig. "If the changes mean you'll be doing more of that"—he gestures to the stage—"I'm happy for you. You're fantastic up there. I mean it. Truly, truly talented."

This might be the first time Carter's done something other than worry about me. It's refreshing. "Means a lot to me that you think so." And his honesty prompts me to admit my own shortcomings. "I'm not sure you know this, but I measure myself against you a lot. Been doing it for years. I'm working on changing that, too."

He nudges me with his shoulder. "There's no comparison. You're way more talented than I'll ever be. Just took you a long time to realize it."

My jaw drops as I stare at him.

"What?" he asks. "I'm serious. I always knew you were the true star in our family."

I shake my head at him. "Okay, now you're just messing with me."

"Nope. I'm dead serious. You want proof?"

I lean back and fold my arms across my chest. "I do."

"You have to promise not to kick my ass when I tell you this."

I laugh. "I will not."

"Promise."

Groaning, I raise my head to the ceiling, but I'm secretly eager to hear his confession. "Fine, I promise."

"Remember when you did that talent show in middle school?"

"Of course I do. Mom and Dad didn't show up."

He bares his teeth sheepishly. "Yeah, about that. I was the one who switched the dates on the calendar on the fridge."

My eyes bug out of my head. "On purpose?"

He drops his head. "Yeah."

I clip him on the shoulder so hard he stumbles out of his seat. "Why would you do that?"

He recovers and slowly lowers himself back onto the stool. "I didn't realize it then, but I was jealous of you. I think I was blown away by your voice, and I wanted Mom and Dad to focus on my acting career. I was fifteen and stupid, and everything was about me back then. I'm sorry. Can you forgive me?"

"I'll think about it."

Looking back on it, I can't say the incident changed the course of my life. My issues about exploring a career in music run deeper than a missed performance. But knowing Carter isn't immune to sibling envy makes it easier for me to accept this part of my personality. "So the great Carter Stone isn't perfect, huh?"

He cocks his head at me. "Perfect? Never. I could have told you that a long time ago. Shit, Tori probably has a spreadsheet listing all the ways I screw up." He rises and throws a few bills on the counter to cover his drink and a hefty tip. "Speaking of which, I need to pick her up at the studio. Want a lift home?"

"No, I'm meeting a band manager about a possible gig. Should be here soon."

"Okay." He pulls me up and out of my seat and enfolds me in a tight hug. "You've got this, Ashley. I believe in you."

That means a lot to me. The best part, though, is that now I can confidently say I believe in myself, too.

Chapter Thirty-Seven

Julian

THE PAST FEW days of soul-searching revealed yet another truth to me: My father and I need to resolve some issues between us, making a trip home well overdue. Which is why I travel straight from the airport to Hart Consulting's headquarters in Downtown Atlanta. The building's new guards have no idea who I am, and an ID showing that my last name is Hart doesn't gain me entry.

A few minutes after my arrival, Nicole meets me in the lobby, the loud click of her heels warning me of her impatience.

"You could have called," she says in a brusque tone.

"Good to see you, too, Sis."

Her shoulders drop, and she holds out her arms for a hug. "Sorry. It feels like the prodigal son is returning, and I'm so exhausted, I almost wish you would take over the reins."

I put an arm around her shoulder, and we walk in step to the bank of elevators. "That's ridiculous. I haven't been to a strip club in years, and my finances are sound."

She sucks her teeth, a hint of a smile lifting the corners of her mouth.

"Seriously," I continue. "I'm sorry you're tired, but I'm not here to usurp your role at Hart. I never could."

She draws back and guides me to the first elevator that arrives. "He still wishes you would, though."

"He'll have to deal. And if he's hell-bent on continuing to be stubborn about it, you could always shave your head and pretend you're me. It might be a good look for you."

She considers me in the small car, her eyes tired and puffy, and then she shakes her head and snorts. "My wardrobe can't compete with yours, and my head isn't big enough, but thanks for the suggestion."

I lay my hand against the railing and nudge her shoulder. "He has the best person in the position. We all know it."

She gives me a reluctant smile. "Thanks."

"How is he?"

The elevator dings and its doors slide open before she answers. "He's fine. We're not even talking about good days and bad days, more like weird moments. It'll change over time, for sure, but I'm overseeing everything, and Mom's his rock."

I guess it's an inevitable consequence of watching my parents age—talking about my father this way—but knowing this doesn't make the reality of it any easier to accept. "I promise to be around more to help."

She links arms with me and steers me through the reception area. "I'm going to hold you to that promise." When we reach my father's office door, she knocks twice before ushering me inside.

My father's sitting at his desk, his thick, black reading glasses perched on his nose. He looks up, cocks his head as though he's trying to place me, and after a few seconds, drops his jaw. "Well, this is a surprise. A good one, but a surprise nonetheless."

"I told Mom I was coming."

"She didn't say."

My mother thinks the element of surprise should be part of anyone's tactical arsenal, and she probably thought I needed any advantage she could give me. "Might have slipped her mind."

He avoids my gaze and glances at Nicole instead.

"I'll leave you two alone," she says, her hand already on the doorknob. "How long will you be here?"

"Just the day, unfortunately. I've got a few important matters brewing at work, so I can't stay longer. But I'll be back soon and I'll stay awhile. I'd like you to meet someone special to me." That is, if Ashley will have me. "Maybe."

She raises a brow. "I'm going to hold you to that, too." Before she leaves, she gives me a hug and grabs a file off our father's desk. "I've missed you. Have a safe trip back."

"I've missed you, too."

When the door clicks shut, my father motions for me to sit. "I'm eager to hear what brought you from LA on a day trip. Can't be very convenient."

"It's not," I say as I settle into the tufted leather wing-back that he's owned for more than a decade. "But this is important."

"Go ahead, then. The floor is yours."

"I've been doing some mental housekeeping lately, and it led me to you." Damn, I wish I had a stress ball in my hands.

He leans forward. "Son, I don't bite. Say what you need to say."

"Okay, fine. For years now, there's been this tension between us because I chose to become an agent rather than join you here, and I suspect you've always regarded that decision as a rejection of you, but it wasn't. It was a decision that made sense for me at the time. I didn't want to be in Atlanta. I wanted my own space, wanted to define my own path."

My father shifts in his chair and lays two fingers against his mouth, his expression contemplative. "Go on."

"Every time you criticized my decision, I double downed on wanting to prove you wrong, figuring you'd eventually see that I made the right choice."

He leans back in his chair and places his threaded fingers on the desk. "If you want to spend the rest of your life chasing someone else's dream, I can't stop you."

I shake my index finger at him. "See there? That's where you're wrong. I'm not chasing someone else's dream. I'm chasing my own."

He purses his lips. "Carter's the actor, not you."

"Yes, I'm the agent. I'm the one who makes the deals. Not just for Carter but for two dozen clients total. I make their dreams happen. And I'm damn good at my job."

He takes a deep breath. "I wish you would dedicate yourself to this business as much as you dedicate yourself to that one."

I wave a hand around me. "This isn't my dream, Dad. This is yours. I know nothing about company branding. I need my own goals, my own reasons for getting out of bed and wanting to show up at the office."

He wrinkles his nose and straightens his cuffs. "And you have that?"

"That's the other piece of the puzzle that I finally figured out. I've been going through the motions lately, but I didn't want to acknowledge that work isn't as fulfilling as it used to be, because it would have meant accepting that you've been right all along. But you're not, and someone in my life helped me to see that. So the short answer is yes, I'm working on it. And you'll be happy to know it involves opening my own agency."

He sticks out his chest and pats it. "So you're following in my footsteps, after all."

I expected him to make one last run at getting me to join his company, so the fact that he doesn't is a huge relief. "There's something else I need to say. I won't play a role in the business, but I'm your son, and I want to be here for you. To help you get through…"

He raises his chin and looks at me knowingly. "Your mother told you."

I nod. "Yes."

"There's nothing to be done. It's just something I'll have to deal with."

"But you won't deal with it alone. I'll be there for you. And so will Nicole. Speaking of which, Nicole is busting her butt trying to be the leader you need. It's time to accept that she's the one who's most qualified to continue your legacy."

"I know." He narrows his gaze, although his expression isn't unkind; it's resigned. "But it was supposed to be me and you."

"That's a tired way of thinking about this company's future, and you're all about innovation and progressive thinking." I rise. "So we're good?"

He shakes his head, his mouth curved into a reluctant smile. "No, we're not good, but I don't appear to have a choice in any of this."

I chuckle. "Now you're catching on."

THIS IS THE visit I've been dreading the most. And because the gods have a sense of humor, too, neither Carter nor Tori answers the door. Instead, a laughing Ashley swings the door open with her head still facing the person behind her.

Only a week has passed since she left my place, but it feels like months. I miss seeing her on the couch or bent at the waist as she rummages through the fridge. I miss shoving aside the toiletries she relocated to my bathroom after the first night we slept together in my bed. I just miss her, period.

When she finally turns to greet me, her eyes grow wide, but then she slips on a mask of polite familiarity. "Hi, Julian. We were expecting the pizza guy."

"Does he have my sausage, and is he wearing white tube socks?" a voice inside asks.

Eva. One day, she's going to make someone very lucky—and exhausted.

She appears behind Ashley, her chin resting on Ashley's shoulder. "Oh, hey, Julian."

"Hey, Eva."

"We're waiting for pizza," she explains.

"Yeah, Ashley told me."

Eva turns to Ashley. "Did you order an XXL? Bahahaha."

Ashley shakes her head. "She's on margarita number four. Ignore her."

Next, Tori stumbles to the door. "Julian, we're having margaritas and waiting for pizza." She burps, ending her sentence with perfectly timed punctuation.

They all stare at me as though I might turn into the very pizza they're obviously craving. "Is Carter here?"

Tori pulls me inside. "He's in the theater room basking in a sentimental mood and watching early episodes of TV shows he appeared in. Gets like this whenever he's thinking about his career." She squeezes my forearm. "Go spend some time with your boy. As a friend."

I grin at her. "Will do."

Before I head back, I place a hand on Ashley's retreating shoulder. She spins around and waits, and for a moment I'm frozen. This isn't the time or place to tell her how I feel, but not saying anything doesn't seem right, either.

"Can we talk later?" I ask.

She bites on her bottom lip as she considers me, and I lock my legs in place to keep from squirming under her inspection. Damn, this woman really is my kryptonite.

Finally, she says, "Okay, sure. I'll be around. But I'm working on my second margarita"—she points a finger at me—"so don't take forever. I won't be held responsible for what I say when I've got tequila in my belly."

I stifle a laugh. She's going to be tipsy soon, so I better get back to her quickly. "I promise I won't take long."

A few seconds later, I find Carter where Tori said I would. He's sitting in a high-back armchair with one foot on the floor and the other draped over the chair's arm. He appears to be aimlessly pressing buttons on the remote.

He swivels around and looks up at me when I enter the room. "Hey, man."

"What's up?"

He returns his gaze to the television. An early audition clip is playing on the screen. He points the remote at it. "Reminding myself of the early times."

I laugh. "The braces were part of the scary times."

"A necessary evil."

I have a lot to say, but I don't know where to begin.

Carter fills the silence instead. "Talk to me, J. I get the sense you're not telling me something I need to hear."

I drop onto the couch. "I'm leaving SCM. Plan to give notice next week."

He straightens in the chair, bringing his feet to the ground, and his mouth falls open. "Whoa. That's not what I was expecting you to say. Where will you go? Worldwide? IMG?"

"None of the above. I'm going to start my own agency."

He stares at me for a few seconds, and then his incredulous grin gradually builds into a megawatt smile. "You crazy motherfucker, that's great news. I'm behind you one hundred percent."

I doubt that'll still be the case when I tell him my plans. "I'll start small, taking on only a limited number of existing clients while I settle into my new role, but eventually I hope to hire a few junior agents and bring on new clients."

He sits up and leans forward, resting his forearms on his thighs. "You don't have to sell me on the idea, man. I'm there with you."

"Here's the thing, Carter. I think you should stay with SCM."

The dazed look on his face guts me, but I forge ahead knowing this is the best outcome for us both. "You're a bona fide superstar, Carter, and you need the backing of a first-tier agency to represent your interests. Plus, I can't give you the expertise you need. But I know someone who can. Sooyin deals with multiyear film deals all the time, and there's no other agent on the planet I trust more. You'd be in good hands. And to be honest, I don't want to engage in a protracted battle with Quinn about poaching you. He won't care about my smaller clients, but he'll go rabid if he thinks you're going to jump ship with me."

He shakes his head. "But we've always been a team, and we're on the brink of sealing a major deal. What's changed?"

"That's just it, man. Everything's changed. Me. You. What we want from our careers. What we want for our lives. And it's fine. Change is good. I want the chance to make mistakes, but I don't want to risk your career while I do it. I know you might think I'm being an ungrateful shit for wanting to drop you, but I need to be on my own. I'll always be around to guide you if you need it, but not as your agent."

He does nothing but stare at me for what feels like minutes. Then he shoves his fingers through his hair and collapses back into the chair. "I'm going to tell you something, and then we're going to be done with this bullshit. Because I don't do maudlin moods. I don't do angst. Not in my real life, anyway. So let's clear the air and move on, okay?"

I nod. "That's what I was hoping for."

"When I realized Simon was altering my books, I wanted to leave the business altogether. It was still early in my career, and I hadn't seen any evidence that I would gain any traction in the business. I even told my dad that I wanted to come home. He told me he'd support whatever decision I made."

"I'm not surprised. Your dad's always been there for you."

He dons a pensive expression and turns back to the TV screen. "Yeah, he has. And I considered tucking my tail under me and running the other way, but then I told you what had been going on, and you dropped everything to help me. I can still picture you poring over stacks and stacks of notes, royalty checks, Simon's emails."

He stands and uses the remote to turn off the TV. "I still don't know how you figured it out, but you did. And I finally had someone I trusted who was willing to dig deep. That made the difference. *That's* why I stayed. I was scared shitless, but I figured if you were around, I'd be okay. So if you think you owe your career to me, I'd have to disagree. I owe my career to you." He grins as he strokes his chin. "And to my fantastically handsome face, of course. Oh, and my unparalleled talent. But you get the big picture." He waves a hand around the room. "All of this wouldn't have been possible without you."

His first agent screwed him, and it's affected how he interacts with anyone in his life. But I never knew he considered leaving the business back then. Now all his side comments about the importance of smart choices make sense. "Thanks for saying so, man. I didn't know."

"Well, now you do. So if you think we need to part ways, I'll deal. Because it isn't all about me. You need to be happy, too. Figure out what's going to get you there and go for it. I won't stand in your way."

"Funny you should say that, because being with Ashley would make me happy."

The words come out without much forethought, and I don't regret them in the least. When I envision a future with someone by my side, Ashley's the person I see.

He drops back onto the chair. "Give me a sec." Then he rubs the back of his neck. "I'm so fucking confused."

"I was, too. But I'm not confused anymore."

"She's my little sister, though. I thought you guys were pretending."

"Something changed."

"During the reunion?"

"Even before then, I think, but I didn't want to see it. Remember when I told you I'd fall on my ass eventually?"

"Yeah."

"It happened, and I fell hard."

He slaps both of his hands on his chest. "Ah, God. You're killing me here." After a beat of silence, he says, "She won't settle down, you know. Not yet."

"I think you're wrong about that. This is one time when I know your sister better than you do. But it doesn't matter. I'm willing to wait."

He leans forward. "Jesus, this is too much."

"Think about it, though. You know me better than anyone. I'll treasure her if she wants me to."

After studying me for several seconds, he throws up his hands. "You need to be having this conversation with Ashley, then."

I shove my hands in my pockets. "You're right about that, but I think she's tipsy, and she needs to be sober when I tell her how I feel."

Before I leave the room, he calls after me. "Don't kiss her in front of me."

I laugh. "I can't make that promise."

"You mean you *won't* make that promise."

"That's exactly what I mean."

Chapter Thirty-Eight

Ashley

I CAN'T STOP pacing and fidgeting as I wait for Julian to return. If he makes me suffer through an apology to assuage his conscience, I will gag. Shit, for all I know he might just want to tell me I left a bra at his place.

Eva waves a lazy hand at me. "Psst. Sit the fuck down. You're making me"—she turns to Tori and snaps her fingers—"What's the word I'm looking for?"

Tori tilts her head. "Horny?"

Eva rolls her eyes at her. "No, that other word."

Tori shakes her head. "Dizzy. The word you're looking for is dizzy."

I sit across from them on the single armchair. "Sorry. He said he wanted to speak with me, and now I'm nervous."

Eva straightens, making a valiant effort to appear sober. "You want my advice?"

I nod. "Sure."

She points her index finger in the air. "There are two kinds of men in this world. Men who have banana-emoji dicks and men who have eggplant-emoji dicks. Choose wisely."

Tori giggles and plays with her hair. "That's such an oversimplification I don't know where to begin. What about the other emojis? The rocket, the syringe, *the plug.*"

"How'd that work out for you, by the way?" Eva asks Tori.

Tori slaps her hands over her eyes.

Eva laughs. "Oooh, there's an emoji for that, too. The see-no-evil-monkey emoji."

Tori jostles Eva with her shoulder. "I love you, lady."

"I love you, too, *chica.*"

"Enough to move to LA?" Tori asks.

The possibility that Eva would relocate to LA never occurred to me. "That's up for discussion?" I can't contain the excitement in my voice.

Eva nods. "I'm thinking about it."

I repeatedly clap my hands as I bounce in place. "That would be awesome."

"And expensive," Eva slurs.

I'm so taken with the idea of Eva moving to LA that I don't hear Julian's approaching footsteps. When I look up, he's standing near me.

A stampede of horses couldn't compete with the pounding in my chest. *Control yourself, woman.* I rise and lick my lips. "Want to talk out on the balcony?"

He motions for me to go with him through the floor-to-ceiling glass doors. I lean against the railing and survey the Hollywood landscape.

"Carter's got a better view than me," he says.

I raise a brow. "You make a better breakfast."

Then there's a brief period of silence; it's not uncomfortable, but it's not welcome, either. I want more than a friendly conversation, more than confirmation that we can be civil to each other. But maybe that's all he's prepared to give.

Julian grips the handrail and stares out at the hills. "Listen, I've been reevaluating some things, and I just wanted to thank you for pushing me to consider what would make me happy."

I study his profile. His strong nose. The scarily perfect eyebrows. His super-soft lips. God, I miss him. He's so close I could taste our togetherness, but he's not budging. "Have you figured anything out?"

"I'm working on it." He turns to face me. "What about you? How's teaching?"

That question elicits a genuine smile from me. "It's great. My schedule's going to be three-quarters full most days. And I'm setting aside five hours of my work week to give free lessons. Benny's granddaughter will be one of my students."

"That's wonderful, Ash."

"Yeah. Tori gave me the idea. Feels good to give back. And I'm giving some serious thought to hooking up with a band."

"I'd be your biggest fan."

"Ha. You'd be my *only* fan."

"You have to start somewhere." He taps the handrail and straightens. "So I've got a lot of projects going on, but when things calm down, I was thinking it would be nice to go to dinner or a movie. I don't want us to lose touch."

Well, that was underwhelming. What's going on here? Is he trying to friend-zone me? Or friends-with-benefits me? He's lucky Tori snatched the butt plug away; I know exactly where I'd put it. I refuse to commit to anything, so I sidestep his question. "I'm sure we'll see each other around. After all, we have Carter in common."

He draws back and puffs out his cheeks. "Right. Take care of yourself."

"You too, Julian."

When he's gone, I lean on the rail, close my eyes, and let the cool breeze kiss my skin. He's unwilling to tear down the roadblocks, and I refuse to follow his detour. I guess we're at an impasse.

THE NEXT DAY, Julian's text arrives minutes before I'm due for a lesson at Musicology.

Julian: Hey, Ash. Wondering if you'd like to
            hang out tonight. Dinner? Movie?
            Netflix?

Me: Sorry. I'm working tonight.

Julian: Sure. Maybe another time, then.

Oh, he's angling for a friends-with-benefits arrangement, all right. Well, he can suck it. Rather than dwell on Julian's audacity, I walk into Musicology and head straight to the back, where I claim my music studio for tonight's lessons. The room's bright and cheery with hand-painted sunflowers on the wall, and the kids love it. Outside the room, a pegboard lists the names of the instructors, and below their names, a peg represents each half-hour of instruction. I experience a small thrill when I discover that I'm completely booked tonight.

The school's manager, Beatrice, wearing a sly grin as she studies her computer screen, waves at me from behind the shop's counter. "Your seven o'clock was just dropped off."

"Thanks," I say as I pass her. "I have a busy night."

Squinting, she reads the pegboard and gives me a genuine smile. "Wow. You sure do. Congrats."

I stride down the hall, readjusting my guitar case in my hand to accommodate the narrow door. Once through, I look up and stumble forward. "What are you doing here?"

Julian lifts the brand-new guitar in his hands. "I need lessons."

I plop onto the bench across from him and tilt my head to the side, placing my guitar case between my thighs to keep me upright. "You need guitar lessons?"

He nods. "Sure do. Want to know why?"

I do. But only after I get my fill of gawking at him. He's doing his best impersonation of a bad boy, complete with a scruffy beard and a sexy smile. If that's not enough, he's wearing worn jeans that are snug against the widest part of his thighs and a gray T-shirt that stretches across his firm chest. Apparently, there's T-shirt porn, too.

"Ash?"

I shake my head. "Yes?"

He makes a V with two fingers and points them at his face. "My eyes are up here."

I cough. "Right. What did you ask me?"

He flares his nostrils, although his lips are still curved into that seductive smile. "I asked if you wanted to know *why* I need lessons."

"Oh, yes. Of course."

"It's simple. This is important to you, so it's important to me." He points at my battered guitar. "That instrument represents a lot of things to me. It reminds me of your talent. It's evidence of your dreams and aspirations. And it brought you here, to Musicology, which tells me you're ready to settle in one place and call it home. I want your home to be with me. I want my home to be with you."

The pace of my pulse increases with each revelation. This isn't a booty call. It's an I'll-love-you-forever kind of call. I'm woozy. "What brought all this on?"

"When I was doing all that soul-searching, I thought about something you told me. You were talking about my career, but it applies equally to us. You said you didn't want me to wake up a decade later and discover I let my happiness slip away because I chose the path of least resistance. Do you remember that?"

Oh yeah, I did say that. Past me is a smart woman. "I remember."

"Well, I gave notice at SCM last week, and soon I'll be opening up my own agency. A small outfit at first. I'll probably work from home to start, but yeah, I'm making it happen."

I'm thrilled for him. Julian has so much to offer, and SCM didn't deserve him. "That's great. I'm proud of you for taking such a huge step. Is Carter on board?"

"Carter's staying with SCM, Ash."

My ears grow hot when I hear this. "What?" I stand in outrage, sending Melanie crashing to the floor. After I scramble to pick her up and lean her against the bench, I face him again. "He's not going with you? I'll kill him."

Julian grabs my hand and tugs me back down. "Ash, he's staying at SCM because I asked him to. You were right. I need my own space, my own passions."

My mind can't wrap itself around what he's just told me. Can this be real? "What does Carter think? Is he mad?"

"Nope, he understands. He did ask me to promise that I wouldn't kiss you in front of him."

I lean over and slap his thighs. "You *told* him. What did you say exactly?"

He leans forward, too, and squeezes my hands. "I didn't say much, because these words are only meant for you. I will never run from what we have again, and I'm sorry I tried to. I need to become the best version of myself, and I can't do it without you. That feeling I've been searching for? The one that'll make me jump out of bed in the morning and want to seize the day? I found it with you. I love you, Ash. And if you feel the same, we can have loud, grumpy sex forever and ever."

All I do is stare at him as I try to process his declaration and everything else he's told me. As a teenager, I doodled his name in my notebook and admired him from afar, and now this man is telling me he loves me. I believe him. More than that, I sure as hell feel the same way. This isn't puppy love or infatuation. We're two imperfect people pushing each other to grow wiser and stronger on our own and *together*. I can't think of anything better than spending the rest of my life loving this man. "I love you, too, and I'd be happy to have loud, grumpy sex with you forever and ever. You're the Twizzlers in my trick-or-treat bag."

He smiles. "King-sized, right?"

I reach across and caress his cheek. "Without a doubt."

His eyes blazing with need, he sets aside his guitar, and I shove Melanie under the bench. When I sit up, he lifts me onto his lap so that I'm straddling him. His mouth grazes my neck and jaw before it lands on mine. I squirm on his thighs, our lips tangling and teasing so hungrily, *kiss* isn't the right word to describe it. Then he grabs my ass and rubs me against him until he hardens under me and we both moan. It's not enough. I grasp his T-shirt and pull it out from the waistband of his jeans, but a remnant of reason reminds me that my next student might be waiting outside.

I pull back. "Wait. You want actual guitar lessons? From me? Seriously?"

Glossy-eyed, he nods. "Seriously. I'll never minimize something you love ever again. So I'm going to learn how to play, too. That way, when you're composing your Grammy-award-winning music and you're frustrated with a chord or whatever it's called, I'll know exactly what you're talking about. Plus, I hear the ladies dig guys who play guitars."

"Then we should get going because I have another lesson soon."

He waggles his brows and places my arms over his shoulders. "No, you don't. I booked the entire night."

Oh. My. God. Guitar porn exists, too.

Life is good. Life is *very* good.

Acknowledgments

I'm always giddy when I reach this point. It means the book I've spent months writing and revising will be published soon. And it's an important reminder that publishing a book is itself a journey, with ups and downs and everything in between.

Here, I extend my heartfelt gratitude to everyone who helped me along the way:

My editor, Nicole Fischer, who offered excellent guidance and let my voice shine;

My agent, Sarah Younger, who listened when I needed to be heard;

My husband, who gave me invaluable advice about Julian's arc, enlightened me about this thing called a push-up, and supported me unconditionally;

And my amazing daughters, who were patient and encouraging as usual.

I'm also blessed to have a wonderful network of friends and first readers whose support means the world to me, including my critique partner, Olivia Dade; my beta readers, Ana Coqui, Susan Scott Shelley, and Soni Wolf; my partner in book crime, Tracey Livesay; and my cheerleaders, Priscilla Oliveras, Sabrina Sol, and Alexis Daria. Empanadillas for everyone!

And finally, a special thanks to the folks at Harper-Collins for this book's gorgeous cover and for promoting me and my books with unparalleled class.

Bianca, you're a gem.

Are you obsessed with Tori's funny, wild, best friend, Eva? Well, then you're in luck because the final installment in the *Love on Cue* series is coming soon!

CRASHING INTO HER

Fitness instructor Eva Montgomery is excited to take a leap into the unknown and accept a position with her best friend's new exercise studio in LA. But then her father reneges on his promise to help fund her relocation and she's desperate for a way to supplement her income before her savings run out. When Eva learns that a person with her skills can make excellent money as a stunt double in Hollywood, she signs up for training.

So what if the lead stunt instructor is the same infuriating (and sexy) man she met at her best friend's wedding? So what if he's not happy about working with her? And *so what* if training involves long hours in close quarters with nothing but physical exertion to stem her…frustration. She'll be on her best behavior. Promise.

Read on for a sneak peek…

Chapter One

Eva

OKAY, SATAN. TODAY it is.

The vein at my temple throbs in response to my father's announcement. I want to kill him, but I'm certain patricide remains illegal in the United States. Blowing out a long breath to compose myself, I tighten my grip on the phone and stifle the urge to let out a string of curse words that would make a Navy SEAL blush and clutch his Glock. Instead, I speak calmly. "You agreed to help me get settled. For a year at least. What's changed?"

My father sighs on the other end of the line. "Well, the more I think about it the more I think this move is a bad idea. Giving you money would just enable you to make poor choices, and I wouldn't be able to live with myself if I did that."

He's telling me this *after* I left my job in Philadelphia and relocated to Los Angeles, which I did based in part on his promise to help fund my move. Manipulation 101 is in session, and he's mastered the material so well he could write encyclopedic volumes about it. "It doesn't bother you at all that you're reneging on a commitment?"

After a brief pause, he speaks in a soothing voice. "Sweetie, don't be mad at me. The money will be here when you return."

When you return. In other words, he's expecting me to fail in LA and come crawling back to Philadelphia before long.

"As soon as you're ready to take those accounting courses," he continues, "I'll gladly pay for them. But if you really want nothing more than to be a fitness instructor, it should be on you to make it work, don't you think?"

Stay calm and don't say anything you'll regret, Eva. He's trying to provoke you. Or he wants you to beg him to reconsider. "Right." My tone is clipped and emotionless. "Okay, I need to get to work. My first class starts at six."

"Give me a call when you're not busy, okay?"

"Of course I will, Dad." But in my head, I make plans to busy myself from now until eternity. "Take care of yourself."

"You do the same, sweetheart."

I end the call and shove my phone into the gym bag my best friend, Tori, gave me as a welcome gift. Rolling my shoulders to ease the tension in them, I scan the living area of my new one-bedroom apartment and mentally calculate how long I'll be able to afford it. Without my father's financial help, the answer is not long at all. Bye-bye, lovely fireplace. *Au revoir*, cute terrace overlooking my quaint neighborhood. *Hasta la vista*, community garden that doubles as a singles hangout.

No, I'm not going to let him steal my joy. Inspecting my reflection in the mirror, I set aside my financial woes and focus on the positives: I'm a single woman with a nice apartment and a fun job who's embarking on an adventure in a new city. Also, my ass looks *amazing* in these yoga pants.

Satan can shove it.

WHEN I ARRIVE at Every Body, my new place of employment in West Hollywood, Tori waves at me from behind the reception desk, the studio's general manager, Valeria, by her side. "You can't begin to understand how happy I am to see you walk through that door and know that you'll be working here now. My heart can't take it."

I'm just as thrilled as she is, honestly. Tori left town over a year ago to join the love of her life, megastar Carter Stone, in California. Philly wasn't the same without her. When she brought me in to tour the space a few months ago, I could easily picture myself working here. "We're stuck with each other, *chica*—for better or worse."

She rounds the desk, hands me a manila envelope, and tackle-hugs me. "This is going to be great."

My arms hang loosely at my sides, and my check is smashed against her chest. Damn, this bitch is tall. "Tori, I need air."

"Oh, sorry about that." She draws back, scans me from head to toe, and points at the envelope. "Your ID, access card, locker combo, and office codes are all in there. Valeria will get you copies of your employment forms. You know your way around, right? Because my class starts in a few minutes."

I roll my eyes at her. "You have four exercise studios in a five thousand square foot space, woman. I think I can figure this place out on my own."

She bumps my hip with hers. "Fine. I'll introduce you in Advanced Zumba at five. The people in that class can't wait to get started. I've been talking you up for weeks."

A wave of jitters hits me. Advanced Zumba has always been one of my most popular classes, but what if the regulars here don't like it? What if the music doesn't suit their tastes? We did a few trial runs while I was considering Tori's job offer, but maybe the students were just being polite when they said they enjoyed themselves. I don't want to let Tori down.

Goodness, Satan's working overtime today. I rub my temples, knowing I'm overthinking everything. *Kill the drama, Eva.*

After placing my belongings in a locker in the staff room, I stroll through the fitness center, trying to familiarize myself with the layout. It's early afternoon, and the place isn't packed yet. I duck into the studio where I'll be teaching most of my classes and walk along the perimeter. Twice the size of my exercise room in Philly, it's bright and airy, with floor-to-ceiling mirrors along the front and back, a soft blue wall to the right of the stage, and a glass door and frosted wall to the left. It's perfect, and according to Tori, mostly mine.

I step onto the stage, its suspended wood floor easy on my joints, and bend at the waist to stretch my lower back.

A whoosh of cool air brushes over my shoulders. I straighten and turn to the door, my mouth falling open when I see Tori's cousin Anthony watching me. His dark eyes are flickering with amusement, and his pretty lips are pursed in interest.

He strides into *my* room like he owns it, the outline of his long muscular legs visible through his navy blue dress slacks. If he were wearing thick black-rimmed glasses, I'd wonder if he were this decade's Clark Kent.

"If you wanted to get my attention, all you had to do was say hello," he says.

I cross my arms over my chest and smirk at him. "This might be hard for you to grasp, but some of us are perfectly capable of existing without your attention."

He smiles at me as he removes his jacket. "But existing pales in comparison to living, no?"

I chew on my bottom lip to stop myself from making a smart-ass comment. Anthony can't fathom anyone would be immune to his charms. I look between us, taking in the differences in our appearance. Wait. Why is he here? "Um, if you're looking for Tori, she's in Studio A."

He drapes his jacket over a chair by the stage and stuffs his very large hands in his pockets. "I'm not looking for Tori. I'm teaching a free self-defense class for women at five."

"Here?" I ask.

"Here."

"In this room?"

He nods. "Yes, in this studio. Two times a week for the next six weeks." He drops his chin a fraction, his eyes downcast. "Just my way of giving back."

Right. How convenient that the class is geared to women. Very Anthony, indeed. "And sharing your many gifts with the ladies, I assume."

He snorts under his breath, and then he gives me a playful smile. "That, too. So get used to this handsome face, Eva. We'll be seeing each other a lot."

My eyes flutter closed. "Lovely."

Well played, Satan. Well played.

About the Author

MIA SOSA is an award-winning contemporary romance writer and a 2015 Romance Writers of America Golden Heart® Finalist. Her books have received praise and recognition from *Library Journal*, Booklist, *The Washington Post*, Kirkus Reviews, Book Riot, Bustle, The Booklist Reader, and more.

A former First Amendment and media lawyer, Mia practiced for more than a decade before trading her suits for loungewear (okay, okay, they're sweatpants). Now she strives to write fun and flirty stories about imperfect characters finding their perfect match.

Mia lives in Maryland with her husband, their two daughters, and an adorable puppy that finally sleeps through the night. For more information about Mia and her books, visit www.miasosa.com.

Discover great authors, exclusive offers, and more at hc.com.

A Letter from the Editor

Dear Reader,

I hope you liked the latest romance from Avon Impulse! If you're looking for another steamy, fun, emotional read, be sure to check out one of our upcoming titles.

If you like a bit of suspense in your contemporary romance or just love a good Channing Tatum movie, then you do not want to miss STRIPPED by Tara Wyatt! The first book in her new Blue HEAT series is a delicious mash up of *21 Jump Street* and *Magic Mike*, as an elite undercover detective must infiltrate a drug ring operating out of a male strip show. What makes this novel extra steamy? His one-night-stand-turned-new-female-partner is in the audience as back up...and watching the whole thing! One-click away!

You can purchase this title by clicking the link above or by visiting our website, www.AvonRomance.com. Thank you for loving romance as much as we do…enjoy!

Sincerely,

Nicole Fischer
Editorial Director
Avon Impulse
Acting on Impulse